Earth Angel

Ray stretched, yawned again, and opened his eyes slowly. Where—? Oh yeah. Old Lady Garvey's basement. He must have fallen asleep on the job. Man, he was stiff, and his eyelids felt like lead. Well, hell, what did he expect, sleeping on a cement floor in this dusty old place.

He stretched again and sat up. The room whirled around him and the furnace split in half, then slid back together. The door did the same thing. He was seeing double. Was he drunk?

Ray struggled to stand. Man, he didn't feel so good. He sure hoped he felt better by the weekend. A honeymoon was no time to be sick.

He grinned at the thought of getting Celeste away from here, of spending the rest of his life with her. She was like an angel, his own personal angel. He didn't know why she loved him, but he sure was glad she did. She was the best thing that had ever happened in his sorry life, and he was going to take care of her like she was made of that crystal old Mrs. Garvey kept locked in her dining room.

With another yawn, Ray lurched to his feet, then looked down. What the—

He could see right through his boots!

EARTH ANGEL

KATE FREIMAN

J
JOVE BOOKS, NEW YORK

HAUNTING HEARTS is a registered trademark of Berkley Publishing Corporation.

EARTH ANGEL

A Jove Book / published by arrangement with
the author

PRINTING HISTORY
Jove edition / November 1997

The Putnam Berkley World Wide Web site address is
http://www.berkley.com

ISBN: 0-515-12175-4

A JOVE BOOK®
Jove Books are published by The Berkley Publishing Group, a member of
Penguin Putnam Inc., 200 Madison Avenue,
New York, New York 10016.
JOVE and the "J" design are trademarks belonging to Jove Publications, Inc.

PRINTED IN THE UNITED STATES OF AMERICA

10 9 8 7 6 5 4 3 2 1

My thanks to my intrepid critique partner, Doretta Thompson, and my love to Mark and Ben, my husband and son, for their love, support, and culinary resourcefulness at deadline time!

This book is dedicated to two very special partners: my agent, Alice Orr, and my editor, Cindy Hwang, who shared my vision of this story, and encouraged me to reach for the stars.

Prologue

Ray climbed the wooden stepladder, steadied its wobbles, and reached for the burnt-out bulb in the spidery brass chandelier. Old Lady Garvey had gone to the grocery store with her housekeeper, leaving him alone with a list of odd jobs. As soon as he'd seen her classic old Hudson sedan lumber down the driveway, he'd switched on his transistor radio. The fifties song by the Penguins, "Earth Angel," was playing, and Ray hummed along, thinking of Celeste Benedict. "Earth Angel" was *their* song.

And Celeste was *his* angel, he thought with a grin. Only his, even if her old man wanted her to marry that doctor who acted like he owned her. It didn't matter what her daddy wanted, even if Old Man Benedict was the banker who owned the factory where he worked. Celeste wanted him, and he wanted her, and next week, they were gone. They were going as far away as they could get from New Harbour, Connecticut, to be together forever.

The front door creaked open behind him as he was tight-

1

ening the new lightbulb. Uh-oh. Old Lady Garvey must have forgotten something. Now he was gonna catch it. She hated rock 'n' roll. She was going to pitch a fit over his transistor. He couldn't afford to get her mad at him now. She'd been good to him, almost like a grandmother. And he needed the extra cash she paid him on top of his factory job. Aw, hell!

Ray started to turn, opened his mouth to say he was sorry for disturbing the peace of the old Garvey mansion. But it wasn't Mrs. Garvey coming in the door. It was a man in a dark coat, with a dark fedora pulled low on his forehead. *How did he know I was here? What the hell does he—*

Fire slammed into his chest. It tore through him, stealing his breath. The force of it threw him backward off the ladder. The floor smashed up at him. The world exploded into heat and pain. Stunning, blinding pain.

"Celeste," he whispered with his last breath. *Oh, angel, I'm sorry . . .*

The heat turned to cold. The pain turned to nothing. The light turned to darkness. All that was left was his love for Celeste.

Chapter One

Assistant District Attorney Renata Moretti took her glasses off and twisted a loose strand of hair around her finger. Frowning, she tried to concentrate on her notes, but images of that dream refused to clear out of her brain. Why was she thinking about it now, when she could barely see over the stacks of files on her desk?

Nevertheless, she couldn't erase the image. It was always the same dream, at least at the start. She was dancing with a tall, dark-haired man, a handsome man with dark-lashed green eyes and a cocky grin. In the dream, she was herself, yet not herself. In reality, she was a petite brunette with brown eyes. In the dream, she was always a tall, willowy blonde with blue eyes. In reality, she'd never been in love, but in her dream, she knew she was totally, passionately, in love with the man who held her in his arms.

Sometimes, she woke up while they were still dancing, and she could hear in her mind the faint, illusive strains of the old song they danced to. It was always the same song, a

3

romantic slow dance, but she could never quite remember it when she awoke.

Sometimes, however, the dream lasted longer, and she woke up while they were making love. On those occasions, the sensations that lingered had little to do with dancing. This morning had been one of those heated awakenings that even a cold shower hadn't completely cooled. Usually, she was successful in pushing the sensual images away, but today the remembered feelings just wouldn't fade. Why . . . ? Oh, maybe because she'd overheard two of the secretaries chatting in the ladies' room, and one had described what had sounded like an extremely close encounter the night before.

Well, now that she knew what had triggered the erotic images, maybe she could forget them—at least for a while—and get back to work. Shutting out the busy sounds from the surrounding offices, Renata opened the file centered on her desk and frowned. She could understand why her colleagues had been eager for her to take this case. She was new in the New Haven office, although senior to most of them, and she'd made it clear when she'd arrived that she wasn't going to pull rank on assignments.

This case was definitely a stinker, although it certainly wasn't high-profile or sensational. For over thirty years, a man named Frank Dane had been a low-grade virus of criminal activity in Connecticut. Because the D.A.'s office was perennially overworked and understaffed, while Dane had a battery of well-paid defense attorneys, he'd successfully thumbed his nose at the law. Despite police investigations for activities ranging from extortion and loan-sharking to running a car-theft ring, Frank Dane had had amazingly good luck: few actual charges, and not a single conviction.

Renata smiled grimly. Mr. Dane's luck was about to end, as he was going to learn when he arrived for a "chat." In the overall "forest" of the justice system, Frank Dane was a relatively small tree, but she loved a challenge. It was a shame that Mick Donovan, the attorney who'd had the case originally, had been so badly hurt in a car accident three months ago. She would have enjoyed working with Mick, and she certainly owed him her thanks. His extended medical leave, which had left the New Haven office more understaffed than usual, had paved the way for her application to transfer. And as little as she wanted to think about her recurring erotic dreams, she wanted to dwell on her reasons for leaving the Hartford area, her home for most of her thirty-two years, even less.

Becoming aware of the general buzz of the offices around her, Renata checked her watch. Mr. Dane was late for their appointment. Deliberately, she was sure, considering his reputation for arrogance. Well, she wasn't impressed. Automatically, she smoothed her hair away from her face and re-fastened the clip at the back of her neck. The intercom buzzed. Renata replaced her glasses, then pressed the reply button and answered the secretary she shared with several other A.D.A.s. "Mr. Dane is here," Judith informed her. Renata told her to send him in.

The door to her little office burst open. The man who strode inside, shutting the door loudly after himself, made her think of a bull. He was in his early sixties, shorter than average, stocky, and led with his chin. He stared at her with narrow-set, small black eyes, sizing her up. Renata almost expected him to paw the floor. He jerked his head up and opened his mouth to speak.

"Thank you for coming to see me, Mr. Dane," she said smoothly, before he could say a word. "We appreciate your cooperation. Please sit down." She wanted to be sure he understood she was in control, but she was willing to let him think he was doing her a favor, if that could get him to let down his guard. "Will any of your attorneys be joining us?"

He stood over her desk. With him this close, she could smell the stale cigar smoke that clung to him. He leered down at her, making her feel as if she'd been touched obscenely. He gave a snort that added to his bull-like image, and broadened his defiant stance opposite her, crossing his arms over his barrel-like chest. Renata forced herself to gaze back evenly. Frank Dane was morally bankrupt, and proud of it, but he was hardly the first such creep—or the worst—she'd prosecuted, and she refused to be intimidated.

"The D.A.'s office must be really hard up," he said, his

voice unpleasantly gravelly. His gaze slithered down to her chest. "I don't need attorneys to talk to little girls." His leer broadened as he met her eyes again.

Renata clenched her fists under the edge of her desk, but kept her expression neutral as she faced Frank Dane's challenge.

"You may want to sit down. This could take a while." She allowed herself a tiny smile. "Unless, of course, you're prepared to cooperate."

Dane's thick brows rose. Otherwise, he didn't move a muscle. "What are you offering, little girl?"

She refused to let herself rise to his bait. "That depends on you, Mr. Dane. Things might go better for you if you were willing to talk candidly now. Otherwise . . ." She shrugged one shoulder, as if to say things would not go in his favor in court, even though they always had before.

He walked toward her bookshelf and studied her diplomas for a long moment. Then, with a dismissive snort, he turned toward her again. "Otherwise, you take me to court and you lose, big time," he commented, his irritating voice full of self-assurance. "Like usual."

"I don't think so, Mr. Dane. Not this time. We have enough evidence about your involvement in the car-theft business, as well as jury tampering, attempted bribery of police officers and threats against judges. In fact, we have enough evidence against you to send you away for a very long time." He turned and raised his brows in challenge. She went on as if she hadn't noticed. "I don't really have to bargain with you, but if you cooperate, I'm willing to discuss a reduced sentence on some of the charges."

He laughed, a low, menacing sound that didn't reveal a shred of humor. Renata felt as if she were trying to bluff a very aggressive pit bull. "Not in this lifetime, little girl. I don't plead. I don't have to." His declaration came out as a feral growl.

"Are you saying you're innocent of any of the charges against you?" With effort, she kept her skepticism out of her voice.

"I'm telling you that *if* you get to court, those charges

aren't going to hold up." He sneered. "You don't have evidence against me, little girl. You don't have witnesses. You don't have a case."

Again, Renata lifted one shoulder, but she felt far from nonchalant under the glare of his snakelike eyes. "We'll see in court, then, won't we?" she said softly. Picking up her pen and the next file folder on the pile, Renata gave him a dismissive smile. "If you'll excuse me . . ."

She lowered her gaze to the open folder, but the sudden forward movement of his bulk startled her into looking up again. He braced his hands on the edge of her desk and leaned down to stare into her eyes. The reek of cigar smoke sank nauseatingly in her stomach. It took all her willpower not to recoil in her chair.

"You're a pretty little girl," he told her, his gravelly voice winding around her like a snake, "even if you dress like a prison warden. Those glasses don't fool me." His lips curled. "Much too pretty for dirty work that don't concern you. You could get hurt. You could end up a lot less pretty." His grin faded. "Wouldn't that be a shame."

"Are you threatening me, Mr. Dane?" she asked as coolly as she could.

His small, dark eyes slid over her again, and his lips pulled back in a parody of a smile. "No, little girl. I'm warning you." His grin widened. "I'm a nice guy. I can be very generous when I want. I'd be willing to protect a pretty little thing like you. All you have to do is ask."

His meaning was all too clear. Renata suppressed a shudder. Didn't this slimebag ever look in the mirror? "This interview is over, Mr. Dane."

He straightened. "You think you're tough, doing a man's job. Don't fool yourself. Most real men aren't tough enough to take me on. You sure aren't. Think about that, little girl." He bared his teeth in a humorless grin. "Think hard, and you'll come to the right decision."

He turned and strode out after yanking open her door, which he didn't bother to close this time. Renata waited until she was certain he was gone. Then she exhaled, unclipped her hair, and removed her glasses. Talk about an inflated sense of importance! With a shake of her head, she turned her attention to the next file. And, between phone calls, the next. And the next. When her eyes started to burn, she folded her arms on her desk and lowered her head. How was it, she wondered as she rested with closed eyes, that the same species that produced incredibly brave and selfless heroes and heroines also spawned so many creeps?

Ray stretched, yawned and opened his eyes slowly. Where—? Oh, yeah. Old Lady Garvey's basement. He must have fallen asleep on the job. Man, he was stiff, and his eyelids felt like lead. Well, hell, what did he expect, sleeping on a cement floor in this dusty old place. The question was, why was he sleeping on the floor?

He stretched again and sat up. The room whirled around him and the furnace split in half, then slid back together. The furnace room door did the same thing. No, it wasn't them. He was seeing double. Was he drunk? He couldn't remember drinking, but he sure had a hangover. Maybe it was that flu that he'd heard was going around. Whatever had hit him, had turned his brain to sand. He never fell asleep like this. What time was it? Hell, what *day* was it?

Aw, jeez, Celeste! He was probably late meeting her. He better get his butt in gear, or she'd think he'd split on her. That's what she said her old man kept telling her, that her "gigolo boyfriend" would dump her if she didn't have her father's money. Like the money mattered. That old bastard had tried to pay him off to get out of town. Well, he was gonna get out of town, all right, but not without Celeste. The old man didn't know he had plenty of his own money, money he'd earned and stashed in Old Lady Garvey's basement, along with a diamond engagement ring. He didn't need Mr. Banker Benedict's money to do things right. And neither did Celeste. All they needed was each other. And they had that, "for all time," just like in their song.

Ray struggled to stand. Man, he didn't feel so good. He sure hoped he felt better by the weekend. A honeymoon was no time to be sick.

He grinned at the thought of getting Celeste away from

here, of spending the rest of his life with her. It was gonna be good; he'd make sure of that. She was his own personal angel. He didn't know why she loved him, but he thanked Heaven every day that she did. She was the best thing that had ever happened in his sorry life, and he was going to take care of her like she was made of that crystal old Mrs. Garvey kept locked in her dining room.

Well, it was time to get going. He had a lot to do. With another yawn, Ray lurched to his feet, then looked down. *What the—?*

He could see the floor through his boots!

"Hey! You sleeping on the job?" A man's voice broke into Renata's consciousness.

Startled, she lifted her head, slid her glasses back in place, and blinked. Then, seeing State Trooper Will McDonald frowning down at her, she smiled. Immediately, he smiled back, a hopeful smile that made her sigh inwardly. Young, blond and model-handsome, Will had a buoyantly good nature, and an apparent inability to take *no* for an answer. He'd been trying to persuade her to go out with him for the past three weeks, after coming to her rescue over a flat tire in the New Haven courthouse parking lot.

Renata had been just as persistently trying to convince Will that their dating wouldn't be a good idea. First, there was the difference in their ages. At twenty-seven, he was five years younger. Will didn't think it was a significant gap, but Renata felt much, much older than her years. And with his boyish energy, Will seemed much younger than his. Then there were the differences in their backgrounds. She came from a wealthy, totally dysfunctional background, while Will came from a traditional, even old-fashioned, family he described as large, happy, and close, but far from rich. It wasn't their relative wealth that worried her, but their differences in expectations. Will made no secret of his ideal of a big family with a stay-at-home wife. Renata wanted a family, too, but she was realistic enough to know she'd never be happy completely giving up her work.

But her most compelling reason for not wanting to get involved with Will was that she knew she couldn't love him the way the woman in her dreams loved the man who danced with her. Nor did she think it was fair to either of them to establish a relationship that was doomed from the start to be temporary. The fear of making the kind of mistake her flighty mother made so often only increased her emotional caution. Her mother believed a woman had to keep kissing toads until she found her true prince. Renata preferred to believe she could skip the toad-kissing and go straight to the true-prince phase. Feeling irrationally guilty because Will deserved to be happy, Renata smiled more brightly.

He gazed down at her, concern in his light blue eyes. "Are you okay?"

"Mmm-hmm. I was resting my eyes and thinking," she told him. "What brings you here?"

"I had some business at the court, so I thought I'd swing by and take you to lunch. What do you say?"

She felt her smile fade. "Will, I—"

"Hey, chill out," he broke in, his tone teasing. "It's just a quick lunch, not a proposal."

Guilt nudged her again, this time for putting him on the defensive. "Fine." She stood up. "Give me a minute to freshen up."

Will tugged a lock of her hair lightly. "You can get as fresh as you want with me," he murmured.

Renata pushed her hair behind her ear and glared up at Will, all traces of her guilt vanishing. "Behave yourself!" she muttered.

Will grinned and lazily moved his long-limbed body out of her way. "I am. Very badly," he drawled, his tone telling her he wasn't taking her seriously.

With a resigned sigh, she made her way to the ladies' room. Sometimes, she thought, Will seemed more like a brother than a potential boyfriend. She didn't think he'd like to know that was how she really felt about him. Chances were, it was the novelty of pursuing a State prosecutor and older woman that would hold his interest only until some gorgeous young thing caught his eye. Will was too social a guy, and she was enough of a workaholic to bore the leaves off a houseplant, so it was surely just a matter of time before he moved along. Still, she didn't want to hurt his feelings.

After brushing her hair and applying a muted rose lipstick, she glared at her reflection. She looked neat and professional in her charcoal wool suit. Prison warden! Hah! And what was wrong with her glasses? Without them, she could hardly see her own toes. Besides, they made her look mature and authoritative. She only wore her contacts for social occasions, which meant she hardly wore them at all anymore.

She was a prosecuting attorney, not a fashion model! Who did Frank Dane think he was to criticize her appearance? It was just another ploy to undermine her confidence. One he couldn't use on a male attorney. Irritated that she'd almost let him succeed, Renata grabbed her coat and purse from her office. Will was leaning his hip against the secretary's desk, gesturing as he spoke, and Judith was laughing. Renata smiled. Will always had amusing stories of his encounters while on duty. He shared the superficial anecdotes readily whenever they met, but stubbornly refused to talk to her about the serious nature of his work, insisting that it was too grim for her. He seemed to forget or ignore that her work often required her to deal with life's less appealing aspects. That was another reason she didn't think they were right for each other. He couldn't accept the realities of her profession, and of her commitment to it. Still, as he'd said, this was only lunch, not marriage.

"Burgers okay with you?" he asked as they walked to the exit.

She would have preferred a chef's salad, but the diner Will mentioned treated greens as if they were only fit for goats. Still, Will needed more food than she did. "Fine with me," she told him. And after those few unpleasant minutes with Frank Dane, she was more than willing to give up salad for Will's cheerful company.

As they sat in a booth in the diner and waited for their orders, Will reached across the table and took her hands in his.

She didn't resist, but if Will was expecting her to feel a spark at the contact, he'd be disappointed.

"I heard you had Frank Dane in your office this morning," he said.

Renata nodded. "What a jerk! The man is pond scum! He thinks he can squeak out of any charges, but not this time."

"Be careful, Renata. He's a shark and you're just a little minnow. I don't want to see you get hurt."

Will's reference to her lack of height and physical power irritated her almost as much as his assumption that he was responsible for her. "Some shark! He's a catfish with a superiority complex. He wouldn't dare hurt me," she said firmly.

Will's strong hands wrapped more firmly around hers. His eyes met hers, gravely serious for once. "He *would* dare, Renata, and he *can* hurt you." Before she could argue, he went on, "Hell, you don't seriously think Mick Donovan's accident was an *accident,* do you? Or that it's coincidence no one ever seems available to testify against Dane?"

Renata felt a chill at Will's words, but swiftly shook it off. "Nonsense! You're making him sound like Attila the Hun, for pity's sake! Dane's a bully and a swine, not a murderer. Besides, the juror who claimed Dane tried to bribe him died of a heart attack. That was just rotten coincidence." Will lowered his gaze for just an instant, but it was enough to make Renata pounce. "What is it? Do you know something we don't?"

His eyes narrowed and his fingers tightened almost painfully. "Damn it, Renata!" he growled under his breath. "I'm a cop, for crying out loud. We're supposed to be on the same side, you and me. Remember?"

Renata immediately felt contrite for implying that Will could be anything but honest and above reproach. "Then what are you suggesting? That Frank Dane is responsible for Mick being in a body cast?"

"If he is, it could be a warning to Mick to back off. I was there when they were prying him out of his car. He's lucky to be alive, you know. I don't want to find your car at the bottom of a ditch, and you hurt—or worse."

She swallowed hard. "I'm not saying I believe it, but if it's true Dane had anything to do with Mick's accident, that's all the more reason to stop him. Besides, the State won't drop charges against him simply to protect me."

"I'm not suggesting the State drop the charges, babe. I just don't want you to be the one to prosecute Dane." This was supposed to be just one of many criminal cases. Now, Will's intensity alarmed her almost as much as his suspicion that Mick had been deliberately injured. She tried to tug her hands out of Will's, but he wouldn't let her go. "Pass his file to one of the other A.D.A.s."

He was treating her as if she didn't know enough to come out of the rain! "I can't believe you're saying this. Frank Dane is an unpleasant bully, but I'm not in any danger from him. That would be too obvious. Everyone knows Mick drove a poorly maintained older car. His brakes failed during a thunderstorm. The police found no evidence of tampering. Besides, even if I suspected Frank Dane intended to threaten me, I have a commitment to my work." A muscle in Will's face jumped as if he were clamping his jaw closed.

The waitress arrived with their food and Will released her hands, but even as Renata busied herself pouring catsup on her grilled chicken sandwich, she felt his gaze on her face. He was serious. She couldn't believe it, but he was truly serious about her dropping out of the Dane case. She looked across the table at him, searching for the right words to tell him how she felt, but not certain exactly what that was. It was hard to be angry at him for caring about her safety, but it was exasperating that he couldn't understand that she wasn't a damsel in distress.

Renata tried again to explain. "The thing is, Will, you don't know me well enough to—"

"Yeah, babe, but I'd like to know you well enough to . . ." He winked. "You know." He leaned forward and touched her cheek with his fingertips. "Give me a chance, Renata. You could find yourself crazy about me." He smiled at her like a naughty boy who knows he can get away with almost anything using charm.

She stifled a sigh. "I'm sorry, Will, but I'm so busy, I can't see when I'll have any free time until Christmas, at the soonest. It wouldn't be fair for me to ask you to wait that long." The words sounded incredibly lame as she spoke, so she smiled tentatively, hoping he would understand that she had nothing against him personally.

Will's jaw set. "That's not the whole story, is it? You think dating a cop is beneath you."

His accusation stung. He really didn't get it. "For pity's sake, no! This has nothing to do with either of us! I don't have time to date! I'm up to my elbows in alligators, trying to protect society from pond scum like Frank Dane," she countered. "I've been taking care of myself for a long time, and I don't need you exercising your protective instincts." Now she was too irritated at his patronizing attitude to feel guilty for her sharp words.

Will stared at her for a long moment, then shook his head and picked up his burger. "Eat your lunch." His stony expression said as clearly as his tone that the discussion was over, and that she hadn't convinced him of anything.

Renata tried to nibble at her grilled chicken sandwich, but the dry meat stuck in her throat. The thought of Mick Donovan being deliberately injured had taken away her appetite. So had her flare-up at Will. She never lost her temper. Neither did Will. Frank Dane certainly brought out the worst in people. She sipped at her diet cola and waited for Will to finish his meal.

"If you're not going to eat that, I'll take it," he said after he'd wolfed down the last of his jumbo burger. There was no trace of the former anger in his voice.

"Go ahead." She slid the plate toward him. He grinned and dispatched it in a few bites.

During the short walk back to her building, Will talked about the young basketball players he coached, but Renata hardly heard him. Instead, she was wondering if he could be right that Mick had been hurt deliberately. And that she could be in danger, too. Trying to shake off that notion, she smiled up at Will. He gave her a sweetly cocky smile in return. She was grateful he had the kind of nature that didn't stew over disagreements. It was such a welcome change from the simmering, angry silences she'd grown up with in her grandmother's house in Avon. She wished she could feel more than simple liking for Will.

With her mind occupied by too many troubling thoughts, she tripped on a broken curb. Will caught her elbow when she stumbled against him, then steadied her gently. She pushed her glasses back up on her nose.

"Thank you," she murmured, feeling vaguely guilty that his touch through her coat sleeve didn't feel extraordinary and exciting. She *did* want to fall in love. She just didn't want to do it over and over, looking for the right man. It would be nice to be as deeply in love as the woman she dreamed of being nearly every night.

Will squeezed her arm before releasing it, but the gesture only felt friendly. Neither of them said anything more as they walked the rest of the way to the steps of her building. Will blocked her way before she could reach for the door.

"Renata, just give me a chance. If it doesn't work out, fine. We'll be friends. Okay? Let me take you out tonight," he said with touching intensity. Looking down at her, he brushed a curl of her hair back from her cheek. She held back her sigh.

"I really can't tonight," she answered honestly. "I promised a very close old friend I'd drop by after work. She's moving today and could use an extra pair of hands." He nodded, but he looked so disappointed, Renata felt her resistance waver. Maybe if she went out with him once, he'd finally get the idea that they weren't destined to become a couple. "I'm free tomorrow—Good grief, that's Friday already!" she exclaimed.

"Damn! Can't Friday. I'm doing a double shift to pay Morgan back. How about Saturday night?"

She felt her lips curve upward. "Saturday will be fine."

He grinned like a cat with a mouth full of feathers. "I'll pick you up at seven. Wear something you can go dancing in."

He turned and walked away before she could answer. She watched him stride toward his unmarked navy blue sedan, a tuneless whistle drifting back to her. Dancing? It looked like her plan to discourage him had backfired.

Renata opened the heavy front door and headed toward her office. But by the time she reached her desk, the only thing on her mind was the somewhat daunting backlog of work that always waited for her.

Ray stared at the floor showing through his black motor-cycling boots. What the—? What the hell was that all about? He lifted his hand and saw the furnace through it, as if he were looking through colored glass. Oh, man! This was too weird! He sure hoped he was dreaming.

But he didn't think he was. He had a sick feeling that something had gone very wrong with his plans. But what? Hell, that didn't matter. The only important thing was to get to Celeste and reassure her that he still loved her, that they were still going to elope. His money and the ring he'd bought to surprise her were in a metal box, hidden behind bricks in a corner of the furnace room in the Garvey mansion.

Ray pivoted and scanned the furnace room. It looked the same as always. He hurried toward his hiding place, but had to stop short halfway there. Whoa! His head was spinning! He reached out to brace his hand against the wall, and sank right through the wall, up to his shoulder. He jerked himself straight again and made his way behind the furnace. Everything was a lot cleaner than the last time he'd been in there. There was no sign of his secret spot, but he knew where the box was. Kneeling, he slid his hand into the space in the brickwork, low down on the wall, and grinned.

And then he curled his fingers around the brick—and right through it. He could see the brick through his fingers, but he couldn't feel it, couldn't touch it, couldn't move it. A terrible desperation filled him. Celeste's ring! To hell with the money, he had to give her the ring, had to let the world know she was his earth angel, now and forever.

Chapter Two

Leaving her office later that afternoon, Renata wondered how the weather knew it was Halloween. This morning had been sunny and mild. Now, the day was appropriately damp, cold, and depressingly gray. Only the prospect of spending the evening with Melissa Hartley brightened her mood. It would be great to live ten minutes away from her old friend, after hardly seeing her in the years since law school.

She clutched her unlined trench coat closed against the bite of the wind with one hand, and gripped the handle of her overloaded legal bag with the other. The briefcase was so heavy that the handle dug painfully into her bare palm and banged against her leg with every other step across the parking lot. Over the past weeks, she'd been too wrapped up in work to remember that Indian summer would soon—and abruptly—turn to autumn. Her gloves were in the pocket of her winter coat. Unfortunately, her coat was in the cedar closet at her grandmother's house in Avon, almost two hours away from the Connecticut shore town she now called home.

Dry leaves eddied around her ankles as she walked. A sudden gust deposited airborne debris in her hair. Movement at the far end of the parking lot caught her attention. A plain, dark car—an unmarked State police car, no doubt—wheeled into the lot, then stopped in front of her, blocking her path to her own car. When she halted, her briefcase banged into the side of her knee again. Annoyed, Renata pressed her lips together and started to make her way around the sedan. The sudden blast of the horn made her jump and set her heart pounding painfully.

Composing herself, she lifted her chin and took another step. The driver's door opened. A moment later, Will unwound his long, lanky frame from the front seat and stood up to grin playfully at her. She should have known. Renata tried to frown back, but the laughter in Will's eyes wouldn't let her.

"Any chance we can grab dinner after you visit your friend?"

Renata shook her head, amazed at his persistence. "Sorry. I promised Mel I'd help her get settled. And then I'm spending a few hours with Frank Dane." Will jerked his head and narrowed his eyes. "Well, not with him," she clarified hastily, dropping her gaze to the legal bag that was beginning to stretch her arm painfully, "but with his files." His, and as many others as she could get to before she fell asleep.

Will seemed to notice the briefcase for the first time. The disapproval left his face and he gave her a sheepish smile, then reached for the handle. She didn't have the room or the strength to resist. Awkwardly, he took the bag from her, his much bigger hand almost crushing hers as it crowded her out of the way.

"Damn, this weighs a ton! It's too heavy for a little thing like you to have to drag around. Why don't I drop this at your place for you?"

"No, thanks. My car is in the next row," she answered tartly. If he hadn't been so patronizing, she would have agreed. But her pride still rankled from Dane's taunts about her youth, stature, and apparent need for protection.

Her grandmother hadn't sweetened her mood by phoning earlier to remind her, again, that she was shirking her responsibility to settle down and produce heirs to the family fortune. She'd gritted her teeth and listened while Gran raved about "that nice young David Mayhew," her best friend's grandson and some kind of businessman in New York City. When she reminded Gran that David hadn't exactly beaten a path to her door, and in fact, had never personally called or asked her out, she'd gotten a lecture about how she should make amends for snubbing the "poor boy" ten years before at a charity fund-raiser. Only when she pointed out how Gran hated the notion of women—her many-times-married mother for example—asking men out, had her grandmother changed the subject.

Apparently reacting to her scowl, Will now lifted his eyebrows, but turned without speaking and started walking toward her silver Infiniti. She almost had to run to keep up with his long strides. He stopped beside the car and waited for her to unlock it. Will set her briefcase in her backseat and shut the door. When he turned toward her again, he reached out to grasp her shoulders in his large, gloved hands, forcing her to tip her head back to look up at him.

"Do me a favor, huh?" he muttered. "Leave the perps and suspects at the office Saturday night, okay? Give me a chance here. Let's find out if we click as well as I think we do."

Oh, dear! Maybe she shouldn't have agreed to go out with Will after all. He seemed to have more on his mind than dinner. She didn't want to mislead him. Where were all her eloquent words, her gift of thinking on her feet, when she needed them? "Will, I . . . I don't think I'm ready to—"

He gave a soft snort of laughter and released her. "Hey, relax. You take everything so seriously," he told her, shaking his head. He stepped back and winked. "Of course, if you'd said yes, I wouldn't say no."

Renata suspected he was joking to protect his pride. She sighed. "Will—"

"Don't say it." His smile faded. "I'm trying not to rush you, Renata, but I like you. I'm just a hardworking regular guy, and you're such a classy lady, and it makes me feel pretty damn special when you even smile at me." He shrugged. "I'm a normal guy. I can't help it if I want more than a smile."

His wistfulness touched the empty place inside her, and brought the sting of tears to her eyes. He could be so sweet, but that wasn't enough. Her mother flitted impulsively from man to man, presenting each one to her own skeptical mother and her insecure daughter as "the right one this time." At least the ones who simply walked out on them had spared them living in a constant war zone. Long before her mother's third marriage, Renata had retreated to the emotional Arctic of her grandmother's house, unable to continue witnessing the results of her mother's emotional mistakes.

Renata started to speak, to explain her caution, but he touched his gloved fingertip to her lips. "I know," he murmured. "Too much, too soon." She smiled gently and nodded. He grinned crookedly. "Okay, go. Drive carefully. Have fun. And watch out for things that go bump in the night."

An hour later, putting dishes away in her friend's newly renovated kitchen, Renata thought of Will's warning when a muffled thump startled a yelp from her and Melissa. They looked at each other as one of the movers emerged from the basement stairwell, then burst out laughing.

"Halloween probably isn't the best day to move into a house that's supposed to be haunted," she teased her friend, but she couldn't resist looking over her shoulder. It was obviously the power of suggestion, but she kept feeling as if someone were watching her.

Ray heard guys' voices in the basement and forced himself to get up. Oh, man! He felt seasick! It took a while for him to catch his balance enough to move around. Then he discovered that he sorta floated instead of walked, and he still could see through his body. It looked like he was gonna have to go around like this a while longer. At least he should see what was going on upstairs, and who those guys were.

Half-floating, half-stumbling out of the furnace room, he reached out for the light switch. Nothing. Damn! He couldn't feel things, couldn't move them. But then the bulb in the ceiling fixture flickered. Hmm. That was interesting. He tried again, keeping his hand on the switch longer this time. He still couldn't feel anything, couldn't move the switch, but the bulb flickered, then flared brighter than normal. The loud *pop!* it made when it exploded made him jump.

A second later, he heard curses in English and Italian from the guys prowling around down there. With a grin, he floated out of the furnace room and looked around the basement. There were two big, beefy guys in sloppy jeans and baggy shirts stacking cartons in the room where Old Lady Garvey kept stuff she collected from her rich friends to give to charities. Last he'd seen that room, it was full of clothes in bags and kitchen stuff in baskets. Now, there were just boxes with big letters that said: LAW BOOKS and MYSTERIES and REFERENCES. Maybe some of Mrs. Garvey's friends were giving books away now.

Feeling bolder, he stood in front of one of the movers. The guy looked right through him, then started to *walk* right through him! Ray jumped away just in time.

The mover cursed. "First that light, now cold drafts! Let's get outta here!" he muttered to the other guy.

Ray grinned. Whatever was wrong with him had its plus side, too. This was the perfect time to see if he could repeat his experiment with the lights. Those fluorescent bulbs—he didn't remember them being there. *Well, here goes,* he thought. He touched the starter end of the bulb farthest away from the two men. No point in hurting anyone if it worked. First the thing hummed, then it dimmed. A second later, it exploded. Bits of glass came down like sleet. The movers both swore loudly, then bolted faster than he thought two blubbery guys could run.

With a snicker, Ray followed them upstairs. On his way up, the sound of female laughter made him curious. He wasn't sure what was wrong with him or what was going on in the house, but at least he wasn't still lurching around the furnace room.

He stopped at the top of the basement stairs. For a flash of a moment, he'd thought he heard Celeste's voice, but he didn't see her anywhere. All sorts of stuff he didn't recognize was piled up in the hallways and the rooms. The rooms looked different, too, especially the kitchen. It looked like a picture in one of those fancy decorating magazines Celeste's mother got. This stuff had to belong to someone else. Where was all of Old Lady Garvey's stuff? How could she move out without him knowing about it?

Ray shook his head. Mistake. The house tilted and swooped around him. When he got steady again, he saw the two chicks unpacking things. His eyes didn't work so well, but he was pretty sure he'd never met them before. How the hell could they move in without him knowing? Not that that mattered. Celeste was the only thing that mattered. He had to get a grip, had to find her so they could elope before it was too late. Jesus! How much time had he lost already, sleeping like a bear?

He forced himself to move around, trying to walk off whatever had hit him. Could these two chicks see him? He'd have to sneak out before they spotted him and called Old Lady Garvey. But who were they? Ray hovered in the hallway, watching the two chicks in the kitchen. Something weird was going on here. And where was Old Lady Garvey? Last thing he remembered, she was getting ready to give him hell for playing rock'n'roll in her house. . . .

Oh, yeah. He remembered now. Somebody sure did give him hell . . . he was dead.

The heavy front door of the old mansion groaned eerily on its hinges as it swung shut behind the movers. Renata and Melissa looked at each other and giggled at the men's hasty departure. Every time the house settled or the wind howled through the surrounding trees, the movers had glanced at each other. One of the men crossed himself furtively whenever he thought the women weren't looking. With dusk settling, the two burly men had scuttled out, muttering about dark, and candy, and kids on the roads.

"Even with the kitchen remodeled, the house does feel like a setting for an Edgar Allen Poe story," Melissa said with a grin. "How about some tea?"

"I'd love some." The quiet in the house, after all the noise the movers had made, seemed to breathe. Once again, Renata had that uncomfortable feeling that someone was watching them.

With a quick laugh at her own foolishness, she followed Melissa, who was flipping on lights on the redecorated first floor. They moved from the living room and dining room and parlor to the kitchen and mud room, stepping around cartons, discussing the lovely detailing that had been painstakingly restored by local artisans. Renata couldn't help a twinge of envy at the gracious home her friend was creating for herself. It was the kind of house she herself would like to have one day. But not until she'd found someone to share it with. Otherwise, it would be an empty shell, like the mansion her grandmother rattled around in.

After Melissa filled the kettle, they went upstairs, laughing self-consciously as they turned on the lights in the hallway and in all six bedrooms, even the three that were totally empty and unfinished.

"Not a ghost in sight," Renata announced, but her cheerfulness sounded forced to her ears.

"So, how about staying over tonight?"

Melissa gave her such a wistful smile that Renata almost gave in. For all her friend's bravado, Renata wondered if Melissa was having second thoughts about buying this house. It might not be haunted, but it was old and huge, and made strange noises. Well, of course it wasn't haunted, she corrected herself. There was no such thing as a ghost.

Renata started to speak, then stopped, mouth open. It was even stronger this time, the uneasiness of being watched. A current of cool air eddied around her as they stood on the landing. It was probably just a draft from a fireplace in one of the unused rooms, she told herself, determined to be logical.

Feeling foolishly guilty at abandoning her friend, she said, "Sorry, Mel. I'd really like to, but I can't. I've got a briefcase full of work to read tonight. I'm in way over my head."

"Sure," Melissa scoffed, but she was smiling. "You're just scared of the old Garvey mansion ghost."

Renata smiled back. "Could be. But I do have piles of cases to sort through. And this Frank Dane creep . . . I'm determined to get him convicted if it's the last thing I do."

Melissa shivered, then propped her hands on her hips and said sternly, "Don't say it like that, Renata! That's too close to tempting fate."

Renata gave a little snort of amused disbelief. "He's slippery, Mel, and he's a crook, but he's not going to rub out an assistant district attorney." The memory of Will's warnings, his suspicions about Mick Donovan's injuries, momentarily stole her amusement. But she refused to let the bad guys ruin her entire evening. "I'll compromise," she offered with a smile. "I'll stay long enough to help you unpack a little more and hand out the Halloween goodies." She tugged on one of Melissa's hands and led her down the stairs. "Now, let's have our tea before we tackle any boxes."

Once back on the first floor, Renata went through the parlor and into the huge formal dining room. She cleared off enough space among the piles of dishes on the table for them to set the mugs she found. As she turned to walk around the table, she saw something move across the room.

Someone was out there, watching her!

Heart pounding, she stared at the tall panes of glass in the ten French doors opening into what had once been a lush garden.

There! She caught sight of a shape in the glass. Human, but indistinct. Shadowy and still, watching her. Oh, God! Renata felt herself trembling and wrapped her arms around her middle to contain her terror.

The figure in the glass moved. Renata's stomach lurched. The figure wrapped misshapen arms around its dark midsection. And suddenly, she nearly laughed aloud. It was her own reflection, distorted by the imperfect panes of old glass!

"Oh, for pity's sake! Get a grip! A simple trick of the light," she muttered.

"Who are you talking to?" Mel asked as she carried the teapot into the dining room. "Don't tell me you've found the ghost already."

"I'm talking to myself, which only proves I'm out of my

mind," Renata answered. "A sane person would spend the evening with you, or Will, instead of going home alone to read about the exploits of career criminals."

"Your Mr. Dane does sound charming." Melissa poured their tea. "I hope he has his own attorney. I'd hate to find him on my doorstep."

Renata settled onto a chair and reached for her mug. The hot tea steamed her glasses. "He has a small army of attorneys, the type who give the profession a bad name. Although, if he knew about you, he's the kind of man who would try to hire you to defend him. Forcing two friends into a courtroom battle on his behalf would probably appeal to his sense of humor."

Melissa sat across from her and shook her head. "Not a chance. When I gave up my entertainment clients in L.A., I swore I'd never take on another sleaze-master."

Their eyes met, and laughter bubbled between them, reminding Renata of the easy rapport they'd had almost immediately after meeting in law school. "Ah, Mel, I'm glad you're here." Renata said with a sigh. "It's been a long time."

"Too long," Melissa agreed, lifting her mug in salute.

This was weird. He was so sure he was hearing Celeste's voice, her laugh, but he could only see the two dames he didn't know. Ray forced himself to stay awake as he made his way along the hallway to see what was happening. He was getting better at moving around, but he still had some trouble controlling direction and speed. Not that it mattered. If he didn't stop in time, he just floated through whatever was in his way. He didn't even really feel the impact. Well, of course he didn't. He was dead.

If he didn't know better, he'd say he was a ghost.

A clock chimed eight times, but it didn't sound like Old Lady Garvey's grandfather clock. In fact, he couldn't see any familiar stuff. Everything looked new, especially the kitchen. He hovered in the hallway and peered into the foyer. The front door was open wide—he was supposed to oil those hinges, wasn't he? They screeched like a banshee—and the two women were standing in the doorway, staring into the darkness outside.

"I guess no one knows you're here yet," one of the women said. The little one, with the glasses and the thick dark hair, who kept shivering whenever he drifted too close. Like she felt him, but couldn't see him. She was the one he thought sounded like Celeste. Didn't look like her, though. Celeste was tall and blonde, with big blue eyes and a figure that didn't quit. This one had dark eyes and looked about fourteen from the neck down. Every time she shivered, he felt like he'd kicked a puppy.

"Either that," the tall redhead answered, "or no one wants their kids trick-or-treating at a haunted house."

Now he got it. Halloween! No wonder he couldn't sleep. It was the night for spirits to wake up and walk. Haunted house, huh? Maybe he should get into the spirit of the night and find some chains to rattle. Not that he believed in ghosts. That was . . .

Oh, yeah.

By eight-thirty that evening, it was clear that none of the neighborhood kids were going to come to Melissa's house for Halloween treats. It was too bad, really, Renata thought, because now there was that big bowl of chocolate bars and just the two of them. Ironically, if she'd gone home to work earlier as she planned, she'd have had to turn off her porch light because she'd forgotten to buy candy and a pumpkin. Will was right; she was eating, sleeping, and breathing her work, although he was the one blowing the case against Frank Dane out of proportion.

With a sigh, Renata lifted the last of Melissa's silk dresses out of the garment box and hung them in the closet.

"You better get yourself some woolies, Mel. All you've got is warm weather clothes."

Melissa turned from smoothing a quilt over the four-poster bed. "I know. It's already colder than I remember."

"That's a beautiful quilt," Renata commented. "Isn't that a wedding-ring pattern?" The suddenly bleak expression on Melissa's face prompted her to ask, "What?"

"I bought the quilt for my hope chest." She sighed. "Back when I still believed Gabe and I would get married."

"Gabe who?" She couldn't recall Melissa ever telling her about someone she'd wanted to marry. She also couldn't recall anyone in law school named Gabe. The only Gabe she knew was . . .

"Gabe Bautista." Melissa blinked as if to clear her eyes. "You probably know him."

Renata felt her jaw drop. "Gabe Bautista? As in New Harbour's youngest ever Chief of Police Gabe Bautista?" Her voice must have gone up an octave by the time she stopped for breath. "You and *that* Gabe?"

Melissa nodded.

"Oh, my! You never said a word, even when you knew I was moving down here. Even when you said *you* were moving here." She didn't mean to sound accusing. "I mean . . ."

Melissa smiled sadly. "I know. I guess I should have. It's an old story, but it still hurts. When I was sixteen and he was eighteen, my father broke us up and sent me away to private school. Said the son of a beat cop wasn't good enough for his princess."

From her short acquaintance with Gabe Bautista, he was a prince, Renata mused. She'd liked him, and respected him, immediately. Most people, except the bad apples, seemed to feel the same way about him. But she understood what her friend was saying. Hadn't Will accused her yesterday of being a snob? It was hard to ignore the tension between cops and lawyers, to pretend the differences in status, education, earning power, didn't exist. She and Melissa both came from wealthy families concerned about proper matches. She herself was the result of her mother flaunting that snobbery, and not a week of her life had gone by that her grandmother hadn't reminded her of that, as if it were somehow her own fault that she'd been fathered by a man her mother shouldn't have married, however briefly.

"Gabe sent back all my letters without opening them," Melissa went on, pulling Renata back from her own thoughts. "By the time I finished high school, my parents had moved to L.A." She shrugged. "I figured he must have found someone else, so I went on with my life." Melissa sat on the edge of the bed. "I'm not carrying a torch for him after all this time. I just never found a man in L.A. I wanted to marry."

Renata sat beside her and placed her hand on her friend's shoulder. Sad as Melissa's story was, Renata envied her. She'd never felt that kind of aching, desperate, profound love for any man, except in her dreams. She wanted to, but she'd always felt as if her heart were insulated. As if she were in some kind of emotional suspended animation.

"Gabe never married, either," Renata told Melissa gently, giving her shoulder a reassuring squeeze when her friend flinched. "He claims he's married to his work and his Harley. I've heard whispers and rumors, because everyone likes to speculate about good-looking bachelors. But I've never heard your name mentioned in connection with his."

"It was so long time ago. Our friends didn't think we belonged together, either." Melissa smiled sadly. "We used to sneak in here whenever we could. We planned to buy this house and live happily ever after."

"Is that why you moved back here?"

"No. I moved back because New Harbour is my real home, and this is where I want to live and practice law. And, before you ask, I bought the house because I always loved it, not because of Gabe. I probably won't ever see him."

"Think again, Mel. You know even better than I, this is a small town. Gabe is very visible, very involved with the community. You're bound to run into him somewhere. Even if you don't practice any criminal law, you won't be able to pretend he doesn't exist."

"I don't intend to," she said with stiff dignity. Renata opened her mouth to apologize for upsetting her friend, but Melissa stood up and smiled. "Let's defrost a pizza, open that bottle of wine you brought, and you can tell me all about this Will person you mentioned earlier."

She should have known her friend would have caught that detail. "There's not much to tell. We aren't dating." Melissa's raised brows prompted her to continue. "He's a State Trooper, and we met three weeks ago." She shrugged at Melissa's smug grin. "He's nice, but he's younger, macho and patronizing."

"Okay, but what's wrong with him?" When Renata opened her mouth to protest, Melissa linked her arm through hers and chuckled.

Ray looked down and discovered he was sunk halfway into the wall he was leaning on. The sight of flowered wallpaper through his leather jacket spooked him. He'd straightened and shook his head. Spooked *him!* Ha! That was a laugh. Hell, *he* was the spook!

This was going to take some getting used to. He'd better pay attention.

The two chicks now were drinking wine in the room Old Lady Garvey called the parlor. They both wore jeans that fit second-skin tight and sweatshirts that fit just the opposite. Music he'd never heard before came from a radio about two feet long, with much better sound than his transistor, wherever it was. Funny, it was the same station he always listened to— the DJ had just given the call letters—but it didn't sound the same.

From what he could put together, the tall one with the long reddish hair was moving in, and the little one with the shoulder-length dark hair, the one who laughed like Celeste, was her friend. Idly, he wondered where Mrs. Garvey was. How long had he been . . . sleeping?

There was something about the friend . . . Did he know her? He drifted closer to get a better look. Oops. A little too close, 'cause she shivered like she felt a draft. He floated back a bit, then studied her. Nope, no one he knew, but there was something about her eyes—not the color, which was dark brown, but the expression behind her glasses—that reminded him of Celeste.

He came fully awake and stood up straight. Aw, hell! Celeste! How were they supposed to get married now? He didn't even know where she was. And he was . . . where he was. And dead. It didn't look good.

They were finishing the last of the frozen pizza when Renata heard the voices outside. Puzzled, she glanced at Melissa, who shrugged and rose to peer out the windows. Renata followed her from room to room, staring into the darkness. She saw no one at the side or back of the house, and wondered if it were just a trick of the wind that voices were carrying as if they were so close.

Then came the thuds on the front of the house. One. Another. Dull thuds. Something soft being thrown at the house. Melissa gasped. Renata felt her pulse pick up speed. More thuds, faster now. And voices jeering and yelling right in front of the wide, wooden porch.

Melissa darted to the closest parlor window. Renata grabbed her arm and pulled her away. "Careful!" she hissed. "They can see you."

"Then I'll put on the outside light so we can see them." Before Renata could stop her, Melissa suited actions to words.

Cautiously, Renata peeked again. There was a group of sheet-covered figures milling around the front lawn, apparently unconcerned about the light now illuminating them. One bent and picked something out of a basket, then lifted an arm and flung the object at the house. It made a soft thud and drew a cheer from the rest of the group. Then the sheeted figures jostled each other to reach into the basket.

Melissa uttered a sharp, angry curse and moved toward the nearest phone, telling Renata she was calling the police. A barrage of thuds hit the house as she dialed. As she spoke, a rock smashed through the pane of glass beside Renata. Her cry echoed Mel's, who urged the police to hurry before hanging up.

"They're on the way," Melissa told her across the mess of broken glass. "The cop says stay away from the windows."

Renata rolled her eyes. "No kidding."

"Are you okay? Did any of the glass hit you?"

"I'm fine. Just mad." Her anger grew by the second, fueled by her sense of helplessness and the fear that the kids could do real harm. She suspected Melissa felt the same way. The thuds against the house continued, along with the wild whooping, but no more glass broke. "I suppose the kids will scatter the second they hear the sirens."

Suddenly, the thuds stopped. Seconds later, the raucous howling they'd heard through the broken window turned indignant. Deeper male voices, their words indistinguishable but their tone authoritative, overrode the protests of the uninvited guests. "We weren't doin' nothin'," and "We were just havin' fun," came through the air several times.

"I'm not impressed by their idea of fun," she said to Mel, who made a face, then moved toward the windows, stepping around the broken glass scattered on the newly oiled hardwood floor to stand beside her. Six "ghosts" were being unmasked by several uniformed police officers, then marched to two waiting cruisers. The sirens wailed as the boys were taken away.

The sharp knock on the front door startled yelps out of both of them. Sheepishly, Renata smiled at Melissa who, with one hand on her throat, retraced her way around the glass. The knock came again as Mel moved out of sight into the foyer. The heavy front door creaked like a prop from an old Dracula movie. And then, a long silence.

As soon as Renata heard the rumbling baritone in the foyer, she recognized Gabe Bautista's voice. Poor Melissa probably wasn't ready to face him without any warning. Of course, she had to know she'd be seeing Gabe again, but not so soon. The Chief of Police seldom made house calls.

"Not much of a welcome back," he commented as he walked into the room. He stared at Renata. She gave him a smile that felt less than convincing and pushed her glasses up her nose self-consciously. "What are you doing here? Do you two know each other?"

She nodded. "From law school. We shared an apartment."

"Figures," he muttered, then turned to Mel. "Jesus, what a mess! Did either of you get hurt?" Melissa shook her head. "What other damage did they do?"

"They broke one window, but I haven't looked at the front of the house." Renata thought Melissa sounded remarkably calm and composed.

"You don't want to," he said. "It's covered with tomatoes and eggs. You going to press charges?"

Melissa glanced from Gabe to Renata. "Do you think I should?"

"I would," he told her. "The two rich kids usually get away with hell, and let the others take the blame. Hell, you've got an assistant D.A. as a witness. Trespassing. Public mischief. Property damage. Reckless endangerment. They might benefit from a little shaking up. I'd like you both to come down to the station tomorrow and give a statement. Okay?"

"Yes. Thank you," Melissa murmured. Renata suspected this was the most awkward moment of her friend's adult life, but she was handling it very well. Except, of course, for this long, awkward silence, and the way she was staring at Gabe.

Actually, they were both staring at him. Renata readily conceded he was an attractive man. He was a good and honorable one, as well. But in that black leather motorcycle jacket, sweatshirt and jeans, he looked more like a biker than the Chief of Police. Age and experience had etched themselves into the lean angles of his face. There was no visible silver in the black curls, and his laser-bright blue eyes usually sparkled with intelligence and humor. Not now, though. Now, he looked grim.

She noticed he was holding a sack under one arm.

"What's that?" Trying to keep her teeth from chattering in the cold draft from the broken window, she unwrapped one arm from around her middle to point. At least *now* she had a reason for feeling drafts!

He swore under his breath. "Add cruelty to animals to that list of charges. A cat," he said, his expression grim. Renata and Melissa gasped. "A black cat. One of the boys gave it a sleeping pill he stole from his mother. They said they found it hanging around and figured it was a stray nobody wanted. God knows what the little bastards were planning to do with it."

"Is it—?" He shook his head. "What will you do?"

"Take it to the pound."

Melissa shook her head and held out her hands. "Give me

the cat, Gabe. The poor thing's been through enough without waking up at the pound."

He held the sack out toward her. Melissa took it. Renata saw their hands touch briefly and turned away to give them a moment of privacy. When she stole a peek at them, Mel was laying her sad little burden on a chair and Gabe was scowling again at the mess on the floor.

He looked at Renata. "Are you sure you're all right?" There was gruff concern in his voice. She nodded and saw him relax a degree. "Good." He turned back to Melissa. "Don't forget to give the desk sergeant your statement tomorrow. I don't want our friends thinking they can do whatever they want because they're just kids. Do you need some help putting something over that window? It's supposed to get pretty cold tonight."

Melissa smiled but shook her head. "We can do it. Good night. And thank you."

Gabe walked away and shut the door quietly behind himself. A few seconds later, his footsteps echoed down the hollow wooden stairs of the porch. Outside the front of the house, a motorcycle roared to life, then slowly rumbled into the distance.

Ray drifted to the front door behind the cop. He caught a quick glance at the little dark-haired chick, Renata, and saw her shiver again. She was kinda cute, even with those glasses, and he felt bad about giving her chills, but he could worry about that later. Right now, he just wanted to hang his head out—or through—the door. The roar of that big Harley was music to his ears.

He stepped out onto the porch to get a better look at the bike and smacked into a wall. What the—? Back in the house, he floated through walls like they were made of air. What was out here? Nothing! Nothing he could see anyway, but he couldn't go past the top step.

Damn it, he was trapped! How was he going to find Celeste now?

Chapter
Three

Gabe grudgingly geared down for a downhill curve, then opened the throttle and roared toward the next bend, as if he could outride the night. If he weren't a cop, he'd take off his helmet so he could feel the cold slap of the wind in his face. He needed something to force the image of Melissa Hartley from his mind.

He wasn't handling this well. Hell, he'd known for weeks she was coming back. New Harbour was a very small town. Her name on the deed was a matter of public record, even if the real estate agent who'd handled the deal hadn't been the wife of one of his cousins. And the renovations she'd arranged long-distance had been contracted to the brother of one of the women on the police force. His next door neighbor was the decorator. But knowing all that, he still felt like he'd walked off the edge of a cliff.

Damn her for coming back! Damn *him* for rushing to her rescue like the fool he was! Sixteen years after she'd left without a backward glance, without a word of explanation, he still couldn't control the reflex to take care of her. Still couldn't stop wanting her.

He was grateful Renata Moretti had been there, to keep him from making a total ass of himself. He liked Renata—had from her first day on the job. She came from the same kind of money as the Hartleys, but Renata really cared about justice, cared about ordinary people. Funny, her being Lissa's good friend. Lissa Hartley probably didn't know what ordinary people were.

The lights of a car behind him swept over the dark road, then dropped out of sight when he sped around the next curve. He knew he should slow down, knew he should take himself back to the station, check on the punks who'd been terrorizing Lissa, then go home. And he would, just as soon as he'd completed the circuit of roads that led into town the back way. Maybe by then, his head would be clear. He eased up on the throttle and downshifted into another, sharper turn, still torturing himself with thoughts of Melissa.

Ray moved aside as the two women walked to the front door, almost walking through him. The one called Melissa watched her friend, Renata, drive away, then carried that limp kitten up the stairs. He drifted back into the living room to check on the cardboard patching the broken window. Hardly any cold air came through. He couldn't have done better himself. Of course, since he couldn't even pick anything up, it was just as well the two women had managed without help.

His head still buzzed from hitting that invisible wall. Hell, he couldn't help himself. Why was he thinking about trying to help anyone else?

He didn't like being alone on the first floor, so he drifted upstairs. Too bad Renata had gone home. She seemed to feel him, even if she didn't see him. He needed to talk to someone, to make some sense out of what was happening. Maybe he'd have some luck with Melissa. She was moving around the bedroom Old Lady Garvey had used. The lights were dim but he could tell the furniture was all different now. Looked like Mrs. Garvey had moved out after all. But when? This was all pretty confusing. How come he didn't know? How long had he been . . . not been . . . whatever?

Melissa suddenly stopped moving around and stood still as if she were listening. *Probably expecting more of those little punks to attack,* he thought. Ray strained to listen, too. All he heard were the usual creaks of the old house and the sounds of nature outside. Nothing else.

As he watched, Melissa took a deep breath, then turned her attention to the kitten she'd placed on a chair. This time, when she stroked the dirty fur, he could hear the little body start to purr, softly at first, then more strongly. *Well, good,* he thought. There was already too much death here. Melissa fetched a damp washcloth and gently wiped it over the black coat. She passed the cloth over his face, smiling when a pink tongue slid out to lick at her fingers, even though the cat's eyes stayed shut. For a while longer, Ray leaned against the doorframe, wondering what it was about small animals that made women get all motherly. Maybe Celeste would like a kitten, too. Or some babies. *His* babies.

"Lucky for you that Gabe came along." Melissa's voice startled Ray. He saw she was smiling, and realized she was talking to the kitten. "Lucky it is," she murmured, scooping the sleeping cat into her arms. "Time for bed, Lucky. I hope you're house trained."

Thinking about the last time he'd held Celeste in his arms, the last time she'd cradled his head against her breasts the way Melissa was holding that cat, Ray hoped the little beast knew just how lucky he was.

Gabe left the police station grimly satisfied that the half-dozen creeps who had besieged Melissa's house were being properly processed. They didn't look so tough now. Too bad the rich kids' parents were already there to bail them out, while the other kids were looking forward to a night in the holding tank. But then, there'd always been that division of privilege between the rich kids and the poor ones. Like the line between Melissa and him. The one he should never have crossed.

He walked toward the space where his bike was parked, his boot heels echoing in the quiet. He heard the racing of the engine up the street, heard the squeal of tires behind him.

Turning, he saw a dark car coming right toward him, aiming at the sidewalk. There was no place to duck into. No way to outrun the car. This was it. In a split second, he was going to die. Why?

Time slowed. Gabe stared hard through the windshield, trying to see a face. The front bumper was inches away, moving toward him as if they were underwater. Gabe tried to vault onto the hood. It had to be a better choice than being crushed against the brick wall of the station. He felt the impact lift him, throw him.

His breath came out in a cry of rage and need. "*Lissa!*"

Suddenly, time sped up until it ran out.

Ray wandered the house in the dark, restless. He still couldn't remember how he got to be . . . the way he was. Or when it had happened. He hated this helpless feeling. Didn't much like being transparent, either.

What was he going to do about Celeste? She must be wondering where he was, maybe thinking he'd stood her up. Maybe thinking he didn't really love her, but was just interested in getting back at her old man for setting him up with the cops. Even his doofus of an attorney had been able to get the charges dropped. And Celeste knew he'd never break into her parent's house to steal anything. Except her. He surely would steal her, if he could.

He almost had.

Damn!

He drifted back upstairs, and hovered outside Melissa's room. He hated to ask a stranger for help, especially a girl, but he was beginning to think he was stuck. He didn't even know how long he'd been . . . Or not been. He had to do something about this stupid situation, before Celeste gave up on him and let her old man force her into marrying that doctor. The guy gave him the creeps, hanging onto Celeste like she was some kind of possession. The same way her father treated her. They never cared that she was smart. All they saw was that she was beautiful.

Poor Celeste. Poor little rich girl, she used to call herself, but he'd seen the sadness behind her smile. No one but him had ever looked after her, cared about her feelings. He had to do something.

He needed to think.

He also needed a cigarette.

His hand went to his inside jacket pocket, and sure enough, his smokes were there. Well, hallelujah! Something was working out right! He shook a cigarette out of the pack, and found his steel lighter in his other pocket. The lighter Celeste had given to him for his last birthday, with his initials engraved on the side. The same initials he'd scratched off his ID bracelet before giving it to her, so her old man wouldn't know she was his girl.

He stroked his thumb over the wheel and lit the wick. Cupping his hand over the end of the cigarette, he held the flame to it and took a long drag. A second later, he thought his lungs were going to explode.

The silence echoed around her. Renata looked at her watch twice, unable to believe she'd worked until after midnight. Even the cleaning staff was gone. She'd stopped by the office, on her way home from Melissa's, with the intention of spending only a few minutes picking up a book to add to the pile of work she'd already stuffed into her briefcase. Now, although she'd found what she needed and more, it was much too late to do any more work, here or at home. Not without at least a few hours of sleep.

Stretching her cramped muscles, Renata stood and glanced at the files and casebooks piled on her desk. She had too many projects going at once, but Will's warnings had piqued her curiosity about Frank Dane. He seemed to have no sense of right and wrong—doing whatever he wanted, acting as if laws and rules only applied to other people. Yet, compared to the rapists and murderers and spouse-batterers who paraded through the courts, he was pretty small potatoes. Ah, well, perhaps Will's cautions had been his way of showing his concern. Certainly, he hadn't meant to frighten her.

The moment Renata stepped outside, she became uncomfortably aware of how deserted the area was. She'd left work this late countless times before, without worrying about the darkness that stretched beyond the streetlights. But now, every bush, every shadow, every unidentifiable night noise seemed sinister. Her breath hung in the crisp air, clouding her vision. Her car was in its usual parking space, but even it looked somehow strange in the mist. She felt in her coat pocket for her keys, closing her fingers around them with relief. Will might not have intended to frighten her, but he'd managed to succeed.

Her car started immediately, its purring engine sounding incredibly reassuring. After snapping her seat belt around herself and locking her doors, she switched on her lights and set the car into drive. The headlights swept through the misty air as she drove out of the parking lot, reflecting back at her more than they illuminated, forcing her to strain to see. Once on the back road to New Harbour, she felt her body relax and her lungs expand, as if she'd been holding her breath.

Just as she turned onto Harbour Street in the center of New Harbour, Renata caught the glare of bright headlights in her rearview mirror. She tried to avoid looking at the reflection, but like a moth, her eyes kept seeking the blinding light. Suddenly, she realized she was veering toward the center of the street. Even though there were no oncoming cars, her stomach leaped. She wrenched the wheel toward the right, overcorrecting, before settling back into her lane. The bright lights seemed much closer now. She must have slowed considerably when she'd gone off course. She pressed a little more on the gas pedal to put more distance between her car and the one behind.

But the lights stayed just as close, just as distracting and blinding. She sped up again, just a little, but the distance between the two cars stayed constant, and much too close for comfort. Probably, she thought, it was a car full of teenagers who thought it was funny to scare a woman driving alone. After all, it was Halloween night, a traditional excuse for pranks. Look what those kids had done to Melissa's house.

She snuck a quick glance in the mirror, hoping to see into the car behind her, but the bright lights stabbed her vision, forcing her to turn her head away quickly. Renata realized her heart was pounding. This wasn't funny. This was frightening. But what could she do?

Her cell phone! She could call the police. Thank goodness her brain was starting to work again! Gripping the steering wheel with her left hand, she used her right hand to feel for her briefcase behind the seat. Her cell phone was in there, but she couldn't reach the snaps to get into the case. Damn! Why had she replaced her console-mounted phone with the more portable flip-phone when she'd bought this car? If she hadn't, she would have had the phone at her fingertips.

Now what? Still trying to maintain a safe distance ahead of the other car, Renata thought quickly. If someone was really following her, she couldn't drive home. But where could she go? The State Police were too far away, but the New Harbour police station was just past the next intersection. She pressed harder on the gas pedal, not caring that the traffic light had turned amber.

As she drove into the parking lot of the police station, she realized that the other car's lights no longer shone in her eyes. Whoever had been following her had turned off. If, in fact, someone had actually been following her. Maybe she was imagining things, after her encounter with Frank Dane and an evening in Melissa's spooky old house. Feeling foolish, hoping none of the officers she knew would be coming outside, she turned the car around and headed back onto Harbour Street.

She drove home feeling raw and edgy, but no lights appeared in her rearview mirror. When she arrived home, a small rented cottage that used to be a guest house on an old estate, she flipped on every light in the four welcoming, familiar rooms. Eventually, she calmed down enough to lie in bed trying to talk herself into falling asleep.

"Lissa!"

Ray jerked himself upright. What the hell was that? It sounded like a guy yelling. He stood in the hallway and listened intently, but he didn't hear the voice again. What he did hear was Melissa rustling around in her bed.

"Who's there?" he heard her call. "Gabe?"

"Mew?"

Ray chuckled.

"Hi, Lucky," she whispered. "You scared the daylights out of me. Are you hungry? I don't have any cat food but I think I have some tuna somewhe—"

"M'raow!" Uh-oh. That damn cat knew he was there! The little rat!

"*Smoke!*" Melissa yelped. "I smell smoke! Dear God, the house is on fire!" Ray looked at the cigarette in his hand and shrugged. "Oh, Lucky! You brave kitten! I have to call the fire department. Then we'll get out of here."

The firemen weren't going to appreciate this call. He better stop her before she got them out here over a Camel. He heard her move around and fumble for the lamp switch. He moved to the open doorway as the light came on. Melissa was sitting up in bed, clutching Lucky and reaching for the phone beside her.

"*Hey, baby,*" Ray said, wondering if she'd be able to hear him. It was worth a try. "*How's it goin'?*"

Melissa let loose a shriek. Lucky hissed. Ray cleared his ears and moved a little farther into the room. Leaning against the doorjamb, he took another drag on his cigarette. Now what?

"It's a nightmare. It has to be," Melissa muttered, hanging onto the kitten. She was looking at him, her eyes huge. "Who . . . ? Gabe? No! Who . . . ?" she stammered.

Well, that answered that question. She sure could see him. The edge in her voice made him wish he'd handled this differently. He exhaled smoke that clawed at his lungs, and straightened. Melissa scooted back in her bed. He could feel her fear and it bothered him. He'd always been a rebel, always caught hell from teachers, cops, ministers, you name it, but he'd never scared a girl like this before.

Lucky growled. Ray grinned. Tough little guy. "*I don't think the cat likes me,*" he said to Melissa, hoping he could calm her down.

"Whoever you are, get out of here!" she screeched, shooting down that hope. "Get out before I call the police!"

Well, he couldn't come out and say he was a ghost—it sounded dumb put like that—but he could show her that calling the cops wasn't going to solve her problem. *"Whatever you say,"* he answered, then took another drag of his cigarette. Melissa coughed.

He moved into the room and gave her a wink. Melissa gaped at him.

"Please . . . don't!" she whimpered as he took another step into the room.

He could feel how she held her breath, sensed her trying to think of some way to defend herself, as he walked closer to the end of the bed. He probably should have just stopped there and told her the truth, but he just couldn't help himself. What the hell, it was Halloween. So he walked past her, across the room to the far wall. Pausing between the two wide windows, he gave her a smile. She was staring back at him, her fear giving him another twinge of guilt. But what the hell? Actions speak louder than words, Old Lady Garvey always said.

He walked through the solid brick second story wall.

From inside, there was a scream and a thump.

Renata awoke with a start. The dream had been so vivid, she was still trembling. It was the same dream as always, but this time, not quite the same. She recognized the man holding her in his arms, and the slow song was the same, even though she still couldn't remember the title. But this time, instead of seeing herself as someone else, this time as they danced close and slow, she *was* herself. Then, somehow, they were lying together, their clothes gone like smoke on a windy day. And he kissed her until she ached with need, stroked her until she felt feverish with desire. As he'd slowly, tenderly joined their bodies, Renata had looked up into his shadowed face. His eyes were an almost otherworldly green, darkened by passion. She didn't know who he was, didn't know who *she* was right then, but she knew he loved her, knew she loved him.

She also knew the man in her dream wasn't Will.

She'd awakened to feel her body pulsing in release that brought no relief. Too much imagination, too little sleep. That was all.

Untangling her covers with a sigh, Renata rose and wrapped her old terry robe around her shoulders. The room was cold and dark, but enough light came in around the edges of her window shades to illuminate her path to the hallway. Hugging herself against the chill, she went to the kitchen and poured herself a glass of chocolate milk. Then, barefoot, she went into the living room to stand by the uncovered picture window to look outside while she drank the milk she hoped would help her get back to sleep.

The images from her dream swirled around in her memory while she stared outside, the shapes of parked cars and silhouettes of bare trees across the street indistinct without her glasses. She could barely see the scattered twinkling of stars above them. Instead, she saw his face, her dream lover. Would they ever meet? Or had they met already and she just didn't realize it yet?

Gabe looked down at the doctors and nurses in their green surgical gowns. That was his body under those bright lights. So what was he doing up here, watching? What were they saying? Coma? Who, him? No, couldn't be him. He was up here, watching them try to put Humpty-Dumpty back together.

What the hell had happened? Oh, yeah! The car. He'd gone flying. Hit his head. Driver didn't stop. Stop? Ha! What a laugh. Driver hit him on purpose. Hit and run. Why? Tried to kill him.

Looked like he'd succeeded, too, 'cause what was left of Police Chief Gabe Bautista was looking like yesterday's news.

Say goodnight, Gracie.

In his memory, the car came at him again in slow motion. In the heartbeat before impact, Gabe saw the driver's face as clearly as his own in a mirror. Surprise turned to satisfaction. Now that he knew, he could. . . .

No, this was wrong! He couldn't die.

Lissa! He had to see Lissa again. And he had to tell someone who had tried to kill him. He couldn't let him get away with murder.

* * *

Ray looked at Melissa lying crumpled on the floor and swore. She must have charged out of bed to see where he'd gone, and fainted. He hoped she hadn't hurt herself. It was his fault for showing off with that floating through walls trick. He'd made his point. And smacked into that damn invisible wall again.

He knelt beside her and tried to think of what to do. He didn't know how to do artificial respiration, and anyway, he didn't exactly *breathe*. And he couldn't feel, either, he discovered when he tried to find a pulse in her wrist. Her hair was draped over her neck, so he couldn't see the pulse in the base of her throat. By concentrating, he could sense her heartbeat. She was okay. But her face was as white as a . . . ghost.

He gave a snort of a laugh. The black kitten growled a threat from under the bed. *"Oh, shut up, Short Stuff! I'm not going to hurt her."* The cat hissed a curse. *"Well, if that's the way you feel—"*

"Oh!" Melissa gasped. "Wha . . . ? What do you want?"

While he was talking to the cat and himself, she'd opened her eyes and lay there blinking at him and looking scared spitless. For the first time, it really sank in that the chick—and the cat—could see and hear him. This was good news. This meant he could get help. He could find Celeste and figure out what was happening to him. If Melissa here didn't die of fright first.

"Hey, take it easy. I'm not going to jump you. You're not my type." That was true. It didn't have anything to do with the energy he'd sensed between this Melissa and the cop on the Harley. He just didn't feel that old spark when he looked at this particular woman. He hoped to hell—or wherever—that just because he was dead, he hadn't lost the ability to feel the old spark, because he was going to find Celeste somehow and—

"Do you want money?" she said in a tight voice. "My purse is on the dresser. Take what you want. I haven't unpacked the CD player or the VCR. You can have them. Just take what you want and leave me alone." She got up on one elbow and pushed herself a little away from him.

He didn't know what the hell a CD player or a VCR were, but he figured he must look like the kind of guy who stole them. And attacked women. Well, maybe that's what he looked like, but it *wasn't* who he was. He wasn't big on rules and regulations, but he also wasn't the kind of guy who hurt people. Unless they hurt him first. Or someone he cared about. Which was, he hated to admit, a kinda short list. Just Celeste, really. And Old Lady Garvey, who had been nice enough to him, in a stuffy way.

"Thanks for the offer," he told the woman, trying to tone down the sarcasm, *"but I can't leave."*

She sat up, looking even more scared. "You *can't* leave? Why? Are you waiting for an accomplice?"

That made him smile. *"Nah. I don't like crowds."*

Melissa scooted a little farther away and got her feet under her. "But if you don't want money or electronics or . . . or . . ." Her cheeks turned pink, and he caught what she was thinking. Damn if his own face felt a little warm. "Well, if you don't want anything, then get out!" Whoa! The lady had a temper. The New Harbour Chief of Police was gonna have his hands full with this babe.

"I can't," he told her again. *"I have to stay here."*

"The hell you do!" she snapped. "This is *my* house. *You* are trespassing. You don't belong here."

That made him wince. Well,, they said the truth hurts. *"Okay, you're right. Sorta. Thing is, I don't exactly belong anywhere, if you see what I mean."* He stood up and started pacing, trying to figure out a way to explain what he didn't understand himself.

"Oh, dear God!" Melissa whispered. "I . . . I can see through you!"

Gabe heard the voices and struggled to wake up. *Paul! Paul Sykes! Gotta talk to Paul.* His friend. Paul had been in the operating room, working on him. Gabe remembered watching, admiring Paul's steady hands. Remembered the pain in Paul's eyes. Friends thirty years. Like brothers. He had to tell Paul he was okay.

Other voices. He was moving. Floating. Where was he going? Why couldn't he wake up? He had to tell Paul he was okay. Had to tell New Harbour cops about the driver. Saw his face so clearly, then *pow! Gotta tell them. Murder. Gotta find out why.*

Lissa. Had to see Lissa. Ask her why, too.

As Ray watched, Melissa shook her head. "It has to be a dream. A hallucination. Exhaustion. Food poisoning. Too much Halloween candy," she mumbled. "I'm *not* sitting on the floor having a conversation with a man who walked through the second-floor wall. *Oh, God, and then walked back again!* It's just a dream. Just—"

"I don't think so," he told her. *"We're both wide awake."*

She glared at him. "Who . . . Who are you? *What* are you? Why are you here?"

He rubbed his stubbled chin, considering how to answer. This was worse than a job interview. And a hell of a lot more than a paycheck was on the line. *"Jeez, you ask a lot of questions. You sound like a lawyer,"* he finally muttered.

"I *am* a lawyer."

Unable to resist teasing her, he grinned. *"I knew you weren't my type. Unless you do criminal law."*

"I do general law."

"Too bad. I don't know any generals, but I know plenty of criminals." It was a lie, but, watching her struggle not to rise to the bait, he felt his grin widen. *"Don't you think you should get up now? It's gotta be cold on the floor, and all you're wearing is that flimsy nighty."*

Melissa shook her head. "Right! What am I doing, sitting on the floor in my nightgown, talking to a figment of my imagination in the middle of the night?" she babbled. "If anyone could see me, they'd have me in a rubber room in a New York minute."

Ray watched her trying to pretend nothing unusual was happening. "Mew?" came from under the bed. Melissa clucked to the kitten. "Come on, Lucky. It's okay. You're safe now."

Slowly, the kitten crept out from under the bed, his green eyes reflecting the lamplight like twin emerald beacons. When he reached the edge of her nightgown hem, she scooped him up and cuddled him close. Celeste or no Celeste, Ray thought, he could envy that cat, snuggled between her breasts, purring like an idling Harley. "That's my boy," she crooned. "Let's go back to bed and forget all the bad dreams.

"Dreams," she muttered, getting to her feet. "No ghost with attitude. Just my overactive imagination and too much pizza. Only a fruitcake would believe in a ghost smoking a cigarette and wearing a black leather jacket!"

Ray snorted at her attempt to will him away. Her body jerked at the sound, then she shook her head and walked back toward the antique four-poster bed, hanging up the phone as she went past it. She set Lucky down at the foot of the bed and straightened the quilt before sliding under with a sigh.

Son of a—! She was gonna go to sleep and leave him hanging there!

"Hey! What about me?"

With a gasp, she sat up and clutched the quilt to her chest. The little cat stood up and growled. His ears lay flat against his head, his coat was puffed out, his back arched, his tail straight up. Ray couldn't decide if he found the kitten's stance funny or admirable.

"Get out! Go away! I'm calling the police! Right now!" Her voice rose shrilly. She grabbed the phone and pressed a button. He wondered what happened to the dial.

"Forget it. You and the cat are the only ones who can see me," he told her, guessing, hoping she wouldn't call his bluff. *"Besides, if you try to report a ghost on Halloween, they'll laugh you out of town."*

"There's no such thing as ghosts. You're a petty criminal, breaking and entering." She pressed another button.

"Oh, yeah? When was the last time you saw someone walk through a wall?" He grinned, trying to look cool, but

he was beginning to feel a little desperate. He had to convince this chick he really was there. Something told him she was all the help he was going to get with his problem. *"I'll do it again, if you want."*

"It was an optical illusion. A trick with mirrors."

She pressed another button and Ray heard the muffled sound of the phone ringing at the other end. He didn't think anyone would believe her if she called for help, but one cop in the house was enough for the night. Besides, he was using up a hell of a lot of energy arguing, and he needed to find Celeste.

"You want to see a trick with mirrors? Here! Look! No reflection. See for yourself!"

Her eyes followed his pointing finger. Lucky growled again as Melissa looked into the wood-framed antique mirror across the room. He saw her eyes widen as she saw herself and the cat. But he knew she couldn't see his image even though he was standing between her bed and the mirror.

She hung up the phone.

"You . . . You're a ghost?"

"Yeah. I guess."

"Oh, my God! The house really is . . . haunted?" she said, her voice a lot higher and thinner than before.

"Looks like it, doesn't it?" Feeling more confident now, he grinned and reached into his black leather jacket for his cigarettes and lighter. He shook a cigarette from the pack, took it between his lips, and clicked the lighter open.

"Don't do that!" she ordered sharply. Startled, he snapped the lighter closed and looked at her. "I'm allergic to cigarette smoke," she said in a softer tone.

"Well, keep your pants on. I won't light up." He replaced the cigarette in the pack and put it and the lighter back into his pocket, after first rubbing his thumb over the initials Celeste had had carved there. *"Tastes kinda stale, anyway."* He shrugged.

"Who are you? And why are you here?" She stroked the purring kitten.

"I'm Ray Lowell."

"Sorry, but the name doesn't mean anything to me. Why are you here?"

A good question. *"Someone murdered me,"* he muttered. Saying the words made him feel foolish. He ducked his head a little, avoiding her gaze.

"Excuse me?"

"I told you." He met her eyes, his embarrassment turning to anger. *"Someone killed me, damn it, but I didn't see who, and I don't know why."*

"This sounds like a bad movie. Let me guess. You're going to find out who killed you, then go happily into the afterlife, right?"

"Right." He smiled, pleased that she'd caught on so quickly, until it occurred to him that he didn't have a clue what was going to happen if he found out who murdered him—and why. *"Sort of. I guess."*

"Sort of? You guess? Can you be a little more specific, Mr. Lowell?"

"Call me Ray." He flashed her a grin, feeling much better now that he was pretty sure she was going to help him. Yeah, he had a good feeling about this now. *"What's your name?"*

"Melissa Hartley."

"And you're a lawyer? Son of a b–gun! You're too cute to be an old maid. Why don't you have a husband taking care of you, and some kids?" He shook his head.

"I'll ask the questions, if you don't mind, Ray."

"Now you sound like a cop."

"Never mind me. Tell me about yourself. Why do you think you were murdered in this house?"

"Why do I think I was murdered here?" He snorted. *"Because I'm dead, and I'm stuck here! Look at me!"*

"Either tell me what happened to you, or fade away and let me go to sleep," she snapped back.

Ray grunted and moved toward the foot of the bed. He sat down, not quite able to control the way he sank partway into the mattress. The mattress, however, didn't give under him at all, which was weird, since he weighed about one-eighty last time he checked. Lucky growled softly, but didn't react otherwise. Melissa studied him, but he couldn't tell what she was thinking.

"Talk to me," she said gently. "I want to believe you. Tell me exactly what happened. If I can, I'll try to help you."

"All I remember was being in the front hall fixing something," he told her. *"I did odd jobs for Old Lady Garvey, for extra money. There I was standing on a ladder, and then I felt something hit me in the chest, and then I was . . . you know."*

"It sounds as if you were shot."

When she said the words, he looked away and shrugged, suddenly uncomfortable talking about his own death. He was glad he didn't remember what had happened after he'd been shot.

"It will be easy enough to verify your story. I have to go to the police station tomorrow anyway. With luck, Gabe might be willing to help me search the records." Ray looked at her, unable to find words to say thanks. She smiled. "Of course, he might think I'm nuts if I tell him my first client is a ghost."

He grinned. *"Hey, at least it's an excuse to see him again,"* he teased, making her blush.

She opened her mouth, shut it, then shook her head and said, "Ray, how could you work for Mrs. Garvey? She died and some distant cousin inherited the house. It's been boarded up for about thirty-five years."

Ray whistled softly, trying to hide his shock. How was he going to find Celeste after all that time? His mind went numb. All he could think of to say was, *"Jesus! No wonder my smokes tasted stale."*

Chapter Four

Gabe woke slowly, but only inside. He couldn't make his eyes open. Couldn't make himself speak. Couldn't move. His body was trapped under a heavy weight. But he was alive.

Voices. A woman's voice. Lissa? No. Damn!

"—help you, Dr. Crandall?" the woman's voice was saying.

"No, thank you, Nurse. I just came by to check on Chief Bautista. A pity about the accident."

Not accident!

"I hope they catch whoever did this." The nurse's voice. Angry. "Who could be so irresponsible?"

"Teenagers, probably." Crandall's voice. "You know how they like to go joyriding, especially on Halloween. They probably stole a car, got good and drunk, then took off scared when they realized what they'd done. I wouldn't be at all surprised to hear they weren't even from New Harbour. But don't you worry, young lady. Our police will do everything in their power to catch those young punks."

No. Only one. Have to tell someone. *Oh, God, someone listen to me!*

*   *   *

Thirty-five years? Ray tried to get his mind around that, but it wasn't easy. He'd been twenty-four when he . . . died, so that would make him almost sixty years old! Jesus! Well, it *would* have, except—

"Ray? I'm sorry if I shocked you."

Melissa's voice broke into his thoughts. She sounded a lot nicer now than when she'd been yelling at him and threatening to call the cops. She said she wanted to believe him. If she did, maybe she could help him. He wasn't sure how, but he was pretty sure she was all he had. Otherwise, he figured Melissa wouldn't be able to see and hear him now. Why her, he wondered. And why now, after all this time? Where was Celeste now? And, oh, hell! Celeste was thirty-five years older, too!

"Ray? Are you all right?"

He had to force himself to answer Melissa. *"Yeah. I'm fine."* Sure, he was. And the sky was green. *"Just trying to get a handle on all this."*

Oh, man, poor Celeste! Talk about getting stood up. . . . She'd think he didn't love her. He'd promised to take care of her, and ended up hurting her worse than anyone. Maybe the reason he was still hanging around was that he had to square things with her, tell her he really did love her, he'd never meant to let her down. Maybe that meant Celeste was somewhere near. But how could he make it up to her when he was like this? And what was *she* like now? She'd be old and alone, because of him. The thought made him sick.

"I guess it must be distressing for you." Melissa sounded like she was talking to that pathetic Lucky.

"Hey! I don't need you to feel sorry for me!" He didn't mean to sound so sharp. The kitten growled a warning. Ray glared at him. *"Quiet, Short Stuff,"* he said. *"Think you can help me, lady lawyer?"* He tried to make it sound like a dare, not a plea. Even a . . . a ghost had some pride.

"I can try," she answered in a very gentle voice. "The first thing I'll do is check the police files and the newspapers' morgues."

"Watch your mouth, huh? Morgue isn't a word I want to hear."

Melissa smiled. "Touché. Right now," she said, "I need to sleep. *If* I can, knowing I really am living in a haunted house. Can you go back to . . . to wherever you were before you broke in and scared the daylights out of me?"

He grinned. *"Yeah. I can fade. I could use a rest myself. I'm kinda new to this haunting business. It takes a lot of energy. Anyway, you've got Short Stuff to guard you. He's one tough little guy. Picked up some pretty rough language living out on the streets, I gotta tell you. Good thing you can't understand what he says."*

The kitten gave him one of those *if you were a mouse* looks. Melissa laughed softly and stroked Lucky. Something about the way she touched the cat sent sadness swirling through him. God, he missed Celeste! It was like a huge bruise where he used to have a heart. Thirty-five years was a long time to be alone, way longer than he'd been alive.

Everything was backward. He and Celeste were supposed to grow old together, but now she was old enough to be his mother. Older. His mother had had him when she was seventeen. Hell, maybe Celeste had forgotten all about him, married that doctor—what the hell was his name?—and had his kids. Her *kids* were probably older than he was! She could be a grandmother!

Oh, man! This was turning out to be some heavy-duty stuff. He started to fade, to find a dark corner where he could think.

"Ray?" Melissa called him back. "Before you go, we have to get some ground rules straight." He pulled a face. She smiled. "Simple rules. I'll help you try to find out who murdered you, but in exchange, my room is off-limits from now on. *And* my bathroom."

"Hey! I'm no pervert!"

"Quiet. No parlor tricks like ratting chains or making the lights flicker. No more scaring me and Lucky, or anyone else. And no smoking, please. It really makes me sick. Okay?"

He pretended to think about her rules, so she wouldn't think he was too desperate, but the truth was, he'd agree to anything in his power—whatever power he had, that is—if she could find out who his murderer was, and help him find Celeste. He had this nagging feeling that he was running out of time.

"Sure. I guess I went cold turkey thirty-five years ago anyway." He shrugged like he couldn't care less, but the smile she gave him made him think Melissa could see through him—in more ways than one.

Renata hung up the phone and stared bleakly up at her bedroom ceiling. She still couldn't believe what she'd just confirmed with hospital admissions: Gabe Bautista was in intensive care, in critical condition. Poor Gabe! And Melissa! Oh, God! Poor Melissa! It would break her friend's heart to hear about Gabe the way she had, on the early Friday morning news that blared out of her clock radio.

With shaking hands, Renata pressed the auto-dial button for Melissa's number. Her friend's voice answered, foggy with sleep.

"Mel, it's Renata." She took a deep breath and plunged in. "Gabe was in an accident last night. He's in the hospital, in intensive care. It was a hit-and-run in front of the police station."

There was a long silence, then a low moan came over the line. "No! No, that's not possible! It has to be a mistake."

Renata could hear the trembling in Melissa's voice. She wished she could lie and spare her friend the pain. "It's on the news this morning. I called the hospital myself, Mel. He's out of surgery, but he's in a coma. I didn't want you to hear it on the radio first."

"Oh, God! Renata!" Melissa's anguished cry twisted through Renata's heart. "Oh, Gabe! Gabe! No! I can't lose him like this!"

"He'll be all right, Mel. We have to keep believing he'll recover. He's a pretty tough guy. He'll make it."

After a long, shuddering silence, Melissa said softly, "I have to go to him, Renata."

"Do you want me to drive you?"

"No. Thanks. I'll . . . Can you meet me there? I'm afraid they won't let me in or tell me anything, because I'm not . . . not . . ." Melissa broke off with a sob.

Renata bit her lip but couldn't suppress the hot tears that slipped from her eyes. She ached for Melissa, and she could only pray that she was right about Gabe's resilience.

"I'll meet you in the hospital lobby," she told her friend. "I just need to call my secretary and tell her I'll be late."

When—not if—whoever hit Gabe was arrested, Renata intended to prosecute that coward into the far side of hell.

A little after four-thirty that afternoon, Renata's intercom buzzer barely broke her concentration on the casebook open on her desk. Without looking up from the page, she unwound the lock of hair she'd been twisting around her finger and pressed the reply button.

"Will's on line three," her secretary told her.

With a guilty glance at her watch, Renata lifted the phone and said hello. She'd intended to phone him earlier.

"Hi. I just wanted to be sure you like Italian food," he said. "For Saturday."

She looked down at the casebook, then sighed. "Uh, Will, I, uh . . ."

"Don't say it," he ordered so sharply that she winced. "We have a date."

She didn't want to hurt his feelings, but she felt swamped by work. Once more, she twisted a lock of hair around her index finger.

"I'm sorry, Will. Honestly, I am. But I've got about twenty new cases to process, and at least two trials to prepare for. I spent most of this morning at the hospital, hoping for news about Gabe Bautista." Poor Melissa had been brushed aside by the medical personnel because she wasn't part of Gabe's family, and had been snubbed by Gabe's distraught parents. Renata hated to leave her alone, but Mel had insisted she go to her office. "My friend is very worried about him. He's still in a coma."

"Yeah. Hit-and-run. That one's getting our full attention. The Chief's a good guy. I hope he'll make it. But what has that got to do with Saturday night?"

"I have so much to do, and so little time to do it. You know how important it is to keep the wheels of justice turning. There are too many bad guys and not enough of us." She winced at how preachy she sounded, but the legal system was, after all, something both she and Will had a vested interest in.

"So I'm taking a back seat to the lower life forms." She could practically see his scowl over the phone.

"You aren't. But I can't afford to make any mistakes, and every hour, more cases come in to the department. Dane refuses to consider negotiating with us, even though we have a very strong case against him. He wants to go to trial, and the date was just moved up. So, in addition to everything else on my top priority list, I have a little over a week to prepare for trial."

"Okay, okay. Call me an idiot, but I'm not giving up without a fight. You have to eat Saturday night anyway, right?"

"Right."

"So we'll go to dinner and save the dancing until we can celebrate your victory. I'll get you home in time for a good night's sleep—alone. Okay?"

She sighed. He really was doing his best to understand. She might as well compromise, too. "Okay."

"So, do you like Italian food?"

That made her smile. "With a name like Moretti?"

"'Nough said. I know a place you'll like. See you at seven, Saturday."

A second later, the dial tone hummed in her ear. She still wasn't sure she should take a few hours off for a restaurant meal on Saturday. She'd be better off having a quick sandwich at her desk. Renata caught her lower lip between her teeth and briefly debated phoning Will back. Then she decided against it. She'd already hurt his feelings too much.

With a sigh, she turned her attention back to the casebook. She found her place and began reading and taking notes. Vaguely, she was aware of her colleagues leaving for the day. She answered if anyone said good night, hardly looking up to see who was speaking. She didn't realize how late it was until she came out of the ladies' room to find the cleaning staff setting up.

By the time she realized that the cleaners had gone, silence had descended over the usually bustling offices. A glance at her watch showed her it was after ten o'clock. Where had the time gone? And she'd just started making her notes for the Dane trial! She needed to make sure there wasn't a single loophole, a single misstep in her prosecution, to allow for an appeal, or worse, an acquittal.

Renata threw down her pencil and stretched. Her back ached and her eyes burned. Also, her stomach was growling like an angry lion. It was, she conceded, time to go home. She gathered her things and went outside. Last night, as befitted Halloween, everything had been so spooky. Tonight, there was no mist and the stars sparkled in a high sky. Her car sat waiting under a light, and a quick glance around the lot showed her there were no other cars lurking in the shadows.

Still, she couldn't help feeling jumpy as she drove out of the parking lot. She really wished Will had kept his misgivings about Mick Donovan's accident to himself! After she'd gone several blocks, a car pulled out of a side street and settled into the lane behind her. Even though it stayed well back, and didn't shine its high beams into her eyes, her stomach clenched and her breathing grew shallow and rapid. When that car turned off, the darkness in her rearview mirror was almost as unsettling.

Sure enough, as she made her way along the state road between New Haven and New Harbour, another car swung into place behind her, with only its running lights glowing dimly. She could just make out the shadowy form of the driver. It looked like a very large man. When the headlights suddenly went on, her heart leaped.

With her pulse pounding, Renata pressed the gas pedal a little harder, speeding ahead. Within seconds, the car behind her closed the gap between them. She reached into her briefcase for her cell phone, her trembling fingers barely able to open the latches of the big leather case.

And suddenly, the lights behind her disappeared. The car that had been there had turned off. Through her side window, she saw the headlights swinging into the distance on the right, before the diverging roads took them too far apart to see anymore.

With a sigh, she put both hands on the steering wheel and willed herself to relax. Eventually, her heart stopped pounding against her ribs, and her breathing returned to normal. An old song, dreamy and romantic, sweetly evocative, poured out of her car radio, diverting her thoughts of crime to thoughts of her recurring dream. This was the song! At least she thought it was. Not that the exact song mattered. What mattered was the message of her dream, that such a deep and beautiful love was possible—was perhaps out there waiting—for her.

Someday, she told herself. Someday, she wanted to believe, she would find the right man to make the lyrics of the song come true.

Without any further false scares, Renata signaled and turned off Harbour Street. Less than a quarter of a mile along Deer Pond Road, the streetlights ended, so she switched on her high beams. The road wound through wooded areas and past small farms and estate homes, as it rose toward the narrow dirt road where her cottage waited. Hours ago, timers had turned on her lights and radio, so she wouldn't be walking into a dark, silent house as she had for so many years after school. Her mother was seldom in the same state, never mind the same house, and her grandmother's days had been filled with her clubs, boards, and societies. Gran's housekeeper had refused to allow her to have any kind of pet, even a goldfish. She'd get a kitten like the one Gabe had given Melissa last night. Maybe two kittens. The pound always had too many kittens that needed homes. They might not replace a Prince Charming, but they had to be better than toads, she told herself with a giddy laugh.

Lost in her thoughts, Renata didn't notice the car behind her until it slammed into the back of hers.

* * *

Ray paced the upstairs hallway, grumbling. After disturbing his rest all day yesterday with her noisy unpacking, Melissa had deserted him to run to the hospital. He felt bad for the cop, Gabe, and he felt bad for Melissa, but he was stuck here. Stuck and restless and impatient. He wanted answers. He wanted action. Damn it, he wanted Celeste! Now. Not soon. Not tomorrow. *Now!* If he could get out and do it himself, he would, but every time he tried to leave the yard, that invisible wall stopped him cold. And how would he even open the phone book and look up Celeste's number? He still couldn't touch anything, couldn't pick up or move anything.

He paused when Lucky scampered past him, chasing imaginary butterflies. The way the little cat swore at him, acting tough before scrambling away, made him laugh. But then, his laugh faded and Ray started pacing again, his steps ticking off the seconds. Time was such a tricky thing. First it dragged, then it raced, then it dragged again. Everything depended on how much waiting a guy was willing to put up with, which in his case wasn't much. Hadn't ever been. He'd always been in a hurry, and look where it got him.

Dead.

There were no headlights shining on her mirror from the car behind her. Her car lurched from the impact. With a shriek, Renata clutched the wheel and tried to decide in a split second whether to hit her brake or her gas pedal. Another, harder, shove from behind sent her foot to the gas. The tires spun and spit gravel but she was able to put some distance between her car and the one following her.

Renata sped past her own street, heading deeper into the woods, where the road writhed and narrowed. She had to fight the wheel, and several times nearly missed the sharp curves that would have sent her flying into the trees and underbrush. If she could stay ahead of the maniac trying to ram her, the road would wind its way back toward the other end of town and she'd be able to get to the main street and the safety of the police station.

Fleetingly, she wondered if Will had been right after all, about Frank Dane. The very notion sent an angry rush of determination through her. Whoever was chasing her, she wasn't going to give up without a fight.

Another sharp curve appeared in front of her, driving away all distracting thoughts. She braked to take the turn, and felt the impact of the bigger car hitting the left rear corner of her car. For the next seconds, Renata had no idea what was happening. All she could do was grip the steering wheel and fight the demons that were grabbing at her tires. Whimpering a prayer that the other driver wouldn't be able to control his car any better than she could hers, she tried to steer through the next curve.

With sickening clarity, Renata realized she was going to fail.

The car seemed to fly into the bushes as if it had left the ground, but in reality it was bouncing with bone-jarring impact toward the trees. Branches whipped at her windows, the sharp sounds striking like physical blows.

Then, the car rammed into a thick tree and rocked to a halt. In the corner of her mind that was still functioning, she expected her air bag to inflate, but nothing happened. Renata pitched forward. Her seat belt jerked her back, sending a jolt of pain up her neck. She fell forward again, hitting her head on the steering wheel even as she tried to stiffen her arms to hold herself back. Lights exploded behind her eyes and for a long while, she wasn't aware of anything except the pain in her head.

As her mind cleared, Renata braced herself for the attack she knew would follow. Any second now, whoever was in the big, dark car would wrench open her car door and drag her outside. And her pitifully meager dabbling in self-defense courses wouldn't do a thing to stop the thug.

Her only chance lay in escape. The car engine had died when it hit the tree, but maybe she could start it again. Maybe it had enough traction to back out of the underbrush and get her safely back on the road. Maybe whoever had been chasing her assumed she was dead already, and would leave her alone.

All her maybes died when the engine caught but the tires spun in vain.

Ray could practically hear old Mrs. Garvey's voice in his mind. "All in good time, Ray," she'd say when he'd confided to her how hard it was to wait for things to start going his way. But no time had been good for him, and now, he didn't know how much time he had left. He'd already wasted over thirty-five years. Why couldn't he remember what happened? Who had murdered him? Why? Where was Celeste? What if he never found her?

What if he did? What was she like now?

How was he supposed to get answers when he was stuck here, haunting this house? As if answers were going to just fall into his lap while he hung around like the curtains! Being dead in New Harbour was just like being alive there. Nothing ever happened.

With a snort that startled Lucky into puffing up his tail and staring wide-eyed, Ray turned and stomped downstairs. Unfortunately, his ghostly boots didn't make a sound, which took most of the satisfaction out of stomping. He couldn't even rattle any chains, assuming he could find any.

Renata felt the night swelling around her, smothering her. Somewhere nearby, the man who had run her off the road lurked, waiting, she was certain, to finish the job. But she wasn't willing to sit there paralyzed like a deer caught in headlights, waiting to be a victim. Will had been right, and she'd been such a stubborn fool.

With trembling hands, she realigned her glasses and pushed open her door. She'd have to leave the casebooks in the car, but they could be replaced. Even if they were the object of her attacker, her secretary had a list of sources in her computer. No, whoever was after her probably knew that. It wasn't the books—it was the prosecutor who was the target. Oh, God!

Despite the pain in her head and the ache in her neck, she was grateful that the air bag had failed. She didn't want to be trapped inside the car now. She had to get out. Gravity

pulled her off balance when she climbed out to the steep
bank of dirt next to her car. Expecting to be grabbed and
wrestled into submission at any second, she scrambled
around the crookedly perched car. Then she staggered away,
following the downward slope of the terrain toward Harbour
Street, an unknown distance below her.

Her feet in her low-heeled shoes sank and slipped in the
ooze of mud. Branches slapped her face, grabbing at her
glasses, stinging her skin, bringing tears to her eyes. Roots
caught at her feet, tripping her, pulling at her shoes, almost
bringing her down. She could barely see where she was
going by the dim light of the full moon. Shapes loomed out
of the darkness at her, each one possibly the form of the
creep who had chased her off the road. Somewhere in her
purse she had a small flashlight, but she was moving too
quickly, too desperately, to search for it now.

Something caught her ankle and flipped her down to the
mud. A root or loose branch, she couldn't tell what, only that
it wasn't the hand of her human pursuer. She fell hard,
barely managing to stifle her shriek of surprise. Her glasses
flew off and landed out of sight. Before she could react, her
purse tumbled away into the dark tangle of underbrush. Pain
streaked up her leg and into her shoulder when she landed,
but she clamped her mouth shut. She couldn't afford to give
her pursuer any hint of where she was. Renata caught her
breath and pushed herself back upright, first into a cautious
crouch, then standing, testing her weight on her ankle. It was
twingey, but she could still use it.

Without her glasses, the woods seemed even darker, the
shapes around her menacingly blurred. But she couldn't afford to search for her lost glasses. Pausing only for a second
to listen for telltale sounds of someone following her, her
own heartbeat drowning out any other noises, she continued
her scramble down the hillside toward the road, toward
safety.

Renata lost track of time and distance, fighting her way
through the woods. Suddenly, the trees and underbrush simply stopped. She fell flat onto wet, muddy grass and lay
panting, trying to orient herself. She was at the edge of a

large yard, still high up in the hills. A huge house stood in the middle of the yard, with lights glowing softly, warmly, in some of the windows. The Garvey mansion! Melissa's house! Oh, thank God! She'd never seen such a beautiful sight in her life!

Impatience warred with caution, but she forced herself to crawl across the yard toward the front of the house. Praying that Melissa was home, she made her way up the porch stairs. Her legs refused to cooperate when she tried to stand to ring the doorbell. Finally, with tears sliding down her face, stinging the cuts across her cheeks, she reached as high as she could and pressed the button.

Deep inside the house, the chimes bonged. Renata sank back down and waited. And waited. She forced her hand up to ring the bell again. *Melissa! Melissa, help me!* she thought desperately.

Slowly, she slumped in defeat. "The lights are on, but no one's home," she said out loud, then nearly giggled at the absurdity. That frightened her more than anything; she couldn't afford to lose control now. She had to hide. She had to call the police to catch her pursuer. She couldn't give up.

The boards of the porch scraped her shins, but her nylons were already history. She managed to make her way back to the ground and around to the far side of the house. Knowing Melissa's caution, the odds of finding an unlocked window were not in her favor, but she had to try. Ironically, she was disappointed that the house alarm had been disarmed last night. If she could set it off by breaking a window, the New Harbour cops would appear in minutes.

The third window frame she pushed against yielded so quickly she almost fell through. With her heart pounding in her throat, Renata forced herself to wait until her vision adjusted to the darkness of the basement. Finally, her fear propelled her forward, hoping she wasn't going to land on anything dangerous. As far as she could tell from the lack of shapes, she wasn't going to land on anything except bare concrete, but it was her only option.

Renata turned around and eased her legs into the opening. The bottom frame of the window pressed lightly on her back. She found the wall with her toes and clutched the window frame under her arms trying to support herself far enough down to shorten her fall.

"Last I looked, breaking and entering was illegal," a man's voice said from out of the darkness.

Renata gasped, but she was too frightened, too exhausted, to scream. Her arms turned to rubber, breaking her grip, and she dropped like a stone. Hot pains streaked up from both ankles, the injured one protesting with breathtaking sharpness. Unable to move, Renata huddled on the cold, hard floor, trying to smother her whimpers.

"Aw, hell! I didn't mean to scare you like that. Did you get hurt?" That voice . . . It sounded so familiar. Did she know him? *"Hey, are you okay?"*

But why would she know someone who was lurking in Mel's basement? Anyway, why was some man in Mel's basement, when she wasn't home? Half-indignant and half-petrified, she demanded, "Who's there? Who are you? What do you want?"

"I could ask you the same thing. You have a problem with doors?" He sounded amused.

It wasn't funny, damn it! Someone had tried to kill her. Indignation gave way to fear. She started trembling. "Mel . . . No one answered. I . . . I'm sor . . . sorry! But I was so sc . . . scared!" The words burst from her. "Can you help me? Please? I think s . . . s . . . someone is trying to k . . . kill me."

The unexpected flare of light stabbed her eyes, forcing them closed. To her disgust, another whimper escaped from her lips.

"Baby, you are a mess! And you're hurt. Is it bad?" No amusement now in that low voice. It didn't matter now that she thought he sounded familiar. He sounded sympathetic, kind. His concern almost undid her determination not to cry.

Slowly, she squinted her eyes open, letting them adjust to the light. Keeping her gaze lowered, she thought she saw a pair of scuffed black boots under the rolled-up cuffs of blue jeans. As her eyes became used to more light, she let her gaze travel upward. The figure standing across the basement room was tall. Even with her poor vision causing everything to appear hazy, she noticed that his jeans hugged well-muscled thighs. A white T-shirt clung to his torso under a black leather jacket that hung open, suggestively framing his impressively flat midsection. His dark hair dipped over his forehead in a James Dean–like wave.

He moved closer and, with a cocky grin, looked her over in turn. Now that he'd closed the distance between them, she could see that his eyes glittered in the light of the bare bulb, a pale, pure green fringed by black lashes. His features reminded her of the actor who'd played Remington Steele and James Bond—definitely the kind of man a woman enjoyed looking at. Even one who was frightened out of her mind and nearsighted, to boot.

But who was he? He appeared to be in his middle-twenties, but Renata knew better than to rely on appearances or her own eyes. This was strange. Melissa hadn't mentioned having guests. He was gorgeous enough—at least to her poor vision—and had a distinctive and sexy enough voice to be an actor or a rock star. But why would Mel have a client from L.A. in her basement? Renata's head ached from trying to make sense of that.

"I thought Halloween was last night," she commented, trying vainly for a light tone.

"Great. A burglar doing a comedy routine." He took another step toward her.

Against her will, she recoiled. "Who are you?" It wasn't likely, but he could be the one who had chased her.

He stopped several feet away and held out his hands, palms up. *"Hey, take it easy. I'm Ray. Ray Lowell. I'm one of the good guys."* The smile he gave her then warmed her like the sun breaking through heavy clouds, making her want to believe him.

"I'm not a burglar," she told him, her own smile wobbling badly. She was still shaking with fright and exhaustion.

"I know that. You're Melissa's friend."

Wrapping her arms around her middle, she tried to control her trembling. "I'm Renata Moretti."

He stepped even closer, smiling into her eyes. *"Hi, Renata Moretti,"* he said in a low, intimate voice. *"I'm a friend of Melissa's too."*

Looking into Ray's eyes, Renata felt herself starting to relax, starting to believe there was a way out of this frightening mess. There was something about him. . . . She knew beyond a doubt that she'd never met Ray Lowell before, yet there was something about him that made her trust him without question. No, there was something more, she thought a little dazedly.

In the middle of the most dangerous, terrifying experience of her life, the man of her shadowy, erotic dreams had appeared as if out of thin air! The realization startled a gasp from her.

"Where are you hurt?" he demanded gently.

"I . . . I don't know. I think I'm too scared to tell yet. I . . . I need to call the police."

He nodded. *"You probably want to clean up, too. Melissa's hanging around the hospital hoping someone will tell her something about her boyfriend, but I think she'll be home soon. C'mon upstairs."*

"Oh, God! Gabe!" Renata sighed. This was all too overwhelming.

"Yeah. He'll be okay."

Ray spoke with such confidence that Renata found herself believing him. He held out his hand to her. She struggled to her feet, determined to make up for those pathetic whimpers of helplessness. She stood, one hand braced on the cool, rough wall behind her, and reached out toward his hand with the other.

Then she looked closer and fear clutched at her heart like the grip of an eagle on its prey. Dear God, she could *see* right through him! It had to be her poor vision, or the pain in her head, or a trick of the light! But no, as he moved toward her, she could see the lines of the banister and the stairs behind him. She could see them *through* him! But that was impossible!

Then his outstretched hand touched hers. Except that it *didn't* touch hers! She saw his fingers cover hers, but she felt nothing! She felt nothing, and she could see her own fingers through his hand!

"You're . . . You're . . ."

Her mind couldn't grasp any more. Darkness closed in on her. As she slid down the wall, she heard a string of curses. Then, *"Aw, shit! Not again!"*

Chapter
Five

Oh, Mom, Gabe thought. *Don't cry!*

The sound of his mother's muffled sobs made him feel even more helpless. And angry. He had to wake up. Had to tell someone who had done this to him. Not an accident.

His father's voice rumbled over his mother's sobs. Gabe wanted to smile. Love. Strong. Steady.

Dad, I can hear you, Gabe wanted to say. *Don't cry. I'll make it. Promise.*

His father's tear-choked words broke his heart. Mario had never, *never* cried, not at death, not for joy, not in anger. But Gabe couldn't break free of this numbing force. He was a prisoner in his own body. *I love you, too, Dad,* he wanted to say. Mario had never said the words before. He showed his love without words. Never doubted him. Need to tell him.

Nurse's voice. Time's up. Too soon. Not tiring me. All I do is lie here. Need to hear voices. Need to fight. Wake up! Need to see Lissa. Someone tell Lissa? Have to see her again. Put the past away. Start over. Not too late. Oh, God, why can't I wake up?

Paul? Do something, buddy! Get me out of here! Best damn doctor. Lousy basketball player. Can't shoot pool, either. Get me out of this mess, buddy. Let you win next time. Promise. Never break a promise.

He felt his mother's kiss on his forehead. Felt the weight of his father's hand on his shoulder. But it was all through a fog, like the sensations were being filtered. Another muffled sob from his mother, then rustling and the silence of his empty room.

The struggle to wake exhausted him. Gabe let himself drift. Suddenly, he was aware of another person in the room with him. Lissa! He could smell her light perfume, the sweet musk of her skin, the way it had been last night, new, yet familiar, sending a rush of memories flooding over him.

He felt the touch of her fingers on his hand, lighter than the brush of a butterfly's wings. No matter how he concentrated, he couldn't make his hand move to capture hers.

"What are you doing here?" Paul's voice, tight, angry. He could picture his friend, tall, wiry, sandy-haired, wearing a white doctor's coat over his shirt and slacks. Would she recognize him? Did she still hate him? Paul had never missed an opportunity to warn Gabe away from her, calling her a spoiled little rich girl who was just using the poor boy until something better came along.

"I . . . I wanted to see Gabe, but . . ."

"Won't do you any good."

"I wasn't thinking of myself," Lissa snapped. *Good girl,* Gabe thought. *Don't let him push you around.*

Paul snorted. "Right," he said. "Did you come back to New Harbour to gloat?"

Gabe wanted to punch him.

"I came back because this is home. I'd had enough of prima donnas and spoiled artistes. I came back to do the kind of law I always wanted to practice, and to live my own life."

He imagined the two of them facing off, each challenging the other without a word, just like in high school. He'd always wondered if Paul had wanted Lissa for himself, or been jealous because Gabe had split his time unevenly after he'd fallen in love with her.

After a long silence, Paul said, "You still care about him, don't you?" Gentler than before. Good.

"I . . . I never stopped caring." Her whispered words made his heart swell. *Oh, God! Lissa, I never stopped loving you!* he tried to say, but he couldn't make his lips move, couldn't force his breath to shape the sounds. He couldn't even cry in frustration.

"Funny, but that's not how Gabe tells it. He carried a torch for a long time after you left." Paul's voice was bitter again. *No good, buddy. Let it go.* "He was so torn up when you seemed to disappear off the face of the earth, I didn't have the heart to tell him I'd told him so." *Did anyway.*

Melissa sighed. "It's too complicated to explain now, Paul. Right now, all I care about is Gabe. Be honest with me, please. What are his chances?"

"I wish I knew." The hollowness behind Paul's words sent ice through Gabe's veins. "Melissa, I'm going to set aside my own feelings here, and take a chance. I don't think it will hurt. Maybe it will help." Gabe felt a leap of hope. What was Paul going to say?

"What will help?"

"Gabe may be able to hear—many patients who emerge from comas report that they heard what their visitors said to them—but he can't respond. Not consciously. If you think you can handle it, I'll let you talk to him for a few minutes every day. You always had a powerful effect on him. Maybe we can put it to good use this time."

"Of course I can handle it. I'd do anything in my power to help him."

Oh, baby, I hope you can work miracles!

"Just steer clear of Mario. He still holds a grudge against you for hurting Gabe."

"All I care about is doing whatever I can to help Gabe recover. If that means sitting with him and talking to him, I'll do it. If it means staying away"—she paused—"then I'll have to stay away."

No! Don't stay away! Need you with me! Don't leave me, Lissa.

"Let's try. I'll give your name to the nurses, and tell them not to let Mario know you were here."

"Thank you," she whispered.

Gabe sensed her coming closer again, and fought to move his hand, a finger, an eyelid, anything to prove to her that he knew she was there. Any way to say he loved her. He felt her touch on his hand, on his forearm, but all he could do was lie there like a rock. When she left him, some unknown time later, he wondered if she'd come back, or if she'd give up because of his silence.

The noises of the hospital came to him as if through a thick filter. Voices on the intercom were muffled, garbled. People came and went from his room, taking his pulse, his blood pressure, scratching notes in his chart, changing the IV bag. He was aware of it all as if it were all part of a strange dream, a nightmare. Sometimes, he thought he slept. He'd wake with a start, but only inside. His eyes refused to open. His vocal cords refused to make a sound. His body refused to move. But when he was awake like that, he was aware.

Lissa's soft voice still seemed to float through his mind. She was gone now. Paul had hustled her out before his parents came in to say good night and cry over him. Had Melissa cried? He thought she had, but silently, as if believing Paul's word that he could hear even if he couldn't react.

Inside, where no one knew, he cried, too.

Ray looked at the woman lying on the concrete at his boot-tips and groaned. He'd really screwed up this time. If he hadn't turned on the light, if he hadn't started making wisecracks, she wouldn't have known he was there. Even that wasn't the worst mistake. Why had he offered Renata his hand, like he was a normal guy? He *wasn't* a normal guy. He was a *dead* guy. He was an idiot! She'd been running for her life, and he'd gone and scared her half to death. He was just trying to help, but . . .

But, hey! She could hear him and see him, just like

Melissa! That must mean something . . . But what? Why
these two? Maybe it was because he'd always had a way
with chicks. At least, he used to. He'd been the bad boy
mothers warned their little darlings away from, and plenty
of those little darlings had loved the thrill of tasting forbid-
den fruit. Sure, some of them had gotten nervous at the last
minute, but none of them had hit the floor in a dead faint. So
far tonight, he was batting a thousand.

Now what was he supposed to do? He couldn't just leave
Renata there on the cold cement floor, but he couldn't exactly do anything to help her. He didn't even know if he
could get her to come to. And if he did, what would he do if
she got scared again?

Come to think of it, what would he do if she *didn't* get
scared again, but expected him to help her up the stairs?
She'd probably think he was some kind of jerk with no manners. Before she fainted, she'd acted like he was a regular
guy, maybe even a guy she thought was worth a second
look. Unless Renata remembered why she passed out, she
wasn't going to believe he was a ghost. Who would believe
it? Hell, *he* hardly believed it, and he was the ghost!

Ray crouched, hands on his own knees, and looked her
over. She was a cute little thing, and she had a lot of guts.
He really felt bad about scaring her. He'd have to be careful
not to do it again. Easier said than done, if she was going to
be around him any time at all. If he just faded out of sight,
he wouldn't be able to talk to Melissa, and then he might not
be able to find Celeste. Then again, if he hung around and
accidentally scared Renata, Melissa might be so mad she'd
never talk to him again, or help him connect with Celeste.

He got to his feet and paced back and forth in front of Renata's unconscious body, muttering to himself with every
turn. *Damn! Damn. And double damn!* And where the hell
was Melissa? It was late. Finally, he stopped short and
crouched again beside Renata. A sudden urge to touch her,
just once, lightly, just to feel a woman's skin again, feel the
warmth of flesh on his, caught him by surprise. He put out
his hand, but inches away from Renata's face, he clenched

his fingers into a fist and drew it back. How could he want to touch Renata when he still loved Celeste?

Loyalty was a big deal to him. He wasn't the kind of guy who cheated on his friends, or on his girl. And he'd made a promise to Celeste. . . . But, hell, even if he found her and she forgave him for getting murdered all those years ago, what was he going to do then? He was dead, for crying out loud! It wasn't like he had a lot to offer. He didn't have anything to offer, not to Celeste or any other chick, except that stash of cash and the diamond ring he'd squirreled away in the basement, and he couldn't get his hands on them.

Anyway, money wasn't what he needed right now. Right now, he needed a body that worked, because he had to do something about Renata. Helping her couldn't be a betrayal of Celeste anyway. She wasn't that kind of person. She'd want him to help. He didn't know what he could do, but he slowly lowered his hand until—if he'd been alive—he would be touching Renata's shoulder.

Something hot and stinging ran up his arm, as if he'd touched a live wire. He pulled his hand back and stared at it. What was going on? What was that? He could see the floor through his body, just like before, but for the first time since waking up yesterday, he *felt* something. It was like a spark in a spark plug, arcing between two points that weren't touching, igniting internal combustion. Hell, he hadn't felt that kind of electricity when he'd been playing with the light-bulbs.

He started to reach out again, then heard Melissa unlocking the front door upstairs.

She called his name. He bellowed back. Renata stirred, so he knew she could still hear him, but she didn't wake. A moment later, the cellar door opened. Lucky bounded down the stairs like he had somewhere to go. Melissa followed, her smile turning to a gasp when she saw her friend lying on the floor at his feet.

"What happened? What did you do?" she demanded as she almost tripped down the rest of the stairs.

"I seem to have this effect on babes," he joked, but the

words sounded hollow. He felt bad enough about Renata without having Melissa rub it in.

Melissa knelt beside Renata and felt her neck. "Her pulse is steady. I don't suppose you can help me . . . No, of course not. I have to get her upstairs. What on earth is she doing in the basement? How did she get in? The front door was locked. And you can't . . . Can you?"

Talking pretty much nonstop as usual, Melissa got her hands under Renata's arms and pulled her up to a limp sitting position. Ray watched, feeling helpless and guilty, even though he kept telling himself he hadn't really done anything to Renata. Besides, it wasn't his fault that he couldn't lift her. He was a ghost! Man, lawyers were all the same. First thing they did was find someone to blame, then grill him until he wanted to confess just to shut them up.

"I didn't do anything," he finally grumbled when she stopped for breath. *"Renata rang the bell about a hundred times, then came in through the basement window. She said some creep was chasing her through the woods. All I did was offer to bring her upstairs so she could wait for you."* And let her see through him, he added to himself in disgust. *"I didn't rattle any chains or yell* boo *or anything. She took one look at me and passed out."* He shrugged. *"Sorta like what you did last night, when I walked through the wall."*

Melissa shot him a dirty look. "Great. Now what am I supposed to say when she wakes up? Guess what, the house really is haunted?"

Before he could answer, Renata moaned softly and blinked. Ray watched her look around, first just with her eyes, then moving her head slowly, cautiously. Poor babe, she needed someone to take care of her, not to scare her half to death. For just an instant, his mind surprised him with a picture of him holding her like a normal guy, telling her she was going to be okay. It was the kind of picture that stirred things up inside a guy, even a dead one, and that made him feel even more guilty.

"Oh! Mel! What happened? My head . . ." Renata looked at Melissa, her dark eyes widening. "That . . . That creep . . . ! Ran me off the road. Chased me." Her voice quavered, like she was mad and fighting tears. Melissa pushed a strand of wet, dark hair away from Renata's face.

It had to be his imagination, or wishful thinking, but whenever Renata talked, he could swear he was hearing Celeste's voice. Maybe that was why his mind was playing tricks on his hormones.

"I rang your bell but you weren't home." She drew a shaky breath. "The window was open, so I climbed in, and then . . . There was someone here. Ray? I think that's what he said."

Melissa gave him a quick look he figured was a warning not to spook Renata again. "That's my cousin Ray. He, uh, dropped in unexpectedly."

"Cousin?" Renata frowned, reminding him an awful lot of the way Celeste used to look when she was trying to work something out in her head. Talk about a one-track mind. "He told me he's your friend."

Hmm. She was pretty sharp, even when she was scared. He was beginning to think girls had changed in the past thirty-some years. For one thing, they weren't girls anymore. And neither was Celeste, he reminded himself grimly. As soon as Renata was taken care of, he was going to have to deal with that.

Melissa cleared her throat. "Well, yes, he's my friend, too. I mean, he's such a distant cousin that we're more like friends than family." Her cheeks turned pink. Ray wondered if her nose was going to grow, too. "He's right here."

"Oh."

Renata turned her head, lifted her chin, and looked right into his eyes. Ray held his breath—or would have, if he could breathe—and looked back. Would she scream and faint again when she saw the wall through him? Or would she run away in a panic, maybe right into the clutches of the guy who'd run her off the road? Or maybe, now that Melissa was back, she couldn't see him at all, and he was just imagining that she was looking at him.

And then she smiled at him, one of those sweet, sexy girl-to-guy smiles that could melt steel and turn a man's brain to mush. Not to mention what it could do to other parts of his anatomy—at least, to guys who *had* anatomy. Her dark eyes seemed to have extra light in them, like looking at him made her feel good. He felt an answering grin tug at his face, but fought it for Celeste's sake.

Suddenly, he was remembering a long time ago, when he'd met a pair of sparkling blue eyes belonging to the most beautiful girl he'd ever seen. Celeste got out of her baby-blue Mustang convertible—they were in the parking lot of her father's factory, her the owner's daughter, him just a no-body who worked a joe job and had big dreams. He idled his motorcycle—a used Harley he'd traded part-time roofing work for—and watched her struggle to open the hood of the car. Without thinking about the consequences, he glided to the parking space beside hers and cut the engine. She looked at him, then *looked* at him, and smiled. Smiled the way Renata was smiling now.

He'd looked into Celeste's blue eyes and fallen like a ton of bricks. He opened the hood of the car. She stood beside him, almost close enough for his elbow to brush her arm, close enough for him to smell her flowery perfume. By the time he'd reconnected a loose plug wire, he'd found his voice and asked her to go out with him. When she said yes, he thought he was going to have a heart attack.

"Hi, Ray," Renata said softly. Something about the smile she gave him then wrenched at his heart. She looked so sad, and as vulnerable as a kitten. "Sorry I, um, dropped in like this."

Melissa groaned and got to her feet. "C'mon, Renata. No more bad puns, please. Let's get you upstairs and figure out what to do next. You're a mess, and we don't know if that thug is still out there."

Ray took a step back when Melissa and Renata stood up, Renata clutching Melissa's arm. He couldn't let her get close enough to discover he was as solid as fog.

Renata let herself lean on Melissa, the slashing pain in her ankle nearly toppling her. She felt as weak as if she had the flu, and pain pounded in her head. Even as she was trying to clear her vision, she felt herself slipping into darkness again.

With a deep breath, she willed herself to stay conscious. There were too many things going on—some dangerous, some puzzling—for her to lose control now.

"Okay," she said after another deep breath. "I'm ready." But when Melissa took a step forward, Renata felt a wave of dizziness wash over her again and sagged against her friend, trying to fight the weakness. She couldn't decide which hurt worse, her head or her ankle.

"Take it easy," Ray muttered.

She looked into his amazingly green eyes and felt another of those strange *déjà vu* moments, as if she'd done this, been here, seen these people, heard the same words, some other time. The feeling had welled up in her when she'd been lying on the floor gazing up at Ray, before the bump on her head had made her faint.

"Renata, do you want me to set up a cot down here?" Melissa's voice broke into her thoughts. "Just until you can get upstairs?"

Renata gave herself a mental shake. "No. I'll make it."

Every step threatened to send her diving back into the darkness, but eventually, she and Melissa stood at the top of the stairs, in the open doorway to the main hall. While she caught her breath and leaned on Melissa, Ray came silently upstairs and stood watching her with more concern than she normally expected from a total stranger. Still, it occurred to her to wonder, if he was so concerned with her well-being, why hadn't he helped Melissa support her on the way upstairs? Small as she was, she would have done that in his place. Then again, he might have offered and Melissa had shooed him away. The stairs were awfully narrow, and only had a railing on one side. There wasn't room for three of them.

Melissa reached for a kitchen chair. "Sit down here. I'll get you some water, and some ice for your head and ankle."

Gratefully, Renata sank onto the chair. Her hands shook so badly when she accepted the glass of water that she had to set it down before she could take a sip. Ray stood in the shadows of the kitchen doorway, studying her so intently that she felt the loss of her glasses acutely. She finally smiled nervously, hoping he would stop. When he didn't, she broke their eye contact and turned her gaze to where Melissa was picking up the phone.

"Wait!" Remembering Melissa's suggestion that the man who'd been after her could still be outside searching for her, Renata felt panic tightening her nerves. "Who are you calling?"

Mel paused in the middle of pressing numbers, her expression puzzled. "The police. Someone tried to hurt you, maybe worse. And you need an ambulance."

"No! No police, no ambulance! Please." She heard Ray's muttered reminder that she'd planned to call the police earlier herself. "I changed my mind," she said hastily, her gaze still on Melissa. "It's not a good idea to call them. Please trust me on this."

Melissa put the phone down and gaped at her. "There's a man out there who intends to harm you. The police need to find him. And you need to go to the hospital, Renata. You were unconscious. I'm not a doctor. What if—?"

"What if that bastard is out there watching for some sign of where I am? If you call in the police, they'll come here to talk to me. They'll follow my path right to your door. And the incident report will be public. The town paper would love another injured prosecutor story. What if the guy who chased me comes here and tries to hurt you or Ray, to find me?"

She heard Ray make a hissing sound that drew her attention to where he stood. Even with her poor vision, she could see he wore an aura of masculine power and authority. He was probably insulted by her attempt to protect him. No doubt, he thought he could deal with these guys himself, and make sure she and Mel were safe. But it was *her* job to protect ordinary citizens, not the other way around.

Mel said her name, her tone irritated. "So what am I supposed to do? Your car is up there, and you're down here. You both need repairs."

"Call a tow truck. I always take my car to Select Car Care, on Main Street. Call them, and I'll leave a message."

She waited, hand outstretched and trembling, for several

long seconds before Melissa turned away to look up the garage's phone number and dial it. Ignoring the way her friend's lips compressed in obvious disapproval, she took the receiver and spoke after the answering machine beeped.

Renata struggled to keep her voice as normal sounding as possible as she explained to Vinnie, her regular mechanic, that she'd had an accident swerving to avoid a dog in the road. Uncomfortably aware of Ray's steady gaze, she described where to find her car, and said she'd call him about repairs soon.

She realized as she hung up that, for someone who revered the truth, she'd become a very accomplished liar in a very short time. But the stakes were too high for her to waffle and take chances. No one had to paint a picture for her now: Will was right. Frank Dane and his business associates probably wouldn't think twice about using Melissa and Ray to get to her. There was no way she could let that happen. Other than not drawing them toward her hiding place, she didn't know what to do, but somehow, she'd think of something.

Melissa took the phone from her suddenly limp fingers. "Renata, why are you trying to be a hero?"

"I'm not." She gave Melissa a halfhearted smile, hoping she didn't look as pathetic as she felt. "I'm trying to get invited to your guest room."

Then she remembered that Ray was staying with Melissa. Her battered face stung with her blush. "If there's room for me. If not, I'll call Will and—"

"There's room." Ray's gruff baritone came out of the shadows, startling her.

"Oh!" She turned toward his voice. "I . . ." But he wasn't there. Puzzled, she looked at Melissa, who looked back with an odd expression.

"He's shy with women he doesn't know," she said with a shrug. "Let's get you upstairs."

As she rose and accepted Melissa's steadying hand on her arm, she thought about her first encounter with Ray. "Shy? He sure didn't seem shy when I was sneaking into your basement. He was positively cocky." And, she thought, he deserved to be. "He probably has women throwing themselves at him all the time."

Melissa hesitated. "Um, no, not really," she countered in a strange tone. "Not until recently, anyway. He's sort of a late bloomer. But he, um, he acts."

"Acts?" She was beginning to suspect she wasn't the only accomplished liar in the house tonight.

"It's not uncommon. A lot of actors are shy when they don't have a part to play. Or they create a persona for themselves and that's what the public sees. Ray, well, he . . . he likes to create a role, be someone else, so he can cope with an awkward or difficult situation."

"Oh," Renata answered through gritted teeth. She didn't believe Melissa for an instant, but she needed something to help her forget she was about to die halfway up the stairs. "So who is he tonight? James Dean?"

From somewhere behind her, she heard a noise that sounded very much like a snort of disagreement.

Ray hovered behind Melissa and Renata, watching them struggle up the stairs to the second floor. With every step, he imagined he could feel the pain ripping upward from Renata's swollen ankle. It was like that with him and Celeste; whenever she got hurt, he felt it. God, he loved that girl! He had to make peace with her, even if that was his ticket to nowhere. Melissa could help him, if he could get her attention. Later, when Renata was in bed . . .

He moved down the hall, thinking it was kinda funny that he was alone with two very good looking babes, and not interested. Or at least, not *very* interested. He'd been pretty wild and free with the ladies from a young age, but as soon as he met Celeste, he couldn't even think about fooling around with any other chick. He'd been her first, and she'd been his last. That was what love was all about.

"Ray?" Melissa's voice startled him. He grunted an answer. "Renata will need watching while she sleeps. We have to wake her up every hour or so, to make sure she's lucid. Think you can manage to take the first few hours? I'm desperate for sleep." Melissa yawned behind her hand while she spoke softly.

"Yeah," he said, even though he wanted to put his time into finding Celeste. Renata needed looking after. *"Lucky and I'll take care of her tonight."* He gave Melissa a grin that felt crooked. *"Hell, what's one all-nighter? I've been sleeping almost forty years."*

Melissa smiled. "Longer than Rip Van Winkle. Wake me if you need help. You know how to check her pupils, to see if she reacts to light?"

"Sure. I don't know how I'm gonna hold a flashlight, but I know what to look for."

"Oh, dear! I hadn't thought of that. I don't suppose you can turn on the lamp by the bed . . ." She shook her head. "What am I thinking? You're not a wizard. You're a ghost."

He knew it was true, but hearing the words still made him want to cringe. *"Hey, relax, I've been practicing with the lights downstairs. With a little luck, the lamp will work the same way. Go get some sleep. Your eyes are at half-mast."*

Melissa yawned again. Lucky blinked up at him and yawned widely, too, giving him a terrific view of tiny needle-teeth. The kitten muttered that he'd probably end up doing all the work anyway, 'cause ghosts couldn't be trusted to tell time, then slunk into the guest room where Renata was sleeping.

"We'll see about that," Ray muttered after the little scrapper.

"Stop bickering," Melissa hissed. "Renata is bound to notice eventually that you're not exactly a regular guy."

He bit off a harsh laugh. *"What do you think sent her into that dead faint downstairs? It's just dumb luck she didn't believe she was seeing through me, and with that concussion, she doesn't remember."*

Melissa let out her breath. "Well, you can't hide it forever from her," she said. "What am I supposed to say when she's over her concussion and realizes that you're still transparent?" Ray didn't like the worry creases between her brows. They seemed deeper every time he looked. He liked her. She didn't need trouble from him, too.

He tugged at the hair over his forehead. *"I don't know. I'll think of something. But let me tell her, okay? I don't think she's ready to hear it yet, anyway. She's got enough rough stuff to sort out first. Someone out there really meant to hurt her."*

Melissa nodded. "Okay. Good night." She started walking down the hall to her own room.

"Hey, wait," he hissed. *"I just thought of something I need you to do tomorrow."*

Melissa turned and her brows went up a little. "What's that?"

"I need you to track down Celeste and find out how I can get in touch with her. I don't remember the name of the jerk her father wanted her to marry. Some doctor. Town Hall probably has a record of her wedding." The thought left a sour feeling deep inside him. *"Then you can look her up in the phone book, maybe call her and ask how she's doing. Her last name is Benedict. Ask her over for tea or something, so I can see her myself."*

"Right." Her back got as stiff as Lucky's. "And do you want me to wear a turban and give her a message from the great beyond for you?"

"Hey, what's your problem? She was waiting for me when I got murdered. We were going to elope. I didn't have a chance to tell her what happened. I need to know she's okay. That she . . . doesn't hate me. I promised I'd take care of her. I have to tell her I tried, and I still . . ."

Man, this was embarrassing! He'd never talked to a chick—or to anyone—about his feelings like this before. But Melissa was listening, not laughing at him. *"I have to tell her I'll always love her,"* he said fast. *"Then maybe I can get out of here."*

Melissa lifted her hand to him, her eyes clouded. "Sorry, Ray," she said softly. "You seem so real, it's easy to forget. I'll do what I can tomorrow, on the way to the hospital."

"Okay," he muttered, cringing at the pity in her eyes. *"That's good enough for me."*

He turned away, ignoring her sad-sounding, "Good night."

Slipping into Renata's room, he settled into a shadowed corner to watch her sleep. Lucky blinked at him twice, then started to wash his face with a front paw. Ray turned away from the cat and concentrated on the soft breathing of the woman under the covers.

He didn't totally understand it, but he wanted to take care of Renata. She was trying so hard to be tough, but she was small and scared. With good reason. It would be easy for a thug to hurt her real bad. The thought made him clench his fists. If anyone tried, they'd have to go through him first. For real. What good was he like this? How was he supposed to protect Renata—and Melissa—when he was about as strong as a shadow? But he would think of some way to take care of her. It would give him something to do while he was waiting for news about Celeste.

Funny, but until now, he'd only wanted to take care of Celeste, but here he was, trying to play bodyguard to two women he'd just met.

He looked at the clock. Not even eleven. It was going to be a long night, he thought. Probably the longest night of his . . . afterlife.

Chapter Six

In the darkness of her mind, Renata saw the car lights behind her, stabbing her eyes, the beams reaching for her as if they had substance and strength and intent. She twisted away from their grasp and tried to run, but deep mud encased her legs. The sounds of snapping branches and heavy boots slapping the wet ground rushed at her from behind. The beams of light stretched and stretched until they touched her, cold as icicles, scalding as steam. Pain seared her nerves, cutting to the bone, lifting her, wrenching a cry of helpless panic from her.

Hands caught at her, holding her shoulders, imprisoning her. She fought, trying to scream, hearing nothing but the heavy breathing of her pursuer and her own whimpers. And then a voice, strangely familiar yet unknown, calm and calming, penetrated the darkness, calling her name. She reached toward the source of that voice, somehow knowing safety waited in that direction.

"Renata, baby, easy now. You're having a bad dream. Wake up, okay? It's just a dream. You're safe now. You're in Melissa's house. Open your eyes, baby. It's me, Ray. Open your eyes and see for yourself."

Slowly, the panic, the darkness receded. Renata blinked and opened her eyes cautiously, afraid to discover her dream was real. But to her relief, Ray stood beside the bed. In the dim light of the room, without her glasses, she could barely see him, but she *knew* him. He wasn't touching her, but she *felt* him, like the kiss of sunshine after a chilling rain. He was the lover of her dreams, the mate her heart yearned for . . . or a compassionate, good-looking stranger.

"Oh! Wha . . . What are you doing here?"

He drew a little closer to the bed. *"I'm watching over you while Melissa gets some sleep. We're taking turns. She's afraid you've got a concussion."*

"Oh." She swallowed. "Thank you."

She saw one broad shoulder lift, stretching the white fabric of his T-shirt under his leather jacket. *"It's nothing,"* he muttered, and she understood why Melissa thought he was shy. No, he wasn't shy. He was . . . *courtly,* in a tough-guy way. In her mind, she compared him to the young Marlon Brando, to James Dean; the outdated images suited him.

He tipped his head, studying her, then gave her a half-smile, that to her nightmare-battered mind, looked rather sweetly sexy. *"There's a glass of water by the bed if you need it,"* he told her. *"You go back to sleep now. But you call me if you want me."*

Call me if you want me. Renata closed her eyes against the temptation to beg him to stay with her and hold her hand while she slept. She'd always taken care of herself, no matter how lonely, how hurt, how afraid she'd ever been. It was such a temptation to give in to her fears and accept comfort from a perfect stranger—a handsome, courtly and sexy stranger—but she didn't dare depend on anyone else. If she did, what would she do when she was left alone again?

Opening her eyes to thank him and assure him that she would be fine by herself, Renata discovered that Ray had already left, as soundless as smoke. Or maybe she'd fallen asleep again without knowing it. With a sigh, she let exhaustion wash over her again, reluctantly comforted by the knowledge that he was watching over her.

* * *

Gabe listened to the silence of the hospital at night. Nothing to mark the passing of the hours, except for the occasional rustle of a nurse's uniform as she checked his vital signs. His body still refused to obey his mind, but his mind hummed with energy anyway. He hated the trapped feeling, like he was suffocating in his own body. He wanted to get out, to see Lissa, to feel her in his arms and tell her that whatever her reasons for leaving him so long ago, he was beyond joy that she was back.

He walked through the scenario in his mind. He'd go back to the Garvey mansion, ring the bell. She'd look surprised, but pleased. Maybe she'd blush a little. They'd talk a while, maybe awkward at first, trying to stay on neutral ground. She'd offer him a beer, take a glass of white wine for herself. When it was time for him to leave, he'd wait till she stood beside him at the door, her face tipped up, her eyes questioning, her lips parted a little. And he'd forget what he was saying and bend and touch her lips with his, just lightly, giving her a chance to think about kissing him.

Maybe she'd be startled, but she'd also be pleased; he'd know by the way she'd respond. She'd let her lips go soft under his, let him hold her against his chest, her breasts touching, then fitting to him. He'd tease her lips with his tongue, needing to taste her, aching to carry her upstairs and bury himself in her body. But he'd make himself stop. She wasn't ready yet. Maybe he wasn't either. They were still strangers who had once been lovers, but so long ago, and for so little time.

With an inner grin, Gabe let the image of Melissa slip out of his arms, let himself drift into a healing sleep.

Ray paced the hallway outside Renata's room, all his senses attuned to the woman inside. She'd been sleeping for two hours again, without any more bad dreams. It was time to check on her, to see if she needed a doctor for her head. He was pretty sure he could get the bedside lamp on—he'd been practicing on a lamp in one of the other bedrooms, and hadn't broken the bulb yet—but he felt kinda funny going back in there and waking her. There was something about being in a chick's bedroom . . .

Ah, hell! Who was he kidding? There was something about Renata that got to him. It wasn't like his feelings for Celeste, but whenever he looked at her, whenever he heard her voice, he felt a strange sort of . . . *something* inside, some kind of tug at some part of him he'd never thought too much about before waking up dead. The sooner he found Celeste and figured out what he needed to do, needed to know, the happier he'd be. He hated this not knowing.

Okay, enough stalling. Melissa was trusting him to look after her friend, and he wasn't going to let her down, no matter how many funny feelings he had to deal with. He slipped into the room and stood beside Renata, calling her name as gently as he could. Lucky lifted his head, yawned, and tucked his head back under a paw. Ray called Renata again, but she only sighed in her sleep.

Impulsively, Ray reached his hand out toward Renata's shoulder, then pulled back. Except for that one quick contact in the basement—and the only thing he'd felt was an electric shock—he hadn't touched a chick since the last time he'd made love to Celeste. Oh, God! He missed her! Where was she? Was he ever going to touch her and hold her again?

His eyes started to sting and an ache shuddered through him. He gritted his teeth until his vision cleared.

Watching Renata stir, sensing her eyes fluttering open, he let himself remember the times that Celeste had fallen asleep in his arms. She would wake to his kisses like a cat, blinking and stretching, almost giving in to the temptation to sink back into sleep. And then she'd snuggle closer and nuzzle his neck, her lips warm and damp on his skin. She'd squirm around until her body was pressed against him, teasing him, signaling that she wasn't ready to go home yet. And he'd stroke her hot, silky skin and discover that she was ready for him to love her again.

Renata stretched and her fingers brushed the air where his belly would have been, if he were solid. A *zing* of electricity raced through his gut as if she'd really touched him. He was *tingling,* like he still had a body, for crying out loud! His jaw dropped and he stood like a statue, watching her give a little start and gasp softly. She must have felt the same shock, because she pulled her hand back. Damn, this could get embarrassing! He better do something to distract them both.

"Take it easy, baby. Don't move too fast. You've got a couple of nasty bumps on your head."

She blinked up at him again. "I . . . No, it's not my head. I thought I felt a shock, but it must have been a dream. I'm okay now, thanks." Her smile looked pretty wobbly.

Impulsively, Ray knelt beside the bed. Now they were eye to eye, which had seemed like a good idea until he realized he could hear her breathing softly. And he thought he could feel the beating of her heart, like the pulsing of butterfly wings in his own chest. The sensations spooked him. He wanted to know why this was happening, but he couldn't think straight when she was staring at him like she was drowning and he was some kind of lifeguard.

Talk, he told himself. Break the silence, break the spell. *"You can probably take a couple more pain pills,"* he told her, remembering Melissa's instructions. *"It's been about four hours since the last ones."* His voice sounded gruff. He told himself it was just because he was trying to speak softly. Not because he felt like he was cheating on Celeste to be feeling Renata's heartbeat inside himself.

She gave him a sleepy smile. "I think I will. Thanks."

Man, oh, man, talk about a bedroom voice to go with those dark bedroom eyes! Why was he even noticing, when all he wanted was to find Celeste? What the hell was wrong with him? He had to get out of there before he did or said something stupid.

"Okay. I'll see you later." He turned and headed toward the door, hoping she couldn't see through him by the light from the hallway.

"Ray!"

There was an edge to her voice that made the hair on his neck stand up. *Uh-oh!* He turned back, waiting for the question he didn't want to answer. She didn't say anything, but he heard a suspicious little sniff. He moved back into the room and looked down at her. Sure enough, he could just see the glint of tears in her eyes. Oh, man! He hated it when dames cried. He couldn't even pat this one on the shoulder without having his hand sink into her. And it wouldn't be fair to Celeste for him to go sinking into any other chick, even by accident. He didn't think even Celeste would understand that.

"Hey, baby, what is it? Do you hurt somewhere?"

"Ray, please don't let Melissa call the police or an ambulance or anyone, until I can think this through." Her voice came out in a husky whisper that seemed to draw him even closer. Or maybe it just held him there, trapped by a connection he didn't understand, didn't want to understand. Didn't want, period.

Before he could answer her, she murmured, "I couldn't bear it if anything were to happen to her. Or to you." And then she lifted her hand to his face—or to where his face should be. It wasn't like he could feel her fingers on his skin. He couldn't feel anything like that at all. But he could feel the spark of contact between them.

He jerked back before she could realize she was really touching thin air, but maybe not quite in time. Her eyes went wide. Her hand dropped.

"You gave me a shock," he muttered, hoping she'd accept that as the truth, which it was, and wasn't.

"Sorry. I felt it, too," she whispered.

"Take your pills and go back to sleep. You don't have to worry about me. I'm a big boy. I can take care of myself. And I'll make sure Melissa stays out of trouble. Promise. Okay?"

She whispered her thanks, and he escaped before she could call him back again. But for the rest of the night, as he kept watch from the hall, he wondered what it all meant. He had some pretty uncomfortable suspicions, but he didn't have any answers that made sense. Then again, being a ghost didn't make a whole lot of sense either, but there he was.

In one corner of her mind, Melissa knew she was dreaming, but everything seemed so real. She heard the chime of the doorbell echo through the house, and when she opened the door, there was Gabe. He smiled down at her, no sign of the injuries that had put him in the hospital. Feeling a little shy and nervous, she invited him in. She could even smell the subtle spice of his aftershave as he walked past her in the narrow entry.

A moment later, they were sitting on her living room sofa. Gabe held a half-empty beer bottle in one hand. She didn't know how they came to be there, or for how long, but then she remembered it was a dream. Her fingers cupped the bowl of a glass of white wine she'd barely touched. They must have been talking, but she couldn't hear what he was saying, didn't know what she was replying.

Then, like one scene in a movie dissolving into the next, she found herself following Gabe back to the door. He was leaving, but she didn't want him to go. When he reached for her, she felt her body jerk in surprise, then go soft with longing. His first kiss was just a light brush of his lips against hers. His next kiss left her no doubt that he wanted her. She clung to him, feeling his heartbeat thudding through her own body as his mouth fed off hers. And then he was gone and her arms were empty.

When she awoke, the sun was shining into her bedroom, and all the events of the past few days flooded into her memory, crowding out the details of her dream. With a sigh, she gathered clean clothes and went to shower. The face that looked back at her was flushed, and her lips were red and swollen as if she had, indeed, been thoroughly kissed.

Gabe heard Paul Sykes talking to someone as he came closer to the bed, but his body still refused to obey his orders and wake up. Damn! He wanted out of this cocoon. He had a hit-and-run to solve, and a dream encounter with Lissa to live out in real life.

" . . . don't understand it," a woman was saying to Paul. "His blood pressure and pulse rate dropped, then went sky-high, for no apparent reason. Look at the chart. But by the time the nurses ran in, he was stable again."

Inside, Gabe grinned. He knew damn well what had sent his pulse soaring. Too bad it was just a dream. But hell, at least he could control *something.*

Renata heard voices nearby and tried to waken. At her first cautious movement, the overall throbbing in her head focused into a searing pain in her forehead that made her close her eyes and forced an involuntary whimper from her. A moment later, Melissa was calling her name in an urgent tone. Renata's first attempt to answer came out as a groan. Finally, she managed to speak, but she wasn't ready to try opening her eyes again.

"Mel?"

"Right here. How are you feeling?"

"Awful." She offered a weak-feeling smile, still not ready to open her eyes. "But I'll survive."

"This is ridiculous! You're hurt badly. You need a doctor."

Fear jolted her eyes open. Will's warning about her safety echoed in her memory. She looked up at her friend, desperate to convince her of the danger. "No! Mel, you promised!"

"Okay, okay! But I'm entitled to my opinion, which is that you're being incredibly foolish. You should be demanding police protection."

"I know, but . . . Give me some time to think this through. I'm not hurt as badly as you think. Just banged up. That fall I took when we were skiing in Colorado last year was even more painful, honest," she lied. She tried to smile, but the skeptical look on Melissa's face told her she wasn't being very convincing.

They stared at each other for a moment before Melissa finally sighed. "Okay. Let me help you get to the bathroom to freshen up."

Even with Melissa supporting her, practically dragging her, Renata barely made it to the en suite bathroom before the shimmering darkness teasing the edges of her vision closed in on her. She clutched at the edge of the sink and sank to the side of the tub, the cold porcelain under her hands and thighs making her aware of the feverish aching of her entire body. Ordering her not to move, Melissa left her for a moment, returning with a nightgown and robe.

Twice, while Melissa helped her strip off her mud-caked clothes, Renata had to sit down to keep the darkness at bay. Nevertheless, she insisted on showering, overriding her friend's protests. The warm water, flowing at the softest setting on the fancy new showerhead, battered her bruises and scrapes like hailstones, but Renata refused to give in to the whimpers welling up inside her throat. The water and soap washed away the dirt and blood and tears, but couldn't erase the sense of violation that lingered from her flight through the woods. Whoever had been pursuing her might think she escaped without significant damage, but he'd be wrong.

Finally dressed in her friend's silk nightgown and robe the color of blush roses, Renata accepted Melissa's help getting back to the bed. Tears filled her eyes again when she saw that Melissa had changed the linens on the bed. Without a word, Mel handed her a tissue and drew the soft quilt up to her chin. That was when Renata noticed how pale and drawn Melissa looked.

"Mel, you have dark circles under your eyes." Her face hurt when she spoke, making her words sound muffled. She was glad she hadn't given in to the temptation to examine her injuries in the bathroom mirror. The pain was enough of a reminder without knowing how she looked. "Did you get any sleep last night?"

Inexplicably, Melissa's ivory cheeks turned pink. "Yes, but I . . . I had some dreams that woke me, that's all."

Renata could well imagine the nightmares that had disturbed Mel's sleep. "I'm sorry. How is Gabe this morning?"

"No change, according to the official report. But I doubt they'd tell me anything, unless I can talk directly with Paul Sykes. If you're okay later, I'll try to visit him." Melissa's voice carried a hint of doubt.

"Please don't stay away from the hospital on my account. I'll be fine here. I'm just going to sleep and think. You don't have to wait on me."

Mel gave her a sad smile. "I can't go when his parents are there anyway. Do you want some breakfast?"

"Nothing, now, thanks." A yawn swept over her. She let herself nestle into the bedding. "I wanted to thank Ray for looking after me last night. Is he around?"

"Um, no. I think he, uh, had some errands to do. He, um, comes and goes a lot. Sometimes I practically forget he's here."

"Oh. I thought I heard him talking to you before my shower."

Melissa turned her back, and Renata could see her giving extra attention to straightening the drapes that kept out the bright sunshine. "He was here then, but now he's not. I'll tell him for you if you'd like."

Renata smothered another yawn, wincing as even that small movement made her ache. "Please. It was very sweet of him to give up his sleep for me."

"I doubt he minded."

Melissa said something else, but Renata was already drifting into a weighted sleep that made her friend's words muffled and unintelligible. Sometime later, she thought she heard Melissa and Ray in the room with her, speaking quietly, but she could also have been dreaming. Even asleep, her mind was on guard, her body tense. But when she dreamed of Ray stroking her hair from her face, she smiled at his shy earnestness and felt her tension and pain evaporating. If she didn't know better, she'd believe he really was taking away the throbbing ache that had imprisoned her body.

Ray stood over Renata and watched her breathing softly and evenly. He wanted to try touching her again, to see if that strange feeling was a fluke, or some kind of quirk of his imagination. But he didn't want to wake her with those shocks that kept happening every time they got close enough to touch. And he didn't want to do anything Celeste could misinterpret. He'd always been true to her, and he wasn't about to cheat now, just because he was dead and she wasn't.

Finally, he settled for putting the tips of his fingers on the fluffy fringe of dark hair hiding some of the bruises on Renata's forehead. No shock this time, but tiny tingles ran up his fingers, like bubbles. He couldn't actually *feel* her hair, but he knew it would be soft and fine and thick.

He used to love playing with Celeste's hair. The long, pale strands would flow over his fingers like champagne, and she would tip her head back and make soft little sounds of pleasure, almost a purr. Sometimes, that would be enough to bring her into his arms, a little shy, not quite bold enough to say what she wanted with words, but one look in her eyes, and he got the hint real fast. But it never really mattered if they were somewhere where they could make love, or not, if he could give her back a little bit of the sweetness she gave him.

And then, as he stared at Renata, the image of Celeste floated in front of him. He tamped down the urge to run—after all, he was dead; what could hurt him?—and waited to see what would happen. Like Renata, Celeste seemed to be asleep, a soft smile curving her lips. And damn if Renata's lips didn't shape a smile, too, as if the two chicks were sharing some kind of girls-only secret. Maybe they were dreaming about him.

Confused by the whole thing, he ran his fingers through his hair and tried to figure out what this could mean. As soon as he moved his hand away, Celeste disappeared, leaving him staring down at Renata. He felt an ache inside, missing Celeste, feeling helpless, feeling angry, and damned guilty for touching Renata.

Still, he couldn't help feeling sorry for her. Someone had tried to hurt her, and she'd been pretty cool and brave to escape, and still think she was supposed to protect her friends. She was badly banged up, and had some nasty looking scratches across her face and on the back of the hand that curled under her chin. He wanted to do something for her, but he didn't know what. Melissa had sure put it right: He was a ghost, not a wizard.

He'd told her he could take care of himself, but that was no big deal. But if the creep who had chased Renata through the woods caught up with her here, was there anything he could do to protect her and Melissa? Not a damn thing.

That helpless feeling gripped him like a vice, but he

quickly turned it into anger, something he understood much better, and knew how to use. Anger at the guy out there for his cruelty, anger at whoever murdered him, and at himself for his uselessness. Muttering a curse, he fisted his hands, then turned and walked out of the room.

Restlessly, he paced the hallway, trying to get past his anger and focus his thoughts.

"Ray? Are you doing something strange?" Melissa called, snapping him out of his concentration.

"Like what?" he answered, moving toward the kitchen, where Melissa was pouring coffee.

"I don't know." She turned and shrugged. "The temperature dropped just now, as if someone had opened a door, and the lights keep flickering."

He shook his head. *"All I was doing was pacing and thinking. You could have a short somewhere. I'll check the windows and see if any of them are open."*

"Oh. I guess that could explain it."

"You sound disappointed. Did you think I was pulling some kind of Halloween gag?"

"No. Sorry. I didn't mean to accuse you. How's Renata? Is she still sleeping?"

"Yeah. She's pretty banged up."

Melissa sighed heavily. "I feel so helpless, Ray. First you, then Gabe, now Renata. I wish there was something I could do besides wait."

"I know what you mean." He started to lean against the door frame, then remembered he'd probably sink into it. Crossing his arms over his chest instead, he shook his head. *"I keep getting this feeling that time is ticking away on us."*

At Melissa's gasp, he tried to explain where his scattered thoughts had been leading. *"There's got to be some reason why I woke up now, right? So what's different now from the last thirty-five years?"*

Her eyes widened, and then she nodded. "I bought this house and moved in. It's the first time anyone's lived here since Mrs. Garvey died. But I never met her, and you and I have no connection. We can't. You were . . . You know, before I was born."

He started pacing across the kitchen, passing her as he spoke. *"No, no connection with me, but with Gabe. And with Renata. And Gabe and Renata know each other."* He halted briefly and met her eyes. *"I didn't wake up until the day the three of you got together in this house. Halloween."* Then he shrugged and continued pacing. *"The only thing I can't figure out is the connection between me and any of you. Like you said, I was long gone before any of you were born, and none of you have any connection with Celeste. You don't even know who she is."*

"No, I don't." He turned in time to see Melissa shaking her head. "Not only that, but Gabe and Renata didn't know each other until a few months ago, and neither of them knew they had me in common until Thursday night. The same night you woke up."

He nodded. *"Halloween."*

She opened her mouth to speak, then closed it and stared at him as he strode past her, frowning.

He paused and lifted his eyebrows at her. *"What?"*

"That cold draft. I can feel it again, but I remember checking that the doors and windows were all closed after Renata went to sleep last night." She gave him a funny look, like she suspected him of switching the sugar for salt. "Are you sure you're not doing it by accident?"

After thinking a moment, Ray shook his head. *"I'm not sure of anything, except that I woke up dead on Halloween night. I don't know why I was murdered, I don't know why I'm here, and I don't have a clue what I can do, except for walking through walls and turning lights on and off."*

He also didn't know why he felt that strange, unsettling connection with Renata, but he wasn't about to tell Melissa anything about that. In frustration, he pounded his left fist on his thigh, but couldn't feel a thing, so he didn't even have the satisfaction of hurting himself.

"I gotta say, Melissa, I feel bad for Renata and Gabe, but I have my own business to take care of here, if I can figure out what the hell it is. I can't do anything for anyone else. I don't have any magic powers. Hell, I can't even pick up a feather."

He couldn't keep the anger out of his voice, but he didn't

care. He wanted answers, and he wanted them *now*. The main problem was, the only people he could ask had more questions than he did. He was definitely on his own here. As usual.

Melissa carried her coffee mug to the table, circling wide of the area where he'd been pacing. She sat and looked at him, wary, like she was too close to a lion's cage. Maybe she was, damn it. He glared back, letting his anger simmer inside him. How was he even supposed to know if he was a "good" ghost, like Casper, or a dangerous one, like the headless horseman? When he was alive, he'd never hurt anyone who hadn't tried to hurt him first, but he'd been dead a long time. Maybe he'd changed.

Cursing under his breath, he turned away, then looked back over his shoulder at Melissa. Damn! She was still eyeing him the same way, like she was beginning to be afraid of what he might do.

"I'm gonna check on Renata," he muttered, then headed for the hallway.

"Ray? Tomorrow I'll try to find out about Celeste," Melissa called.

He grunted his thanks, not caring if it sounded rude. But as he stood at Renata's doorway, he felt something like the hairs standing up on the back of his neck. If he didn't know better, he'd swear he was afraid of hearing whatever news about Celeste Melissa could find. Nothing worse could happen to him, so what was there to be afraid of? Not a damn thing, except finding out that something bad had happened to Celeste.

He shook off that thought and stepped into Renata's darkened room.

Cold. So cold. Renata shivered helplessly under covers that couldn't warm the chill within her. She lay in the fetal position, her arms curled tightly around her. Everything hurt, but she couldn't make her muscles respond to her brain's orders to relax their grip on her limbs. Even her ribs were clamped in a vice of tension, pressing on her heart. Breathing hurt, so she barely sipped at the air, taking only enough to live. Through her closed eyes, she could feel the icy light that tempted her to give in, give up. She squeezed her eyes shut tighter. She didn't want to know what was out there waiting for a moment of weakness to engulf her. And then, with sudden clarity, she understood.

She was dying.

Chapter
Seven

She was . . . She was someone else. Herself, but not herself. Alone and cold, she was dying. Alone and afraid of the dark, of the unknown light that pulsed like a living thing. Afraid of the pain that was tearing her apart. Afraid of not feeling anything ever again. Afraid of never knowing . . .

Electricity tingled along her nerves, hot and cold, stinging her all over. It hurt! It hurt so much, she couldn't breathe, couldn't cry! At first, she thought it was part of dying, and she held herself rigid, calling up all the shreds of strength left in her, determined not to give up. She wasn't finished living!

There was something she had to do, something important. But what? And who was she? Why couldn't she remember? Was it because death stole all memories? Was she dead already, and still caught in this choking, constant pain?

But no, the electricity that surrounded her was warming her now, thawing the grip of her muscles, easing the crushing pain that had been wrapping ever tighter around her. She took a tentative breath. Air whooshed into her lungs. She exhaled slowly, afraid the warmth was a final illusion, that this would be her last breath. But when she inhaled again, her lungs filled easily and sent warm blood singing through her veins.

Her nerves tingled with the warming that seeped into her, unlocking her joints. When she told her limbs to uncurl, they obeyed, stiffly, painfully, but they obeyed. Finally, her shivering stopped, and when she relaxed her tightly squeezed eyelids, the aura of light around her was soft, dim, soothing.

She wasn't dying. She was sleeping. Warmth hummed through her body like an embrace. She was sleeping, but she felt herself healing. And she felt the comforting strength of that warm embrace, the embrace of her dream lover. *Ray.* He held her close, his body curved around her, his arms wrapped around her, infusing her with his warmth. She felt his breath stirring her hair, felt his heart beating against her back, felt his vitality flowing into her.

He was no stranger, this dream lover with Ray's face and voice, Ray's smile. She knew him with her heart. He loved her with tender hunger, with careful strength, with reverence and earthy passion. But was it only in her dreams, when she was someone else? Outside her dreams, was her heart still waiting?

Her body hummed with renewed life. She knew she was dreaming, that Ray wasn't her lover, except in her dreams. But the memory of a promise lingered in her dreams, a promise given in good faith, broken but not broken. Something hid at the edge of her memory, taunting her to discover it, but whenever she reached toward it, it slid further into the darkness of memory.

Maybe, if she kept dreaming, her dream lover would help her remember.

Pouring himself into his efforts, Ray felt Renata's shivers vibrating through him, and let himself absorb her pain, her fears, sending the energy back to her as warmth and healing. He heard her draw a deep breath, felt her relax in his arms, and smiled to himself. Damn, he was good! Even if he'd only been guessing, feeling his way, whistling in the dark, his instincts had been right on. Think how good he would be if he'd paid more attention to all that stuff about energy in physics classes.

He opened his eyes again, and stiffened. Like a memory come to life, Celeste lay with her head on his biceps, her bottom tucked into his thighs. It was Renata he felt breathing quietly and steadily, but for one incredible moment he saw Celeste in her place. And then she was gone, and he was looking at Renata again. Losing Celeste pierced him with the sharpness of a sliver of glass. He had to close his eyes against sudden tears.

And then he realized something he'd been too busy trying to heal Renata to notice before. He could *feel!* Oh, man! He could feel! Well, almost feel. More like he could *sense* the feeling of Renata breathing against him. But hell, it was more like feeling than he could do till now. He almost laughed out loud, then frowned. Why now? What was it about Renata that made him think he was seeing Celeste? What was it about Renata that reached inside him and turned on sensations that had been dead for thirty-five years?

Oh, Celeste! He'd sworn he'd always love her, look after her, always be with her. That no one could keep them apart. He'd broken his promises when he'd died. His body ached for her. His heart ached for the pain he'd caused her. He needed to tell her he hadn't meant to break his promises. Now, for that magic instant, he'd touched Renata and seen Celeste. It wasn't enough. He wanted to wake her, kiss her, make love to her, but she was already gone, leaving Renata sleeping in his arms.

Could he reach Celeste through Renata? Or was he imagining things?

It wasn't Renata who turned him on, who sent the lightning through his veins. It couldn't be. Only Celeste—still and always—Celeste who made him ache with a hunger that was beyond physical. Renata brought out raging protective instincts no one but Celeste had ever stirred in him. But Celeste wasn't there with him, and Renata was. Did that mean something? It had to mean something, didn't it? Or was he crazy as well as dead?

* * *

Renata floated to the surface of consciousness, momentary disorientation abruptly shifting into sharp focus as her senses awoke. The first thing she noticed, before opening her eyes, was that the pain was gone. All the pain, even in her sprained ankle. The next thing she realized, without having to open her eyes, was where she was: Melissa's guest room. And that she was alone.

But she hadn't always been alone. Lucky had snuggled up to her before she'd fallen asleep, but later, Ray had come to her. He had held her against him as she'd slept, his powerful body shielding her, infusing her with warmth and strength. She'd felt the energy of his embrace even in her dreams. No, especially in her dreams. He was all she had dreamed about.

And what dreams! A smile curved her lips as she turned onto her back and stretched. Dreams of making slow, leisurely love, as if their bodies and minds were intimately in tune with each other. As if they knew each other, soul to soul. His hands had trembled as they'd eased her out of her nightgown, and his tightly leashed eagerness had fueled her passions. When their dream-bodies joined, his control had snapped, and he'd driven them rapidly to a shattering climax. And then, as her dream-self caught her breath, he'd held her and whispered sweet love-words. And all the while she was dreaming, a remote corner of her mind insisted that making love with Ray, with this complete stranger, was unmistakably, totally familiar.

Definitely a dream, since she'd never had a lover, and she knew she would have awakened if he'd actually tried to make love to her. Besides, even as she had savored the sensual delights of that erotically charged dream, she'd been aware of him holding her gently in the curve of his body, not moving as she slept. Obviously, the attraction was one-sided: hers. Ray had been protective, not seductive. She'd be well-advised to keep her fantasies about him to herself, and not embarrass them both.

Cautiously, she sat up, taking stock of her injuries. It wasn't her imagination: the exhausting pain of the day before had faded almost entirely, leaving her feeling only mildly achy.

After swinging her legs over the side of the bed, she tried flexing her twisted ankle. It was still slightly twingey, but when she stood and gingerly put weight on it, there was just a vague tenderness to remind her of the searing pain that had made her feel so faint. The phrase *time heals all wounds* popped into her head.

How long had she been asleep?

Melissa had left clean clothes on the chair in the bedroom. Grateful for her friend's thoughtfulness, Renata carried them to the bathroom, bracing herself for the renewal of pain that never came. She showered, then braved a look at her battered body. The sight of the bruises, already fading, made her wonder, again, how long she had slept. Even the scratches on her face and hands looked as if they were partially healed.

The leggings Melissa had left for her fit well enough, although they reached down past her ankles. Heavy socks covered the rolled-up edges. The oversized sweatshirt nearly swallowed her up, but even that wasn't a problem. But there was no way her B body was going to fill out Mel's C bra. There was a limit to where she was going to wear socks!

When she came out of the bathroom, she followed the sounds of soft rock music and clanking china downstairs to the kitchen. Mel stood on a stepladder, arranging her dishes in the new cupboards. Ray sat at the table, reading a magazine. Wishing she had her glasses or her contacts so she could see him clearly, Renata took advantage of being unnoticed for a moment to study him.

What was it about him that sent awareness crackling through her like static electricity? Was it simple attraction, the kind she'd never felt for any other man? She'd certainly never been even mildly attracted to a man like Ray, except in her dreams. He was so blatantly masculine, so natural and unpolished, so unapologetically bold. Usually, men like that made her run, not walk, the other way.

Was it her current vulnerability that made her receptive to the sexual signals his direct green eyes and knowing grin gave her? Or was that magnetic sexuality the reason that she hadn't forced herself to wake up last night and demand that he leave her bed? She could have, she knew, but she hadn't wanted to. She'd wanted him to hold her. Why? Remembering how she'd always before dreamed she was someone else, she had to wonder, was it ever her own feeling of attraction to Ray? Why was she more attracted to Ray, a virtual stranger who was so much younger, who treated her like a friend, than she was to Will, who wanted to be more than a friend?

Will! Oh, no! Their date!

Renata didn't realize she'd gasped until Melissa turned around and Ray lifted his head. They both looked at her, but Mel smiled a welcome, while Ray studied her without any reaction—at least, none she could see at this distance.

"Hi, sleepyhead," Mel said brightly. "How are you feeling? Do you want some ice for your ankle?"

"No, thanks. It feels almost perfect now." She glanced at Ray, thinking of the way he'd held her most of the night. Her cheeks tingled with sudden heat, and she felt grateful now that, without her glasses, she couldn't see his face clearly. Too bad her nearsightedness didn't work both ways!

Mel came down from the stepladder. "Great! Looks like you heal fast. How about some breakfast?" Mel glanced up at the wall and grinned. "Or lunch?"

"Um, sure, breakfast, I guess." She followed Melissa's gaze to the clock on the wall and squinted. One-thirty? She smiled lamely. "Or lunch."

"The fridge is full, and there's a fresh pot of coffee. Help yourself. You can talk to me while I'm unpacking this stuff." Mel grinned. "Ray found a motorcycle magazine in the basement, which has rendered him utterly useless as company."

Renata half-smiled, then blurted, "What day is this?"

"Saturday," Mel told her. "Why?"

"Thank goodness!" she breathed. "I didn't know how long I'd been sleeping. Would you excuse me? I have to use the phone. I, um, I had a, um, a date for tonight that I have to cancel. I'll call from the other room."

Renata looked away from Ray, but she could feel his stare, as if he were actually touching her. As she was turning, she saw Melissa glance over her shoulder at Ray, and he seemed to frown.

"A date with Will, the trooper?"

Fighting irrational embarrassment, she nodded. "And I'm afraid that if I simply stand him up, he'll start looking for me. He knows I was visiting you on Halloween. I don't remember if I told him where you live, but he's a cop. He can find out. This would probably be one of the first places he'd look. He suspects the prosecutor who was on this case before was deliberately hurt in a car crash, and he has this theory that I'm in danger too."

"Looks like he was right," Mel muttered.

Again, Renata couldn't resist glancing at Ray. His handsome face was set in a fierce scowl, his gaze shifting from her to Melissa and back. When he met her eyes again, she read a challenge in his piercing look, but she couldn't tell if he was wondering about Will, or about why she was apparently putting herself in danger.

What she could tell was that, regardless of Melissa's opinion, Ray was definitely *not* shy. He was quiet, contained, rather mysterious. But underneath the surface, he simmered in ways that she found compelling, dangerously compelling. He was the kind of man she knew she should avoid at any cost, the kind of man her mother had been helplessly attracted to so many times. So why, when she should be thinking of her safety, bodily and emotional, when she should be calling Will to ask him to hide her where thugs couldn't get to her, was she drowning in the inexplicably familiar light of Ray's eyes?

"I'll be right back," she said hastily, hoping neither of them saw the blush she could still feel tingling in her face.

She dialed Will's home number. He answered on the first ring, his voice momentarily shocking her into an odd feeling of watching herself doing something.

"Hi, babe! I was just thinking about you," he said when she replied to his greeting. The warmth in his voice made her cringe.

"Were you?" she asked inanely. How was she going to find the words to tell him she was cancelling their date?

"Yeah." He chuckled. "Nothing too risqué, since this is our first date. Maybe a PG-17."

She took a deep breath. "Will, I'm sorry to do this so last minute, but I . . . I . . ." She what? Inspiration struck. "I think I've got a stomach flu. I feel awful. I can hardly stay awake, and I hurt all over." That much, at least, was true. "I'm sorry, but I can't go anywhere tonight."

He swore softly. She unsuccessfully pushed away the stab of guilt at the mental picture of him composing himself. "That's too bad, babe. Do you want me to come over with chicken soup? My mother always brings some for my freezer when she visits. I've got plenty to spare." He sounded a little too hopeful.

"No, thanks. I . . ."

She stopped herself from admitting she wasn't home. Some instinct, probably the same one that protected any prey from predators, warned her not to tell even Will where she was. She felt foolish to withhold the information from him, when he was a policeman, sworn to protect. Fear had apparently heightened her self-preservation instincts beyond blind trust. After last night's incident, she knew it wasn't wise to talk herself out of being cautious.

"That's really sweet of you, but I'm not fit to be seen, and I don't think I have the energy even to answer the door. Besides, I'd hate for you to catch this bug."

After a silence, he answered, "Okay, Renata. I'll let you get your rest. Call me if you want company." His dull tone told her he didn't believe her excuse, didn't expect her to call.

"Thanks, Will."

"Yeah. Take it easy. Hope you feel better soon."

He hung up before she could say goodbye. With a sigh, Renata replaced the receiver. She hated to lie, even when it was justified, and especially when she didn't know for sure if it was or wasn't. Maybe she should call Will back and tell him what had happened. He could protect her, protect all three of them, better than they could protect themselves. She reached for the phone again.

"Hey! Leave the guy a little pride," Ray ordered gruffly.

She gasped in surprise and turned to find him lounging in the doorway, arms folded across his chest. Even though she couldn't see his face clearly, she didn't need her glasses to feel his disapproval. How much of her conversation with Will had he overheard?

"It's rude to eavesdrop," she snapped.

He grinned. *"Yeah, I know. But enlightening."* His grin faded. *"You feeling okay now? You still look a little pale."*

Her annoyance fizzled at the concern in his voice. "Better than I thought I would. I'm glad I let Mel bully me into a shower and those painkillers." *And,* she added silently, *I'm glad you held me and made me feel safe in the dark.*

He gave her a lazy, cocky smile, vividly reminding her of the erotic fantasies, the heated images that had swirled through her sleep.

"Maybe it wasn't all Mel's doing," she blurted, immediately regretting it. Revealing her attraction to Ray would embarrass him. Revealing her yearning for a man who didn't exist would make him pity her. No wonder her mother was still kissing toads, looking for her prince. The need to love someone, to be loved in return, was overwhelmingly powerful. She wanted to turn away without another word, but his gem-bright gaze seemed to be challenging her to explain. Well, she'd gotten herself into this situation. She'd get herself out.

"I appreciate your watching over me, especially after my nightmare," she told him, willing herself not to blush, knowing she wouldn't succeed. "I was able to sleep peacefully after that."

"I wasn't just watching you, Renata." He gave her an unexpectedly sweet smile that made her wonder if Melissa had been partly right about her cousin being shy. *"I hope you didn't mind,"* he added in a low, suggestive tone that didn't fit his words at all, and sent the idea of him being shy up in smoke. Or maybe it was just her imagination again, filtering impressions through her fascination with him.

Suddenly tongue-tied, she nodded.

Before he could reply, Lucky streaked into the room, tried in vain to stop, and slid halfway across the slick hardwood floor, his little paws scrambling wildly for traction. Renata watched the kitten shake his head, then sit and regard them with a regal *I meant to do that* expression on his face. Ray snickered, triggering Renata's laughter. Lucky scowled, then rose and stalked out of the living room, his tail as straight as a flag pole.

"You better go have something to eat," Ray told her when they'd stopped laughing. *"You need your strength."*

Nodding her agreement, she went into the kitchen. When she got there, she realized he hadn't followed her.

"What are you doing down here?"

Melissa's voice suddenly came from behind him. Ray jumped, then turned and tried to shrug off his spookiness. *"Just looking through the junk."* He nodded his head toward the corner of the back basement room he'd been haunting since Renata went to have lunch. It was a good place to think. And maybe figure out some way to get at his hidden cash and Celeste's engagement ring.

Melissa looked around the room and sighed. "I never even noticed that stuff before. What's in there?"

"Old magazines and newspapers. I don't know what's in the trunks." He grinned. *"Bodies?"*

Melissa shuddered. "Stop! One ghost per house is enough, thanks."

That hurt. He thought they were getting along pretty well. *"Yeah, well, thank you, too. If you don't want me hanging around here, you know what you can do."*

"I'm sorry, Ray. I didn't mean it like that. I don't mind you here. I'll miss you when you leave. But I don't think I can handle any other spirits looking for help right now."

"Yeah."

Melissa gave him a quick smile, then crossed her arms in front of herself. Now what? He leaned against the wall and willed himself not to sink into it.

"Ray, what did you do to Renata last night?" Her voice was hushed, urgent, like she was afraid of being overheard.

He glared at her to cover the fact that her question made

him feel pretty damned uncomfortable. *"What do you mean, what did I do to her last night? I didn't do anything to her."*

"That's not what I mean. I mean, you must have done something to help her heal. No one gets better that fast. Not with the kinds of bruises she had."

He'd been wondering the same thing, himself. *"I didn't do anything,"* he told her again. *"Nothing I knew I was doing. She had a nightmare, so I woke her up, gave her some water and another pain pill. Then I...I..."* Jeez, he couldn't believe it, but he could feel his face burning! *"I held her while she slept, that's all,"* he muttered.

"You *held* her?" Melissa's eyes went wide. "Did she know you were there? Could she feel you? Could you feel her? Did anything special happen?"

Ray put up his hand to stop the questions coming at him like darts. *"Hey, whoa! You're doing that lawyer-cop thing again. Yeah, she knew I was there, so she must have been able to feel me. I couldn't exactly feel her, but I could feel something."*

"What? What could you feel?"

He thought about how to describe the sensations. *"It was like heat-lightning, all over, wherever I was touching her. Freaked me out the first time, but I'm getting used to it."*

"That must be it, then. Some kind of energy that you produce or channel, that can heal."

This kind of talk was beyond him. He knew about the energy produced in an internal combustion engine, not the kind that could heal. *"If you say so,"* he told her, hoping she'd be happy with that much and leave him alone again.

She didn't take the hint. "That's amazing!" Her eyes narrowed on him again. *Now* what? "Why do I get the feeling you aren't telling me everything about last night?"

Damn! He shrugged.

"Ray? Renata is just about my best friend in the whole world. I love her like a sister. Did anything else happen last night?"

He had to be haunting a lawyer's house! *"No, damn it!"* he growled. She jerked back, making him feel guilty.

"Look, Melissa, I need to do some thinking, and I need to be alone to do it. Okay? But ... There's something I've

gotta know. You can see through me, right? I don't have a shadow, and I don't show up in mirrors, right?" Melissa nodded slowly. *"So, how come Renata doesn't notice that I'm transparent?"*

Melissa sat down on an overturned wooden seltzer-bottle box. She was quiet for so long, Ray wondered if he'd said something to upset her. Finally, she looked up at him and shook her head.

"Renata is very nearsighted, and she lost her glasses in the woods. She has a concussion, so she probably thinks I look pretty fuzzy, too. But . . . Now that I look at you . . ."

Her eyes widened. "Ray, you don't look as transparent as you did at first. I can still see through you when the light is very strong, or when you're in front of something with a strong pattern. But it's not the same as before." She shook her head again. "That's very strange. I wonder why."

"Yeah, me, too." He had a theory, but he wasn't ready to share it yet. It was so wild, he wasn't sure even he could believe it.

Gabe couldn't help feeling relieved when his mother kissed his forehead and whispered that she would be back later. He hated hearing her cry softly over him without being able to reassure her that he was alive and fighting to recover. It made him feel even more helpless, which was bad enough. But sometimes, he wondered if she was already mourning him.

He sure as hell hoped not. He wasn't ready to cash out yet. Not until he nailed the bastard who'd run him down, and not until he'd made some kind of peace with Lissa. If he was lucky, it would take him every day of a very long lifetime with her to do that right. Too bad last night's dream hadn't been real. He'd have to see what else his imagination could conjure up. The thought of winning her back made him smile inside.

He must have drifted off to sleep, because the feel of cool fingertips on the back of his hand startled him. Lissa was back. He could smell her delicate scent, or at least he thought he could. Her touch was as light as a butterfly, but he felt her trembling and ached to be able to comfort her.

"Hi, Gabe," she murmured. "Paul said your mother just left, so I'm sneaking in for a few minutes. I had the most vivid dream last night, or maybe it was this morning. I dreamed you came to the house, and we sat and talked. You had a beer, and I had wine, and we listened to music until you had to leave." She gave a soft little laugh and added, "I know it sounds ridiculous, but it felt so real, I expected to find the wineglass and beer bottle in the living room when I woke up this morning."

Surprised disbelief streaked through his mind, followed immediately by curiosity. Was she going to mention those kisses that had sent his pulse racing, or had that happened only in his version of the dream? How could they both have the same dream, anyway? Frustration gnawed at him, but all he could do was wait for her to speak.

"Remember the first time we met?" She let her fingers rest more firmly on the back of his hand. He could feel her silky skin, but it was like there was a layer of gauze between them. "I was six, and you were nine, and some bullies were chasing me. You seemed to come out of nowhere, and at first, I thought you were one of them. I was crying so hard I thought I would be sick. I was almost as afraid of my parents as I was of the boys, because they told me to stay away from the park, but I'd disobeyed. And then you started chasing the bullies away, even though there were four of them."

He smiled inside at the memory. Even then, he'd thought she was cute. He'd told Paul he was going to marry her. Paul had howled as if he'd heard the funniest joke in the history of the Western world.

Lissa stroked his hand. "I thought you were the bravest boy in the world. And the handsomest. You even had a handkerchief in your pocket, and you dried my tears and cleaned my face. I fell in love with you that day." His heart leapt at her confession. He'd never known she'd felt the same way, at the same time. Maybe there was a lot he didn't know about Lissa. *And whose fault was that?* he heard his conscience ask. He winced inside.

"I forgot to ask you your name." He could hear the smile in her voice. "And I was so afraid I'd never see you again."

Lissa gently picked up his hand and cradled it in hers. He fought to make his fingers respond to her touch, but nothing happened.

"I can't remember how long after that, I badgered my nanny into taking me to the carnival, and you were there. I wanted to go on the Ferris wheel, and my nanny was afraid of heights, so you said you'd go with me. Your friends laughed at you, remember? But you told them your father always said it was important to take care of people who needed help."

Talk about ironic, Gabe thought. His father would have a fit now, if he could see Lissa holding his hand and trying to draw him out of the blackness of this damn coma.

"That was when I started to learn about the difference between your father and mine. Yours was a dedicated cop who wanted to help people, and mine was an ambitious lawyer who wanted to win no matter which side he was on. The good guys were always the ones with the most money."

Some things, he thought grimly, *never changed.* But it didn't matter now. They weren't children. And when he and Lissa had their own kids, he'd have a lot of hard lessons to remember about being a parent. Be a lot easier if they only had sons, though. Lissa's father was a snob, who used money to measure people's value. Gabe judged people by their actions, not their income. But if any horny punk tried to touch a daughter of his . . . Gabe wanted to laugh at his sudden sympathy for Lissa's father.

"You held my hand on the Ferris wheel," Lissa reminded him, her voice quiet and dreamy. "I was petrified when the thing stopped with us at the top, but you just took my hand and you didn't laugh at me. Do you remember? And do you remember when I was fourteen and you were seventeen, we snuck out to the carnival and rode the same Ferris wheel? And that time, when it stopped with us at the top, you kissed me on the lips for the very first time."

He felt the butterfly kiss of her fingertip on his lips. *Damn, damn, damn!* he raged against his immobility.

"Melissa?" Paul's voice now. "Sorry, but you have to go now. We don't want to tire him out, and his parents will be back soon. Try again tomorrow, okay?"

She lifted his hand and pressed it to her cheek. He felt the hot sting of tears, the soft brush of her lips, and ached inside.

"I'll come back, Gabe. I promise." She squeezed his hand gently. He tried to squeeze back, to tell her he heard her, but his body couldn't obey his orders yet. "We'll fight this together," she whispered. "And somehow, we'll win."

Gabe heard his father clear his throat, a sure sign he was having trouble with his feelings. *Me, too,* Gabe thought, *but I can't even clear my throat.* A moment later, his father muttered that he was going to the coffee shop, did Linda want anything? She didn't. When he heard his mother sigh, Gabe knew his father had left the room. Gabe fought the straightjacket trapping him in silence. His mother was doing most of the emotional work for both of them, and she had to be wrung dry. He wanted to tell her he would be okay, but he couldn't even manage to squeeze her hand.

"Gabriel, I don't know if you can hear me. Paul says maybe you can. Mario says you can't. I don't know what to believe, so I'm going to try anyway. There's something I have to tell you, and I only have a little time until Mario comes back. This is for you."

His mother let go of his hand, and then he felt something cool and heavy on his right wrist. Not a watch. That would go on his left wrist.

"I want to tell you the truth now, because . . . because maybe I . . . I won't have another chance. Mario and I love you. You are our son. But we aren't your real parents."

Gabe wanted to cry. That was what she needed to confess? Hell, he'd known that ever since he was a little kid! He was the only blue-eyed Portuguese kid in the neighborhood, and he didn't look anything like anyone in the family. He just never mentioned it to his parents. At first, when he was too young to understand about adoption, he was afraid they'd give him back. Then, later, he didn't want to hurt them by bringing up something they obviously didn't want to discuss. By then, it hadn't mattered. They were his parents because they'd raised him and loved him. And he loved them. He was their son.

"Mario never wanted to tell you that we adopted you. He was ashamed that he couldn't give me children. He was afraid you'd turn your back on us and want to know about your real parents."

Aw, hell, Mom, he wanted to say, *you're my real parents.*

"This . . ." She closed her hand over the thing on his wrist. "This belonged to your real father. It was his high school ID bracelet. Your mother left it for you. Mario never wanted you to have it. He thinks I threw it away when you were a baby."

He waited. He had no choice. Finally, she sighed. "I wish I could tell you his name, but I never knew. No one did. She never told. Not even his initials. They were scratched away before you were born. But I knew your mother . . ."

Linda's voice trailed off. Gabe strained to hear.

"Shhh! Mario is coming. I'll tell you about her another time," she whispered. He felt her tuck the cover over his right arm again, hiding the bracelet.

Paul came into the room with his father, no, with Mario. No, damn it! With his *father*. He heard their voices, but he wasn't listening. He was thinking about the bracelet on his wrist. An ID bracelet that gave no clue about his biological father's ID. He used to believe he didn't care. But now, the questions burned inside him. Like nailing the bastard who'd tried to kill him, and starting over with Lissa, it was one more reason not to give in to the darkness that waited for him to give up.

Chapter
Eight

A car door slammed in the driveway. Startled out of her thoughts, Renata dropped her pen onto the kitchen table. She waited, hardly breathing, until she heard the scratch of a key at the front door and Melissa's voice calling her name. Then, feeling foolish, she rose and met her friend, who was carrying several grocery sacks. Automatically, she began helping Mel unpack, pausing several times to chuckle at Lucky dashing in and out of the paper bags, his eyes wide, his tail puffed.

Listening to Mel talk about her visit with Gabe, Renata wondered where Ray was. She hadn't given his absence any thought while she'd been working on her notes, but they could have used his help with the second load of groceries. Melissa wouldn't let her outside to go to the car, fussing that Renata's ankle wasn't perfectly healed and the driveway was uneven. Renata knew the real reason was her friend's worry that her unknown pursuer was still lurking in the woods, but she hated feeling like a prisoner to caution. Still, she decided that the least she could do was try to stay cheerful, for all their sakes.

"Good grief! You bought enough for an army!" she teased as she sorted out the packages of meats and vegetables and cheeses. "I hope you have a freezer."

Mel gave her a look that was much too serious for comfort. "I do have a freezer, downstairs. But this isn't for an army. This is in case of a siege."

Renata put down the package of frozen bread dough. "Mel, for pity's sake, we aren't expecting a siege. No one knows I'm here. That's why I won't let you go to my place for my spare glasses, in case there's someone watching it."

"I know. This is just in case I can't get out to shop for a while . . ." Mel shrugged. Her eyes looked troubled. "You might want to get out of sight soon. There are a couple of guys coming to fix the broken window. It will probably take them about an hour."

It irritated Renata to know Melissa was right. She helped put away the food, then collected her legal pad, and went upstairs to the room Mel would use as her real office. The enormous antique pine rolltop desk, Currier and Ives prints, and comfortably overstuffed seating arrangement in Mel's first floor office were strictly for meeting clients. The room upstairs contained cleanly modern furnishings to accommodate Melissa's computer system, phones, fax and copier machines, and hundreds of books, all still in cartons around the room. It made Renata smile to see that her friend had put into practice an idea they'd cooked up way back in law school.

Shortly after she settled herself at the writing desk, the doorbell rang. By then, she was already deep in thought. Losing track of time, she scribbled what she could recall of her notes about the Frank Dane case. Then she sat back and twisted a strand of hair around one finger as she pondered the possibilities. Assuming Dane was responsible for two prosecutors'—Mick Donovan's and her own—car "accidents," it was possible that the charges the State was laying against Dane were just the tip of a much larger criminal iceberg. The D.A.'s office had always seemed to consider Frank Dane a chronic nuisance, but it looked as if everyone, including her, had been underestimating him. Winning in court against him was all the more important if he really were capable of vehicular assaults against State attorneys.

Even the sudden blare of the stereo downstairs couldn't distract her from the chilling certainty that Melissa and Ray were in real danger because of her. Somehow, she had to do something to make sure nothing happened to them.

Ray touched the power switch of Melissa's stereo. A second later, the lights came on in the front panel and the radio came on. Boring, middle-of-the-road, easy-listening. In the two days since he woke up on Halloween night, he'd discovered that rock 'n' roll had turned some major corners in thirty-five years. Melissa had given him a crash course in history during one of Renata's long naps, but she'd left him to catch up on music and movies on his own. It had been an education.

Right now, he was bored. Somewhere, there was a station that played rock, not this lullaby stuff. Yesterday, she'd interrupted him before he figured out how to change the station. Today, she was doing something in the kitchen, and her mind was on her cop boyfriend. Renata was upstairs working. After sleeping for almost forty years, he was entitled to a little activity.

He touched his fingertip to the *seek* button. Sure enough, the green numbers in the little window changed. Ray grinned and tried again, then listened. Nope, he didn't like that station. He tried another, and then another, until he heard a hard-driving song by some band called the Rolling Stones. Now, that was more like it! He passed his fingers over the volume control and cranked up the sound until he could feel the vibrations in the floorboards. From inside the kitchen, he heard Melissa say something that sounded like "Aaargh!"

"Hey, lady?" One of the glaziers bellowed over the blast of sounds pouring out of the speakers. "How do you turn this thing off? We're going deaf in here!"

Melissa came out of the kitchen with her hands over her ears. She opened the glass cabinet and touched something on the black metal box on the top shelf. The noise stopped.

The silence echoed. He tried not to snicker, but the look on her face when she folded her arms and glared at him was too funny.

"Thanks," the glazier muttered. "Don't know how that thing came on. We were just minding our own business. Nearly dropped your new pane."

She switched her focus to the two guys in their white overalls. "I'm so sorry. I think there's something wrong with the connection."

"Better get that thing fixed, or it'll give somebody a heart attack." The other guy shook his head.

"That wouldn't help," Melissa muttered, turning her glare back in his direction. He laughed out loud. He couldn't help it. Well, after the glass guys left, he'd try to refine his technique.

He gave Melissa his best grin. She made a huffing sound and was turning to go back to the kitchen when he reached toward the power button. "Don't you dare!" she hissed at him. He jerked his hand back and flashed her another one of those smiles that used to melt all but the hardest of teachers' hearts. From Melissa's expression, she wasn't impressed.

"What's that?" The taller of the two guys stared at Melissa.

"Nothing. Sorry. I wasn't talking to you. I was talking to . . . to the cat, who is being an absolute jerk!"

She walked out of the room with a look on her face like she was sucking lemons. Too bad Melissa didn't understand about guys and dares. Now, he was going to have to find something else to do to get a rise out of her. He knew she had a lot of stuff getting her down—so did he, starting with his failure to find Celeste—but Melissa really needed to lighten up before she had a nervous breakdown. He'd be glad to explain all about how short life was.

Renata absentmindedly tapped her pen on the legal pad, her attention on the list of loopholes Frank Dane's clever attorneys had pulled him through in the past. Without her notes, she had to rely on her memory, which was fortunately pretty close to photographic. Countless arrests, yet either charges were promptly dismissed for lack of evidence, or he was acquitted the few times he'd gone to court. But she'd wager her soul that he couldn't be innocent. Too many threads led back to him, despite the circumstantial nature of so many of them, and he was too damn smug about that. Somewhere, there had to be a courageous witness, some concrete proof. So what was she missing?

Were there any patterns in the information she'd compiled? Certainly, the charges tended to fall into the same categories: the *alleged* "chop shop" operation for disguising stolen cars and motorcycles and shipping them out of state; the *alleged* illegal gambling and loan-sharking; the *alleged* sales of stolen weapons and electronics; the *alleged* dealing of controlled prescription drugs; the *alleged* prostitution business. And the latest, *alleged* jury tampering.

But no matter how close the evidence came to pointing at Frank Dane, no witnesses ever put him at the scenes of crimes, nothing conclusive could be found. Unfortunately, the juror who had tipped off the police about Dane's offer of money in exchange for a "not guilty" verdict had suffered a fatal heart attack shortly after the case had been dismissed anyway. Lack of evidence again.

If she hadn't faced him in person in her office, she might have given some credence to one journalist's tongue-in-cheek theory that Frank Dane didn't actually exist. No fingerprints or phone calls, no paper trail, led back to him, yet he had a long history of attracting police attention. Ordinarily, she would be willing to concede that the police occasionally charged an innocent person, but if Frank Dane were innocent, his arrest record was blatant, organized harassment. She simply couldn't believe in a three-decades long, statewide, multi-jurisdictional police conspiracy against Frank Dane.

She also doubted that all the criminals currently and previously serving sentences for crimes alleged to have been masterminded by Frank Dane were organized and clever enough to create a shadow crime boss and convince that sleazy man who had been in her office to play the role for them.

Well, maybe she was looking at this the wrong way. Instead of trying to find patterns in the charges, maybe she should be considering—

"I'd hate to be the guy you're trying to nail."

Without warning, Ray's voice came out of the shadows of the darkened hallway. Renata started and yelped. Her pen flew out of her fingers and slid across the floor. Lucky scrabbled in from wherever he'd been lurking and pounced on the pen. Grasping it between his front paws, he flipped tummy-up and raked at her pen with his back feet. Even with her heart pounding, she had to laugh at how silly the kitten looked.

Hearing Ray's warm chuckle, she met his eyes. Suddenly, Lucky's antics, even Frank Dane's alleged crimes, became insignificant. Every nerve in her body flared with awareness, like tiny electrical storms exploding in the sun's corona.

Ray snorted and shook his head at the kitten, apparently unaware of her sudden sensitivity to his presence. *"What a tough guy,"* he commented. *"Look at him go for the jugular. Must have been a lawyer in a past life."* She couldn't be certain, because she couldn't see clearly enough across the room, but she thought he winked at her.

She barely registered the jibe at her profession. All she knew at that moment was that, despite her nearsightedness, the sight of the man stepping into the room did something devastating to her equilibrium. All she could think of was the way his gaze locked on hers until he was all she could see. Once again, the unnerving memories of her imaginary lover rushed into her mind. The logical side of her brain refused to believe she could conjure such a perfect likeness of a total stranger in her dreams. *Who cares? He's here now. See where this leads,* the emotional side of her brain countered. The logical side seemed to be losing badly. She was so sure Ray was the man who had haunted her dreams for years, making love to her dreaming self with tender passion. So sure he was the man she'd been waiting to love, that she had to restrain herself from reaching out to welcome him the way she often did in her dreams.

As Ray drew closer, she saw that his full lips were curved

in a smile, and she imagined she could feel their warm pressure on her own lips. His thumbs were hooked into the waistband of his jeans, his hands leading her gaze downward to the masculinity tantalizingly revealed yet hidden by the snug fit of his jeans. As her gaze lowered, she couldn't help noting how his white T-shirt outlined his tautly muscled torso. Part of her wished she could see him more clearly, while part of her was grateful she couldn't. She didn't want to test the possibility of spontaneous combustion.

Renata lifted her gaze to his face again to find that his smile had faded, but his new expression was still too indistinct to read from this distance.

He tilted his head. *"What are you doing?"*

The utterly neutral tone of his question made her realize that Ray didn't share her intense recognition, her almost painful need to feel his embrace. And why should he? The dreams were hers, her own private longings. How could he possibly know he was the star? To cover the sharp disappointment she feared showed in her eyes, Renata glanced down at the diagrams on her legal pad.

"Working," she told him, not looking up. Her voice sounded husky, almost sleepy. She cleared her throat before speaking again. "Trying to figure out how a man can keep sliding out of the legal system without a shred of physical evidence and not a single living witness willing to testify."

He walked farther into the room and settled on a chair. She felt her face grow warmer when she realized she was staring at him as he moved, frankly admiring the feline grace of his limbs, the aura of pent-up power in his broad shoulders. It took all her self-control to turn and reach down to take her pen from Lucky's possessive grasp. The little monster batted at her hand with sheathed claws and gave her a plaintive *meow,* then sat up and began scrubbing a front paw with his pink tongue, as if that had been his intention all along. Renata gave him a light stroke with her fingertips, and he repaid her with a quick rasp of his tongue that made her smile.

"This guy sounds like a ghost," Ray said. They were

close enough now that she could see he'd cocked an eyebrow in playful challenge.

She summoned her self-discipline to match his casual friendliness. Smiling, she shook her head. "No, this guy's real enough. I had the pleasure of a meeting with him the other day. He's so smug about being untouchable. It's clear we've all underestimated him. There's something about him—his gravelly voice, his piggy eyes, even the sleazy *smell* of him—that made me feel ill."

Ray sat up a little straighter. *"Smell, huh?"* He swore mildly, then offered her a sheepish-looking grin. *"I, um, lost my sense of smell in a, uh, in an accident."* All thoughts of Frank Dane fled from her mind. Renata couldn't restrain her slight gasp. How awful to lose such an essential sense. She was about to offer sympathy, but Ray lifted one leather-clad shoulder. *"Hey, no big deal. It was a long time ago. I'm used to it now. What the hell? At least I can see and hear."*

"I'm sorry." At his scowl, she hastened to add, "Sorry for my reaction, not sorry for you."

His grin softened into a smile, a rather naughty smile. She wondered if he knew what kind of effect that smile could have on a susceptible woman—any woman, she suspected, who was alive.

"If I had a choice, I'd give up smell before I'd give up touch." Ray wasn't smiling now. He was looking at her so intently that she felt heat rise to her cheeks.

"Renata, this is weird, 'cause we just met, but I feel like there's some connection between us, like we know each other from somewhere else," he said, his voice so low that it drew her senses toward him. *"You know that feeling? Like we could just take up where we left off, if we could only remember where that was."* Transfixed by the emerald gleam in his eyes, she could only nod: yes, she certainly knew that feeling. *"Do you—?"*

"There you are!" Melissa rushed into the office, her cheeks pink, her hair straggling out of the knot uncurling itself at the top of her head. "I lost track of time and I have to get to the hospital before Gabe's parents come back. They always take a break for a couple of hours every afternoon."

Renata forced herself to recover quickly, to consider practical matters, and ignore the galloping of her heart. "Is the window repaired?" she asked. Melissa nodded. "Then get going. We're fine here."

"Don't try to answer the phone or the door. I finally got the answering machine hooked up to the house and office phones, and I'll turn on the alarm when I go out." Melissa made a rueful face. "I'm sorry to treat you as if you're under house arrest, Renata, but I'd rather be safe than sorry."

Renata carefully avoided Ray's gaze and smiled at her friend. "Speaking for myself, I feel like a pampered guest."

Mel gave her a suddenly jaunty grin Renata suspected had been forced for her sake. "Good. So maybe you won't mind setting up my computer while I'm gone? In exchange, I'll get you another pair of glasses tomorrow, when your optician is in."

Recalling Melissa's love-hate relationship with computers, her answering smile was real. "No, I don't mind. In fact, it will make my brainstorming easier. And tomorrow is soon enough for my glasses. Thanks."

Mel let out an exaggerated sigh of relief. "Bless you! The components are in those boxes. The manuals are all in the blue carton, and if you need any of the software, the disks are in the fireproof box in the closet. The fax machine and the modem both run off the same phone line. I marked which one it is on a piece of masking tape on the wall jack." She smiled, her hazel eyes twinkling with mischief. "I'm sure Ray will be glad to help," Mel added with a chuckle.

Renata was still trying to reconcile Ray's apparent lack of interest in her with his sudden assertion that he, too, thought they knew each other somehow. With Melissa's obvious hint hanging in the air between them, she couldn't bring herself to look at him. Instead, she grasped at the first computer-related thought that popped into her head. "Do you have an Internet server yet?"

"I set up my account yesterday. All you have to do is plug in the phone number and password to log on. The info is in the manual for the modem." Mel looked at her watch. "Gotta go! Thanks!"

A second later, she was alone with Ray, and all too aware of the silence stretching between them. Renata had no sooner swiveled her chair toward the computer desk beside her, when she heard the front door downstairs shut. Still not ready to test Ray's reaction to Mel's suggestive remark, she surveyed the cartons Melissa had pointed to, then assessed the desk space. Finally, she looked at Ray.

Brows raised, he glanced from her to the cartons and back to her again. His face clearly expressed the smug skepticism she'd often seen when men didn't believe a woman could deal with something more mechanical than a nail file.

Her mother always exaggerated her helplessness to manipulate her husbands and lovers into taking care of her. From a very early age, Renata had found her mother's performances nauseating, and had taken fierce pride in doing things for herself. So much pride in being independent that people often complained that she wasn't very good at accepting assistance, even when she needed it. Personally, she thought *needing help* was a matter of interpretation. What others might think she couldn't do alone, she considered a challenge. Anyway, she'd assembled so many desktop computer systems that the task didn't even rate a glance at the incomprehensible manuals.

Feeling smugly confident, she met Ray's skeptical gaze evenly. "I suppose you don't think I can do this alone."

He shrugged. She saw his mouth twitch as if he were trying to suppress a smirk. *"Did I say that?"*

"You didn't have to." She opened the carton labeled "CPU" and reached inside. Over her shoulder, she smiled at him. "Relax. I'll have this powered up and running in fifteen minutes or less."

Ray sagged in relief, then bolted up before he sank right through the chair. Renata had just saved him from making a fool of himself. Damn, Melissa had almost undone him right there. Help assemble a computer? Sure! The only computers he knew about were those room-size things at NASA, and he was no rocket scientist. Hell, even if he was, he couldn't pick up a screwdriver, let alone one of those cartons. Renata might be a little nearsighted, but she'd have to notice something like a cardboard box floating through his gut.

It was, he thought, kinda cute the way she'd talked her way into doing the job herself. He hadn't meant her to think he didn't believe she could set up a computer. He just couldn't believe a computer could fit into a few cartons. This was probably the first and only time he'd been glad a chick had mistaken his meaning. Usually, being misunderstood got him *into* trouble, not *out* of it!

Renata bent over to lift something, and the long, baggy top she wore rode up, giving him a great view of a very trim little rear end in those black tights. Ray sat up straighter. Holy cow! Women's clothes had sure made some interesting progress in the past thirty-six years! He was getting those tingles without even touching her.

Sorry, Celeste, baby. Guess I'm only human, he thought, then had to stifle a snort of laughter.

When Renata started to turn, gripping a metal box against her middle, he slouched back and tried to look a little bored. Let her think he was cool, like he saw women assemble computers out of a couple of cartons every day. No big deal. Like he even knew what was in the rest of the cartons, or had a clue how the pieces went together. Or what the hell anyone was going to use a computer for. Oh, yeah, he was cool all right.

Damn, he had a lot of catching up to do! He'd only just found out Elvis was dead, too. Unless he believed the doughnut shop or the space aliens theories. Hell, he was a ghost, but *that* was more of a stretch than he was willing to make!

Now Renata lifted a TV out of a carton and set it on top of the first box. Well, at least he recognized something, even if it didn't look like any TV he'd ever seen. For a moment, Renata ducked out of sight behind the desk. When she stood up again, that big shirt had slipped off her right shoulder. Her *bare* right shoulder. No bra? Now, that got his attention. The smooth curve between her earlobe and her shoulder looked like a very promising place to do some kissing. Celeste always melted in his arms when he kissed her neck. He couldn't help wondering if Renata would, too, then cursed his impulses under his breath. Damn! He was supposed to be protecting Renata, not fantasizing about her. And he was supposed to be looking for Celeste, not betraying her.

Renata suddenly looked at him. He met her eyes, thinking about how he saw Celeste when he touched Renata. *Why?* he wondered again. Was that feeling he had, that he and Renata had some kind of connection, someway, somehow, the reason she made his pulse crank up a few notches? Or was the connection between Renata and Celeste? Long-lost relatives or something? Hell, it was enough to make a guy crazy, even if he was already dead!

Renata's cheeks turned pink and her chin went up a notch. "What?"

"I didn't say anything."

"Yes, you did. You said something." Her dark eyes shot sparks. "Don't think you can confuse me. I can put this together in the dark."

He grinned. *"I can turn out the lights."*

She smiled back. "That's not necessary."

Suddenly, he wondered what it would be like to be alone in the dark with Renata, when she wasn't sleeping off her injuries or waking from a nightmare. He wanted her to finish putting that damn computer together so he could test his theory about Renata and Celeste again. She must have read something in his eyes, because hers widened, then shuttered, like she was trying to hide.

He couldn't help probing. *"You feel it, too, don't you?"*

"Feel what?"

"That connection between us. Some kinda spark."

"You mean, like sticking a paper clip into an electrical socket?" She made a tiny snorting sound. "In your dreams," she told him, then turned back to the wires she was connecting.

"Yours, too," he shot back.

Renata jerked her head up and glared, then looked away again. Sudden guilt slapped him hard. Damn! She didn't know about him and Celeste. And she didn't think about him as a bodyguard. She didn't know he was a ghost. She thought of him as a man, and she sure as hell felt something going on between them. Maybe she knew less than he did about the facts, but she wasn't nearly as confused as he was about the feelings.

He thought about the way she'd snuggled into his arms and his pulse suddenly kicked into higher gear. Guilt hit him again. How could he react to her the way he reacted to Celeste? Sure, he'd gone without sex for almost forty years, but hey, he'd been dead the whole time. It wasn't like it had been much of a sacrifice. Before he'd gotten killed, the only woman he'd loved was Celeste. Before Celeste, he hadn't known what love was. He needed to find her, make amends, and go to whatever reward good ghosts went to. Meantime, he was going to try to protect Renata and Melissa from some bad guy. He was their guardian angel—or guardian ghost. And he was pretty sure that job description didn't include lusting after Renata.

But there was something between them, something that Renata felt, too. Something that, for her own reasons, she didn't want to feel, either. Maybe she understood what was going on here. *He* sure didn't.

"You know what I mean," he tried again. *"Like we recognize each other. We're not really strangers."* Her eyes went wide and she sucked in a little gasp. Looks like he'd hit a bull's-eye. He said the first thing that popped into his thoughts, stupid as it sounded afterward. *"You know, that* déjà vu *feeling. Like we had something going in another life."* Oh, man, talk about a lame pick-up line!

But Renata didn't look like she thought it was a stupid idea. She caught at her lower lip with her teeth. "Yes. No! I mean, I don't know. I mean, yes, there's something, but . . ." She blew the fringe of dark hair off her forehead. "I don't want to talk about this right now. I have to set up this system and try to figure out how a petty criminal gets away with everything except murder. Maybe even murder, too. I don't have time to think about *déjà vu*."

She might not have the time, he thought, but she sure was thinking about it. Now what?

*   *   *

Renata turned her back on Ray and burrowed into another carton of computer equipment to hide her confusion. Was this how her mother felt, whenever she was infatuated with a new man? This fluttery, heightened awareness? The tingling of skin at just the thought of touching and being touched? A sense of communicating without speaking, of *feeling,* for example, that he was thinking about kissing her when he was staring at her bare neck and shoulder? And the sharp ache of longing for him to do so, immediately and repeatedly!

Nothing like this had ever invaded her senses before, and she wasn't sure she liked it. In fact, she was positive she didn't like it at all. She'd never been the kind of person who did anything without a safety net. She'd even been cautious about accepting a date with Will, and he was a State cop, for pity's sake! Falling for a stranger, even the cousin of a good friend, was definitely a dangerous thing to do. Dangerous despite the almost overwhelming feeling that she knew more about him than she could easily say. But was this something she could even make a decision about? Or, was she ultimately going to be drawn to this man like steel thread to a magnet? She felt out of control, out of her element. Out of her mind. Out of her self, the way she did when she dreamed.

Trying, with absolutely no success, to ignore Ray's presence, she sorted the cables to connect the computer peripherals. With several cables in her hand, she knelt behind the desk and squinted at the plugs in the back of the computer.

"Tell me more about this guy who's slipping through the cracks in the law," Ray said as casually as if he'd never said anything to make her recall her heated dreams.

She swallowed, determined to match his cool tone. "He's got an arrest record going back forty years, but no convictions. The only evidence we have leading to him is circumstantial. And he's so arrogant." She snapped one connector into place, then picked up another. "He enjoys rubbing our noses in our failures. He practically admitted to me that he's guilty of the current charges against him, but he was so smug about getting off again. How does he do it?"

"Sounds to me like he's got people doing his dirty work for him."

She stood up and glared. "I figured that one out already."

He grinned. *"Smart babe."*

Before she could stop herself from rising to the bait, she snapped, "I'm not a babe!"

His gaze slid over her and his grin widened. *"Coulda fooled me,"* he drawled.

She exhaled sharply, as irritated with herself as with him, and ducked back down to connect the printer cable. He was a sexist jerk for calling her a *babe,* for teasing her like that. And she'd asked for it. She was a fool for reacting, for wanting him to see her as more than a smart attorney even as she was hoping for the sanity to stop wanting him at all. Heaven help her, could Frank Dane have been right about her hiding her sensual, passionate side behind matronly clothes? How ironic!

After a moment's silence, she heard Ray ask, with only a hint of amusement in his deep voice, *"Okay, tell me what this guy does that's got you so fired up to nail his hide to the wall."*

Contrite about her temper tantrum, she appreciated his peace offering. From her hiding place behind the desk, Renata told Ray about the charges against Frank Dane as she finished connecting the rest of the cables to the computer. He whistled when she came to the end of the list.

She stood again, not quite meeting those piercing green eyes. "That's all we know. The one witness we had lined up recently died of a heart attack, and the prosecutor originally assigned to the case had a terrible car accident."

"And the chief of police was run down and put in a coma, and the new prosecutor got run off the road and chased through the woods," Ray added, his tone harsh.

The suddenly rather fierce look he gave her sent shivers up her spine, but she told herself he was angry on general principle at whoever had pursued her. The possessive, protective glint she thought she read in his eyes had to be a product of her overactive imagination. Of her wishful thinking, that someday, someone would want to take care of her, would be willing to fight for her, even if she would insist on fighting beside him. It was better to believe that Ray's insistence on some connection between them was just a little harmless flirting, to pass the time. How could he know she'd been so alone all her life?

Renata forced herself to set that line of thought firmly aside, and concentrated instead on Ray's theory. "Oh, my God! We hadn't even considered that Gabe's hit-and-run traces back to Frank Dane!"

Musing over that possibility, Renata sat in front of the computer and pressed the master switch of the power bar. With a shrill *beep!* and a few internal chugs and whirs, the computer began its warm-up sequence. Watching the system information scrolling down the screen, Renata slowly realized that Ray hadn't said a word in several minutes. Curious at his silence, she peered around the side of the monitor.

He was gone.

Gabe sensed Lissa even before he felt her fingertips on his cheek. He fought to turn his head into her touch but his body stubbornly refused to obey.

"Hi, Gabe," she murmured. "I'm sorry I'm late. Things have gotten a little complicated at home."

Home. The old Garvey house. Lissa's home now. Did she come back because of their teenage plans? He wanted to believe that she had.

"Can you imagine, the old place really is haunted?"

He wanted to laugh. Haunted? Only by the memories they'd left there. Memories of first love. Of first lovers. Of fumbling kisses and bumping noses, and hands shaking so bad that they couldn't unhook the damn bra strap on the first try. Memories of whispers, of soft murmurs and muffled groans and sighs. Those were the ghosts of the Garvey place. At least, they haunted him whenever he thought about sneaking in with Lissa holding tight to his hand and following so close behind that she bumped into him with every step.

"I know it sounds silly, but the ghost's name is Ray Lowell, and he was murdered at the house way back when Mrs. Garvey was alive. He used to work for her, thirty-five or -six years ago. I guess we woke him up on Halloween. He's trying to find out who killed him and why. And he wants to find out what happened to the woman he was in love with."

So did he, Gabe thought. Right now, she sounded a few cards short of a full deck. Was this what happened when the daily horoscope in the newspaper wasn't enough? Ghosts? What next? Fairies and elves?

"It's really sweet, but sad. I promised I'd help him find out if she's still alive. Thirty-six years ago, he was twenty-four, and she was twenty-one, so she'd be in her late fifties now. I can't imagine what will happen if they meet again. I don't think Ray's thought it out that far. He just wants to see her again, and tell her he's sorry for getting killed before they could elope."

When she stopped speaking, Lissa ran her hand down his left arm, and he forgot about her wacky story. He wanted to curl his fingers around hers but they wouldn't move, damn them! Her hand rested on his.

"He's rather appealing, in a tough-guy kind of way. And poor Renata lost her glasses when someone chased her through the woods. You know how nearsighted she is. So she doesn't question why Ray looks hazy to her, because everything looks hazy to her."

Lissa's soft voice flowed on. He got it now. She was making up a story, a real whopper of a tall tale, to get him to respond. Like he would believe sensible, grounded Renata Moretti would believe in ghosts. Well, Lissa sure had his attention, but not because of some outrageous ghost story. Her energy was pulsing into him from the touch of her hand. It was like the heat of a good single malt Scotch spreading from the center of the belly out to the skin. Except this was a healing energy, not a numbing warmth. Hungry for more, he tuned out her words and focused on the energy surging through him.

"—so I think Renata is attracted to Ray, which really could complicate things," she was saying when he finally tuned in again to her voice. "It's bad enough that he's forever twenty-four, while the girlfriend he's looking for is middle-aged. But a relationship between a ghost and a living person . . . It's totally impossible. Still, they say opposites attract, and I guess this is about as extreme a case of opposites as you can get."

Her fingertips stroked the back of his hand, stirring sparks on his skin the way they always used to do. Inside, he raged at his inability to respond. *Forget that stupid story and touch me,* he wanted to tell her. *Touch me anywhere, everywhere! Keep touching me until my body wakes up.*

Her fingers went still. "I wonder which of us is in the more impossible situation," she murmured. The sadness in her voice fed his helpless anger. "Renata can't feel Ray's touch. And you can't feel mine. Even if they fall in love, they'll never be able to do anything about it. And you may never know . . ." —she made a soft sound like a stifled sob— " . . . I still love you."

Oh, Lissa! I do know! Don't give up, baby. Don't believe the doubters. I can hear you and feel you. Keep loving me, Lissa. I love you, too, baby. I need you to stay with me. Somehow, I'm going to get back to you, I swear it! The effort to will her to hear his thoughts exhausted him. He began to drift to sleep. Lissa was wrong about him being unable to hear and feel her. Maybe she was wrong about Renata being unable to feel the ghost's touch, he found himself thinking. He hoped so, even if it was a silly story. Someone deserved a little happiness.

"Mel, you better hustle out of here." Paul Sykes. Felt Lissa startle. Couldn't hear Paul's footsteps. "Mario and Linda will be back any minute, and Mario will pitch a fit if he catches you."

Damn! Why can't they make peace now?

"Thanks, Paul." Her fingers lifted from his hand, then slid over his cheek like the brush of a feather. "Can you tell how he's doing?"

"He's stable, but there's no way to predict how long he'll be like this." Lissa made that soft sound again, like she was trying to bottle up her distress. "Hang in there, Mel," Paul told her. Gabe didn't like the low, intimate sound of his friend's voice. *She's mine!* he wanted to growl. *Don't you dare put any moves on her when she's vulnerable!* But he couldn't do anything, damn it.

"Gabe needs you to stay strong," Paul went on. "Mario's starting to give up hope. I think even Linda is starting to wonder. You have to keep believing, even when you don't see any proof. Especially when you don't see any proof. Okay?"

Amen! Gabe wanted to say. And the same applied to him. He'd been too hasty judging Paul. Paul was his best friend. He'd saved his life, and kept him alive. Somehow, with help from Lissa and Paul, he'd get out of this dark tunnel and back to the light. And then he was going to nail the bastard who'd put him here. If not, he was going to haunt him until he scared him to death.

Chapter Nine

Gabe strained to hear his mother's hushed voice. She'd come back alone, explaining to Paul that his father was resting.

"I know it's foolish of me," she was saying, "because you probably can't hear me. But maybe in your soul you do. That's why I want to tell you this. In case . . . in case you never wake up." She drew a long, shaky breath, and her hand tightened on his wrist. "Then, when you . . . get to Heaven"—a soft sob—"you can find her . . . your real mother. She would like that."

Oh, Mom! Don't do this to yourself. I'm going to wake up. I promise, I'm going to wake up. Gabe fought to make his muscles obey, so he could move his hand for her. When nothing happened, he cursed inside.

And then, he realized what his mother had said. Whoever his biological mother was, she was dead.

The thought registered like a lump of ice in his gut. He'd wanted to meet the woman who had given him life, to learn where he'd come from, to ask her why she hadn't kept him. Maybe even to thank her for choosing Linda and Mario. Now, he couldn't.

" . . . beautiful blue eyes, like yours," his mother—the only woman he could think of as his mother—was saying. Inside his mind, Gabe snapped to attention. "So pretty. Her family was the richest in the area back then. My mother worked for them, first as a housecleaner, then as a cook. Summers and vacations, from the time I was twelve, I worked there, too."

"The father was a banker, a cold man. He thought nothing of foreclosing on people down on their luck. But the mother was nice. She never raised her voice to the servants. Always gave us little bonuses for our birthdays and bigger ones for Christmas. Your mother, your birth mother, was their only child, their princess. Her father wanted her to marry a young doctor, also from a rich family."

Gabe was grateful for Linda's pause. He had a lot of information to process. Ironic, after he'd been so hard on Lissa and her family for being rich. His birth mother was a pampered princess who had somehow fallen off her pedestal to conceive a bastard. Was the rich doctor his father? Probably not, or they would have married. So who—?

Wait. Linda—his *mother,* damn it!—had said something before about no one knowing who his father was. The princess probably wanted to sample the wild side before settling down to her mansion. Hell, for all his stiff-necked morality about fidelity and respect for women, he was the result of a sleazy one-night-stand. Wasn't that a kick in the teeth?

" . . . could tell she was so in love with someone, but not with her fiancé," his mother was saying when he caught up with her voice again. "She tried not to show it, but she didn't like him. The engagement was her father's idea. Ah, but when she finished with a private phone call or when she said she had gone out with her girlfriends, she would glow with a special light. When she found out she was pregnant, she was so happy she couldn't help telling me. I was only a little older, but Mario and I had been married for four years, and we wanted children so much. God forgive me, I envied her. Not for her money. For you."

His mother was silent for so long, he was afraid she was

too consumed by her sense of guilt to go on. Finally, she gave a deep sigh.

"Before she could tell her young man about the baby," she continued, her voice even softer, "he disappeared. One day, she was dancing on air, planning to elope, confiding in me like a sister. The next day, she cried until she was sick. All she would tell me was that the father of her baby was never coming back for her, and that she had refused to marry her doctor. Soon after, her family sent her to Boston, to her mother's sister, to have her baby where no one would know her."

Then what happened? Gabe wanted to shout. *How did I end up being your son, if she was so happy about being pregnant?*

"Oh! Look at the time! Mario will think something happened to me if I don't get home to make his dinner."

He felt her warm, dry lips on his forehead and cursed his prison of silence, his inability to reach for her.

"Good night, Gabriel. Sleep . . . sleep well. I'll tell you more about her another time. So don't . . . don't decide . . . to go to Heaven to find her yet. She was a good person, and she loved you very much. She would want you to live a long time." Another kiss, a quiet sob, and then he heard her muffled footsteps fading as she left him alone with all his unanswered questions buzzing in his brain.

Ray found Melissa in the kitchen after her return from the hospital, stirring something in a big pot on a stove that could belong in a fancy restaurant. He sniffed the air, but couldn't smell a thing. Damn! He hadn't really noticed until he talked about it to Renata. Funny the things you miss when you're dead.

Lucky was sitting on the counter next to the stove, the tip of his tail twitching. The crazy cat was watching Melissa's movements like he was taking a cooking class. Probably dreaming of mouse and catnip stew. Ray grinned at the thought, then remembered why he needed to talk to Melissa and lost his sense of humor.

"Damn it! You didn't tell me Renata was tangling with Frank Dane," he said.

Melissa shrieked and dropped the wooden spoon into the pot. She spun around to glare at him, one hand pressed against her chest. Lucky flattened his ears and hissed at him.

"Oh! For crying out loud, Ray! Stop sneaking around like a ghost!" Melissa scolded him, but he could see she was shaking. She crossed her arms in front of her body. "Make some noise like a normal person, would you please? Living in a haunted house is getting on my nerves."

He leaned against the doorframe, careful not to let himself sink through the damn thing. He crossed his arms, too. *"Cut the jokes,"* he snarled. *"This is serious, damn it!"* He must have sounded as mean as he felt, because her eyes widened and she took a half-step back. Lucky arched his back, coat puffed up like a black dandelion. Showing his needlelike teeth, he hissed again.

"Sorry," Ray muttered through a mouthful of guilt. *"Ol' Frank brings out the worst in people."*

Melissa relaxed and even gave him a quick smile. "That's what Renata says, too."

He scowled. *"Renata shouldn't know Frank that well. She shouldn't know him at all, damn it!"*

Melissa's smile faded. "How do you know him?" she asked.

"Frankie and I go way back."

She gave him a funny look. "Way back? But . . . Oh. I keep forgetting . . . You know . . ." He knew. Sometimes, for a little while, he forgot he was dead, too. She shook her head. "He must be about sixty-two or -three, now."

"He was older than me by a few years. Always a bully. Always getting other people hurt. I never thought he'd live this long." He gave her a shrug. *"Then again, I never thought I wouldn't."*

Melissa's eyes went wide. "You don't think Frank Dane . . . ?"

He considered it, then shrugged. His memory of that particular moment was still totally clouded. *"With Frank, anything was possible."*

"How can you be so casual about your own murder?"

He gave her a grin he didn't really feel. *"I'm not."*

"Ray, do you think Frank Dane ran Renata off the road?"

"Hard to say. In the old days, Frankie didn't do his own dirty work when he could get someone else to do it. And he always found some way to use people. The man was a magnet for ugly. But I never heard of him getting into murder."

Ray clenched his jaws at the rush of memories about Frank. If Frank was trying to get at Renata, she'd need plenty of protection. He looked down at himself, where the lines of the doorframe showed faintly through his torso. Helpless! That's what he was, damn it. He wasn't a man, he was a shadow. He heard a soft noise, looked at Melissa, and knew she'd followed his gaze. And his thoughts. Her pity fueled his anger.

"Damn it all! How the hell am I supposed to protect Renata?" he growled.

"You aren't," Renata said from behind him so suddenly that he nearly fell into the wall. By concentrating just about all his energy, he managed to stop himself in time.

He swore and swung around to face her. As soon as their eyes met, her chin went up a notch. And so did his temper.

"Damn it, woman! You scared the hell out of me!" he bellowed, hoping she wouldn't notice he was *A.* embarrassed, and *B.* transparent.

"I doubt that," she answered. "You're probably as full of hell as before." Her soft mouth curved into a smile that reminded him of the way Celeste could tease him. He really wished she would stop doing that.

"Anyway," Renata went on, her voice soft and sweet, but an edge of steel in her dark eyes, "gallant as your protective urges are, it's my job to protect *you* from the bad guys. I refuse to allow that . . . that monster to intimidate me."

Ray opened his mouth to tell her she didn't have to protect him from anything, but the phone rang. Melissa reached across for the phone, knocking Lucky off his perch on the counter, and grabbed the receiver.

"Yes, Paul! What's wrong?"

A panicky light came into her eyes. The receiver shook in

her grasp. Bad news about her cop friend? He didn't like cops on principle, mostly 'cause they'd never liked him on principle—just 'cause you're paranoid doesn't mean they're not out to get you—but in this case, he hoped the guy was still on the right side of the Great Divide.

Renata went to Melissa and put a hand on her shoulder. When Melissa let out a sigh and said, "Thank God! You scared me!" Renata smiled and moved away.

Damn! He wanted Celeste to be there to touch him like that! He wanted to feel the weight and the softness and the heat of her hands on him. Almost as much as he wanted to be able to touch her. Just like it used to be. Wanted to stroke her silky body until she was crying with hunger. Wanted to massage the tension out of her shoulders when her father and that jerk of a doctor got her wound up. Hell, he wanted to find her ticklish spots again, just so he could hear her laugh.

He could want, but he couldn't have. Man, if he wasn't already dead, he'd want to be.

"Let's give Mel some privacy," Renata murmured to him, breaking into his self-pity. She was standing a little too close for comfort, close enough to touch by accident. Probably close enough to see through him even without her glasses. After she moved past him and into the living room, he followed at a safe distance.

She sat in a corner of the sofa and curled her feet under her. Her eyes looked huge and dark. Damn! She looked beat and scared and brave and a lot like she could use a friend. Friend, nothing! She could use the Three Musketeers, the Lone Ranger, Zorro, and Spiderman to look after her. Maybe he should tell her to call that State cop.

Renata spoke first. "Tell me how you know Frank Dane."

That SOB was the last person he wanted to talk about at any time, but especially now, when he was trying to figure out how to protect Renata and Melissa and find Celeste. That was enough to worry about without talking about something one step lower than sewage. Leave it to Frankie to screw someone else up, without even trying.

Renata was waiting for his answer. Ray shrugged. *"Lots of people know Frank. Most of them probably wish they didn't. He gets around."*

"True enough, but how do *you* know him? He's a lot older than you, isn't he? He's over sixty."

Close enough, Ray thought. He wondered what she'd say if he told her he'd known Frankie in high school. Old Frankie had set up drag races, made himself the bookie, charged the drivers to get into the races, and welshed on everyone when the cops put a stop to a race Ray was winning in his souped-up '57 Chevy. Somehow, everyone but Frank got busted. And no one ever did find out what happened to the best of the cars. They just disappeared. But Ray had a feeling that Renata, being a straight-arrow Assistant District Attorney might not understand how bent out of shape the guys were, being cheated in the middle of an illegal race, then having their cars stolen.

"I know some people who know him," he said instead. *"Not friends. Frank doesn't really have any. He uses people. He sets them up, then turns on them. Or scares them into doing things for him they never would do themselves. He's like the guy in the song, 'Mack the Knife.' The body isn't cold yet, but you won't find Frank hanging around to take the blame."*

"He's never been charged with any kind of assault," she said as if she were thinking something through, "but now I can't help wondering." She frowned. "Will—that State trooper I know—doesn't think it was an accident that the prosecutor originally assigned to this case was badly hurt in a one-car crash."

"He could be right." The thought made him feel sick. *"You didn't drive off the road and run through the woods like monsters were after you by accident, did you?"*

She shook her head. Lucky flew into the room, raced up the side of the couch, jumped over Renata, bounced down to the coffee table, then off. He couldn't get any traction on the wood floor, so he looked like he was running in place for a few seconds. Then he launched himself across the room again. Melissa came into the doorway, and moved just in time. Lucky yowled and disappeared behind her.

Good thing the little maniac hadn't stepped through him, Ray thought, or he'd be doing some fast explaining to Renata. This act was getting to him. Maybe he should just take his chances and tell Renata the truth. But how? Being a ghost wasn't the kind of thing that came up in casual conversation. And what should he say about Celeste? How could he tell Renata that when he "touched" her, he saw the image of Celeste? The more he thought about that, the more sure he was that he wasn't ready to face the only explanation that made the most sense. How could he expect Renata to . . .

Melissa came into the room. Lucky streaked past her, did a bank-turn on the far wall, and took off again, eyes wild, tail puffed. "Good grief!" Melissa shrugged into a jacket. "He's a regular heat-seeking missile, isn't he?"

Renata laughed, too. "You'd think he'd seen a ghost."

Ray wondered what she'd say or do if Melissa told her they'd all been seeing a ghost. Well, all except him. He couldn't see himself in any mirrors, and as far as he knew, he was the only ghost around.

Renata's smile faded, and he could guess what was on her mind. "What did the doctor say about Gabe?" she asked Melissa.

"He's still pretty much the same, but Paul said Gabe's parents left early today but they plan on returning later tonight, so I could sneak back for a short visit if I hurry. Dinner's ready, so help yourselves. I'll grab something later, okay?" Melissa was practically out the door already. It was too late to warn her she could really blow it for him with those few words.

"Sure. Thanks. Drive safely," Renata called after her. She stood up and looked at him. Gave him a smile. "Would you like wine with dinner? Mel picked up a bottle of Burgundy to go with the stew."

She expected him to have dinner with her! If he could make it past holding a fork and knife, the food would probably fall through him and end up on the chair. Then, if he could hold a glass, he could wash it down with some red wine, like pouring water through a strainer. Not his idea of a hot date.

"Thanks, but I've got to see someone," he muttered, hoping if she couldn't see through him, she wouldn't see through his lies.

"Oh." She said it softly.

Some of the light went out of her eyes, like she was disappointed. That made him feel guilty, too, but not as guilty as he'd feel two-timing Celeste. Anyway, he had some heavy-duty thinking to do, about Celeste, Renata, Frank Dane, himself, and the meaning of life. That would keep him busy at least through dinnertime.

Gabe floated out of sleep at the sound of Lissa's hello. Was he really awake? No, damn it! Dark. His eyes wouldn't open. His hands wouldn't reach for her. His mouth wouldn't say her name and kiss her. Only in his mind, in his dreams. No pain, no pleasure. He would gladly take the pain just to feel the pleasure again.

"Paul snuck me in again," she said softly. "I'd stay all night if they'd let me, but I don't want to press my luck. I'm afraid that someone will tell your father I've been seeing you. Paul said Mario holds me responsible for you not marrying and giving him grandchildren."

Paul has a big mouth, Gabe thought.

Lissa's fingers stroked his cheek. "I'm sorry he feels that way, but I . . . This is so selfish, but I'm glad you aren't married. When you get better, I'd like us to start over again. Only if you want to, of course."

Only if he wanted to? He couldn't think of anything he wanted more. Not even catching the bastard who'd tried to kill him. All he wanted was to wake up out of this nightmare and have a second chance with Lissa.

"Remember the ghost I told you about?" Lissa picked up his left hand and held it in both of hers. He wanted to yell at her not to change the subject, to keep talking about them, but the words only echoed in his own mind.

"Well, it turns out he knew Frank Dane when they were in school. Of course, he didn't tell Renata that, because he doesn't want her to know he's a ghost."

Her cheerful tone made him want to chew tinfoil. She couldn't believe that ghost crap, so she had to be thinking he couldn't understand her words, just the sound of her voice. Damn! *Believe in me!* he wanted to shout, but the words were trapped inside.

"I think he wants to see if his girlfriend, Celeste, is still around. He's loved her all this time. Isn't that sweet?"

Sweet enough to gag on, Gabe thought.

Lissa touched his shoulder. "I promised I'd try to find her for him, but I haven't made any progress. She's not listed in any of the state phone directories under her maiden name. Monday, I'll stop by the Town Hall records room and look her up."

Gabe wanted to laugh and cry at the same time. Lissa was going on with this crazy ghost story—obviously making it up as she went along—to try to break through his silence. But all he wanted to hear her say was how much she still loved him. And he wanted to tell her about the things his mother had been telling him. Lissa would understand his feelings. Probably better than he could. He wanted to show her the bracelet on his right wrist, wanted to tell her it was his only link to his biological parents. But she sat on his left side, and he couldn't move.

Lissa bent over him to fluff his pillows. She smelled so good. He breathed deeply, filling his memory for later. "Ray can't remember the name of the doctor Celeste was engaged to," she went on. God, he'd forgotten how persistent she could be when she got an idea in her head. It might be a good trait in a lawyer—Renata was one persistent woman, too—but not in a woman he wanted to shut up and kiss him.

"If I could find an obituary in the newspaper archives for someone in her family, that might give me some leads. Her father was a banker in southern Connecticut, and they lived in a real mansion, not just a large house like the Garvey place. Ray worked in one of the factories he owned, and did odd jobs for Mrs. Garvey, too."

He didn't care. Gabe wanted to shout at her, pull her into his arms and kiss her senseless. He didn't want to hear about some poor dead schmuck who had a crush on some rich girl who was engaged to a doctor.

"In a way, they were a lot like us," Lissa said softly. "Her father didn't want Ray near his daughter. But he really loved—loves her." Gabe heard a tiny sniffle. He couldn't believe it! Lissa was holding his hand, and crying over some dead guy's hard-luck story. Some *made-up* dead guy, at that! Hell, if she wanted to cry, she could cry for him.

He felt a hot tear on his forearm. Aw, hell! Maybe she *was* crying for him. It wasn't until much, much later, alone in his silence, that Gabe mulled over some of the details of that crazy ghost story Lissa had been telling him.

Renata sat in Melissa's kitchen, shifting her meager portion of stew and noodles around her plate and considering her options. There weren't a lot of them. She could stay hidden here, possibly—*probably*—endangering Melissa and Ray, stealthily working on the State's case against Frank Dane until their court date. Or she could request police protection, thereby eliminating the threat to two innocent people but effectively putting herself under house arrest. But then she could openly catch up on all the work that was going to pile up by Monday. It wouldn't be long before Dane's day in court.

She captured a mushroom with her fork, pretending the mushroom was Dane and the fork her legal arguments, and sank her teeth into the tender vegetable with some glee. Whatever she decided to do, she intended to work on this case until even the Devil himself couldn't find a loophole with her proof and her reasoning. Spearing a morsel of meat, Renata indulged in a brief moment of professional discourtesy toward her opponent. Frank Dane's attorney might be a slime mold, a bottom feeder with the ethics and conscience of a shark, a hired gun with a lump of ice where his heart should be, but, she told herself, he probably had a pet piranha or python or pit bull he loved. And, grinning an ironic and unrepentant grin, she bit into the savory meat.

The blare of music nearly made her choke. It stopped as suddenly as it started. Someone was in the house! Oh, God! Her heart pounded as she set her fork down as carefully as her shaking hand allowed. Ray and Melissa were gone. She was alone, unarmed, too far from the phone to—

The music blared again. Her heart leaped, stopping her breath. Instinct hollered to flee, to run into the night through the back door, but her body was frozen.

And then the volume lowered considerably, and Ray's voice called *"Sorry!"* from the living room. With her pulse still racing and her stomach churning from the rush of adrenalin, Renata forced herself to breathe.

She would kill him, she thought. It would be totally justified homicide. There wasn't a jury in the civilized world that would convict her.

Ray appeared suddenly in the dimly lit doorway to the hall. His sheepish expression drew a forgiving smile from her even as she was framing her defense for strangling him with her own hands. *So much for that,* she thought. Whatever he had, it sure worked well. Subtly, but effectively, he'd defused her fright, turning it into a keen awareness without any lingering hint of threat.

Still, she wasn't *comfortable* around him. Maybe it was that feeling of knowing him from her dreams. There was some edginess to it, a nervous energy that she usually only felt when she began a new trial. An eager edginess, waiting for something to happen. Something special. Something she wanted, but might not be willing to admit *how much* she wanted it.

"Sorry," Ray said again. *"I must have hit the wrong thing when I turned the music on."*

"I thought you were going out," she said in the most even tones she could muster. Immediately, she wanted to bite the words back. She sounded jealous, possessive, nosy—all those things men said they hated in a woman.

He leaned one shoulder against the wall, as if getting comfortable for a longer conversation. *"I'm back."*

"Ah." She glanced down at the congealing stew on her plate, and decided that Lucky was about to live up to his name yet again. "There's plenty of wine left, if you'd like. Or beer? Mel has some cold bottles."

Lucky, apparently reading her mind from wherever he was in the house, flew into the kitchen like a tiny black tornado and slid to a stop against a table leg. He made an indignant little sound halfway between a chirp and a meow, then scrubbed a paw to compose himself. Chuckling, Renata bent and placed her plate on the floor. Lucky sniffed delicately, then purred like a tractor as he began gobbling the stew without a trace of delicacy. Renata stood and raised the bottle of wine Mel had chosen for dinner.

Ray shook his head. *"No, thanks. I, um, I don't drink."* He shrugged and offered a smile. *"Must be getting old. I don't have the head for it anymore. But I don't mind if you do."*

Renata hesitated, then refilled her wineglass. She needed something in her hands, to keep them busy enough not to give in to the temptation to reach out to Ray. With alarm, she realized her fingertips seemed to think they knew—they *remembered*—the feel of him. The warmth of his skin, the smooth, hard contours of his muscles, the silk of his black hair, and the slight rasp of his clean-shaven cheeks. Could dreams be so vivid?

He moved away as she walked toward the doorway where he'd been standing. To get away from her? Had she been so obvious?

"If you aren't going to work anymore tonight, how about keeping me company?" he asked.

No, he wasn't trying to get away from her. He was simply showing surprisingly good manners in allowing her to precede him. Grandmother would approve, although she'd have a more negative view of the way he dressed. With Ray behind her, Renata indulged in a small smile. *She,* on the other hand, liked the way he dressed. It was a refreshing change from all the somber suits and crisply pressed uniforms she saw most days. And he certainly wore those jeans and T-shirts well.

Wiping the smile off her face, she sat as demurely as she could in one of the comfortably overstuffed chairs and sipped at her wine. Ray sat on one end of the sofa, so that the coffee table stood between them. He looked at the stereo system set up in a beautiful custom-made wall unit, and frowned. Scowled, actually. Well, she hazarded, perhaps he didn't like the easy jazz station Mel was tuned to.

"You can change the station, you know," she told him. "Or put on a tape or a CD. Mel won't mind. She's got pretty eclectic taste in music."

He looked startled. *"Oh, yeah. I, um . . ."* He gave her another one of those megawatt grins that made her glad she'd lost her glasses in the woods. She wasn't sure she could take the full force. Thank goodness the man in her dreams never smiled! She'd never want to wake up!

"Why don't you pick something to put on?" he said. *"My taste is pretty, um, eclectic, too."*

Setting her glass down on the coffee table, she went to the cabinet that housed Melissa's dozens of CDs, and ran her index finger along the spines of the cases, looking for the right album. When she stopped at a boxed set of vintage rock she felt momentarily surprised, but as she took the case from the shelf she realized her choice felt right. As she turned to open the drawer of the CD player, the phone rang.

With an apologetic glance at Ray, Renata reached for the living room extension phone.

"Hi, I'd like to speak with Melissa Hartley," a male voice said in her ear.

"I'm sorry, Melissa isn't available right now, but I can give her a message." She reached for the pad and pen lying nearby.

"I know it's late to call about business, but I need a local attorney pretty quickly. First thing tomorrow morning, in fact. I heard through a friend in L.A. that Melissa just opened a practice here in town, so I figured she could use the business."

Was it her imagination, or did his voice sound vaguely familiar? "Your name and number?"

"David Mayhew," he answered, then recited a local phone number.

"Lydia Mayhew's grandson?" she asked in surprise, putting down the pen.

"Who is this?" His suspicious tone made her smile. "Do we know each other?"

"Our grandmothers would like us to." Had it only been Thursday that Gran had mentioned David? The day before her life had been turned upside down.

"Then you'd have to be Renata Moretti." His clipped baritone warmed up only slightly when he asked how she was.

Not that she blamed him. Their one and only close encounter, about ten years ago, had been an unmitigated disaster. Their grandmothers had tricked them into attending a black-tie fundraising dinner together, with the mistaken notion that if they'd only meet, they'd fall madly in love. At first glance, David had looked promising. He'd been tall and lean, with dark blond hair cut short, emphasizing palely sculptured features. But he'd sat like a statue, hardly speaking, all evening. Then he'd gone home early, handing her a twenty-dollar bill for cab fare. To add further insult to injury, the two grandmothers had blamed Renata for David's behavior.

Renata had resented being manipulated away from her studies and into an evening with a stuck-up jerk who'd left her sitting alone at their table while the other couples were dancing. His obvious lack of interest had made her feel even more of a fool for letting Gran's stylist arrange her hair and apply dramatic makeup. Gran had insisted on buying her a designer gown cut daringly low and clingy. Renata had been alternately convinced she looked like a child playing dress-up, or a wanna-be bimbo who'd been in the wrong line when cleavage was being handed out.

Nevertheless, over the past decade Gran persisted in mentioning David from time to time. Renata knew he'd made a bundle of money, lived in New York City, and according to his grandmother, had beautiful women falling at his feet wherever he went. His grandmother always noted his available bachelor status, but Renata didn't think that made him a toad worth kissing.

"I'd heard you were with the D.A.'s office in New Haven," he told her. "What are you doing here?"

"I live in New Harbour. What about you? I thought you were in New York." Behind her, Ray cleared his throat. She turned and smiled apologetically. He shrugged. She returned her attention to David.

"Yeah, well, I was, but I decided to take a break from the rat race. I've been doing some traveling this past year, and I'm buying a business here in New Harbour."

Odd that Gran hadn't told her any of this. "Really? What business?"

"Right now it's called Harley Heaven, but I'll be changing the name, to get away from the biker image. Touring bikes is what I want to feature."

"Harley Heaven?" she repeated, puzzled by this strange turn of events, and wondering if Gran even knew about it. She couldn't imagine Lydia Mayhew being delighted that her brilliant grandson was planning to rub elbows with motorcycle riders. "Well, congratulations," she said as warmly as she could. "I'll give Melissa your message as soon as she comes home."

"Thanks."

He disconnected before she could say goodbye. Feeling snubbed yet again by that rude jerk, she returned to her chair and picked up her wine. Then she glanced up at Ray. His stare unnerved her. There was something . . . Something hard and uncompromising in his eyes that was eerily familiar. But it couldn't be familiar. No one had ever looked at her with such a . . . a what? A proprietary expression? The idea almost made her laugh out loud. No, it had to be the poor lighting in the living room, and her own poor vision, that made her imbue Ray's questioning expression with some deeper hidden significance.

"An old boyfriend of yours?" His tone was light and he smiled, but he showed a lot more teeth than usual.

"Not at all." Briefly, she explained the tenuous connection between David and herself. When she finished, Ray nodded.

"Harley Heaven? Sounds like my kind of place."

Renata smiled at the way his voice lingered over the word

Harley. "I take it you like motorcycles. You should check out David's place, then."

"Yeah, I should," he answered, but he was frowning, and he looked lost in his thoughts.

Renata sipped her wine, lost in her own. Her fascination with Ray was an aberration she didn't have time for. By Monday—Oh, Lord! That was tomorrow!—the people in the D.A.'s office were going to start wondering where she was. So was Will. She'd have to decide soon—tomorrow morning—whether to call Will and arrange for police protection at her house and office, or to stay with Melissa and risk—

"So," Ray said softly, but suddenly enough to startle her. *"Do you have someone special?"* She shook her head. He flashed another wolfish grin. *"What about this trooper?"*

"Will? No, we're just friends," she answered. Then, hoping her interest wasn't too transparent, she asked, "What about you?"

He hesitated, breaking eye contact. *"There was someone, Celeste Benedict, but we sorta lost track of each other for a while."* His too-casual tone told her he wasn't telling her the whole truth, and she could read between the lines.

He turned his piercing gaze back again to her. Renata quickly lowered her eyes before she revealed the keen edge of her disappointment. She shouldn't have asked, she berated herself. She should have known. Enchanted princes were only in fairy tales and dreams.

Chapter
Ten

"Finally!" his mother whispered, clasping his hand a little tighter.

Finally, echoed inside Gabe. Finally, his father had left them alone for a while. Now she would tell him who his birth mother was. Then he could start making peace with his past. The first thing he would do when he woke up was tell his parents he loved them. And then he would ask Lissa to marry him.

"Mario was so ashamed that we couldn't have children. The doctors said it was his problem, not mine, but he didn't want to believe them. Your father is a man's man, the son and grandson of strong men who fathered lots of babies. But nothing helped. He didn't want to adopt. He said he couldn't love a child who had brought shame to his mother first, and who would be a constant reminder of his failure." His mother sighed. "Your father can be a hardheaded fool sometimes."

This wasn't news, Gabe wanted to remind her. His father's persistence as a police officer had solved a record number of crimes that had been considered unsolvable.

Mario's doggedness had seen them both through hours and hours of practice with baseballs and hockey pucks. His determination had been Gabe's inspiration every time he'd opened a textbook or sat down at an exam. But Mario's stubborn pride had driven a wedge between Gabe and Lissa that he still wasn't willing to admit had been a mistake.

For now, though, Gabe wanted to hear his mother's side of the story.

"Your poor mother came to me, so sad, after her young man went away. She wanted to keep her baby, because she loved the man who was your father, but her own father wanted her to have an abortion. Oh, Gabe, we cried!" A telltale sniff. His mother could still cry for a young woman in trouble, almost thirty-six years ago.

She took his hand in both of hers. He struggled to move his fingers, but nothing happened. "We were both scared. Her father was so angry, so powerful. He wanted her to 'erase her mistake,' as he put it, and marry her doctor fiancé. She told me she'd rather kill herself!"

Gabe pictured his mother crossing herself, warding off the terrible decisions facing her friend. No, her employers' daughter. His birth mother. She had died, though. How? Had she given in to despair? Or did she die giving birth? How did the unwelcome bastard son of a rich banker's daughter end up as the much-loved son of a hardworking cop and his wife?

"I didn't even ask Mario first," his mother continued, as if she had heard his question. "I offered to raise her baby as my own. We planned it very carefully. She told people she was going to school in Boston before she married, and I told people I was going to Boston to help an aunt who was sick. Mario was furious, but I knew it was the right thing to do."

His mother paused. A nurse bustled in and fussed with his tubes. Gabe simmered with frustration. Her professionally cheerful voice was like nails on the blackboard. When she finally bustled out again, Gabe felt his mother listening for his father's return. *Don't stop now!* he wanted to shout.

"We did stay with an aunt of mine. Do you remember Auntie Lucia, my mother's third sister? She was a good woman. She took us in and never asked a single question.

You were born in her house. Auntie Lucia delivered you. And, oh! you were a beautiful infant! Your poor mama cried with joy when she held you. We all cried—your mama, Auntie Lucia, me, my cousins Isobel and Dorotea. You were the only boy in a houseful of weeping women." He heard her laugh softly, to herself. "It's a wonder you didn't sprout gills, with all those tears!"

All those tears, Gabe echoed silently. He shouldn't have prejudged his birth mother so harshly. He owed her.

"Your mama told me to name you. We called you Gabriel from the first. But sometimes, when she held you, she'd whisper her name for you. I'm sure it was your father's name, because she always cried then. Not out loud. Tears would slide down her face and drop on your swaddling blanket, and she'd whisper to you. When she left you with me, she gave me that bracelet. I promised to give it to you, but she said not to promise, just to wait until the right moment came. She got herself in trouble because she was a spoiled little girl, but she did the right thing for you because she turned into a strong woman."

His mother stopped talking. The silence stretched, only punctuated by odd noises from down the corridors and in other rooms. Gabe wanted her to tell him everything she knew about his birth mother. He wanted to tell Lissa what he'd learned. He wanted to . . . Oh, man. Later. Too tired to focus. Need to rest.

"Your poor mama didn't want to marry that doctor her father got her engaged to." His mother's voice jerked him out of his trance. "I never believed what they said," she murmured, so softly that he could hardly hear her. "I never believed she killed herself."

Ray almost missed Renata's reaction when he mentioned Celeste. Just a brief tightening around her mouth as she looked away. That quick flash of the tiny worry line between her brows. She was already smiling by the time he put the clues together.

Damn! This was getting complicated, and it was his fault. He shouldn't have kept after her about feeling a connection between them, like *déjà vu*. He was only trying to figure out why he got those images of Celeste when he touched Renata. But how would Renata know that? She must have gotten the wrong idea and—

Don't flatter yourself, he told himself. No way she felt that way about him. He was imagining things that weren't there. Renata liked him, but she didn't *like* him, not that way. She was in a tight situation, he was trying to protect her, she trusted him. It was that thing about danger and sex. Like the good girls sneaking out at night to catch a ride behind him on his motorcycle, turned on by the thrill more than by him. Of course, before Celeste, he wouldn't have cared why those good girls wanted to be with him. He just would have enjoyed the benefits of being the bad boy of their fantasies.

But after Celeste . . .

"Tell me about her. About Celeste," Renata said. She was still smiling, as if nothing was changed between them. Maybe it was his imagination. He hoped so. He didn't want Renata to be hurt on his account. "That's a pretty name. Is she from around here?"

She wasn't ready for the truth. Or maybe he was a coward. He'd just play it as straight as he could, and lie when he had to. Like his old man used to say just before whipping that thick leather belt, buckle first, across his back, it was for her own good.

"She used to be, but I don't know if she's still living here," he answered. *"I haven't seen her in a . . . a long time. We sorta drifted apart."*

She nodded, the look in her dark eyes soft, understanding. He cursed himself for lying to her. But then, everything she thought she knew about him was a lie. What was one—or a hundred—more?

"Ah. So now you're trying to get back together with her. Were you high school sweethearts?"

"High school? No, not till later. We didn't . . . It wasn't . . ." He shut his mouth. He didn't have a clue what he was trying to say, or why his first impulse had been to deny that he and Celeste had been lovers.

That frown line came back between Renata's brows. "It sounds as if you didn't part amicably."

"Yes and no." He would have left his answer there, but she lifted a brow, and he didn't want to just clam up on her. *"It was one of those things. Her father had a different guy in mind for her. He got his way."* He shrugged. *"I just want to contact her, make sure she's okay."*

An ugly thought occurred to him. Could Celeste's father have hired some goon to shoot him? He had the bucks, and he had the brass to do it. But Ray didn't think Old Man Benedict would risk losing his daughter, if she ever found out. And secrets like that were hard to keep forever. He was gonna make damn sure of that.

"I'm sorry," she said softly. "Almost the same thing happened to Mel and Gabe. Now they may never have a chance to start over." Tears made her eyes glisten. She blinked. One tear slid down her cheek to the curve of her jawline.

He wanted to wipe the tears away. What would happen if he touched her now, when she was awake and looking right at him? Would she feel his touch? Would he feel her? Or see Celeste again? If he saw Celeste, would Renata see her, too? Or was the whole vision thing in his own mind, because he thought about her so much?

He didn't get a chance to find out any of those answers. Lucky tore through the room, banked off the walls, knocked over a vase full of peacock feathers, and raced off. Renata started laughing, and he couldn't help laughing with her. Lucky trotted in again, and sat watching the doorway to the hallway, the tip of his tail twitching. Renata caught him in mid-leap when he dove for the feathers as she was putting them back in the vase. A few seconds later, Melissa opened the front door and called out to them. Ray realized he was disappointed not to be alone with Renata any longer.

She gave him a halfhearted little smile and announced she was tired. On her way to the stairs, she gave Melissa the message from the guy who was buying Harley Heaven. He watched her climb the stairs, then glanced at Melissa. She looked worried.

"Renata is still so pale," she said quietly. "Will you look after her again tonight? I'd do it, but I'm about to fall on my face and go to sleep right here."

He couldn't say no. Hell, he didn't want to anyway. He wanted to look after Renata. It wasn't much, maybe, but he figured it was a way of making it up to Celeste for dying before he could take care of her. Something along the lines of that old saying, what goes comes around, comes around.

"Gabe?" Melissa knew she was sleeping, but Gabe looked so real standing beside her bed.

"Hi, babe," he said in his deep man's voice, no trace left of the boy's timbre. His smile was a man's smile, too. Lazy, sexy, knowing. Knowing that the woman smiling back loved him. He sat on the edge of the mattress, his hip touching hers. "Got room for me? Getting around like this takes a lot of energy."

She moved over, making room for him to stretch out. His big body radiated heat through his clothes, through her quilt. Yes, she was dreaming, and it was impossible for Gabe to be there with her, but she found herself in his arms. For timeless moments, she simply dreamed of clinging to him, savoring the feel of him against her. When his hand slid over her body, tracing the shape of her through the covers, she gave herself over to the heat that followed his touch.

"Remember?" he whispered, his lips brushing her neck. "Remember the first time I touched you like this?" His hand covered her breast. "I was shaking. I was so afraid you'd get scared, or mad."

Melissa smiled in her sleep. "I wasn't either," she whispered, arching her neck to his lips. "I loved the way you touched me." She slipped a hand between his thighs and laughed softly to feel him shudder. "Do you remember—?"

"How could I forget?" he answered.

Taking her hand in his, Gabe showed her that he did, indeed, remember the way she'd touched him, boldly, shyly, with wonder and delight. And later, when his breathing had slowed to normal, he eased the covers off her and reminded her of the way he'd reciprocated. She knew it was only a dream, but when her climax gripped her, she wanted to believe she was lying in Gabe's arms, crying out at the pleasure he was giving her. And when she came down to earth again, dreaming she was sleeping close to his heart felt so right.

She felt him move restlessly and murmured a protest. She didn't want her dream to end. He smiled and kissed her.

"I have to go soon," he said, "but first, I want to tell you something about my mother. My birth mother. Linda, my mother, told me about her. There's too much to tell you now, Lissa, but this will make you laugh. She was a rich girl, like you. Her father was a banker. He had some doctor picked out for her to marry, but she got pregnant with some mystery guy, and gave me to Mario and Linda to raise."

"Your mother told you this?"

"Yeah. She thought I didn't know I was adopted."

Melissa smiled. One of the first things Gabe had confided to her was that his parents could never know. It would have hurt their feelings, he'd explained.

"Mom wanted to square it with me, in case I don't make it out of this coma," he added, and Melissa's smile faded. Reflexively, she clung tighter to him. "Don't worry, babe. I'll make it. But Mom wanted me to know, just in case, so I could find my birth mother in Heaven."

Tears slid down Melissa's cheeks and onto Gabe's chest. "I'm sorry," she whispered.

"Me, too. She must have been very unhappy. I hope Mom was right, that it wasn't suicide." The dream began to shift and fade. Cold air swirled around her. Melissa shivered in his arms. Even his kiss couldn't warm her. "Hush, babe, it's okay. Kiss me now, Lissa. I have to go. I'll be back. Promise. And when you visit tomorrow, you can tell me more of your ghost story."

Gabe's farewell kiss lingered sweetly. When he drew away, disappearing into the swirling fog, Melissa reached for him, plunging into the chilling darkness. She awoke with a jolt, her covers gone, her nightgown twisted so that her body was bared to the cold air seeping in through the window she'd left partially open the evening before. Outside, it was still pitch dark.

Melissa lost track of how long she sat there, replaying every bittersweet detail she could recall from her dream encounter with Gabe. It had all seemed so vivid, so real. Not just the reprise of their earliest lovemaking, but everything. She was so sure she'd been talking to him. But she must have confused her thoughts about Gabe with the story Ray had told her, because in the dream . . .

No! It couldn't be! But what if . . . ? She needed to think. She also needed a glass of hot milk strongly laced with something to help her sleep. There was a bottle of "B and B" somewhere in the packed crates. Melissa bolted out of bed and wrapped herself in her robe. She had a feeling it was going to be another long, strange night.

"You must be dreaming up a storm." Paul Sykes stood near the bed. Gabe smiled inside. "Second time you've cost me a night's sleep since we put you back together. Nothing wrong with you, nothing wrong with the equipment."

He heard Paul shuffling papers, felt his friend poke around, doing doctor things to the body he didn't have much connection to these days. Then the snap of a chart being closed.

"I don't want to embarrass the nurses, but I'd bet my classical jazz collection you were dreaming about Melissa Hartley."

If Gabe could have laughed out loud, he would have. Instead, he promised himself he'd take Paul out some night and get him very drunk. Then he'd tell him exactly what he'd been doing to make those high-tech monitors go ballistic.

Ray watched the television in the living room until his eyes burned. After three hours of—what was it Melissa called it? channel surfing—he realized it was just dumb luck he hadn't said anything to Renata to give himself away. Man, the world had changed in thirty-five years! If he hadn't gotten killed, he would have seen all this stuff happening, could have gotten used to it. Most of it was pretty cool. But trying to catch up was like being at one of those "all you can eat" buffets.

Changing channels was easy, now that he'd figured it out. And he'd figured out how to work the volume control, so he didn't blast everyone's ears. He could even make it look like he was touching the remote control, since it was the electricity in him that did the trick. Everything was energy. He brought his fingertip toward the remote and the channels flipped by until he made them stop. He was probably pure energy. Or as close to pure as a guy like him ever got, he thought with a grin. That was why Renata got a shock whenever they touched.

There were those chicks in those skimpy outfits again, doing exercises. This time they had a guy with them, all muscles and teeth, grinning like a fool and hopping around in time to the music. Wouldn't catch him doing that in public!

'Course, no one would catch him doing anything, 'cause no one could *see* him. Except Renata and Melissa. That was the one problem he had with his energy theory. Why was it only those two could see him? Would Celeste be able to see and hear him when he found her? What would he do if she couldn't?

Hell, he'd figure something out. He didn't even know what he'd do if she *could* see him. Would she be able to feel him? Feel him for real, not like Renata did, only like an electrical shock? It would be nice if there was someone he could ask, but he didn't think the people on the "psychic answering service" would be much help. They looked like they were the ones who needed help.

The chicks on the screen were bending over. The camera angle, Ray decided, was just too tempting for a guy who'd been celibate for almost forty years. He flipped channels again. A huge hand filled the screen. On the third finger was an enormous ring that the hand was twisting back and forth to show off. Blue topaz and cubic zirconia. People were buying things right off the television!

That ring was nothing like the engagement ring he was saving for Celeste. Remembering made him sad and angry and lonely. He'd socked away every penny his old man didn't drink, and put a down payment on the ring. Then, after his day shift and Saturdays, he worked part-time for the jewelry store, between odd jobs for Old Lady Garvey, to pay the rest of his bill. The day he'd finished paying for the ring, he'd hidden it, in its little blue velvet box, in the furnace room here, along with the rest of his savings.

He planned to give Celeste the ring before they left town, so she'd never doubt he meant to marry her. It was a pretty ring, delicate to fit Celeste's slender finger, with a small diamond. The wedding band was designed to fit around the base of the diamond, and surround it with tiny diamonds. He'd been so sure she'd love the rings. Couldn't wait to put them on her.

Funny thing: He was still waiting.

Well, even if he couldn't touch the strongbox, maybe he could see if it was still hidden in the furnace room wall. Turning off the television, Ray got to his feet. Lucky, asleep on the other end of the sofa, lifted his head, blinked and yawned, then curled around onto his back and closed his eyes again. Ray stepped over the kitten, who growled softly but not very seriously. He was about to ease through the door to the basement when he heard Renata cry out.

Run! Run! Run faster!

Renata ran. Trees blocked her path. Low bushes grabbed at her when she tried to dodge them. Sharp branches tore at her. They tripped her. She fell and fell and fell. Her glasses fell away. It was so dark. Where was the path? Was there a path? She couldn't see where she was going, but she had to keep running.

He was after her again. The man with no face was chasing her through the forest. She ran and ran, but she could still hear him panting behind her. He growled, snarling threats. He was going to catch her, and kill her. The branches grabbed at her and she fought them. *Let me go! Let me go!* If he caught her, he would—

"Renata? Wake up, baby. You're having a bad dream." The man with no face disappeared behind her, fading into

the softening shadows. A new voice called to her, soothing her, leading her out of the darkness . . .

That voice . . . Who . . . ? Ray! Oh, Ray! Yes, Ray would take care of her. He promised he'd always take care of her. She smiled, safe now. No need to wake up now. She was safe in a new dream, one she wanted to stay in forever and ever.

"Wake up, baby," he said again.

Silly man, she didn't want to wake up. She was dreaming of him, of them. Such a delicious dream! It felt so real. Maybe it was real. If she didn't wake, she could keep the dream forever.

Ray was kissing her face and neck, soft, teasing kisses that tickled and sent sparks shimmering along her skin. She squirmed and giggled, but he knew she liked it. She liked everything about him, especially the way he loved her.

"Mmm, come hold me," she invited. "Sleep with me. We never spend the night together."

He didn't respond. Pouting, she reached out to him, put her hand on his chest, over his heart. It was like touching fire! She loved his heat, needed his heat. Everyone, everything around her was so cold. But Ray was the sun in her universe, warming her. His arms were so hard under her seeking fingertips. His chest was wide, his belly flat. She grasped his belt buckle and gave a playful tug.

"Hey! Behave yourself!" He made it sound like scolding, but he laughed softly.

This was such a wonderful dream! She giggled. "I am. Very badly!" She flattened her palm against him, and felt him respond. Through his jeans, his arousal fueled her own. Her playfulness dissolved into breathless anticipation as he grew thick and hard under her touch. When he moved her hand away, gently but firmly, her disappointment cut like shards of ice.

Something was terribly wrong. Sudden fear squeezed her heart. This wasn't the way the dream was supposed to go.

"Oh, Ray! Make love to me!" She needed him to anchor her, but she could feel the dream shifting around her, turning into a nightmare. "I'm so afraid of losing you! I'm so afraid something bad will happen. *Is* happening. I need to love you. Please hold me and love me!"

He sighed, and then she felt the heat of his touch as he sank down on the bed with her. Softly, music started to play. Their song. Something about an angel . . .

Enfolding her in his arms, he cradled her against him like spoons in a drawer. His lips nuzzled her neck, teasing her nerve endings into eager awareness. One of his warm, strong hands gently kneaded her shoulder, easing away the tensions trapped there. Her panic faded and she moaned softly in satisfaction.

"Ray, I love you so much! I'm afraid to wait too long. Let's run away now! Henry scares me."

"Easy, baby. We can talk about that later." Ray's deep voice murmured huskily against her neck. *"You go to sleep now. I'll hold you all night, okay?"* He pulled her a little closer to his beautifully muscled body, settling her bottom against him. *"I love you, baby. I'll love you forever. Never forget that."*

She smiled. She could sleep now. "Love you forever, too," she mumbled. "Never forget. Never, ever forget, love you forever. Forever and ever and even after."

Ray opened his eyes and cradled Renata in his arms, waiting for her to go back to sleep. He didn't dare close his eyes again while he was touching her. And he *was* touching her! He could feel the way her breath moved in her lungs, feel the tension in her back slowly dissolve. It wasn't exactly like feeling skin and hair, or being able to hold a fork, but it was progress. As long as he didn't close his eyes . . .

Anyway, he didn't have to close his eyes to see the images that swirled through his mind. It was happening all over again: Renata and Celeste together yet apart, as soon as he touched Renata with his eyes closed. The instant he opened his eyes, Celeste was gone, and he was still holding Renata. But that wasn't what had him spooked.

How did Renata know how he used to make love to Celeste? How did she know how to touch him the way Celeste did, making him hot and aching with wanting her, hot as a firecracker, and ready to explode? How did she know the things Celeste said to him, the things he said to Celeste? *How the hell did Renata know about Henry?*

This was too weird. *He* was the ghost, for crying out loud! He wasn't the one who was supposed to get chills running up his spine! He was the one who was supposed to cause them in others. What the hell was he supposed to do now?

He knew what he *couldn't* do. He damn sure couldn't make love to Renata, even if he *could* make love the way he was. Even if she was dreaming she was Celeste. Even if holding her had him turned on and ready to rock. He wouldn't betray Celeste, wouldn't break his promise to love her forever. He did love her. Wasn't that the reason he was hanging around, haunting this place? He had to find the real, living, breathing Celeste and make amends. This thing with Renata wasn't in his plans. Unless . . . But no, that was crazy.

He didn't want to hurt Renata. It would be easy to take advantage of her—she was scared and she trusted him. But using *innocent* women had never been his style when he was alive. He'd be damned—probably was anyway, but he was gonna make the effort—if he was going to start taking advantage of chicks now that he was dead.

And that, he realized, was the major problem. He *was* dead. He couldn't even use the phone, for crying out loud! He sure wasn't about to do any horizontal slow-dancing with Renata or Celeste or anyone else.

Muffling a growl of frustration, he carefully slid away from Renata. She sighed but didn't move, didn't wake. He gave his own sigh, straightened his jeans, tucked in his shirt, and faded out of the room. He needed to get away from that woman, so he could think.

Ray drifted downstairs. A light from the kitchen shone into the hallway. Must be Melissa. Guess she couldn't sleep, worrying about her cop and her friend. Everyone had their demons, he thought. Even the demons.

He peeked inside and saw her standing at the sink, staring out the window. She had a small glass of something that looked like whiskey in her hand, but she seemed to have forgotten it. Maybe Melissa could make some sense out of what was happening between him and Renata—and Celeste.

"Trouble sleeping?" he asked quietly. He didn't want to wake Renata.

Melissa gasped. Her glare made him almost glad he was already dead. "Don't creep up on me like that!" she hissed. "You'll scare me to death!"

"It beats a bullet any day," he snarled back. The look on her face made him want to take the words back.

"Oh, Ray! I'm so sorry!"

She covered her face with her hands, looking worse than he felt. He hated feeling guilty. Without thinking first, he went to her and put his hand on her shoulder.

Nothing.

No spark. No . . . No feeling. Just the shoulder of her green robe showing through his hand.

"You didn't feel that, did you?" he asked, but he didn't need to.

She lowered her hands and met his eyes. "Feel what?"

"I touched your shoulder. You didn't feel anything, did you?" She shook her head, her eyes wide. *"Neither did I. But when I touch Renata . . ."* He shrugged, then moved away. After the third time he'd crossed the kitchen, he realized he was pacing. He looked at Melissa. She had her arms wrapped around herself as if she were cold. His pacing must cause a draft. *"Did it again, huh?"* When she nodded, he muttered, *"Sorry."*

He tried to stand still, but he couldn't. He had too much trapped inside. As he paced, he sensed Melissa watching him. Suddenly, she stepped into his path. He stopped short, noticing he had a lot more control over his movements now.

"Can we sit down?" she asked. "You're not only freezing me, you're making me dizzy."

It was like his teachers hollering at him for being jittery in class. He leaned his hip against the counter. Melissa sat at the kitchen table and sipped her drink. He couldn't sit still, so he settled for flexing his hand open and shut, open and shut, waiting, thinking. Trying not to think. Ready to explode. Afraid to let it all out. Man, that talk show woman was right. Guys had trouble communicating.

"Ray, what's the matter? Is something wrong with Renata? Or is it . . . ? *You're* okay, aren't you?" She pressed her hands to the edge of the table, rising. "Nothing's happening to you, is it? I mean, you're not . . ."

She sounded more bent out of shape than he was! He shook his head. She sat down and sighed. Jeez, she cared. He wasn't used to that. Before Celeste, no one had cared about him. They'd been nice to him if they could use him, like the girls who wanted their taste of the wild side, but didn't want to stay for the whole meal. The guys who were his buddies until their wheels were fixed, then somehow couldn't put together the cash to pay for his work. His old man, who cared about keeping him around until he was too big and strong to beat up. Being cared about was, he decided, a nice change. Would he have time to get used to it?

Melissa was still looking worried. He felt bad. She had a lot to worry about between her cop and her friend. He could take care of himself. Hell, he was already dead. What was the worst that could happen to him?

"I'm okay," he told her. "Renata's okay. She's sleeping. But . . ." He took a step forward, then caught her eye and stopped. "It's like this: Whenever I touch Renata, I see Celeste, too. Like a double image on a movie screen. It happens every time. I figured it was just 'cause I'm so focused on finding Celeste, that my imagination was working overtime. But tonight . . ."

When he didn't finish, Melissa arched a brow at him. He took a couple of steps, not really pacing. Thinking. Moving around helped. She cleared her throat quietly. He stopped walking and looked at her.

"What about tonight, Ray?"

"Tonight was . . . different." Ah, hell, the only way to get wet was to jump in the pool. "Renata had another nightmare. I went in and tried to wake her up. Next thing I know, she's talking in her sleep. But that wasn't the problem. It was what she said."

He jammed his hands into his jacket pockets and looked

at Melissa. She gave him one of those little half-smiles that he could tell meant *get on with it*. For the first time since Halloween night, he wished he had a cigarette.

"What she was saying . . . Hell, Melissa, she said things only Celeste knew. It wasn't like those cheesy movies where people go into a trance and talk in funny voices. In her own voice, Renata said she was afraid of Henry and she wanted me to take her away. Henry was the guy Celeste was supposed to marry. Did you tell Renata about me and Celeste?"

Melissa got a huffy look on her face. "I did not! Besides, you never told me his name. You couldn't remember it."

He felt his face burn. *"Oh, yeah. You're right. I didn't remember it until Renata said it. Sorry."* He ran his hands through his hair, then grabbed on and tugged hard. It didn't exactly hurt, but the tingles weren't the kind he felt when he touched Renata. Finally, he gave up and paced the kitchen floor, feeling more wound up with every step. When he couldn't stand the pressure anymore, he stopped and faced Melissa.

"How the hell would Renata know about any of that?" he practically shouted. She jumped at his voice. He toned it down. *"Tell me that, would you? How can Renata know about Henry? How can she say the things Celeste used to say to me? And how can she know how to . . ."*

The heat rose in his face again. No, better not say what else Renata did the way Celeste used to do it, even if it was proof that Renata sure could feel him. He didn't know Melissa *that* well. He shrugged and hoped she wouldn't notice he was turning beet red.

"I don't know, Ray." Melissa's eyes got wide. "Unless . . . ." She stopped talking and clapped one hand over her mouth. Her eyes got even wider.

"Yeah," he said, knowing what she meant. *"Unless."* Hands jammed in his pockets again, he paced, thinking. Melissa was quiet. When he stopped and looked at her, he could see she'd turned pale. *"That thought's already crossed my mind a couple of times. I need to know . . . I need to know that Celeste is alive or . . ."* The words stuck in his throat. He forced them past the sudden ache. *" . . . or not."*

Chapter Eleven

"Hi, Gabe."

He jerked awake. Lissa was back. How long since his parents had left after their morning visit? Couldn't tell without a clock. Couldn't see a clock even if he had one. Didn't matter. He wanted to see her smile, to touch her face, to kiss her and caress her the way he could in his dreams. Have to wait till he woke up and got out of the damn hospital bed. But then . . . Dreams couldn't match the real thing.

The chair scraped nearer to the bed. Melissa picked up his left hand. "I met with my first client this morning," she said. She sounded happy. "His name is David Mayhew. He's taking over Harley Heaven and wants an attorney on retainer. Renata knows him. She said he used to be a jerk, but he seemed quite nice to me." She laughed lightly.

He didn't like the way Lissa said that. Didn't like that little laugh, either. Like she was attracted to this guy. Not that he could do anything about it . . . now.

"You'll like David," she said. Gabe didn't think so. "He's really keen on New Harbour. His plans for Harley Heaven are very wholesome. No choppers, no gang-types. He's in-

terested in the weekend touring biker. And some of the bikes
he's going to stock are beautiful. He sent some magazines
and catalogues for you, for when you wake up. If you don't
mind, I'd like to bring them home for Ray first. He's as
crazy about bikes as you are. It might help him catch up with
what's been happening in the past four decades."

*Terrific. This guy, who isn't a jerk anymore, sends bike
mags home with Lissa, and she wants to lend them to a dead
guy.* He had some opinions about that, but there wasn't
much he could do about them. This was probably a good
time to develop the sense of humor some people claimed he
lacked.

Lissa lifted his hand. "I told you about Ray trying to find
out about Celeste, right? Well, the strangest thing happened
last night." She placed his hand on her face and he felt her
lips on his palm, but he couldn't make his finger move to let
her know. "Well," she said, "two strange things happened
last night." She rubbed her cheek on his hand like a kitten.
"I'll tell you what happened to Ray first."

*Oh, great! Another episode of "The Dead and the Rest-
less." Or "All My Spirits." Or "General Haunting."* Inside,
he snickered. Who said he didn't have a sense of humor? If
he never made it out of this coma, he could get a job writing
soap operas for the afterlife. *How about "As the Crypt
Turns?"*

"Poor Renata's been having nightmares," Lissa said, jolt-
ing him back to reality.

Damn, he'd forgotten Renata was hiding out at Lissa's
house. And why. Another reason for him to wake up and get
his butt in gear. It was his job to protect Renata, so she could
do her job, not lie around here while some creep terrorized
her.

"She probably had a mild concussion, but she's as hardheaded as you are. Absolutely refused to go to the hospital
or let a doctor come to her, no matter how bruised she was.
She's afraid that would alert whoever was after her and put
Ray and me in danger. Not that anything can hurt Ray. I did
tell you that Renata lost her glasses, didn't I? She's so nearsighted, but she's afraid to let me go to her place for her

spare glasses, in case someone's watching it. I'm supposed to pick up a pair from her optician today. Can you imagine, she still doesn't suspect Ray's a ghost?"

Probably, Gabe thought sourly, *because he's really a con man.* Renata was a hell of a prosecutor. He never would have suspected she could be so gullible. But falling for a con man, or even a ghost, was better than tangling with whoever ran her off the road like that. Damn! Why didn't Renata get someone from the department to watch over them? She knew they would send a car around the clock. Hell, they'd bring her spare glasses to her, too. Although she did have a point about her place being watched. Sensible woman.

"Anyway," Lissa said, "Ray told me last night that when he touches Renata, he sees Celeste. And last night, Renata said things in her sleep that only Celeste could know." Lissa made a soft little laughing sound. "I think she must have gotten fresh with him, too, because he got embarrassed and clammed up. It was rather touching seeing this big, strapping ghost in denim and leather blushing."

Touching didn't begin to describe that scene, Gabe thought. *Seriously touched was more like it.* When he got out of this coma, he'd have to give Lissa the credit. He was desperate to wake up, so he wouldn't have to hear any more of this loony ghost story of hers.

"Poor Ray," she said. *Poor me,* Gabe wanted to say. "He's in love with a woman who is either about fifty-eight years old, or deceased. Either way, what's he going to do? And now, I think he believes Renata . . ." Again, she laughed softly. "Never mind. It's too weird for words. Let me tell you about my dream."

Ah! Now you've got my attention, Gabe thought.

She moved closer. He could smell her sweetness, feel her warmth. She still held his hand. When she bent down to him, her breast pressed against his arm. Her breath feathered his skin. Her words made his pulse thunder in his ears. It was like they'd had the same dream. Or like he'd been there with her in spirit, at the same time he'd been lying here unconscious. Everything he remembered saying, everything his mother had told him about his birth mother and his adoption, she repeated. And everything he'd imagined doing . . . apparently, he'd done it. Or they'd both imagined doing it together. And all the things he'd dreamed she'd done—the way she'd touched him, the way she'd made him shake like a leaf in a storm—she whispered to him now.

He wanted to pull her down to him and do it all again.

"Gabe? Gabe! You moved your fingers! Can you do it again?" Her excitement gave him enough energy to try. "Oh, Gabe! You *can* hear me! Wait right here! Oh, what am I saying? I'll be right back. I have to get Paul!"

He could hear the tears in her voice. Her lips pressed kisses and tears into his palm. Then she was gone, and he was waiting. Waiting and trying to make his hand move again.

"Hey, bro'," Paul said. "I heard you're making some progress." He lowered his voice and said, "Told you Melissa would be good for something." If Gabe could have, he would have punched Paul.

"Did it again!" Paul was close to shouting. Gabe wanted to grab his old friend by the collar and shake him. "And again! Well, all right! Hang in there while I get the neurologist to poke at you. It's guaranteed to be the highlight of your day."

To hell with the neurologist. He wanted Lissa to poke at him—and vice versa. Where was she?

"Your mother just came back," Paul announced in a normal tone. "She'll be ecstatic." Then he added, almost too quiet for Gabe to hear, "Especially since she caught Melissa sneaking out of ICU. Good thing your dad wasn't there. He's having enough trouble with the stress. You better get out of never-never land soon, buddy. You've got some serious damage-control to do."

Tell me about it, Gabe thought.

Renata peered at the computer screen, highlighting the information she needed. Uncertain whether or not she should go to the office today, she finally decided to call in sick. From downstairs, she was vaguely aware of music. Ray must be back from his latest errand. He'd been out all morning, and like a love-struck teenager, she'd been both relieved he was gone and anxious to see him again.

Gran would probably smile and tell her it served her right for being so persnickety about men. She'd finally found a man who made her blood sing and her nerves synapse like millions of tiny lightning strikes, but only when she was dreaming. And when she was dreaming, she felt she was someone else. Not that it mattered who she was or whether she was awake or asleep. Ray was apparently still carrying a torch for an old girlfriend who was married. Her mother would be amused at her expense, also, but for totally different reasons. Mother would probably propose seducing Will or Ray for the experience; one gorgeous young man was as good as another.

Well, she didn't think either one of them was right. Not that it mattered. She could practically hear her work piling up while she was stuck hiding here at Mel's house, where she was handicapped by lack of resources, and stalked by villains. She had no time or energy for the man of her dreams, whoever he was, even if he walked in the front door. Falling in love would have to take a number and wait in line.

"Oh, poor me," she muttered. "Poor, poor me." Those words reminded her of a Linda Ronstadt song along the same theme, and she started humming under her breath as she scrolled through the files she'd downloaded from her office.

Once she'd cleared her mind of all distracting thoughts, she worked intently. Frank Dane's previous trial transcripts were fascinating, like an accident scene on the side of the road. He had all the guile of a snake oil salesman, and all the charm of a snake. She couldn't stop reading, convinced somewhere in the back of her mind that she'd find some sign pointing the way to winning the State's case against him. When Lucky leapt into her lap, she barely noticed.

But when Ray entered the room, she knew without hearing a sound, without seeing him. She just *sensed* him there with her. The air felt warmer, electrically charged, and she felt different in some intangible way.

"How's it going?" he asked, suddenly behind her.

Deliberately, she kept her eyes focused on the screen. "It would be going great if there were more hours in a day. I've got so many other cases to deal with, and I'm afraid I'll leave Dane's attorneys room to squeeze him through. He's got at least four lawyers on his defense team. The State has me and some students and clerks."

"Doesn't sound like a fair fight."

"It isn't. But if the State can't prove its case beyond a reasonable doubt, then it's right that Frank Dane goes free. Justice isn't necessarily fair."

"It'll catch up with him, you know." Ray spoke with such quiet assurance that Renata couldn't help glancing up at him. He was scowling at the computer screen. Before she had a chance to guard her own expression, he looked directly into her eyes. *"What goes around, comes around, right?"*

Renata couldn't hold his gaze. It was too intense, as if his eyes could see into her heart and mind. He made her yearn to be the woman she became in her dreams, the one he made love to so sweetly and wildly, and that was too unsettling to consider. She turned away and concentrated on her Internet surfing.

"Hey, that's wild," he said as a list of files popped onto the screen.

In spite of her discomfort at his hovering presence, Renata grinned. "It is, isn't it? There doesn't seem to be anything you can't find out about on the 'Net. And some things no one in their right mind would want to know."

"Oh, yeah? Like what?" Laughter lurked behind his challenge.

Renata felt herself blushing. "You don't want to know," she assured him. "Trust me. A lot of these people don't get out much, but they have very rich fantasy lives."

He snorted softly. *"Yeah, well, they aren't the only ones."*

Meaning her, Renata understood. To hide her sudden hurt, she focused on the screen. Numbly, she selected a file, downloaded it, and scrolled through it before realizing it wasn't the article she was looking for. Damn! She didn't have time for hurt feelings.

"That's a newspaper!" Ray sounded genuinely surprised.

"Of course it is. I'm looking for stories about the kinds of criminal activity we suspect Dane of being involved in or being behind. This issue is from about five years ago. The State police and the FBI broke up a chop shop ring but they couldn't get a lead on the Connecticut contact. There! See that tiny news brief? The man whose car flipped into a ravine and burned?"

Ray leaned forward to peer at the screen. *"Yeah. So?"*

He was so close that Renata felt his heat on her back. Suddenly, concentrating on crimes and criminals became a major task for her overly aware brain. Even breathing was becoming a challenge. She swallowed hard before speaking. "The man who died in the crash was supposed to testify against Dane. The cops caught him red-handed with several stolen cars he was crating for export. He copped a plea: testimony against Dane in exchange for a reduced sentence. He was out on bail, arranged by one of Dane's attorneys, so he wasn't in jail or protective custody. Bye-bye only witness. Bye-bye charges against Frank Dane."

Renata saved the article to a diskette, then called up another article. "See this one? This gentleman claimed that Dane offered him a bribe when he was serving jury duty. He held out for a guilty verdict, and the trial ended in a hung jury. The juror was more than willing to testify, so the State brought charges."

Ray leaned over her shoulder. Her skin tingled with heat and she felt as if her sense of reality was shifting away from her. "He had a heart attack," she said, forcing herself to concentrate. To her relief, Ray moved far enough away to break the electrical connection between them. "Good timing, wasn't it?" Again, after saving the article, she searched for another name connected with Frank Dane. "Here we are." She pointed to the small news article. "What do you think?"

"It says the lady died of an accidental drowning in her pool." She waited for Ray to read further on. When he whistled softly, she knew he'd seen the key line. *"She was Dane's bookkeeper,"* he said.

"Not exactly what I'd call career advancement. Frank Dane is like Typhoid Mary. Wherever he goes, people drop dead, but no one seems to have put it together until now."

Ray settled himself on the arm of the overstuffed reading chair. Renata could breathe again, but, perversely, part of her wished he'd come closer.

"There are more?" he asked.

"Four more that I'm sure of. Two or three more that I'm not positive about. The trouble is, they're all accidents or natural causes, so there was never a reason for further investigations."

"Who says they're accidents or natural causes?"

Renata looked at him. Her jaw dropped as the pieces of an idea slid into place. "You're a genius!" It took all her self-control not to jump up and hug him.

He straightened and frowned. *"What did I say?"*

Renata laughed with delight. "You gave me an idea. A fantastic idea. If I'm right . . ." Her glee turned to dismay. "Oh, Lord, if I'm right, this is worse than stolen cars and jury-tampering."

"What was that woman doing in my son's room?"

His mother sounded more hurt than angry, Gabe thought. Like she'd been betrayed. By Paul, who'd saved her son's life? By Lissa, who was helping her son come out of his coma? By him, for never giving up loving Lissa?

"Mrs. Bautista, please sit down." Paul was good with his mother. Respectful. Affectionate. She'd always liked him. "I'd like you to hold Gabe's hand and talk to him. Tell him you're here, and praying for him."

He felt his mother close her hand around his. "Every day I tell him I'm here, I'm praying for him. What good does it do? Does he hear me?"

Gabe understood what Paul was trying to do. He concentrated all of his energy into the hand his mother held. If he could give her some reassurance . . .

"Oh! He squeezed my hand!" A volley of Portuguese, mostly prayers mixed with thanks to Paul, filled his room. He felt her tears on his skin.

"Don't thank me, Mrs. Bautista," Paul said. "Thank Melissa Hartley."

His mother's hand went stiff against his. "Why should I thank her? She broke Gabe's heart and he never got over her."

"And she says he broke her heart and she never got over him," Paul countered gently. Gabe could feel his mother preparing to argue. "It's a long story," Paul added, "and I'm not sure of all the facts. But I do know that Melissa loves him. She's here every day, between your visits, holding his hand, talking to him, bringing him back to us. Gabe responded to Melissa earlier. She had just run out to tell me when you saw her."

The silence thundered. Gabe strained to move his fingers again. He wanted to give his mother hope, and he needed her to trust Paul and Lissa. He couldn't feel his fingers move, but he could feel his mother's grip tighten.

"Then tell her . . ." his mother paused. Her hand trembled slightly and his heart seemed to stop while he waited for her to announce her decision. "Tell Melissa she has my blessings. If Mario doesn't like it, too bad. He won't interfere. My son's recovery is more important than my husband's pride."

Gabe squeezed his mother's hand again and felt her tears fall onto his skin.

Renata dialed the phone number of her friend Susan, the wizard of the State's records department. She explained what she needed Susan to look up, heard her friend whistle softly, and knew her warning to keep her request totally confidential wasn't really necessary. Susan had provided her with enough information about Frank Dane to appreciate the need for secrecy.

When she hung up, she found Ray looking at her oddly. *"What was that all about?"* he asked.

"I asked for the names of the doctors who had signed the death certificates of people who died before they could testify against Dane. And then I asked for the names on all the other death certificates those doctors signed. If I'm right,

I'm expecting at least a few more hits between the list of potential witnesses and the lists of people whose deaths those doctors attributed to accidents or natural causes."

He frowned and ran his fingers through his hair. *"Let me get this straight,"* he said, his eyes intense as he studied her face. *"You think the doctors who signed death certificates for those guys in the articles lied about the causes of death?"* She nodded. *"So that would mean they had some connection to Frank, too, right?"*

Renata nodded. It was too horrific a possibility to be happy about discovering it, but she was pleased at how quickly Ray followed her logic. At the very least, he confirmed that she wasn't stretching credibility too far.

Ray swore under his breath. *"Okay, but that's going to take forever to find out, isn't it? And how are you gonna get those lists without anyone finding you here?"*

"No problem. Knowing Susan, if the data is in her computer, she'll be E-mailing it to me within the hour."

He frowned again. *"And then what?"*

"And then I arrange for an investigator to talk to the doctors involved. If they don't want to cooperate, it probably won't be too difficult to convince a judge to subpoena them. I think I can figure out a way to question them without running up against doctor-patient confidentiality. Besides, the patients are all deceased."

"What if Frank gets wind of what you're doing? The more people you contact, the more chance you're taking that he'll find you."

Renata tried to ignore the little flutter of pleasure at Ray's concern. "He won't. He isn't clever enough to crack into the State's computers. And he's not big enough to have that many people in his pockets." She smiled, hoping to reassure Ray that she wasn't foolhardy. "Besides, if I'm really worried that Dane might come after me, I can always call Will and get police protection."

Ray scowled and stood up abruptly. *"Yeah. You do that,"* he practically snarled.

Startled and puzzled by his sudden change of mood, Renata blinked. When she looked again at the chair where he'd been sitting, Ray was gone. She tried to tell herself it didn't matter, but the room felt much, much colder without him.

Ray slouched onto the pile of cartons in the basement and tried to figure out why he was so ticked off about the idea of Renata calling the State trooper to protect her. It would be the smart thing for her to do. Even if Melissa could be home all the time, she sure wasn't going to fight off an attack by Frank or his boys. And he was about as useless as a wet noodle.

Damn it! That was why he was acting like he had a burr up his butt. He wanted to protect Renata. She was such a brave little thing, tackling that creep Frank. And old Frankie never cared who he hurt. If Frank found her, Renata would be like Superman in a room full of Kryptonite. She deserved better.

The way she used that computer, and the way she figured things out . . . She was a smart little cookie. He stood up and stretched. Maybe that was why he wanted to take care of Renata. He hadn't been able to stick around for Celeste, and Renata reminded him of her. Sure. That made sense.

A yowl from somewhere in the basement made the hair on the back of his neck stand up. What the hell . . . ? He heard it again, louder this time. If he didn't know better, he'd say the place was haunted.

The third yowl was even closer. Ray moved toward the sound, trying to convince himself that he was already dead, so nothing worse could happen, but he had to admit, he didn't know if that was true. He looked around the corner.

Lucky dropped the mouse in his teeth and made that bloodcurdling yowl again. Damn cat! Almost gave him a heart attack. He let loose a few well-chosen words about the little beast's parentage and IQ. Lucky just sat and grinned like he knew exactly what he'd done.

The mouse suddenly got to its feet. It didn't take the time to look back. It just took off and scrambled between the boxes, gone before Lucky could catch it. This time, Ray grinned while Lucky flattened his ears and hissed.

"Better not let the ladies hear you use words like that," he told the cat. *"They think you're such a sweet little thing."*

With another hiss, Lucky stalked up the basement stairs and nudged the door open. His tail stuck straight up like a flagpole. Ray was still chuckling when he heard Renata shriek.

Mom, there's nothing to cry about, Gabe wanted to say. He never could understand why women cried when they were happy.

"Mrs. Bautista?" Paul's voice again. "Melissa's here."

Gabe braced himself. His parents had never given Lissa a fair chance. They'd disliked her even before meeting her. His mother might agree in principle to letting Lissa spend time with him, but how would she react to meeting her?

"Hello, Mrs. Bautista." Lissa's voice. Soft. A little shaky.

"I was wrong," his mother said.

His heart fell. She was going to change her mind and refuse to let Lissa be with him.

"I was wrong to judge you without knowing you." He heard the tears in his mother's voice. His heart expanded with love and pride. She was one in a million. "Paul told me what you've done for Gabe. He told me you love my son. Together, maybe we can love him enough to bring him back to us."

Lissa's slim fingers curled around his, joining his mother's broad hand. "I believe we can, Mrs. Bautista," Lissa said softly, firmly. "If love is what it takes to bring him back, I believe we have more than enough."

Gabe heard tears in her voice, too. Oh, God! He didn't think he could stand it if they both started crying! He focused his energy on the hand they clasped between theirs. When they both gasped, he knew he'd succeeded in squeezing their fingers with his own. His mother started murmuring in Portuguese. And then, sure enough, both of them were sobbing.

Hell, he felt a little choked up himself.

* * *

Renata's shriek sliced through him. Ray charged up the stairs and through the half-closed cellar door. His boots didn't touch the steps on his way up to the second floor. By the time he reached the upper hallway, his heart was racing. What was wrong? And what the hell was he going to do if she was in danger?

Chapter
Twelve

"Renata!" he bellowed, rounding the corner of the doorway. *"What is it? Are you all right?"*

He stopped in his tracks and jammed his hands into his jeans pockets. She was alone, sitting in front of the computer where he'd left her, holding the phone to her ear, and looking at him as if he was crazy.

From hero to zero in less than thirty seconds.

"I heard you scream," he muttered.

Her smile took some of the sting out of making a fool of himself over nothing. "I'm sorry. It was more of a whoop than a scream."

"You hit pay dirt?"

She nodded. "Serious pay dirt. Give me a second and I'll explain." He wandered into the office while she thanked whoever was on the other end of the phone and hung up. "In about five minutes, all the data I asked Susan for will be in Melissa's computer. She wouldn't tell me any details, but she warned me to be sitting down when I read the lists."

Ray couldn't help scowling at her. *"Hell, woman, you nearly gave me a heart attack."*

Renata smiled again. "I'm sorry. Honestly. This has been so discouraging that anything positive feels like a major breakthrough."

He'd already forgiven her, but he liked seeing her smile. It wasn't like he was cheating on Celeste if he felt something special between him and Renata, was it? Aw, hell! Celeste! He combed his fingers through his hair. Damn! He'd let this stuff about Frankie distract him from finding Celeste.

He settled carefully on the arm of the big chair, hoping he wouldn't sink into it and that she wouldn't be able to see the pink flowers through him. *"Can you look up people using the computer? Sort of like a phone book?"* he asked, trying to sound totally casual.

Renata swiveled around in her chair. "That depends on who they are and where I'm trying to look. I can get into the files at my office and tap into the phone directories for all fifty states and Canada, but if someone doesn't have a phone, that won't help."

"Gotcha." Melissa hadn't found Celeste in any Connecticut phone books. What if she'd moved away instead of marrying that doctor? *"How would you look someone up? Out of state, maybe."*

Renata's brows went up. "Celeste?" He nodded, a little embarrassed that she read his mind so quickly. She turned back toward the computer and started typing. "What's her last name again?" she asked without looking at him.

"Benedict, if she's still using her maiden name. If she isn't, I'm stuck. I can't remember the name of the doctor she married." No point in giving her just a first name. He didn't think there was only one M.D. named Henry in the U.S. and Canada.

Renata nodded. "If I don't get any hits using her maiden name, I'll ask Susan to check into marriage records. That would take her about a minute, less if you remember the date of her wedding."

Not if she got married after I got killed, he thought, but decided that wouldn't be the best way to tell Renata his little secret. Instead, he watched her fingers flying over the keys. After about a minute, she sat back in her chair and looked at him.

"I'm in. Want to watch?" she asked.

He almost choked. *"What did you say?"* he asked, standing up. No matter how fast some girls were when he was wild and free, not a single one had ever said anything like that. And he'd bet Renata didn't have a clue. She might tackle slimeballs in court, but she was so innocent she needed protection from herself.

She looked at him over her shoulder, her brows pulled down in a frown. "I said . . ." Her mouth snapped shut and her cheeks turned pink. No way he could hide his grin. "You have a filthy mind," she muttered, turning away.

"I was thinking the same thing about you," he teased, hoping she would lighten up.

It didn't do any good. She kept staring at the computer screen, not looking at him. Her back was as stiff as a soldier's. Damn! He didn't mean to embarrass her. He moved to stand behind her and put his hands on her shoulders before he remembered that was a bad idea. The jolt of electricity that surged through him shook a gasp from her, too.

Ray lifted his hands, but the sensation of touching her felt like a brand on his palms. This time, though, he didn't see even a hint of Celeste. He stood there, waiting for the double vision, refusing to let his mind sift for possible explanations. He didn't want to know.

Renata cleared her throat softly. He saw her face reflected in the glass of the computer screen. She was frowning at the words in front of her.

"No hits anywhere in North America for a phone listing under Celeste Benedict, Ray. Sorry," she said quietly, not turning around, not even looking up. He could tell by her reflection in the screen. "She must have taken her husband's name. I can get that from Susan and try again, but first, I have to sort through the data she's sending me. I'm running out of time, and I need something concrete I can use against Frank Dane."

Man, she could be fierce. He wouldn't want to be old Frankie when Renata got him on the stand. Wouldn't mind watching, but he couldn't leave the Garvey house. Oh, well. News at eleven. *"Sure thing."* Still, he couldn't resist teasing her again. *"But this time, I want to watch."*

He moved to her side and grinned. Her smile told him she didn't mind his teasing anymore.

"Okay," she said. "But pay attention. There's a quiz at the end." She typed something too fast for him to catch. Words and pictures flashed on and off the screen. "I'm getting out of the phone directory program, and I'm going to check my E-mail."

He watched her type. The computer made sounds like a phone, then let out a bloodcurdling screech. A moment later, different words and pictures flashed on and off the screen. Renata touched the keys a few times, then sat back and took in a deep breath. Her tension, her eagerness vibrated through him, too. It was like they were still connected, even though he'd barely touched her, and he'd let go like she was a live wire. It was like those perfect times making love with Celeste, when he could feel her pleasure and she could feel his. Beyond sex. Beyond touch. Beyond words.

"Yes!" she breathed. Her excitement tingled along his nerves. "She did it! Oh, Ray! This is gold! Pure gold! Susan gets a double-Dutch chocolate cake and a box of Godiva truffles!" She looked up at him, her eyes shining, and something like an electric shock tore through him, even without touch. He was beginning to think his suspicions weren't so crazy after all, but he hated like hell to consider the consequences. "It was your idea," she told him with a big smile. "You deserve something rich and wonderful as a reward."

He knew what he wanted—at least, he thought he did—but it didn't have anything to do with candy. He smiled back at her. *"Forget it. It's enough to see you nail Frankie Dane."*

Her cheeks got pink and her lashes drifted down, hiding her eyes. She turned back to the computer screen. "Here's the list of potential witnesses against him," she said, pointing to a long column of names. "And here are the dates of their deaths and the names of the doctors who signed . . ."

She stopped talking and leaned closer to the screen. Ray got as close as he dared—too close right in front of her and

she'd be able to see through him even without her glasses—
and squinted at the list of names she was frowning at. Renata tipped her face up toward him and met his eyes.

"Am I seeing things?" she asked. "There's only one doctor signing death certificates for all the people who were
supposed to testify against Frank Dane. Look, Ray! This is
the list of all the death certificates signed by this doctor. All
the way back to nineteen-sixty-one, and right up to the juror
who had the heart attack before he could testify, just this
year. Oh, my God! Susan highlighted the names I gave her.
All of them are here! Oh, Ray! That could mean . . ."

She looked at him, eyes wide, then looked back at the
screen and swallowed hard. He knew how she felt. The
causes of death for all the names in gray boxes were listed
as accidental or natural causes like heart attacks, or suicide
by barbiturate overdose. One at a time, they didn't look suspicious. One after another, they added up to Frankie having
his enemies bumped off, and his tame doctor chalking their
murders up to something else that took the heat off Dane. A
doctor whose name was suspiciously familiar.

"Dollars to doughnuts this cat is Frankie's own doc," he
said. He didn't know how to share his suspicions about the
doctor without causing Renata to develop some of her own
about *him*.

Renata groaned softly. "Even if he isn't, we can put him
on the stand, but we can't force him to incriminate himself.
Dane must have some powerful hold over him. Which probably means that this doctor himself did something that left
him vulnerable to blackmail."

She didn't have to say what that something could be. Ray
felt the shudder that raced through her body. "I have this
awful feeling I may be in over my head," she murmured. "I
need to consult with . . ." Her voice trailed off and she
leaned closer to the screen. "No, that isn't possible. Ray?"
She glanced at him, then back to the screen.

Gabe heard voices, women's voices, weaving soft patterns of sound around him. Must have drifted to sleep again,
he realized. Concentrating, he made out his mother's low,

rich voice and Lissa's lighter, softer tones. So it wasn't his imagination. Wasn't a dream. The two most important women in his life had finally met. Sounded like they were getting along fine, too. Now if only his father could accept Lissa.

" . . . telling Gabe the story of his poor mother and how Mario and I adopted him," his mother was saying when he finally tuned in enough to catch words. "Mario never wanted him to know he wasn't our real child."

"He knew, though," Lissa told her softly. "We talked about it when he figured it out, after a science class on genetics. He said you were his real parents because you were the ones who were raising him, and he didn't care if he never met his biological parents."

Gabe wanted to thank Lissa for saying what he couldn't, at least not yet. He just wished his mother would stop sniffling.

"He's a good son," she finally said. "His birth mother would have been proud of him."

"You knew her?" Lissa asked breathlessly.

Funny, Gabe thought, Lissa said he'd told her already, in her dream, or whatever it was they shared. His mother repeated what she'd told him, what he thought he'd told Lissa.

"She was a sweet girl, but she had backbone. She'd made up her mind not to marry that doctor her father wanted her engaged to. She was planning to go away, to start over on her own, a few months after Gabe was born. She had some money from a grandmother, she said. But she begged me to send her pictures of Gabe on his birthdays, and she promised she'd help if we ever needed money. She wanted the best for him."

Gabe stored that information away. His birth mother hadn't been selfish. Hadn't abandoned him. Sounded like she'd loved him. Then why—?

"That's why I don't believe she killed herself," his mother said, as if she could read his mind.

Lissa gasped. He didn't want to believe it, either. His birth mother was just starting to seem real to him. Every time his mother talked about her death, it was like losing her again. Even so, he was hungry for any details.

"She told me it made her happy to give Gabe to Mario and me. Her fiancé still wanted to marry her, but she didn't love him. After she came home from Boston, she acted afraid of him. She decided to move in with friends back in Boston and get a job. I helped her pack and buy a bus ticket. Poor girl." His mother's voice caught. "She died in her sleep that night."

"Oh, no!" Lissa said softly, echoing his thoughts. "What happened?"

"No one knows. We heard later that a doctor said it was suicide from sleeping pills. But what about her suitcase and bus ticket? The ones I helped her hide. They were gone the next time I went to clean, but no one said a word about that. And why would a girl who was planning to start a new life kill herself?"

Gabe suspected the answer to that question could be very ugly. He had to wake up. Had to decide what to do: avenge his birth mother's murder, if that's what it was, or let her rest in peace.

Something had caught Renata's attention enough to stop her in mid-sentence. Ray moved closer to the computer and studied the lists on the screen. It took him a moment to see what was bothering Renata. There, in the list of deaths certified by one doctor in nineteen-sixty-two, was the name Benedict, Celeste Marie. The cause of death was a self-inflicted overdose of sleeping pills following severe postpartum depression.

He felt like he'd been sucker punched. In a deep corner of his heart, he'd known Celeste was dead, had been for thirty-five years, but until now, he'd been able to hope she wasn't. Now, he had to face something worse than his own death. Self-inflicted . . . ? No, not his Celeste. She'd never do that. She was too full of life.

What the hell had happened? Didn't postpartum mean . . . ? Oh, God, she'd had a baby! *His* baby! He hadn't known. Someone killed him before he could find out, before he could marry her. She was gone. Their baby was gone. Boy or girl? Alive or not? He'd never know what happened to the baby. *Their* baby. He'd had a lot to live for, but nothing to come back to. Not anymore. No reason why he'd been hanging around the scene of his murder. He couldn't care less who'd shot him. It didn't matter now. Nothing mattered now.

He closed his eyes to blot out the sight of Celeste's name on the computer screen. He couldn't believe she really was dead. Shouldn't he be able to feel it somehow? What was the point of being a ghost, if he didn't have any special powers? Something inside him, some extra sense, should have told him she was gone. Wishful thinking let him fool himself. He'd been so sure he'd felt her there with him, especially the times he'd touched Renata and seen Celeste.

And there he'd been, thinking that because he wanted to find Celeste, he couldn't touch another woman without seeing her. She was probably trying to tell him not to bother looking for her. Damn! How was he supposed to know? Sure, he was a ghost, but that didn't make him an expert on this stuff. He was having enough trouble figuring out what he was supposed to do. Anyway, none of it mattered anymore. Celeste was dead.

How did a ghost mourn?

"Oh, Ray! I'm so sorry about Celeste," Renata was saying softly. She had a tragic look on her face.

When she lifted one hand, he moved away before she could touch him. He didn't deserve her sympathy. He was a fraud. He'd been trying to use Renata to take Celeste's place, but what was the point? He was dead, for crying out loud! By his figuring, he was here to do two things: find Celeste, and identify his own killer. Okay, so he'd found Celeste. She was gone, and maybe she'd been trying to tell him. Well, he had the message now. He was fifty percent closer to going wherever good ghosts went when they'd solved their problems.

"Obviously," Renata murmured, "the date of her death is a typo, but—"

It was time. *"No, it's not. It's correct the way it is."*

He owed her the truth, even if she didn't believe him at first. A couple of what Melissa called parlor tricks, and she'd have to be convinced. Walking through walls wasn't his favorite thing to do—it felt real weird the way the bricks and insulation and everything sorta got sucked through him—but he'd do it a hundred times if he had to, if that would take away the suspicious look in Renata's eyes. Not to mention, as soon as Renata knew the truth about him, he could kiss their friendship good-bye. He didn't want that to happen, but he didn't matter. It was Renata that counted, especially now that Celeste was gone.

He hoped she wouldn't faint away again. She was a tiny thing, as chicks went, but he'd never be able to get her up off the floor. All the time he spent practicing, when no one was watching, he'd only managed to lift really light things, like Melissa's silk scarves, and only a little. Even that took a lot out of him.

Renata frowned and her hand dropped to her side. "The date of her death has to be wrong." She shook her head and gave a soft laugh. "If it's correct, that would mean Celeste died thirty-five years ago. That was before you were born. So how could you even meet her?"

Ray stared at her, stumped for the right words. She looked back, like she was expecting some pearl of wisdom from him. Like she was more than a little nearsighted, and couldn't see him clearly. Like she cared a lot about him.

Damn! Damn! Damn! He couldn't just spring this on her. This was going to be even harder than he'd thought. Why had it been so easy to tell Melissa? Why couldn't he make himself say the words *I died before Celeste did. I'm a ghost. Think you can help me nail the guy who shot me and find out what happened to our kid?*

He tried. *"I know it sounds crazy, but I . . . Celeste and I . . . We were engaged . . . I was twenty-four. We were planning to elope, but someone shot . . ."* He could see the hurt in her eyes, and figured the best thing to do was just keep going. *"Try to believe me, Renata. I was murdered in nineteen sixty-one, right here in this house."*

Renata made a soft sound, somewhere between a groan and a whimper, and leaned away from him. "It's just not possible," she whispered. "You expect me to believe you're . . . you're a *ghost?*"

The look in her dark eyes made him want to squirm. *"I don't expect you to believe it, but I hope you will. I've been . . . dead for thirty-six years. I woke up Halloween night, when you came here, which makes me think there's a damn good possibility that—"*

"I won't listen!" she wailed. "It's just a trick to get you close to me. Someone sent you to set me up. You knew I'd find Celeste's name on this list."

He couldn't stand the look on her face. Hurt. Betrayed. Her eyes got shiny from tears. If he'd had a heart, it would have broken for her. But that couldn't change the truth. He stood there and waited for her to look at him, really see him. Instead, she closed her eyes. A tear escaped and slid down her cheek. It might have been a knife tearing him apart. How could he hurt so bad if he was dead?

When she opened her eyes again, she looked at him like he was something that lived under a rock. That hurt. "You work for Frank Dane, don't you?" That hurt even more. How could she think that? "Dane got someone to tamper with the computer data, then sent you to trick me into framing this poor doctor, didn't he?"

Her hand shot out and grabbed the phone beside the computer. She glared up at him. "I'm calling Will to pick me up and get me police protection."

It was the right thing for her to do. This was no game. She was in danger. The cops could keep her safe. It was too clear that he couldn't. Protecting Renata was more important than anything else. But something wouldn't let him stand there while she turned to some other guy. Something he'd tried to say, that she wasn't ready to hear.

"Put the phone down!"

"No!"

He could tell she wasn't going to listen, really listen, until he got her attention. He reached out his hand to touch the phone and the energy inside him shorted it out. She stared at

the dead phone, then glared at him and hung it up. It was a
dirty trick, but he could apologize later.

*"Listen to me, Renata. I don't work for Frank Dane. I
don't work for anyone. And I didn't know Celeste was dead,
but I sure as hell knew her when she was alive, because
that's when I was alive. And damn it, I'm not alive anymore!"* By the time he finished, he was nearly shouting.

Renata didn't back down. There was fire in her eyes now.
She put her hands on her hips and shook her head. Before
she could open her mouth, he said, *"How far back do those
lists of deaths go?"*

She didn't move. "Why?" He should have known she'd
want to know that.

"Check back to 'sixty-one."

"Why?" Damn! She was like a terrier after a squirrel.
Couldn't a lawyer take anything on faith?

*"Because if your theory is right, and my suspicions are,
too, you're going to find my name on the list of death certificates signed by that doctor."* He gave her a grin he hoped
was charming. *"Please?"*

Her chin went up, and she blinked away some tears, but
after a few very long seconds, she sat down again in front of
the computer and pressed a key. She was one gutsy babe.
The lists rolled backward and stopped at nineteen sixty-one.
He saw what he was looking for right away. It took Renata
a little longer. He could tell when she found it, because her
head tipped forward, like she was having trouble seeing—or
believing—the words, then slowly turned toward him. Her
dark eyes were huge, and she didn't seem to be breathing.

"Raymond Lowell, previously identified as John Doe," she
said in a hollow voice. "That's supposed to be you, right?"

He stepped toward her. *"I told you—"*

"You . . . You *jerk!* You're a total fraud, and I'm a total
fool." Her chin quivered and she made a tiny sound in her
throat, like a hurt kitten.

Aw, jeez! She thought he was using the name of a dead
guy, acting some role so she'd fall for him. Then, he
guessed, he was supposed to get her under Frankie's thumb.
It was almost funny that she thought he could do that, like

some guy in a movie. But it wasn't funny that she was hurt and sad because of him.

"Renata, baby, please don't cry. It's not what you're thinking." Man, that sounded lame.

Her eyes flashed at him. She was mad as hell, and the madder she got, the more he wanted to grab her and kiss her. And the more he thought about kissing her, the more he felt that old spark. Electricity was practically crackling between them. Everything was going to hell, but he felt more alive than he had in thirty-five years.

But Renata didn't seem to be noticing the energy pulsing from her to him and back. Her words came at him, and he stood there doing the Bambi-in-the-headlights routine. "First you want me to believe you're hung up on a woman who's been dead longer than I've been alive. Now you expect me to believe *you're* dead! I know what you're doing. You're working for Frank Dane, trying to distract me so I'll screw up the prosecution's case. How stupid do you think I am?"

She bent her head down so that her dark hair swung forward and hid her face from him. "Oh, God! Stupid enough to almost fall for it. Go away!" Her voice was suddenly thick with tears. "Just go away."

He saw another opening to explain. *"Baby, I can't go away. Don't think I haven't tried—"*

But Renata slammed that opening shut, just like she slammed her hand on the desk. She stood up and pushed the chair away. "Try harder!" she cried.

Without looking at him again, she just about ran out of the room. A sob from down the hall tore at him. He started to follow, to make up with her, then stopped short. Lucky suddenly sat in the doorway and stared at him. He stared back. Lucky yawned, then went on staring.

"You think you're pretty smart, don't you?" he muttered. Lucky blinked. *"Yeah, well, tell me this, Short Stuff: How am I supposed to convince Renata to believe me? Because as long as she doesn't, she's gonna be hurt, and I really don't want her to hurt on my account."*

Lucky lifted a front paw toward him, almost like he was offering to shake hands. The damn cat was right. If the truth

had been a snake, it would have bitten him by now. He'd
practically been touching the answer without seeing it.

Renata threw herself down on the bed and buried her face
in her pillow to smother her sobs. She was an idiot! A total
fool! Her mother's daughter all over again. All those years
she'd thought she could make her head rule her heart. Ha!
Her heart was going to have the last laugh on her. She'd
thought she'd nipped her feelings for Ray in the bud, as soon
as he'd mentioned Celeste. There was no way she could
have missed his meaning: He would be nice to her, but he
was unavailable. His heart belonged to another woman, and
no amount of dreaming was going to change that.

Oh, God! And she'd just accused him of being in league
with Frank Dane. Thank goodness he was a gentleman, despite
his gruff manner. He was too decent to take advantage of her
vulnerability. His sweetness was one of the things that had attracted her, immediately. But it seemed he could be cruel, too,
claiming he was dead, to avoid telling her straight out that he
wasn't interested in her. That would have been kinder.

Finally her tears were cried out. Head aching, Renata sat
up. She sniffled and wiped at her wet cheeks with the sleeve
of the sweatshirt she'd borrowed from Melissa. Now what?

Ray was Melissa's cousin, so as far as her friend was concerned, he was welcome to stay in her house. That was as it
should be. But she was afraid to go home yet. Afraid even
to go to her own office. She still had work to do, and she was
still in danger from whoever had chased her into the woods.
Could she face Ray after making such a fool of herself? Was
her pride worth more than her safety? She could phone Will
for protection, the way she'd originally intended, except that
fact might end up on the police activity report, to be picked
up by a crime reporter. No security system was foolproof
when people were involved.

Her face burned when she recalled how she'd accused
Ray of trying to distract her. That didn't make a bit of sense.
It was much too iffy that she would be attracted enough to a
stranger to let her guard down. How would Dane even know
where she was, to send Ray to seduce her? Besides, why

would a man as vain and arrogant as Dane send another man to seduce her in his place? How could she be so paranoid?

"Renata?" It was Ray's voice, muffled by her closed door. *"Can I come in? We've gotta talk."*

Her heart leapt and started racing. Self-preservation warned her to refuse, but her heart urged her to open the door and make peace with him This time, her head won. "Not now."

"Renata, I'm telling the truth. I was just guessing my name was on that list." His words came through the door with the clarity of the truth, but she wasn't ready to face him. When she didn't answer, he spoke again. *"Until this afternoon, I'd never seen a computer. I couldn't help you put it together because I can't hold anything. Honest, baby. Please let's talk."*

"Later. Please," she managed to choke out.

There was a long silence. Finally, she heard him sigh. *"Okay. Not now. But soon. It's important."*

"Okay," she echoed. "Soon." But she had her fingers crossed.

"Good evening, ladies." Paul's voice, coming closer. "I hate to break this up, but I don't want Gabe to get tired out."

"How can he get tired if he's just lying here, sleeping?" his mother demanded. He was wondering the same thing. *Good going, Mom!* He didn't want her and Melissa to leave. He wanted to hear his mother telling the woman he wanted to marry all about him as a baby. After all, according to his mother, he'd been perfect. And he was hoping Melissa would be inspired by his perfection to have a few babies with him.

"He might not be sleeping, Mrs. Bautista. His mind might very well be alert, and we need him to rest and put his energies into healing."

"Paul's right," Melissa said. He could listen to her sweet voice all day. "I'll go now, and let you have some time alone with Gabe."

No! His mom could go home to his dad. He and Lissa would be apart, alone all night. He needed Lissa with him.

Hell, he'd even put up with those ridiculous ghost stories if she'd stay.

"Thank you, Melissa," his mother said. "Please, come back tomorrow. Gabe and I will both enjoy your company."

"I will, Mrs. Bautista. As long as it won't upset Mr. Bautista."

"Call me Linda. And don't you worry about Gabe's father. I'll take care of my thickheaded husband."

"Okay. Good night, Gabe. I'll be back tomorrow and tell you more about Renata's new friend. Sleep well, and maybe tomorrow will be the day you wake up." She kissed his forehead, too softly, too quickly. Gently but firmly, she started to tug her hand from his. He tried to close his hand tighter around Melissa's to hold her there with him, but he was getting too tired to get results.

"You and Melissa will bring him back," Gabe heard Paul tell his mother. "The two of you have more faith than a city full of people. Don't give up."

"Never!" That was his mother. Gabe knew she meant it. She squeezed his hand and pressed his knuckles to her cheek. Then, like Lissa, she released his hand.

"I forgot to ask you. Did you put that bracelet on Gabe?"

His mother started telling Paul the history of the bracelet. Their voices faded as they walked out of his room.

He was drifting to sleep. He should save his energy for healing, but it was too tempting to dream about Lissa again. Inside, he gave in to a wicked grin. It was also fun to hear the nurses and residents panicking at the unexplained peaks and valleys in his vital signs. They'd never know why his heartbeat suddenly started to gallop. But when he finally woke up, he was going to enjoy watching Lissa blush when he told her about it.

If he concentrated, he could feel the weight of the bracelet on his right wrist. Until he could get out and buy her a diamond ring, he thought, he wanted Lissa to wear the bracelet, just like in the old days. The way his birth father, whoever he'd been, had done with his birth mother.

Chapter
Thirteen

Renata leaned her aching head against the bedroom door and waited for some sign that Ray—or whoever he really was—was no longer standing on the other side. She had to get back to the computer, had to finish compiling the information she'd been collecting, but she couldn't face the man who called himself Ray Lowell just yet. There was too much to do and too little time. If she focused her mind only on her work, she wouldn't be able to think about anything—or anyone—else. Surely, that would work. It had to. She wasn't ready to contemplate the bizarre lies he expected her to believe, and she couldn't afford to dwell on how betrayed, how hurt, she felt. Oh, God! How could she care so much, so soon? How could she let herself be influenced by foolishly romantic dreams?

Renata took a long, shallow breath and forced herself to think about the nest of snakes her investigations had uncovered. Her own feelings could wait until she settled the more urgent matter of Frank Dane's criminal activities. After several minutes, she heard music coming from the first floor and sighed with relief. Grateful for the carpeting that muffled her footsteps, she hurried to Melissa's office and closed the door.

Blessing her friend Susan's data processing expertise, Renata printed out the list of all people who had been pronounced dead by the same doctor. Then she went back to the local newspaper archives and located obituaries for as many of the names as she could find. With this list, she kept cross-referencing stories about Dane's cases, and sure enough, she found several more people who had been involved with him. None of them had lived to testify against him, yet according to their death certificates and to their obituaries, they had died of natural causes, or by accident, with an occasional suicide. It was diabolically clever, she conceded with a shudder. Because none of the deaths were considered suspicious, and none occurred too close to the others, they only looked like a crime spree when they were compiled in a list.

Finally, she steeled herself to seek information on the two names she couldn't erase from her mind: Celeste Marie Benedict and Raymond Lowell. Celeste was easy. There were stories about her debutante ball, about her charitable work, about her engagement to a promising young doctor from another prominent New England family, and finally, about her tragic death by her own hand at twenty-one.

It all would have been so innocent, she thought, except that Celeste's official fiancé had been the doctor who signed her death certificate. The same doctor who had signed Ray's original death certificate. But not, she noticed, the doctor who had amended Ray's identity from John Doe to Ray Lowell.

With her heart pounding so hard that her hands shook, Renata sifted through articles until she found the story, dated about ten months before Celeste's obituary. A young "John Doe" who had broken into the home of Mrs. Barnaby Garvey had been shot and killed by a rival burglar who had eluded the efforts of police to apprehend him. As a result of the shock, Mrs. Garvey had suffered a fatal stroke. Again, it all looked innocent. Except that Celeste had died only a few days after the name on John Doe's death certificate had been amended to Ray Lowell. And when Renata rechecked her lists, she found that Mrs. Eunice Garvey's death certificate had also been signed by Celeste's fiancé.

So many deaths. So many questions. Renata's mind whirled like a cyclone. Had Celeste figured out what her fiancé had been doing? Had she been the one to identify John Doe as Ray Lowell? Had there been a baby? What had happened to him or her? Who was the baby's father? The doctor or the real Ray Lowell were the most logical possibilities.

Each question led to others: Had that Ray Lowell been a petty criminal? Or an innocent victim? Did the rival burglar even exist? What if poor Mrs. Garvey witnessed Ray's murder? What if she'd been murdered because she could have identified his body? But why? To whom was it important? At least that answer was easy: Whoever murdered Ray Lowell didn't want anyone to know who the victim was. But what, if anything, did that have to do with Celeste? Unless Ray's killer also murdered her.

A shudder ran through her and Renata closed her eyes against the nightmare she'd uncovered. But she had to press on. Later, she'd allow herself the luxury of giving in to her emotions.

With a sigh, she opened her eyes and focused on the computer monitor. More questions. How did Frank Dane figure in the deaths of Ray Lowell and Celeste Benedict? Or did he? *That* Ray seemed to be the first in a horrific string of cleverly concealed murders, but *this* Ray didn't seem to think Frank Dane had murdered him. Was that true? Could Dane be behind only some of the other deaths certified by the same doctor, the ones that seemed to have logical connections to his arrest history?

If so, who had murdered Ray, Celeste, and Mrs. Garvey? The doctor? Ray—or whoever was downstairs listening to a Bryan Adams CD—had said Frank Dane had a knack for finding people's vulnerabilities. Was murder the hold he had on this doctor? Was that how *he* had been getting away with murder? With shaking hands, Renata flipped through the New Harbour phone book. Her stomach clenched at her next chilling discovery. The doctor was still practicing. What irony! With one hand, he could be saving lives; with the other, he was taking them.

She was probably next.

In a sudden wave of paranoia, Renata made a half-dozen copies of her discoveries on diskettes to hide in various places throughout Melissa's house. She even placed two in envelopes, addressing one to herself at her office, and another to her grandmother's lawyer, to be examined in the event of her own sudden death. Considering that possibility made her shake so badly she almost couldn't write. But she had to be practical. Clearly, she was dealing with people who took no prisoners. If anything happened to her, she wanted to make sure that the truth would come out somehow.

With one of the labeled computer disks in her hand, she peeked out the door of the office. The hallway was dark and silent. Ray must have finished listening to music, and Melissa probably wasn't home from the hospital yet. It was a perfect opportunity to hide the last disk. Renata flipped the switch, lighting the long hallway. Squinting, she tried vainly to focus on the details of the painting Melissa had hung on the far wall, then gave up. She needed her glasses to see clearly farther than the length of her arms. Since crawling through Mel's basement window Friday night, she really hadn't missed them, because she'd been asleep or resting most of the time.

But now that she was up and around, now that she understood the kind of danger she could be in, she felt vulnerable not being able to see well. Today, she had phoned her optometrist and ordered a duplicate pair of glasses. No one would have any reason to suspect anything if Melissa picked up a pair of glasses. Thank goodness Mel was so new in town that almost no one knew they were friends.

Halfway down the stairs, she heard a noise in the living room and froze. Was that Ray or Mel? Or—?

Music poured out of the speakers and Renata felt as if the world had suddenly begun spinning the wrong way. Oh, God! That song! The song she heard in her dreams. The song she could never quite remember. The music swelled and swirled around her as a man's sweetly earnest voice sang the opening words of "Earth Angel," a song from the fifties. Old-fashioned and romantic, it was a real love song. A slow-dance song. From the first time she'd heard it on an oldies station years ago, it always made her feel little wistful, wondering if she'd ever be loved like that.

The wave of *déjà vu* that washed over her was like nothing she'd ever felt before. Closing her eyes against sudden dizziness only intensified the sensations. She knew she was standing on the stairs, but she felt as if she were dancing to this very song. Her dream lover was holding her close and singing softly to the words of the song, leading her in a lovers' dance.

It couldn't be a real memory. It just *seemed* real. That was what people said about *déjà vu*. It wasn't a memory, it was a moment, a sight, a sound, an action that *resembled* some memory.

But the longer the song played, the clearer the image in her mind that she was dancing to the dreamy tune, her senses remembering her dream lover. With her eyes closed, she felt the heat of his embrace, the power of his aroused body, the melting hunger of her own desire. With her eyes closed, she became the woman in love with the familiar stranger in her dreams. The man who looked like Ray, the man in love with the woman she became in her dreams.

Oh, God! It was all so confusing. She didn't know who Ray was, this man who claimed to have died nearly four decades ago, who expected her to believe he was a ghost. She didn't believe in ghosts. Did she dare believe in her dreams? If she did, then who was she? With her eyes open, she knew exactly who she was. With them closed, when she dreamed, she fell under the hypnotic, romantic spell of this song, as if it had some special resonance she didn't understand on a conscious level.

The song ended, and Renata opened her eyes to face reality. Shrugging off her odd mood, Renata started walking down the stairs again, pondering where to hide the disk. As she reached the bottom landing, she heard "Earth Angel" starting again, casting its romantic spell again, wrapping her heart in yearning. It was just the song, she told herself, frantically trying to resist its power to make her dream. It was the kind of song that made anyone want to be in love.

But she couldn't lie to herself. The song was only a small part of something mysterious and powerful that she didn't understand. As if there were an invisible cord leading her, drawing her, she found herself walking into the twilight-shadowed living room. She knew he would be waiting there, the man who called himself Ray Lowell. He would be waiting—for her? Or the woman she dreamed herself to be?

She knew she should turn and hurry away. She knew she wouldn't. She couldn't. Listening to that song, she finally, suddenly felt the pieces of the puzzle falling into place, fitting so neatly, so perfectly, that there was no room left for doubt. She knew who Ray was. She knew who she was. And she now knew exactly what to believe: the unbelievable.

Ray watched Renata walk toward him. She had a dazed look on her face, like she didn't know where she was. The song was almost over when she reached the middle of the room. She stopped about a foot from him and looked up into his eyes. They were so close that her energy reached out to join with his, crackling and surging between them.

Her lips curved into a smile that sent a jolt of need straight into him. "I keep hearing this song in my dreams," she said softly, her voice slightly husky, the sound stroking him like fingertips on his bare skin.

Ray shivered in the heat and felt himself tingling and getting hard and heavy at the thought of her touching him. All he could do was stare into her dark eyes, too stunned to answer.

She tipped her head to one side. "It's over."

"It'll start again," he managed to choke out. Once he'd gotten the hang of that fancy stereo system of Melissa's, with the two hundred CDs inside listed electronically, he'd been able to use his energy to play whatever he wanted. He'd found some oldies on CD earlier, and the title of this one special song had practically jumped up and bit him. He'd caught himself smiling in anticipation while he cued

the CD, but the instant the first notes played a vision sprang into his head that erased his smile.

Clear as day, he could see himself listening to the Penguins singing "Earth Angel" on his old transistor radio, and thinking about Celeste, about how much he loved her. And then, he'd turned toward the front door and seen the face of his killer. Closing his eyes, he tried to force his mind to show him the face again. No matter how he concentrated, the identity of his murderer stayed buried.

"Earth Angel" continued to play. Memories of how he and Celeste had danced to this song, called it "their" song, had started the familiar ache in his heart. Then he'd sensed Renata coming down the stairs, and opened his eyes. Suddenly, the pain of losing Celeste turned into something very different, something so sweet and fragile that it scared him to reach for it. Now, looking into Renata's eyes, he understood the electricity between them, finally understood that his attraction to Renata wasn't a betrayal of Celeste.

The song started again. She smiled. Her lashes drifted downward. When she started swaying to the backbeat, the force of the energy between them pulled at him to sway with her, like a magnet he couldn't resist. Didn't want to resist. He closed his eyes, too, letting himself tune into her with his heart, mind, and soul. Renata's every heartbeat, every breath, drew them closer, until there was barely room for a sigh to squeeze between them. He felt the tingling, hot sting of contact and opened his eyes.

She smiled, a slow, sweet smile, then opened her eyes and looked straight into his. And just like that afternoon in the factory parking lot, when he's first fallen for Celeste like a ton of bricks, he knew he'd crossed an invisible point of no return.

He had a feeling that Renata was already a step ahead of him.

Slowly, he bent his head toward hers. Anything more than this explosion of feelings between them should be impossible, but he couldn't stop himself. Renata closed her eyes again. Energy flowed around her, like a halo around the moon. She didn't seem to notice it. She was waiting for his kiss. At the last second, he hesitated.

"I always loved this song," she murmured. "Would you dance with me?"

Her words—the words Celeste had said to him that first night—stunned him. *"Dance?"*

With her eyes shut and her face tipped up toward his, she smiled again. "I want to dance, I want to touch the stars. I want to do all the things I've never done. Now, with you."

It was a good thing, he decided, Renata had her eyes shut. He had a feeling his expression was like an open book. Chapter one was confusion and surprise. Chapter two was raw hunger. The last chapter was going to be regret, because neither of them was going to get their wishes.

"Why now?"

"Why now?" she echoed softly. "Because I've been waiting an eternity for you. And if we wait any longer, we might never have this chance again."

Her words disturbed him. *"What do you mean?"* Stupid question. He already knew the answer. He was living . . . no, *dying* proof of the answer. But he had to be sure she understood, too.

Her eyes opened and focused on his. Something in her expression shook him, but he couldn't put a name to it. "I mean, I have definitely opened a bag of snakes, and one of them probably knows it. I don't intend to do anything heroic and stupid, but I have a job to do. And that means I'll be wearing a target."

It wasn't just what she was saying that tightened the knots inside him. It was the accepting way she said it. He'd lost her once. He wasn't going to stand for it again, damn it! No matter what it cost him, he wasn't going to leave her unprotected this time.

"You'll get police protection, or I won't let you leave this house!"

Renata gave him a sweet smile. "I will, I promise. But not yet. First, I want to dance with you." She lifted her arms. It was an invitation to reach for her. His arms moved, like they had a will of their own. Just in time, he stopped himself. He

could reach for her all he wanted, but he could never hold
her. The damn song finally came to an end.

"Baby, we have to talk," he said in the silence.

She just kept smiling at him, like she knew she could
wear him down without saying a word. Why not? She always had before. Without warning, "Earth Angel" started
playing again. Damn! He'd thought he was so clever to
make the CD player do tricks. Looked like he'd outsmarted
himself.

"Talk later. Dance with me first," she murmured, closing
her eyes again. "This is our song. Don't you remember?"

Remember? Even death couldn't steal that memory!
"Earth Angel" had been playing on his tinny old transistor
radio the first time he'd held her in his arms and danced
close and slow with her. Dancing had been Celeste's idea.
He'd refused at first. A deserted parking lot was no place for
romance.

He'd wanted to take her someplace special, someplace
where people wore nice clothes and knew which fork to use.
He'd buy her a fancy dinner, dance to a band he could slip a
few bucks to play a favorite song. But that kind of date took
money. Money she told him she didn't care about. Instead,
they'd ridden his old Indian Chief motorcycle to the back
parking lot, behind her family's factory. Celeste had taken
his transistor out of his jacket pocket, turned it on and
stepped into his arms before he had a chance to wonder if
she was going to let him kiss her good night. And to the
strains of "Earth Angel," she'd murmured. "This will be our
song from now on. Whenever we hear it, we'll remember
the first time we danced."

It had also been the first time they'd made love. He would
have waited, given her time to realize what kind of mistake
she could be making. But it wasn't so easy to say *no* to Celeste. He'd been her first. She'd been his last.

But that was before someone had stepped in and separated them forever. If he didn't talk fast, she was going to
find herself hugging thin air. *"Renata—"*

She moved too fast for him, her arms looping around his
neck, her body fitting to his. His reaction came from pure

shock, and pure instinct. He wrapped his arms around her and looked down into her face. Her eyes were closed, her expression dreamy. It was always like that when they'd danced. She'd press right up close, turning him on until he could hardly stand. They'd dance like that, hardly moving, deliberately forcing themselves to wait as long as possible. And when they couldn't wait any longer, they'd make love like storm clouds coming together, all lightning and trembling and release.

It was happening again, here and now. Some kind of force, like static electricity, shimmered and spiraled around them. He could almost *feel* Renata against him like that. No, he *could* feel her! Could she feel him? Or was he still a trick with smoke and mirrors? He tensed. No point in hoping for the impossible. But Renata sure moved like she could feel him. Her arms locked around his neck. Her small, high breasts pressed against his chest like he was solid. Her belly cradled him. Oh, man, he sure *felt* solid!

Ray didn't know what was happening to him, to them. They were wrapped in that invisible, crackling force field. When he dipped his head to touch her lips with his, he didn't expect to feel anything. But he did. He felt the soft heat of her lips on his.

Renata or Celeste? Memory or reality? Maybe both. He was in love and it was wonderful! The energy swirling around them pulsed and sizzled. He tightened his hold, drawing her lower body against his and feeling his body respond. Just before he closed his own eyes, he saw the shimmering, colorless light around them turning white with gold sparks.

He knew that what was happening was impossible, but he didn't care anymore. She moaned softly and opened her mouth to him. At any second, the fantasy was going to disappear into a puff of smoke, so he accepted her invitation to deepen the kiss. The crackling and snapping of that electric force wrapped around them got louder and louder, the longer and deeper they kissed. She clung tighter. Her tongue met his. He stopped trying to think of her as Renata, stopped trying to hang on to the little bit of reason he had left.

The force around them got hotter with every thrust of his tongue, every stroke of hers. It seemed to be taking its strength from them, but he didn't feel weaker. If anything, he felt like he could move mountains and hold the sun back from setting. He heard her whimpering, but it sounded very far away.

The energy around them started changing. The heat and noise increased. Now, he felt like he was being squeezed, like they were being crushed by the roaring force around them. He should protect her from whatever this was. *Could* he protect her? Hell, he didn't even know what it was or what it meant. But if whatever it was could harm her, it would have to get past him first.

The roaring and the pressure got even more intense. Now she was trembling. Ray broke the kiss and held her against him, trying to calm her. She opened her eyes and looked straight into his. Sparks flashed around them. She stroked his cheek with her cool fingers and smiled. He saw her lips moving. The storm of energy drowned the sound of her words, but he felt her say, "I love you."

Renata felt as if she'd stepped out of herself and into a lightning storm. She clung to Ray, drank in the sweetness of his kisses, and gave herself to the blissfully familiar sensations swirling through her. She'd waited so long to be in his arms again! A lifetime, and more, had separated them. Joy swelled her heart, even as his touch sent her pulse racing.

"I love you!" she repeated when he broke the kiss. This time, she didn't have to shout the words. The roaring of the energy swirling around them had gradually dimmed to a soft hum.

Ray cupped her face in his hands. Light shimmered around them, teasing her skin with heated tingles. She smiled up at him, smiled at the amazement in his eyes. He seemed to be having trouble grasping this sudden turn of events. She didn't blame him for that. The logical part of her mind was tied in knots, trying to work this out. Her heart, however, understood perfectly.

"What happened?" Ray asked. *"Was it the song?"* She nodded. *"Are you . . . ? Were you . . . ? How . . . ?"* She laughed at his confusion. He gave her a rueful grin. *"Hey, don't laugh at me. I thought I was the one with the weird confession. I've been trying to tell you for days that I'm . . . I'm . . ."* He huffed, but he couldn't get out the word.

She felt tenderness for him welling up inside her. "I know," she told him. "I couldn't believe it until I heard the song. Then it all came back to me. Oh, Ray! I don't know how it happened. I was so afraid we'd never find each other again."

He kissed her gently, then gazed at her with an eternity of sadness in his beautiful blue eyes. *"We still have one little problem, baby."*

His meaning was all too clear. Some of the joy seeped out of her heart. "I don't know if I can bear losing you again," she said, fighting back tears.

He pulled her close again, cradling her head against his shoulder, rocking her in time to the music. *"How much do you remember?"* he murmured into her hair.

She considered. "Feelings. I remember feelings. Everything else is hazy, like a dream you can't quite remember, except in bits and pieces. But I remember loving you. And I remember losing you. And I remember—"

"Hi, guys! I'm home!" Melissa called from the foyer. She started to move away from Ray. He tightened his hold. "You wouldn't believe—" Melissa gasped.

Feeling like a teenager caught necking, Renata met her friend's stunned eyes and smiled sheepishly.

"Oh, my God! What . . . ? I mean, how . . . ? Renata?"

Renata couldn't hold back the sputter of laughter that Melissa's reaction caused. Even Ray grinned, and she understood he was feeling far from lighthearted at that moment. They needed to talk, to assess the situation, to figure out how much time they might have left. Any interruption could be stealing precious seconds they couldn't afford to lose.

But she loved Melissa like the sister she'd never had, and since her friend had brought them together again, albeit accidentally, she couldn't find it in her heart to tell Mel to leave them alone. Not yet, anyway. Besides, they owed Melissa the truth.

"What won't we believe?" Renata asked.

Lucky wound himself around Melissa's ankles. She lifted him and leaned against the doorframe. "From the looks of things, you two would probably believe almost anything," Mel said dryly.

"We'll take turns. You first."

"Gabe is starting to respond! He squeezed my hand, and then he squeezed his mother's hand. Paul says he could wake up any time." Tears filled Melissa's eyes.

"Oh, Mel! That's wonderful!" Renata cried. Tears misted her own eyes.

"Yeah, that's great," Ray added, suspiciously gruff-sounding.

Mel nodded. "I got caught visiting by his mother. She was furious at first. But we worked out a truce, for Gabe's sake. We both love him. She told me a little about how she adopted him. It's a really sad story. Sort of like *Romeo and Juliet.*" Melissa gave them a quick, rueful smile. "Or like Gabe and me." She nuzzled Lucky, who purred loudly enough to be audible across the room. "Okay, your turn. What's going on here?"

"It's a long story," Renata warned.

"Fine. I'm going to pour us some white wine, and then you can tell me your long story."

Melissa carried Lucky out of the living room. Renata could hear her murmuring to him about his choice of kitty foods. She smiled up at Ray, then stopped smiling and closed her eyes for his kiss.

Heat and energy swirled around her, enveloping her, changing her. She felt herself melting into him. His mouth settled over hers, his tongue stroking the sensitive skin of her lips, lighting tiny fires that skittered along her nerves, all the way to her breasts, all the way to the center of her lower belly. Only the sound of Melissa clearing her throat stopped her from sinking to the carpet and drawing Ray down with her.

Drawing a shaky breath, she stepped back, out of the

heated circle of Ray's arms, back to herself again. When she sat on the sofa, he settled beside her. She tried not to notice that the cushion didn't sink under him. Melissa carried two wineglasses, with a bag of gourmet vegetable chips in the crook of one arm. Lucky trotted behind her, licking his chops. After Mel gave Renata her wineglass and sat on the overstuffed chair, Lucky hopped onto the coffee table. He stepped delicately into the wicker bowl in the center, and curled up, nose tucked under his tail, and closed his eyes.

"Okay," Melissa prompted. "The best place to start a long story is probably at the beginning."

Renata looked into Ray's eyes. He put his hand over hers, brushing her skin with gentle sparks. "Unfortunately, neither of us remembers the beginning," she told her friend. "At least, not very clearly."

"That's okay," Mel said. "Ray gave me a thumbnail sketch the night he walked through my upstairs wall."

It took a moment for Renata to realize what Melissa meant. When she did, she felt betrayed. Melissa *knew!* She'd known about Ray all along. All this time, Melissa knew, and didn't tell her. Didn't even *try* to tell her. How could her best friend let her make a fool of herself without stepping in? Melissa had even *lied* to her, claiming Ray was her cousin.

"Renata, I'm sorry," Mel blurted. "I wanted to tell you, but at first, you were so disoriented, and I was so upset about Gabe. And then, I figured you'd notice, but you didn't. I couldn't decide if it was because you're so nearsighted, or because Ray seemed more . . ." She shrugged. "More substantial."

The hurt and anger dissolved when Renata realized Melissa was right. And she knew that no words would have convinced her about Ray. What rational person in this day and age would believe anyone who claimed that one of their houseguests was a ghost? The only way she could recognize the truth was to see it herself, if not with her eyes, then with her heart. And that she had done.

"Blame it on me," Ray offered gently. She met his troubled gaze. *"I made Melissa promise she wouldn't tell you.*

You were kinda fragile at first. And after that, you just sorta accepted me." She lifted a challenging brow. He gave her a crooked grin. *"Okay, I made an effort not to let you figure it out before I was ready to tell you. I sure as hell didn't expect you to find my name on that list with Celeste's."*

Mel's eyes brightened. "What? What list? What did you find? Oh, Ray! I'm sorry. I've been so tied up in knots over Gabe, I never got around to checking the newspaper and town records."

Ray smiled and shook his head. *"No problem. Renata did some magic tricks on your computer, and pulled a couple of rabbits out of a hat."*

Melissa sat up straighter. Renata wrinkled her nose. "More like a couple of bottomfeeders," she corrected. Watching her friend carefully, she said, "Okay, since you've already accepted that Ray Lowell is a . . . a ghost, I'll give the rest of it to you straight. Ray and I found Celeste, alive and well."

Melissa's jaw dropped. "How? Where?"

"Here." Renata smiled at Mel's frown. "He played 'Earth Angel,' the song we danced to the first time we met." She looked up at Ray, then smiled at Melissa. "The night in nineteen sixty that we became lovers."

Renata watched her friend struggling to process her words. Mel's eyes grew wide and she gasped. "You?" she croaked.

Renata nodded. "Me."

Chapter Fourteen

Melissa pulled the quilt up over her shoulders, but she doubted very much she'd fall asleep easily. Her mind was reeling from her conversation with Ray and Renata. Or Celeste? It was very confusing. Her best friend was convinced she and the resident ghost had been lovers in a previous life. And that they'd both been murdered back in the early sixties.

Well, if she could accept Ray's claim to being a ghost, and Renata's theory about the murders and cover-ups connected to Frank Dane, it was hardly a stretch of imagination to accept the rest of it. Was it any less believable than one of her former clients claiming he'd missed performing at a contracted rock concert because he'd dreamed he'd already been there?

Drifting toward sleep, her thoughts played over and over, until she was no longer aware of anything more than the yearning in her heart, the barely checked panic in her mind. She wished Gabe would hurry up and wake from his coma. She wished there really was something she could do to bring him back, instead of waiting helplessly. He was showing signs of progress, but Paul had warned her, the longer he was like this, the worse his chances. She didn't know how she could bear losing him now, after only just finding him.

"Lissa?"

She didn't know if she was awake or dreaming. Gabe's whisper sounded so real, but he couldn't be there with her when he was lying in a hospital bed in a coma. She must be dreaming, then. Resolutely, she kept her eyes closed and hugged the quilt around herself, willing herself to slip further into sleep. If she was dreaming Gabe was with her, she didn't want the dream to end.

"Lissa, honey, move over and make room for me," Gabe murmured. "It's cold in here, and I know you're warm in there." Melissa squeezed her eyes closed, but just in case, she released her grip on the quilt and slid toward the middle of the bed. Even when she felt the mattress give, as if under someone's weight, she didn't open her eyes. If she was dreaming, she wouldn't be able to open them. If she wasn't, if Gabe was there with her, opening her eyes wouldn't matter. The truth was, she was afraid she was dreaming, and she really didn't want to know.

"You know something?" he said, drawing her into his arms. "We've never spent a night together in a real bed. Now that I'm here, I've got some great ideas how we can spend the time, and none of them have anything to do with sleep."

She shivered. "Gabe?"

"Yeah?" His gravelly voice caressed her, just as his large, warm hands were doing.

When he slid his hand under her nightgown and cupped her breast, she had trouble concentrating on her thoughts. "Are you really here? Are you real?" she whispered, hardly daring to believe, desperately afraid not to believe.

He stroked her skin in teasing circles. "As real as you want me to be." He bent and pressed his lips to her throat, where her pulse raced wildly.

She'd never wanted anything more in her life.

Alone at last, Ray thought after Melissa went upstairs, *and not a second too soon. Thirty-six years is a hell of a long time to wait.* He looked into Renata's dark eyes, wondering what she was thinking. She gave him a funny little smile.

"Are you looking for Celeste?" she asked.

"I don't know. Does it matter?"

"No. What matters is, somehow, we're together again."

Yeah, he thought, *but for how long? There has to be a catch.* Sooner or later, something had to happen. He didn't want to know now. Didn't even want to think of the questions. Not yet. All he wanted was the woman he loved, whatever name she had now, in his arms.

She held her hand out to him. No mistaking the meaning in her eyes now. He stood up and touched her fingertips with his, expecting the usual shocks. It was different this time. Still electric, but softer. Gentler. More like the way he remembered her touch could be. She felt it, too, his touch like it used to be. He could tell by the way her eyes went wide, then darkened.

"It'll be okay," he told her, all choked up, having trouble with his voice. He still could hardly believe that after all this time, they were together.

She swallowed, then nodded. He let his fingertips trail from her cheek to her neck. Watched her pulse jump under her skin. Felt her breath catch in her throat. So delicate. It was a good thing that weird energy thing that kept happening between them had gone tame. He'd never forgive himself if his touch hurt her.

She closed her eyes and tipped her head back. Ray figured he could take an extra minute to sample what she was offering. He closed the distance between them and bent to press his lips to the hollow of her throat. Her pulse surged through him, shaking him, binding him to her. When he stepped back, she sighed.

"Oh, Ray!" Her whisper was like a summer breeze at midnight. "Let's go upstairs."

It was the longest walk he could remember taking. He wanted to hurry, to float through the ceiling and floor, drift through the walls, carry her in his arms. He had to float and drift alone, and he didn't want to be away from her for a second. No way he could carry her, though. Once upon a time, he'd imagined carrying her across the threshold of some little house, after they eloped. Looked like he'd have to settle for whatever he could get, and forget dreams like that.

Ray walked beside her up the stairs, wishing he could read her mind. Was she nervous? Hell, *he* was! He was thirty-six years out of practice! When he'd met Celeste, he'd had plenty of the right kind of experience. Even so, she'd surprised the hell out of him. He'd been expecting her to act cool, to keep her distance, maybe to use the excuse that she was only slumming. Nothing in his wildest days had prepared him for the heat, the hunger, the innocence and eagerness he'd found in Celeste. She'd made him crazy with need, refused to let him stop until he couldn't have to save his life. It was like pouring gasoline on a bonfire. The flesh and the spirit had both been very willing.

At least back then, he'd known what to do. Things were a little different, now. *He* was different, that was for damn sure! He still knew how to make love, but what if he couldn't . . . ? Dead or alive, that was a nightmare no guy wanted to face. And he wouldn't know until it was too late.

She opened the door to the guest room she'd been using. She smiled at him, and he followed her inside. He watched her glance at the bed and swallow. Yeah, she was nervous. He'd try to do what he could to make this right for her . . . *if* he could figure out what he could do. *Instructions would sure be useful right about now,* he thought. Maybe this was his punishment for not reading repair manuals until he'd gotten himself in trouble.

When her fingers started working at the buttons of the big shirt she wore, Ray forgot about motorcycles. The room was pretty dark, but he could see her clearly. Nervous. Trusting. Probably confused about what was happening between them. Well, hell, so was he! Her eyes were huge. He could sense her heartbeat, her breathing, the tremors that ran over her skin and made her hands shake.

"I want to undress you, baby, but I can't," he murmured. *"Wish I could, but I can just about pick up a silk scarf or a feather."* Her soft "Oh" came out like a sigh. *"Close your*

eyes and pretend it's me taking off your clothes. In between kisses, I'm unbuttoning your shirt, one button at a time. Can you feel me touching your skin under the shirt? I can. My hands are a little rough. Your skin's so hot, and soft, like silk."

He'd never been much of a talker when he was making love, but right now, it was the best he could do. He didn't know where the words were coming from, but he could see the effect they were having on her. With her eyes closed, her lips parted, she undid her shirt. He heard her breath catch when he described touching her. It was almost as if she could feel him doing everything he was saying. His own fingers tingled as if he really was touching her. If this was the best he could do, he didn't feel like stopping now.

"You're not wearing a bra, are you?" She shook her head. He grinned. *"I like that. I'm teasing you now, stroking your breasts under the shirt. Your nipples are hard, aren't they? You want me to touch them, don't you?"* Her gasp gave him her answer. He could imagine the feel of those tight buds under his rough fingertips. *"I want to see your breasts. Do you want me to kiss them?"*

Renata swayed a little as she opened the shirt and let it slide down her arms to the floor. He caught himself before his jaw dropped. She was so beautiful! Bare from the waist up, she was rounded and perfect and her skin was creamy. She practically glowed, like a pearl. Like moonlight. The gray pants she still wore fit like a second skin. Her waist was tiny, her belly flat, her hips curved above slim legs that he wanted to feel wrapped around his back. It was his turn to tremble. How could she be real?

"Can you feel my mouth on your breasts?" he asked in a hoarse whisper. Her answer was a cross between *yes* and a gasp. *"I'm using my tongue and teeth to tease your nipples. Does it feel good?"* Her head tipped back and she arched her breasts toward him. She wasn't alone in her reactions. His voice was getting more and more hoarse. *"My tongue is hot and wet. You feel what I'm doing all over, don't you?"*

"Oh! Ray, that was . . ." Eyes still closed, she stopped and shook her head.

"Amazing?" he suggested, maybe a little too smug about it.

She blinked her eyes open and gave him a dazed look. "Well, I think I finally understand the appeal of phone sex," she murmured. With her thumbs hooked in the waistband of the pants, she gave him a shy smile. "What about you?" she said in a husky whisper.

What about . . . ? Aw, hell! He looked down at his leather jacket, his jeans, his white T-shirt. The clothes he'd been murdered in. No bloodstains, at least. But no matter how he tried, and he'd tried a whole bunch of times already, he couldn't take them off. They were part of whatever he was, just like they used to be part of who he was. Damn, this was a big mistake. He never should have let things get this far. Now, he didn't know how to go forward or backward. Whatever he did was going to let her down. Again.

The weightless clothes he wore felt like a straightjacket. It was like a message telling him it was useless to pretend he was anything more than a ghost. A reminder that he was only supposed to find Celeste and solve his own murder. He was halfway there. What happened after that was anybody's guess.

He shrugged. *"Would you believe I'm shy?"*

She gave a tiny laugh that sounded almost like one of Lucky's sneezes and shook her head. But then she gave him a long, serious look. "This isn't going to work, is it?" He heard tears behind her voice.

"Yeah, damn it! It's going to work. Close your eyes and keep taking your clothes off. I'll think of something," he sort of growled at her. She blinked. He swore. *"Sorry, baby. What I meant was, never mind about me."*

"But that's not fair."

"Life's not fair." Neither is death. *"You and I sure know that by now. I want to make love to you so bad I could explode, but it isn't gonna happen like this. So get into that bed and let me love you in our imaginations."* He gave her a smile he could feel slipping. *"We never spent a whole night in bed together, did we? Here's our chance."*

She didn't answer, just looked at him a little longer. What

was she thinking? Was she changing her mind? No, she was starting to smile. She closed her eyes again, and started pushing those skintight pants down a couple of inches. A couple more inches. And a couple more. Then she stopped, gave him a sly little smile, and turned her back. If he'd had a heart, it would have been pounding, he thought, watching the pants slide down her legs. She kicked them into the corner and stood there looking at him over her shoulder, letting him admire her perfect little behind. No complaints from him on that score.

She turned around and smiled while he gawked. She was so beautiful. Like a perfect sunset. One of those goddesses carved in marble. Her pale nipples tightened under his stare. All of her was pale and smooth, and her hair and the curls at the top of her thighs were dark and silky. The way she offered herself so sweetly made him hot and hard.

He closed his eyes, searching for Celeste in his heart, and found Renata there instead. He expected guilt. Instead, a weight lifted from his soul. He wasn't betraying Celeste by making love to Renata, because Celeste's love for him lived in Renata.

When Renata moved to the bed, he waited for her to draw the quilt down and slide toward the middle, leaving room for him. Then she smiled and patted the space beside her, inviting him. It was the kind of thing a wife would do, he thought. No, damn it, life wasn't fair. Right now, all he could do, all they could do together, was close their eyes and make believe.

One thing he'd learned about being dead: it was a lot like life. You had to appreciate whatever unexpected gifts came your way, because you couldn't predict what might happen next. Celeste's love, now Renata's, was a gift like that. Perfect and precious. All he had to give her in return was his own love. It was a little tarnished, but it was still strong.

He stepped toward the bed and looked down into her eyes. *"Whatever happens, I love you."* A tear slid down her cheek and fell just over her heart. *"Oh, baby, don't cry."*

He settled beside her and stretched out. With his fingertip, he touched the tiny teardrop that glistened on her skin. The sparks that shimmered and pulsed between them seemed to draw strength from her heart. He felt a current surging through him. Renata felt it, too, he was sure. Her eyes were wide and nearly black, her breathing shallow.

"Close your eyes, sweetheart," he told her. *"Imagine I'm holding you. Who knows what might happen if I keep talking?"*

She closed her eyes and moved into his arms. The heat between them got so intense, he was sure they were going to set the bed on fire. Suddenly his clothes seemed to have disappeared. Renata gasped. Was she sharing this part of his fantasy? He opened one eye to see her face, and discovered he was still dressed. As soon as he squeezed his eyes shut again, he was buck naked and holding a warm armful of equally naked woman. So far, so good.

He found her mouth with his, and kissed her until they were both breathless. Funny that with his eyes closed, making believe like this, he was breathing, his heart was pounding, his . . . Well, he was definitely ready to make love. He could feel Renata's sleek skin against his rougher hide, everywhere they touched. He could even feel the wet heat of her mouth when she parted her lips for his tongue.

Only two things he couldn't do: taste her and smell her. Must be the price of this gift, he decided, covering one small, perfect breast with his hand, and worth the price.

She moaned softly and arched into his hand. Her nipple beaded under his touch. He lowered his head and captured the peak of her other with his mouth. Her pulse surged through him. He felt that he was sharing what she felt. Her legs tangled with his, offering, teasing, caressing. Her fingers closed on his upper arms, then tightened when his hand slid up the inside of one of her thighs. He drew circles and patterns on her skin while he suckled her breast. The sounds of her soft cries sent lightning bolts of desire through him. He slid his caressing fingers past soft curls, finding her hot and slick and ready.

Her hand closed around him, and he didn't care if it was all in his imagination. He had to lift his head from her breasts and grit his teeth when she stroked him. Pressing himself into her palm, letting her feel how ready he was, he fought to hold back and let her set the pace. There was no way of knowing how long he could last, and he didn't want to leave her behind. He stroked the sensitive inner folds that held the key to her pleasure. Her gasp told him he still remembered what he was doing.

"I can't believe this is real," she murmured into his neck.

The ache in his loins was definitely not an illusion. But who knew how long this could last? He didn't want to waste time talking now. Not when they were so close . . .

Gabe held Lissa close and stroked her hair, thinking about what was happening. Damned if he understood how it worked, but he knew he was in the Garvey house, with her, not in the hospital. That was his body, lying alone hooked up to monitors. But his spirit—that whatever-it-was that made him who he was inside—that was here, with the woman he loved. Now was all that counted anyway. Later might not ever happen.

Lissa's fingers traced patterns on his chest. He didn't need the light on, didn't have to look, to picture how pale and fine-boned her hands were against his skin. His fingers closed around her wrist, reminding him.

"Lissa, remember I told you about the ID bracelet my birth mother left for me?"

"The one with the initials scratched out?"

"Yep. The one that belonged to the guy who fathered me, then took off and left his girlfriend pregnant."

She lifted her head to meet his eyes. "That really bothers you, doesn't it?"

"Yeah. Guess it serves me right for being so straight-laced and class-conscious. Turns out I'm the bastard son of a rich banking heiress who committed suicide, and some guy with a Houdini complex."

"Your mother doesn't believe she committed suicide."

"My mother believes the best of everyone."

"What if she's right?"

"If she's right, we've got a very old unsolved murder to tackle when I wake up."

"Maybe more than one."

Gabe listened to Lissa describing Renata's findings, ready to believe her until she brought up the ghost again. Then he placed one index finger over her lips.

"Enough about that stuff," he told her, ignoring the way her green eyes flashed at him. "We're way off the track here. I mentioned the ID bracelet because I want you to wear it until I wake up. Then we'll go shopping for a ring."

She sat up and gaped at him. "Ring?"

He grinned at her stunned expression. "Yeah. The engagement type." She looked as if she didn't believe him. "We're not kids anymore, Lissa. I want to marry you, and if our parents don't like it, that's too bad. Between them, they came close to ruining our lives. At least, our fathers did."

The shake of her head told him she didn't know the whole story. Not so surprising. His father and hers weren't about to confess to their involvement. They both still thought they'd been justified, each one thinking they could force their children to find other, more suitable mates. When that never happened, it was easier for both fathers to blame each other for the unforeseen results than to admit they'd been wrong in the first place. But he'd learned that the two mothers understood that no amount of interference could manipulate love into disappearing. Not when it was meant to be, the way theirs was.

"My mother's been spending hours with me," he explained, "telling me everything about our family, going back about a century to Portugal, and a lot of other things she's had on her mind for years."

Lissa nodded. "Paul told us both to keep talking to you."

"I suspect Mom figured I couldn't hear her, 'cause she's unloaded all sorts of stuff. My adoption. And Dad's part in our separation. Seems he sent back some letters you wrote to me."

"*He* did?" She clapped one slender hand over her mouth and peered at him over it, her eyes wide.

"Yeah. What did you think? That *I* sent them back?" He'd been a cop long enough to recognize guilt when he saw it. "You did, didn't you? Oh, Lissa, I thought you trusted me."

She brought her hand down and made it into a fist. "How was I supposed to know? I was so hurt when they came back. It was bad enough being yanked away from you and sent to that private school. My father made me promise not to contact you until I graduated, or he would tell my mother we'd been lovers. She was sick then, and he knew I wouldn't do anything to upset her. But when the letters came back, I thought you didn't care anymore."

"I didn't get your letters," he pointed out. When she opened her mouth to speak again, he held up his hand, traffic-cop style. "It's gonna be interesting married to a lawyer. I better brush up on my debating skills," he teased. "When do you want to tie the knot?"

She touched his cheek and he saw tears glazing her eyes. "As soon as you can stand long enough to say your vows," she told him.

Drawing her down into his arms again, he said, "Guess that means I better get my butt outta that hospital so we can start making up some of this lost time."

He fumbled with the catch of the ID bracelet, finally getting it open, and slid it off his wrist. As he rolled Lissa over onto her back, he clasped the steel links around her wrist.

"There. Just like they used to do it back in the sixties. You're mine, and I'm yours," he told her. "Now it's official."

Like father, like son after all, he thought as he bent to kiss Lissa.

Ray ran his hands over the sensitive skin of her back, trailing tiny sparks that made her tingle. Renata risked opening her eyes, and felt only heat sliding along her skin. She closed her eyes and arched into Ray's touch, shuddering at the tightening inside her. It was like dreaming, yet being awake.

Her need to understand what was happening dissolved when one of his hands slid around to cup her breast. His thumb stroked her already taut nipple, sending currents of arousal to the heated part of her that ached for his touch. Then he bent over her and his lips closed over her breast, suckling her. She caressed his shoulders, unable to reach more of him, and a tiny cry of both pleasure and impatience escaped her.

When Ray lifted his head, the cool air on her kiss-moistened nipple made it tighten, heightening her pleasure. She tangled her legs with his much thicker legs, savoring the slight rasp of crisp male hair and heated skin on her own legs. She was busy exploring the contours of his muscular chest and belly when he shifted and pressed his erection against her thigh. Goodness! He was very hard, and . . . she took a breath . . . *very* big, and felt very, very real for a ghost!

He dropped a kiss like a tiny flame on her shoulder. He shifted again, nudging her thigh with his heavily aroused manhood. When she tried to capture him, he manacled her wrists to her sides with his strong fingers, and slid his body down hers. His lips and tongue left fiery trails of sensation from her throat to her breasts, and down to the hollow of her belly.

His mouth sought the center of her pleasure, and his tongue found the hidden bud that drew all the currents of desire into a streak of white-hot flame. She gave herself over to the flaring arousal his caressing tongue created. Only dimly aware of her own cries of pleasure, she arched toward the heat until sensations seemed to explode from within her. Even as she shuddered with her first release, Ray's stroking drove her toward another, impossibly intense climax. Waves of flames pulsed through her, consuming her and re-creating her like a phoenix.

In a daze, she felt him shifting, moving over her. Bracing himself on his elbows, he covered her with his body. She reached up and stroked his shoulders and chest with tingling fingertips, learning the contours of bone and muscle. *If this is a dream, I never want to open my eyes,* she thought. Ray dipped his head down to her and sparks brushed her lips as his mouth found hers. He branded her with heated kisses until she was breathless and restless. Her parted legs embraced his muscular thighs, offering him an invitation he seemed in no hurry to accept. When he continued to share his kisses between her lips and her breasts, she slid one foot up the back of his leg, wordlessly communicating her impatience.

Ray moaned softly against her neck, stirring her hair, tickling her skin. Distracted by those sensations, she didn't notice how he'd subtly changed his position, until she felt his hips pushing her thighs further apart. And then, his manhood was pressing into her tingling, aching flesh, and she was holding her breath in anticipation of the unknown. Like the lover of her dreams, Ray entered her slowly, teasingly at first, striking sparks inside the molten core of her body.

She felt his shoulder and arm muscles straining under her hands, the muscles of his buttocks bunching between her thighs, and then, with a growl low in his throat, he thrust hard and deep. She gasped at the shock of being invaded, consumed, conquered. He filled her and surrounded her with a heat and power that danced along every nerve ending within her, and for a moment, she felt totally overwhelmed. But when he kissed her, so tenderly, all her doubts, all her fears, evaporated. When he began to move his hips, stroking her aroused flesh, reaching deep before withdrawing, she realized her body had accepted his. This joining felt so right. A sense of joy filled her heart.

Now, as she met his thrusts with her own movements, an electrical storm began to gather inside her. Just when she was certain she would burst into flames if he pushed her higher, the storm within her broke into a shattering climax. A heartbeat later, Ray gave a last, soul-deep thrust and his muffled shout answered her own startled cry of completion.

Shaken, close to tears, she clung to Ray and waited for her breathing to calm. He had rolled onto his side, cradling her close, murmuring softly into her hair. She was drenched from their exertions and the heat surrounding them, but too content to consider moving. No matter what happened tomorrow, she told herself with only a trace of desperation, they would always have this perfect night of love they'd stolen from death.

Chapter
Fifteen

Even before Renata nestled back into the curve of his body, he knew something was wrong with him. He felt like an hourglass with the sand pouring out. He didn't have enough strength to move his arm from her limp body. Hell, he couldn't even move his fingers. He was . . . so . . . so sleepy. Hadn't felt . . . like this . . . since . . . woke up . . . Hallo . . . ween. Only . . . fi' nights . . . 'go. Gotta sleep.

Some time later, Ray fought gravity to force his eyes open. Big mistake. All he saw was Renata, lying alone, curled on her side in the middle of her bed. He couldn't see himself! He knew he was there. Who else could be doing the looking and thinking? But whatever made him visible to Renata and Melissa—and to himself—wasn't working. Would it ever again? Or was he always going to be invisible?

So his high school football coach was right about sex: It took a lot out of a guy. Looked like the trade-off for getting hard like that was getting soft like this. But he wouldn't trade making love to Renata for anything—except being alive. Nothing less was worth what he'd just had with her.

Ray drifted again, not exactly asleep, more like stuck in neutral. The next time he woke, he didn't feel so much like a wet paper bag. He waited a while before he opened his eyes, not sure he wanted the truth. Sunlight was already flaring around the window shades. Morning. When he finally got up the guts to peek through one eye, he saw he was lying in bed, with Renata next to him and all his usual clothes on. Even his boots. Damn! On the other hand, he was thankful for all miracles. And Renata was a miracle.

He took a few minutes to watch her sleep, smiling dopily at the memories they'd made last night. It was like someone had given him something fragile to take care of. Renata was so damn special . . . He was just this regular guy, not dumb, but no genius. No hero, either, even if he wanted to be. He was a ghost, a shade, a shadow, a homeless soul. Not good for much.

This wasn't fair to Renata. Maybe it was better for both of them that he was dead. Renata had her own life to live. He couldn't expect her to spend it with a ghost. What could he offer her, besides love? He was—had been—a motorcycle mechanic and part-time handyman. Just a regular guy with an alcoholic old man and a mother so worn out by miscarriages, beatings, and factory work that she was dead by his tenth birthday. He talked like a thug. She spoke like a lady. Just 'cause she'd loved him in two different lifetimes, and he had loved her past his dying day, didn't mean they were a good match.

Renata awoke slowly, reluctantly. She'd had the most wonderful dream. . . . It had felt so real, but it couldn't be. It had only been an illusion that she and Ray had made love last night. Mad, passionate, tender, and incredibly satisfying love. Several times. Or so it seemed.

Stretching, Renata felt for Ray beside her, but she didn't really expect him to be there. Nevertheless, she felt a twinge of disappointment when her hand encountered cool sheet instead of electrifying heat and the illusion of hard male muscle. Sighing, she opened her eyes. He was nowhere in the room.

Fifteen minutes later, showered and dressed in more borrowed clothes of Melissa's, a long denim skirt and a soft
cream cotton sweater this time, hair still damp, she found Ray
in the kitchen looking at the newspaper. Or rather, trying to
peer at the portions of the front page that Lucky wasn't covering as he sprawled over as much newsprint as a little cat
could. His contented purring reached her ears from across the
room. The scene made her smile.

Ray looked up and grinned, his emerald eyes sparkling at
her. Renata felt her heart stop. Her breath caught and her answering smile faded. What was going to happen to him? To
her? She couldn't sit on her discoveries much longer. And it
probably wouldn't be long before they discovered who had
killed Ray.

Then what? She would pursue his killer through legal
means, and try to keep out of Frank Dane's way until he was
convicted and locked away. For her, work would proceed as
usual. But what about Ray? Presumably, he would have ful-
filled the two things he believed had been keeping him here:
finding Celeste and solving his own murder. If they were in a
movie, there would be a flash of lightning or something
equally dramatic at that moment. Ray would ascend to his just
reward, smiling beatifically and flapping his new wings or
floating away on a cloud. But this wasn't a movie, and even
if anyone really had the answers, she didn't want to know yet.
She knew it was selfish, but without the illusion, the magic,
the dreams, she was going to be very lonely. Was it so wrong
for her to long for the kind of love Ray and Celeste shared?

Just then, Melissa came into the kitchen. Renata caught
herself about to gape and tried to study her friend more subtly. Melissa looked awful. Her long hair was tangled, her
skin pale, her eyes puffy. Renata's first thought was that Mel
had gotten a call with bad news about Gabe.

"Mel, what is it?" Renata saw Ray's head lift, but she was
too far to read his expression without the help of glasses.
"Are you sick?" Ray came toward them, and Renata saw he
was looking at Mel with concern.

Melissa shook her head. "No. I'm not sick. I'm losing my
mind. Gabe gave me his ID bracelet last night, the one he

got from his biological mother. Except Gabe is in the hospital, in a coma, so he couldn't have. It had to be a dream, right?"

Melissa suddenly opened the refrigerator and grabbed a bottle of iced mocha drink. "I'm going to the hospital to talk to Linda and find out for certain who Gabe's birth mother was."

Renata nodded. Ray slipped his arm around her waist, searing her with his heat.

Ray waited for Melissa to leave the house, then ordered Renata to sit in the living room with him.

"Renata, what is it? You look so sad."

Renata lifted her head and looked into his eyes. "Last night . . . Oh, Ray! Last night was wonderful. Magical. But it wasn't real." A tear slipped down her cheek. "Even in my dreams . . ." She blushed, then smiled. " . . . my *wildest* dreams, making love with you wasn't that incredible. But I don't see how it can work."

That little frown line came back between her brows. He waited for her to finish what she wanted to say, but he had a feeling he knew where she was heading. He wished she wouldn't. It was like poking at a bruise, just to see how much it hurt.

"Ray, even if we went on pretending, we'll never be able to have a child, will we?"

Damn! Sometimes he hated being right. *"No, babe. This is about as safe as sex can get."* He wanted to cheer her up. Time was too precious to waste it worrying about what they couldn't have. *"Maybe we can get ourselves on* Oprah? *Women who love ghosts, and ghosts who lust after them."*

She gave him a weak smile, but it didn't take a mind reader to see she didn't think his joke was funny.

The doorbell echoed through the house. Renata gave a start and clapped her hand over her mouth. Her eyes were enormous, almost black. He could feel her heart leap as if it was his own.

"Renata?" A guy's voice came through the door, muffled, but clear enough. "Renata, open up! I know you're there!"

* * *

"Gabe!"

Lissa was back. Gabe focused on her. On sensing her. She was standing next to him. He felt her warmth. Heard her breathing. Smelled her perfume, and her skin. Everything was sharper now. Like he was coming out of the fog of this damn coma.

He concentrated on moving his fingers. It must have worked. Lissa clasped his hand in hers and pressed it to something soft. Ah! Inside, he was grinning from ear to ear. Lissa held his hand between her breasts. What would she do if he moved his fingers now?

"Gabe, we only have a few minutes. I met your mother in the hall. She's going for a cup of tea, and then she'll be back." For one insane moment, he wondered if Lissa planned to do something wicked and fun to his immobile body. But that wasn't her style. Too bad. He'd have to work on that. "Last night," she said softly, "I dreamed you were with me, that we made love and you asked me to marry you. Please wake up so I can hear you say those words for real. I love you so much, Gabe!"

He knew what she was doing, and he tried to respond, to let her know that all he wanted was to recover, get married, and father lots of babies. And nail the bastard who'd tried to cancel his ticket with a speeding car. By concentrating, he managed to flex his fingers against hers.

Her fingers trembled as they meshed with his. He felt the steel bracelet press between them and remembered that, in his own dream, he'd given it to her as a pledge. Had she dreamed that, too?

"I brought you a coffee," his mother said from across the room. "Black, extra sugar." She was closer now. There was a smile in her voice. Good. That meant she liked Lissa. Now they only had to win over his father. And hers.

"Thank you, Linda. I . . . I won't stay long. I don't want to usurp your place—"

"Stop! We both have a place in Gabe's life. Stay as long as you like. Mario knows not to say a word against it. He knows I believe you're helping Gabe. That's all that counts."

"Thank you," Lissa said again, much softer this time. Deep in his heart, Gabe added his own thanks to hers.

"Oh! You startled me!" his mother said. Gabe could tell by the way her voice sounded that she'd turned away from his bed.

"Oh. So sorry, Mrs. Bautista. I didn't realize you were still here." Gabe strained to hear the voice. Who was that? "I just came by to check on the Chief's progress. I won't disturb you."

"Thank you, Doctor. Every day, he's better."

"Yes, so he is. And we have you faithful ladies to thank for that, don't we?" The words came out sounding oddly insincere. Who was that? Gabe knew he should recognize the speaker. Well, he'd probably wake up in the middle of the night with the guy's name on the tip of his tongue. "Good night, ladies."

Gabe heard chairs being moved, clothes rustling. His mother cleared her throat. "Where was I? Oh! Melissa, do you see that bracelet Gabe is wearing?" she asked. "Gabe's biological father gave it to his mother, when they planned to get married. I think Gabe would want you to wear it until he can get you a proper engagement ring."

Mom, you're a mind reader! Gabe felt Lissa's hesitation and squeezed her hand, trying to tell her he definitely wanted her to wear his bracelet. He heard some telltale sniffling, some rustling of clothes and blankets, and felt both women touching his wrist. The weight of the bracelet lifted, but a moment later, he felt Lissa wrapping his fingers around her wrist, closing them over the links. More rustling and a little jostling of the bed, then more sniffling, and some soft laughter.

"May I ask you a question?" he heard Lissa say a while later.

There was a pause. "That depends on the question. You ask. I'll decide whether to answer."

"Fair enough. I've been fascinated by your story of

Gabe's birth mother. Can you tell me her name, or have you promised not to reveal it?"

His mother sighed. "Even if I promised, she's been dead for thirty-five years. Her family is gone, too. What harm can it do? She was Celeste Benedict. The Benedict family is the *B* in the old B and R Small Motor Factory. They owned banks and factories all around here."

Lissa squeezed his hand hard. Her gasp was muffled, but he heard it. If he could have, he would have made noise, too. *Celeste?* The same Celeste that Lissa had been babbling about, the long-lost girlfriend of the ghost she claimed she had in her house? No, it couldn't be that Celeste. It had to be a coincidence that Lissa picked that name for her ghost story. Not that Celeste was one of those everyday kinda names, but his birth mother couldn't be the same woman as this dead guy's lover. 'Cause if she was, then . . . And *he* was . . .

Nah. No way. He was just confused from being unconscious for so long. Time to get up. He was engaged to be married. He was a cop with bad guys to catch. His clock was running, and lying here was just wasting time.

Ray's first impulse was to block Renata with his body, to shield her from whomever was out there, but that would be useless. No one could see him. He couldn't stop a feather. He touched her shoulder, wanting to reassure her. She was trembling like a scared kitten, and there was nothing he could do to help her. When she made a smothered noise in her throat, he put his fingers to his lips. She nodded.

The bell rang again. "Renata, it's me, David Mayhew. I've got a check for Melissa."

It was the "Harley Heaven" guy. Renata relaxed. She moved her hand away from her mouth and took a breath, like she was going to answer. *"It could be a trick,"* he warned her.

"I doubt it. How would anyone else know I'm here, or that I know David from years ago?"

Damn! She would have to use logic. He didn't have a good answer, so he just shrugged. *"Might as well open the*

*door and take the check from him before he yells a little
louder. He's only said your name three times."*

Renata gave him one of those looks, the kind that didn't
need words, and stood up. "I don't want David to see you
and start asking questions. He was a lawyer, too, you know."
She glanced at the door, then back at him, and her cheeks
turned pink. *Now what?* "Ray, I hate to ask but . . . Can you
um, disappear? Or something?"

*"Ashamed to be seen with me, huh? Guess that means no
guest shot on Oprah."* She gave him another one of those
looks. *"You and Melissa are the only people who can see or
hear me. At least, so far."*

Halfway to the front hall, Renata turned back. "Please,
Ray, don't do the *Topper* thing, okay?" He gave her his best
innocent look. "I mean it," she said. Her dark eyes flashed.
"Don't you dare make me look like I'm talking to myself in
front of David. He'll tell his grandmother, who'll tell *my*
grandmother, and I'll have psychiatrists beating down the
door."

The bell rang again. *"Hurry up,"* he told her, *"or you're
gonna have lawyers beating it down first."*

While she was opening the door, he settled into a corner
of the living room. He never planned to embarrass her, but
it was fun to tease her. She took things so seriously.

"A glass of cold water would be great. Thanks," this guy
David Mayhew said. Ray watched him follow Renata into
the living room. "I think I'm coming down with a flu or
something. Or maybe it's the change of seasons," Mayhew
added, standing in the middle of the room and looking
around. She went toward the kitchen, and he called after her,
"Nice place. I've heard people say it's haunted."

Ray heard Renata make a soft startled sound from the
kitchen, but she looked totally calm when she came in with
two glasses of iced water. She handed one to Mayhew. He
gave her a nice enough smile, and didn't sit down until Renata did. That was worth a bunch of points.

Lucky strolled into the room, sniffed Mayhew's jeans,
and hopped up onto the guy's lap. Ray watched the other
guy look surprised, then smile and lift a hand to pet the lit-

tle monster. Lucky purred like he was gonna explode. Traitor!

Forget the cat, he ordered himself. *Concentrate on this guy.* "Melissa said you're hiding out here," Mayhew was saying to Renata, "trying to work without distractions from the office. Can't blame you."

Renata nodded. "I've got a case going to trial and I intend to close every loophole, if it's . . ." *Don't say it,* Ray pleaded silently. " . . . if it's humanly possible."

Ray watched Renata's face carefully, wondering if she had a soft spot for this Mayhew guy after all. That could work in his favor. Something was going to happen to him after he solved his murder. He'd get his wings or his pitchfork, and go wherever ghosts go when they solve their riddles. But he'd be leaving Renata behind. What would happen to her then? He didn't want her to grieve for him. She'd done enough of that as Celeste. Enough for two lifetimes. He wanted her to be happy. To have what she wanted and needed. If he couldn't be the one to make her happy, who else was there? Renata deserved the best. And not just any Joe out there deserved Renata.

He looked at Mayhew with new interest. The guy was about his height, maybe a little taller. Looked like he knew his way around a gym without turning into a no-necked, muscle-bound jerk. He'd have to be fit to move the heavy motorcycles around the showroom. And that was another couple hundred points in his favor. As far as looks, well, he was a guy. What did he know about what girls—no, *women*—liked in a guy's looks? Mayhew was clean-shaven, his hair was sorta dark blond, and a little shaggy. He didn't look like an ax murderer, but who could tell? Anyway, Renata didn't seem to be having trouble looking at this guy and smiling, so he probably wasn't so hard on her eyes.

Okay, Ray decided, *unless Mayhew does something really dumb, or unless he's already got a babe, he's the one for Renata.*

Ray only half-listened to them talking. He was paying more attention to the *way* Mayhew talked to Renata. No loudmouthed bragging. No sneaky lines. He was . . . *respectful.* Yeah, that was the word. Mayhew was treating her like they were equal. Not like he was doing her some big favor just by talking to her.

He wasn't ready for the knife-edge of jealousy that sliced into his heart. The pain caught him hard and twisted. He had to use all his concentration to pretend nothing was happening, in case Renata saw him. Oh, man, it *hurt!* It shouldn't be such a surprise. He'd loved her when she was Celeste. It was gonna be damned hard to leave her behind forever, but that was the way it was gonna have to be. The last thing he had to do was make sure she was okay. Make sure she was loved. If it hurt him, so what? Life was for the living, and Renata needed a *live* guy, not a dead one.

The sound of Renata's soft voice pulled him out of his thoughts. " . . . might be coming down with a flu. You look pale," she was saying to Mayhew.

"I feel pale, but I'll live." Mayhew shrugged. "I better go. Thanks for the water." He stood up. Ray agreed with Renata; he did look a little gray.

"It was nice seeing you again." Renata sounded like she was at a formal dance. She stood up beside Mayhew. Ray looked away. He could handle them being together after he was gone, but he didn't want to see it before then. Renata walked with the guy to the front door. He heard their voices. "I think you'll like living in New Harbour." The phone rang. "I have to answer that," she said. "I'll make sure Melissa gets the check."

"Thanks. And Renata? Tell Melissa she's probably got something wrong with her thermostat. The heat keeps going on and off."

Oops. Ray caught Renata's eye as she closed the front door and raced for the phone in the kitchen. She was giving him that look again, the one that didn't need any words to explain it. *"I didn't do it on purpose,"* he muttered.

Seconds later, he hear a cry that drove everything but her safety out of his mind. Cold fear settled inside him. No time for hallways and doors. He pushed himself through the wall, ignoring the sickening sensations pulling at him. None of that mattered. All he cared about was Renata. She was leaning against the back door and sliding slowly down to sit on the floor. This time, when she looked up into his eyes, hers were wide with shock.

Gabe was glad to be alone for a while. He needed to think. He needed to rest. Between his mother and Lissa fussing over him, he didn't have a chance for either. He knew they were helping pull him out of this damn fog he was in. He was grateful. Humbled by their love. But all that concentration was wearing him out.

He let his mind drift. *Celeste*. He couldn't get that name out of his head. His birth mother's name was Celeste Benedict. No one knew who his biological father was, but Lissa claimed that her ghost was Celeste's working-class lover. Dead lover. But Celeste also had a fiancé, a rich doctor, she didn't want to marry. One of them was probably his natural father. Okay, he could accept that.

But this theory of Lissa's, that Renata used to be Celeste . . . No way he could accept that *Renata* was his mother. Not on the word of some guy who's been dead thirty-six years. Okay, he'd liked Renata right away, felt they could be friends, but that didn't prove anything. He'd felt the same way about that silly mutt he'd adopted ten years ago. Didn't mean Zelda used to be his mother in another life. Sure, people sometimes called him a son-of-a-bitch, but they meant it professionally, not personally.

Jesus! He was losing it.

Okay, look at it as if it were an investigation, he told himself. Look for the logic. The simplest explanation. The facts. Celeste's boyfriend jilts her. Does he know she's pregnant? If yes, he's pond scum. If no, what happened? The fiancé still wants to marry Celeste. She refuses—why? She goes away to have her baby—me—and turns the kid over to my adoptive mother, then dies before she can go away again. Suicide? If yes, why? If no, who killed her? And why?

This wasn't working. His head was swimming with questions, but he didn't have enough facts to come up with any answers. And he still couldn't get around the problem of basing anything on the word of a figment of Lissa's imagination. He was in a coma, damn it, he wasn't insane.

Forget it. He needed to rest. Oh, damn. The door was opening. Figures someone would come in to change his IV drip or check his electrodes just when he was about to fall asleep. A faint trace of men's cologne caught his attention. Must be one of the male nurses.

"Hello, Gabe."

He knew that voice. Not a male nurse. Oh, shit! He was in trouble.

Ray crouched beside Renata. She was white as a sheet and shaking. *"Baby, what's wrong?"*

"You just walked through the wall!" She sounded like she was accusing him of a major crime. It was just a little B and E.

"Yeah. I'm a ghost, remember?" He gave her his best grin.

She didn't seem impressed. "Don't do it again!"

Why was she mad at him? Women! *"Hey, I didn't do it for fun. It feels awful. But you scared the hell out of me. I thought something horrible happened. What's going on?"*

Renata pointed to a spot on the floor but he didn't see anything. "A mouse. Lucky brought a mouse upstairs, and it got away from him and ran right at me . . ."

He couldn't help it. He started to laugh.

"It's not funny!" she snapped.

"Yeah, it is." He forced a straight face that he knew wasn't going to last. *"Who was on the phone? I thought you got bad news."*

"No." Renata got to her feet and dusted off her cute little rear end. "That was Mel, from her car, to warn us she's on her way home, in case we had baseball bats ready."

As if on cue, Melissa came in from the hallway.

"Geez, Mel, you look like you've seen a ghost," he teased.

She didn't seem to hear him. Looking at Renata, she held out her arm. "Gabe's mother gave this to me to wear until he wakes up," she said in a strange voice. He looked at the familiar heavy steel links, the scratched plate where engraved initials should be. "And she told me—"

"That's my bracelet!"

Ray heard Renata say the same words, at the same time, and turned to see her staring at him. *"Celeste and I scraped my initials off so her old man wouldn't know who gave it to her,"* he explained.

"And Gabe's birth mother gave it to Linda Bautista, to save for Gabe, because it belonged to . . ." Melissa looked from Ray to Renata, back to Ray, and lowered her arm.

"It belonged to Gabe's father," Renata finished for her, her voice barely over a whisper. "He gave it to Celeste . . . because he didn't have the money yet for an engagement ring."

"No," Ray broke in. *"I did have the money. Celeste said she didn't want a ring if it meant spending money we needed to start a life somewhere else. But I wanted her to wear my ring. I kept it stashed in the basement here, with our money, so my old man couldn't find it and spend it on booze and gambling. Probably long gone, but it was there thirty-six years ago."* He shrugged. *"Anyway, that's our engagement bracelet."*

"That means . . ." Melissa said, then stopped. "But that's impossible." She walked away from them and paced the length of the kitchen several times. "It could be a coincidence," she suggested. Ray snorted and shook his head. "I guess not," she agreed. "So that means Celeste and Ray are—were . . ." Melissa stopped and gaped at him.

"Gabe's birth parents," Renata finished for her.

Chapter Sixteen

Renata heard her own words dropped into a silence that swelled like an ocean tide, threatening to drown them. She glanced from Ray to Melissa, unable to think of anything to say. Or, rather, unable to say the next logical thing that came to her mind. Finally, Ray broke the tension with a deep, infectious chuckle. Renata gazed at him, wondering what he'd thought of that could be so funny.

"Jesus!" he said. *"It's gonna take me a while to get used to having a cop for a son."*

Melissa just gaped at him. Renata gave him a sad smile. "One more piece of the puzzle. I wonder if she was depressed because she gave up her baby, or if she gave him up because she was depressed."

Mel covered her face with her hands for a moment, then looked into Renata's eyes. "Don't you know? You said you're Celeste."

"I *was* Celeste. I'm Renata, now. I don't remember everything. I dream about Ray . . . Maybe I'll dream about . . . our son." She shook her head, feeling slightly giddy. "Oh, dear! I can't think of Gabe as my son. He's three years older than I am."

"Hell, he's eleven years older than me," Ray offered with an endearingly crooked grin that brought a smile to Melissa's tense face.

"Linda said no one knew who Gabe's real father was, but that a couple of days before they planned to elope, he disappeared without a word. She thought he'd abandoned her. It broke her heart."

Renata stared at Ray. Her heart pounded so hard against her ribs that she wondered if he could hear it. He was looking back at her with anguish in his eyes.

"That's when I was murdered," Ray said softly. He felt like he was being smothered in a black cloud of sorrow and guilt. The tears in Renata's eyes were like shards of glass in his heart. *"Oh, God, baby, I'm sorry. I never knew you . . . Celeste was going to have my baby."*

He'd let Celeste and their son down. If he was stuck haunting this house until he found some way to make it up to her, he was gonna be here a long, long time. How could he do anything for Celeste? For Renata? What kind of future did they have together? He couldn't marry Renata the way he was. What could he do? Wait till Gabe recovered and offer to take him fishing, maybe take apart a couple of motorcycles? Do a little, what did the talk-show people call it? Father-son male bonding. Sure. Hell, Gabe couldn't even see him.

Renata touched his shoulder. Sparks traveled down his arm. She must have felt them, too, but she didn't flinch. He had the feeling she'd been reading his mind.

"I'm okay," he told her. *"We still have a couple of murders to solve."*

She stood up. He couldn't even offer her a helping hand. Not that she needed help. But he hated not being . . . real. "It bothers you that you didn't know about the baby, doesn't it?"

Her quiet words hit him like sucker punches. *"Yeah."* Suddenly, he couldn't sit still. He got up and started pacing, cursing silently. It was anger that made him restless. Anger at his killer. At himself for letting Celeste down. At Celeste for not telling him about their kid. At the kid, for picking such a dud for a father.

"I feel like I should have known. Should have done something . . ."

"To avoid being murdered?"

He felt stupid. *"Right."* He paced the room again, then turned to her. *"I feel like I was robbed. Like we were robbed."*

Renata stared at him a long time. Then she held out her hand to him. He went to her like she was a magnet. Pain lanced through him like a bolt of lightning. He was only dimly aware of Melissa slipping away and the sound of the front door closing.

"Maybe that's why I'm a prosecutor, Ray. I've always had this thing about protecting innocent people from the bad guys. No matter how much my grandmother argued and pleaded and ordered and bribed, she couldn't interest me in corporate or civil law. My mother thinks I'm a fool not to specialize in divorce, where I could make a fortune. But I always felt as if I'd been born to be doing what I'm doing."

"Maybe you were," he agreed, touching her hair, watching the way the sparks from his fingertips shimmered on the shiny strands under them.

"I wish we knew what will happen when we find out the truth." The sad note in her voice made him ache.

"Finding out is only the first step," he said, working through the ideas he'd been mulling over. *"I think we have to do something about it. Tell someone. Have him arrested. Clear my name, and Celeste's. Everyone thought she killed herself."*

"She didn't, did she?" She looked in his eyes, but he could see she already knew the answer. "Something's been nagging at my memory. Really bothering me. Even before we knew any of this. Before you knew who I was, and I knew who you were. When I was hurt and had nightmares, they got mixed up with what was really happening."

He opened his arms and she stepped closer. He wrapped his arms around her, wanting to comfort her as a friend, but it was only illusion again.

"One time," Renata went on softly, "I remember you told me to take my pain pills. I had a nightmare about being forced to take pills. Too many pills. I was too weak to fight. They tasted so bitter. I got so cold, and I knew I was going to die." A shudder went through her. He held her, warming her, soothing away the chills.

"Why? That's what I want to know," he said, trying to keep his anger from burning her. *"Why kill you . . . I mean, Celeste? Because you . . . she had my baby?"*

"No. That was incidental. It was because Celeste . . . *I* . . . knew something I wasn't supposed to know." She said it so quietly, so simply, that he believed her. It made sense.

"Now what?" he asked.

She took a deep breath, then let it out slowly. When she looked at him, her eyes had tears in them again. "Oh, Ray! It's *all* so sad! You died never knowing you were going to be a father. Celeste thought she'd been abandoned, and had her baby alone, then died never knowing you'd been murdered." There were sudden sparks behind her tears. "I'll get him, Ray. I'll get him and bring him to justice." The sparks faded, and she gave a little hiccup of a sob that tore at his heart. "I promise."

He touched her face. Heat crackled between them. She turned her cheek into his palm and closed her eyes. He wanted to do something for her. Wanted to tell her everything was going to be all right somehow. The words wouldn't come. He couldn't lie to her.

"Or should I say, hello, *son?*" that familiar voice asked quietly, almost as if he were talking to himself. "But you aren't my son." Gabe's relief tasted like cold water on a hot day. "You could have been," the voice went on, "if Celeste hadn't fallen in love with that motorcycle mechanic."

How long, Gabe wondered, before someone came in to change his IV or take his temperature?

"Poor fool. She could have had anything she wanted. I was willing to take her back, after she was rid of you. The mechanic was easy to get out of the way. She thought he'd run off without her. I didn't think she'd ever find out. I was too careful to get caught. But Mario Bautista, a plodding, methodical cop, stumbled onto something that made him suspicious. Never figured it all out, of course, but enough to inconvenience me."

Gabe felt sick. That voice went on.

"Thanks to his interference, my John Doe was identified as Raymond Lowell, a motorcycle mechanic and factory worker. Celeste saw the article in the paper and knew her lover hadn't run off. She figured out the rest on her own and threatened to tell the authorities. That would have ruined me. I couldn't let her get away with that."

Gabe felt himself choking. The man was a lunatic. A murderous lunatic.

"Now, you've inconvenienced me almost as much as your father did. You're a fine young man. An intelligent police officer. Why would you want to concern yourself investigating something as petty as supplying steroids to athletes? Those boys depend on me to help them win, and you were going to spoil that for them. And it wouldn't have stopped there. I can't have you sniffing around, upsetting all my apple carts."

Rustling. The scrape of a chair. Something bumped his bed. The scent of cologne got stronger. He heard the rush of labored breathing.

"You shouldn't have survived the accident." The reasonable tone of voice was shocking. "I'm afraid you're going to have a setback. The postmortem will show that your heart wasn't able to stand the strain of prolonged surgery. Such a shame, but you've left me no alternative."

Gabe felt a hand on his face. The bastard was going to cut off his air. He couldn't move, couldn't yell for help. He was trapped inside his own body, more helpless than a newborn. Oh, God! Where was everyone? He couldn't breathe. Where was Lissa? He needed her. *Lissa, I love you!* His lungs burned.

"Hey, Gabe!" Paul's voice.

The hand jerked away from his face. *Thank you, God!* Gabe felt giddy with relief at being alive.

"Oh, hi, Crandall." No hint of suspicion in Paul's voice. He probably hadn't seen what the good doctor was doing.

"Are you thinking of kicking in a few bucks on the pool? Whoever guesses closest to when this boy wakes up wins the pot." *Jeez! They almost had it backward.*

"Oh. No, no, I'm not interested in betting on that sort of thing. I was merely checking to see that Chief Bautista was resting quietly." *Just about had me resting in peace, the bastard!* "A fine young man, a credit to his family. Have the police made any progress in their investigation of the accident?"

The voice moved farther away. Leaving? *Please! Paul, get rid of that buzzard!*

"No new information." Gabe would have laughed if he could. He had plenty of new info, and no way to report it. *Stick around, old buddy.* "Listen, thanks for checking on my patient, but I have some things to do before his family gets back from dinner."

"Certainly, Paul. He's in good hands with you, but don't hesitate to call on me if you need someone to relieve you. I understand the strain of watching over a dear friend."

Pompous bastard!

A moment of silence. Then Paul stood beside the bed. "Man, that guy gives me the creeps," he said, as if Gabe could hear and reply. "He's like a really well-programmed robot. He looks human, but there's something missing."

Yeah, like a conscience. Maybe a soul.

A chair scraped the floor again. Paul, sitting down next to him. "So here's the deal, old buddy," Paul said. "It's about six in the evening. I'm betting you come back to the surface before midnight tonight. There's a lot riding on this. Your wedding present, for one thing. Those other ghouls want to win the pot for their own selfish reasons. Not me. I'm doing this for you and Melissa. Call it motivational therapy. If you want any kind of wedding present from me, get your butt in gear and wake up tonight. Hear me?"

He heard, Gabe thought, wanting to grin, wanting to tell Paul he'd already given him the best possible wedding present by accidentally saving his life.

Renata stepped back slightly and saw love and regret in Ray's emerald eyes. "Ray, I think it's time for me to bring in some of the big guns in the department. This case is too big for me to handle alone."

"Will you come back?"

The question, the quiet way he asked it, broke her heart. "Oh, Ray! You know I will, as soon as the trial is over and Mel won't be in any danger from my company. Even if I lose, Frank Dane is facing multiple charges of murder and conspiracy to commit. He won't get bail so easily. And we have another murder to solve." Two more murders, she amended silently. She wanted to solve the murder of Celeste, but even more urgently, she was determined to avenge Ray's killing. He'd paid too much for loving her, then and now.

Ray gave one of those little male grunts that sounded like agreement, but usually meant the opposite. Renata couldn't help smiling a little. He lifted a brow, but didn't smile back.

"Promise you'll be careful," he demanded. *"Don't go anywhere without police protection. Promise?"*

She blinked back tears at the huskiness of his voice. "I promise."

"Call whatsisname, the State trooper, to get you a guard. He'll look after you. He's a cop who's in love with you. Can't get more secure than that, can you?" He gave her a crooked grin. *"Can you believe I'm telling someone to call the cops?"*

The grin, the teasing tone, didn't cheer her. Her tears spilled down her cheeks. "Oh, Ray! I'm afraid . . ."

He opened his arms to her again, and she moved toward him. Closing her eyes, she nestled her head against his chest. With his arms around her, she was surrounded by that familiar tingling energy, no longer shocking but softened to an encompassing caress.

"Don't be afraid, Renata," he murmured. *"Be brave. You're gonna win this time. You're gonna put Frank away, and you're gonna nail the bastard who killed me and Celeste. We're so close to the truth, I can feel it."*

"But . . ." She didn't want to say the words, but time was running out. "When we solve . . . ? What will happen?"

"No way to know until we do." His hand stroked her hair, trailing waves of electricity over her back and shoulders,

making her scalp tingle. *"I won't leave you without saying good-bye this time. Not if there's anything I can do about it."*

There were so many things she could say, but none of them could come close to the complexity of her feelings for this man. She looked up into his face. "Ray, would you like to make love to me?" *For the last time?*

"You have to ask?"

She closed her eyes and felt herself slipping away into a maelstrom of desire. Heat flared around her as his mouth came down on hers. Her lips opened to his tongue and she gasped as desire flared inside her. When he lifted his head, an endless time later, she was shaking.

"Renata, maybe we shouldn't." She started to protest, but he stopped her with a sad smile. *"Baby, I want you so much, but I don't want to put you in danger. Give Dudley Do-Right a call and tell him to get the cavalry mustered. The sooner you get this case sewn up, the sooner we can get back where we left off, right?"*

Renata stepped back on unsteady legs and nodded. She hated to admit it, but Ray was right. They were so close to the answers. It was just a matter of time. But how much time would *they* have, after the dust settled?

His butt was asleep. Gabe didn't know if that was a good sign or not, but it was not a pleasant sensation. The door whooshed open, and he went on the alert. Lissa's soft perfume drifted to him, and he let himself relax. She took his hand between hers and he felt her hip against his when she sat on the mattress.

"Hi, Gabe. I'm supposed to help Paul motivate you to wake up. He really wants to win that pool. I think it's the least we can do for him. He's been wonderful. Your mother adores him. He even got your father to loosen up about my being here. Besides, he's still paying off that Porsche, so if we want a wedding present from him, you have to wake up in the next few hours. There's also so much I need to tell you . . . about everything."

He was *trying*, damn it! He didn't care about the pool or

any wedding presents. All he cared about was waking up to Lissa for the rest of his life, nailing a killer before there were any more victims, and getting some feeling back in his butt. *Can't you tell I'm trying?* he wanted to shout.

"What! Gabe! What did you say?" Lissa sounded shrill.

I'm trying to wake up! he shouted in his mind.

"Gabe! Wake up! Oh, Gabe! Talk to me!" Aw, hell. Now she was crying.

"Don't cry," he muttered. His throat was so raw, each short word hurt. The rusty sound of his own voice shocked him.

Lissa started blubbering. She dripped tears on him and fumbled for something on the bed, probably the call button. Then she started touching him, stroking his face, rubbing his shoulders, clasping his hands. It felt so real, so good. He was hoping she'd be willing to take suggestions for other places to rub, when suddenly, everything, including his butt, tingled with the rush of waking nerves. Man, it hurt like hellfire! He'd never felt anything so wonderful in his whole life!

Cautiously, he opened his eyes. The lights stabbed at them and he shut them fast. Lissa held his hand, shaking like a scared kitten, while he tried again to open his eyes. This time, he took it slower. Shadows. Light and dark shapes. Movement. Images swam, then started to come into sharper focus.

He blinked once, and his vision cleared perfectly. And what he saw was perfection: Lissa, tears streaming down her pale cheeks, smiling at him.

Suddenly, all hell broke loose. Paul. His mother. His father. Nurses. It sounded like the Fourth of July and New Year's Eve in his room. Laughing, crying, babbling. And kissing. His mother kissed him. She kissed Paul. She kissed Lissa on both cheeks and called her *daughter*. His father kissed his mother, shook Paul's hand about a dozen times, and finally, offered his hand to Lissa. She hesitated, then gave his old man a bear hug and blubbered all over his shirt.

Paul finally shooed everyone out to the hall to do some official poking and prodding. He was about as tough as an overcooked noodle, and he was going to have to wait a while for a pepperoni and black olive pizza, but he was awake. The best news was that most of the tubes and electrodes and Frankenstein-type attachments he was sprouting would be going back to storage soon.

When Paul let his parents and Lissa return, Gabe caught her wrist and closed his fingers around his ID bracelet.

"I'll bet there's a hell of a story to go with this," he said, enjoying Lissa's crimson blush. "It's official, okay? We're getting married." She gave him a dazed smile and nodded. "The first thing we're doing when they let me out of here is buy a diamond ring." He looked at his parents. His mother was beaming and mopping her eyes. His father looked like he'd swallowed something tough—like his pride. Gabe waited until his father nodded, too. Then he grinned. Everything was finally the way it should be.

"I can't wait to tell Renata," Lissa said. "She's been so worried about you."

Something nagged at his memory. Something about Renata and him . . . ? About Renata being . . . Nah. That was impossible. He must have been dreaming. Except . . . Damn it, there was something he had to do. Something important. What . . . ?

It all came back in a rush of images that took his breath away.

"Lissa, call the cop shop." Her eyes went wide but she let go of his hand and picked up the phone. While she dialed, he told her, "Get ahold of Tom or Brian, whoever's on duty. I need as many men here as he can spare. No sirens. No noise. I'll brief them when they get here."

Their celebration turned to a silence that echoed. He could hear the phone ringing in the police station. He could see the questions in her eyes. His parents were gaping at him, but he waited until Lissa had given his message to Tom, and told him three officers were on their way.

"Gabe, what is it?" Lissa asked.

"I remembered," he told her. "I know who tried to kill me, Lissa." He looked at his parents. His mother was twisting her handkerchief in her fingers. His father's face had hardened into a familiar expression. "Stay here, Dad," he said when his father started to stand up, eyes on the door. "I need you to look after Mom and Lissa. He's in the hospital, and he isn't going to spare anyone who gets in his way."

Renata set the phone back in its cradle and turned to Ray with a shaky smile.

"Will said he'll arrange an escort for me, and pick me up himself in two hours."

Ray sat on the chair across from her. She was too far away to see his face clearly. It seemed symbolic of the separation they were facing. Not for the first time, she feared she didn't have the courage to let him go without knowing that everything would work out for him. But what about them? A sob burst from her throat before she could stop it.

"Easy, baby. You're gonna forget anything bad that might happen. When this is over, you're gonna find someone who'll make wild, crazy, passionate love to you in this life, better than I did." He smiled. *"Soft, tender love,"* he added in a gravelly murmur. *"And you won't have to close your eyes to make the magic happen."*

She closed her eyes and let illusion take the place of their future, a tribute to their undying love. In her mind, his mouth came down on hers and heat pulsed between them and around them as his lips and tongue mated with hers. The kiss seemed to last forever. Her clothes melted away from her. She felt as if she were falling into warm, tingly water. In her mind's eyes, Ray's clothes had disappeared, leaving his beautiful body naked and tangled with hers. His fingers skimmed over her breasts.

The heat of his touch seemed to seep into her bones, turning her languid. When his mouth traveled from her lips down the curve of her throat to one breast, she clutched at his shoulders and held him. He lashed her with heat and electricity that swirled and pooled deep in her belly. She imagined that she was looking at him as she let her fingers and her lips explore his broad chest and flat belly, his powerful arms and narrow hips, his strongly muscled thighs and his hot, throbbing shaft. Her own arousal intensified as she felt him swell and pulse. His gasps and groans summoned echoes from her. Ray's hand cupped the heated place between her legs. His fingers slid into her slick cleft, trailing tiny sparks with every stroke. The swiftness of her climax startled a cry from her.

When their bodies joined, a smile played across her lips at the sight of his face, strained by his fight for control, totally masculine, harshly beautiful. She didn't care if all she was seeing was an illusion. What she was *feeling* was love, and that was real. There were so many things she wanted to say to him, but the words burst into flames when the sensations gathering within her caught fire and stole her voice.

Gabe couldn't believe the timing. The four of them were waiting in tense silence for his officers to arrive, and damn if the door didn't open slowly, and a familiar face appear. Their eyes locked. He watched the expressions crossing the other man's face. Disbelief. Recognition. Shock. Anger. Fear. Especially fear.

"Hey, doc," Gabe said, exaggerating his hoarseness a little. He grinned, hoping the man intent on murder would believe his victim didn't have a clue what was going on.

"You . . . You're awake!"

"Isn't it wonderful?" his mother blurted, then burst into tears again.

Gabe offered another grin, trying to look guileless. "I'm still trying to figure out what all the fuss was about," he told his visitor. "The last thing I remember, I was riding my motorcycle. Then I wake up in the hospital to find out I've been in a coma for four days."

The answering smile looked more than a little sickly. "You gave us quite a scare, my boy. You're very lucky."

"Yeah. I know." Let him figure out what that meant, Gabe thought. "Is my buddy Paul Sykes on duty now?"

"I haven't seen Paul all day, but I'll check for you." The door closed on that bold-faced lie and Gabe let his breath out slowly.

"That's him, damn it!" he muttered, afraid to speak too loudly and give himself away. His parents and Lissa were gaping at him in horror. He couldn't blame them. "Where the hell are those cops?"

* * *

Ray woke with a start. Renata lay curled in his arms, still asleep. This time, he didn't even bother to check. He knew he wouldn't be visible. Reality was closing in. He'd be gone soon. And Renata would be left alone. But not for long, he hoped.

"Renata, honey? Better wake up. Your trooper escort is gonna be here in a half hour."

She moaned softly and stretched, rubbing her soft little bottom against a part of him that was suddenly not so soft. He could tell when she woke up, because she made a startled little sound, then settled back against him with another soft moan. He gave in to temptation and caressed her until she'd turned in his arms and opened herself to him. These last moments might be all they could have together. The love they made now would have to last an eternity. Maybe longer.

Renata drifted back to reality reluctantly. It was time to open her eyes. Time to face the calculated risks and possible consequences. Steeling herself for one last look at her dream lover, she opened her eyes.

Ray was gone. Torn between sorrow and gratitude, she went into the bathroom for a quick shower. With warm water pouring over her, the temptation to give in to the tears crowding her lids was overwhelming. The only way to hold them back was to promise herself that she could do all her crying after Frank Dane was convicted, after she'd avenged all those murders beginning with Ray's.

She was dressing in the bedroom when she felt the heat of Ray's touch on her back. She gave a start, then let out a soft sound of relief that he hadn't left her alone. Just knowing he'd be with her as long as possible gave her strength.

"Don't turn around." His low murmur had an urgent undertone that sent a chill of alarm to her heart. *"We don't have much time before your police escort gets here. I need you to listen to me very carefully. This is important. Okay?"*

"Yes," she breathed. "But why can't I turn around? I want to see you."

"You can't. Making love takes a lot outta me. Just trust me, okay? It's better if you don't remember me like this. Remember me like a normal, real guy, okay?"

Shock stole her voice. Finally, she simply nodded.

"I've been thinking about this a lot. We don't know for sure what's gonna happen to me when you get the answers to who killed me and why. But we both have a feeling I won't be around after you do."

At his words, she stiffened. The heat of his hands on her shoulders and neck seeped into her, but she couldn't make herself relax. When she tried to protest, he shushed her gently.

"Listen to me, Renata. When I'm . . . gone . . ." He paused. Tears stung her eyes. She shook her head, but he spoke again. *"Listen. When I'm gone, I want you to give Mayhew a chance."*

That wasn't what she expected to hear. "David? Give David a chance for what?"

"Give him a chance to love you. To take care of you. I have a feeling it wouldn't take much for him to fall for you. He's a decent guy. He'll be good to you."

A tear spilled over and trailed hotly down her face.

"Renata, what we've had these few days isn't real. You know that. I can't taste your kisses or smell your perfume. I can't marry you. I can't give you kids and watch them grow up. I can't grow old with you. I love you, baby, but I'm not exactly husband material. I want to take care of you, even if it has to be in an indirect way. Do it for me, because I love you."

Renata drew a ragged breath. "Oh, Ray, I love you. I don't want anyone else. I can't stand losing you again!"

"You won't lose me, ever. Don't you know that by now? I'll always be with you."

His energy crackled around her, warming her, seeping into her, and filling her with a sweetness, a sense of peace, the certainty that this was right. She stood quietly and let his strength flow into her. When the doorbell rang, announcing Will's arrival to escort her to safety, Renata was ready.

Chapter
Seventeen

Gabe examined the tangle of tubes and wires connecting him to monitors and drips and cursed his helplessness. His three best officers were combing the hospital, searching for a madman, but he was stuck here like some science experiment. His father's right hand went to his hip every few moments, as if searching for the gun he'd retired with his badge. His mother stood on one side of his bed, obviously trying not to look scared out of her mind. Lissa stood at his other side, her eyes huge, her face pale. Her hand trembled in his.

His mother's sudden gasp startled him. Ignoring the stabbing pain, Gabe jerked his head around to see her press one hand over her throat. She was staring past Lissa. His father had frozen with his hand on his hip, his dark eyes trained on the door behind Lissa. Gabe turned his head slowly, just as Lissa gave a soft cry. He saw the .38 pressed against her temple and felt his blood turn to ice.

The eyes that met his were pale blue and glittered with a strange light. "I knew you were lying. You remember the accident, don't you? You recognized the driver."

"Let her go," Gabe said quietly. "It's me you want."

"That's true," the doctor holding the gun agreed. "But it would be too easy to kill you like this. Where's the satisfaction in that?"

Gabe's stomach clenched but he kept his gaze steady. Lissa still clutched his hand. He could feel her shaking. She pleaded with her eyes for him to do something, but he didn't dare do anything to add to the danger she was already in. Just out of his line of vision, he could sense his father trying to think of something to do.

Before Gabe understood what was happening, the doctor was seized by a sudden fit of sneezing. Cursing, he pushed Lissa away and glared a warning out of watery eyes at Gabe and his father.

"Damn it! Cat!" He sneezed again, the gun waving wildly. Gabe felt his heart stop every time the gun jerked from another violent sneeze. "Allergic," the doctor gasped, then cursed Lissa as he stepped back from her. Gabe saw cold fury in his eyes now, and knew the man holding the gun in unsteady hands had gone past rational thinking. He was beyond worrying about the consequences of murdering four more people.

Gabe felt time slowing down, and desperation clawed at him. He held Lissa's hand tighter, pressing it against his chest, and felt something unfamiliar under his forearm. The call button for the nurses! The cord was pinned to his sheet, beside his hand. Could he . . . ? He moved a millimeter at a time, until the button itself was under his hand. He tried to press it but it moved away from him. Lissa lowered her eyes, then met his. She used her fingers to brace the button long enough for him to press it. Then he waited, praying that this madman would spare his parents and the woman he loved.

Will stood on the front porch, tall and handsome in his uniform. He gave her a smile that lacked his usual open friendliness. Feeling regret at putting him in this awkward situation of fetching her after she'd canceled their date, Renata smiled back with more enthusiasm than she felt.

"Hi. Come in while I get my things from upstairs. I'll just be a minute."

He walked past her and into the hallway. "You look kinda pale. How are you feeling?"

Renata gave a guilty start. She'd completely forgotten her white lie of having a flu. "Much better, thanks. I really appreciate your picking me up on short notice. I'm looking forward to going home, and getting back to work."

She followed him into Melissa's living room, watching him look around. "What kind of arrangements were you able to make for police protection?" she asked when he turned from peering out the front window to face her again.

Will didn't quite meet her eyes, which struck her as odd. "I'll be your escort for the next few hours, until someone relieves me for the rest of the night," he told her.

Poor Will, Renata thought. No wonder he looked uneasy. He was stuck baby-sitting for her himself, only three days after discovering that she didn't yearn for his company as much as he did for hers. She'd try to make this as painless as possible for him.

"That sounds fine," she said, forcing a cheerful tone. "I'd like to stop at my office for a while first," she improvised. It would be less awkward for both of them if they spent as little time alone together in her small cottage. "Have a seat. I'll be right back with my stuff."

He nodded without smiling, and sat on the edge of the love seat, his big body visibly taut, as if ready to spring into action at a second's notice. Renata hurried up the stairs and into the guest room she'd been using since Thursday night. Her meager belongings were already packed into a tote bag Mel had loaned her, but it was the excuse she needed to look for Ray, for one last good-bye.

She called his name softly. The answering silence stretched so long that she began to tremble. Oh, God! He was gone already. An aching hollowness invaded her, consuming the joy she'd thought was so safely tucked away in her heart.

Then she felt that tingling, electrical rush of heat that always accompanied Ray's touch. He was behind her. Renata spun around to fill her eyes with one last look, but Ray wasn't there. A cry burst from her lips, and she clamped her hand over her mouth to stifle the low moan that followed. Had she wanted to see him so badly that she let her imagination fool her?

"Renata, I'm here," he murmured. *"You can't see me now, but I'm here."*

Relief flooded her heart, but it was relief mixed with dismay. "Oh, Ray! I wanted to say good-bye," she whispered. "I'll miss you so much."

"Close your eyes, baby," he ordered gently. She did so, without questioning him, trusting him completely. As soon as she closed her eyes, she saw him in her mind, smiling a little sadly, a lot roguishly. *"Remember what I told you. You'll never lose me. I'll always be with you, no matter what."* She felt his heated energy surround her, and stood quietly to absorb the love and strength he infused her with.

"Promise me you'll give Mayhew a chance to love you," he demanded, his voice tenderly gruff in her ear. *"Promise you'll give yourself a chance to love him, too. Okay?"*

Tears stung her eyes. A heaviness weighted down her heart. Reluctantly, she whispered, "I promise."

"I don't want you to be lonely, Renata. Don't waste your life grieving for something impossible. It's up to you to make up for whatever was lost. Okay?" he went on in that low, gravelly murmur. *"And the next time you come back to this house, look in the basement, behind the bricks in the southwest corner of the furnace room. Use it for your future, okay? Promise me."*

She blinked against the tears. "I promise. But what about you? I wish I had something more than just some answers to give you."

"That's all I need, now, Renata. Go on, before Dudley Do-Right down there comes up here looking for you. Dry your eyes and go get the bad guys for me."

Before she could choke out another word, the coolness of the room replaced the heat of Ray's embrace, and she knew that this time, he was gone for good—except from her heart. Renata wiped her cheeks and grabbed the tote bag that sat on the freshly made bed. After a deep, calming breath in and out, she headed for the hallway, to set out with her police escort.

Renata reached the bottom stair and turned to look toward Will. The sudden cold kiss of metal under her ear stopped her in her tracks, trapping the breath in her lungs. A second later, she smelled the rank odor of stale cigar smoke and knew who was behind her. With her heart racing painfully, she took shallow breaths. Moving only her eyes, she searched frantically for some sign of Will. *Where was he?* He was supposed to be protecting her. What had Frank Dane done to him? *Oh, God, let him be safe!*

"I told you, little girl, I always win." Dane spoke too close to her ear, with grating smugness. Renata winced. "You didn't know your boyfriend has a little gambling problem, did you?" It took Renata a moment to realize Frank meant Will. "Soon as I got wind of that choice bit of information, I bought up all his IOUs from his creditors. That's not gonna look too good to an Internal Affairs investigator, him being in debt to me." Dane's *tsk, tsk* made her flinch. Her reaction made him chuckle.

"What did you do to him?" Renata demanded, almost afraid to hear the answer. What she'd already heard sickened her.

"Aw, ain't that sweet? He sold you out, and you're still worried about him." The hard, cold metal pressed under her ear now slid along her skin in a deadly parody of a caress. Renata shivered. "We made us a deal, Will and me. He delivers you to me, and makes dead certain you don't get into the courtroom without you agreeing to bungle the case. And in exchange, I tear up his IOUs and no one ever hears about his little problem."

How could Will have been so foolish? How could he leave himself so vulnerable to blackmail, knowing how close she was to the case? Or was that why he'd gotten close to her in the first place? He could have gotten professional help for his gambling problem. He could have told the truth, and taken away Dane's leverage over him. Instead, to protect himself, he'd served her up like the daily special, putting Melissa in danger at the same time.

Maybe she could plead with him. Could she appeal to the sense of decency she knew had to be inside him, under his desperation? Would she be able to persuade him not to let Frank Dane ruin his life?

"You gave him a run for his money, little girl. He had some time trying to get to you. But you played right into his hands, just like I told him you would. Show your face, McDonald," Dane ordered in his grating voice. The uncanny way he'd read her mind gave her chills. "Your girlfriend wants to tell you to come clean and double-cross me. Don'cha, little girl?" His mocking tone made his cleverness seem even more diabolical to her.

Will appeared from the living room. He glanced briefly at her face, then refused to meet her eyes. "Do what he says, Renata. It's not just you he'll hurt. He'll do whatever it takes to convince you to bungle the case enough for him to walk," he muttered.

Dane pressed the gun a little harder under her ear. She could hear her pulse pounding under that taunting nudge. The hollow tone of Will's voice frightened her almost as much as the cold ruthlessness of the man with the gun. He believed the situation was hopeless. Understanding how resigned Will was to following Frank Dane's orders, Renata felt utterly helpless.

Suddenly, she felt that familiar tingling heat slipping around her. *Ray!* He was still there!

"Hold on, baby," Ray murmured. *"I don't know what I can do, but I'll think of something."*

"I know," she answered without thinking.

"See?" Dane chuckled. "She's not only good-lookin', she's smart." Renata was shocked to realize her captors both thought she'd been speaking to Will, agreeing to cooperate with Frank Dane in order to spare herself and Will. "Now, here's how it works. Your police escort will stick to you like plaid on a cheap suit, and you'll let my attorneys know everything you got against me. They'll tell you how to screw up without it being obvious. And you'll do it, like a good little girl."

"What if I decide not to cooperate?" The trembling in her voice betrayed her fear, but she knew both men expected her to be afraid. She suspected Dane was absorbing her fear, growing strong from it, the way a vampire took sustenance from his victim's blood.

"Don't make him too mad yet, baby," Ray told her. *"I'm still thinking."*

Her heart sank at Ray's warning. A second later, Frank's stubby hands lifted her hair off her neck and ran the edge of the gun barrel across her throat, making her stomach clench in disgust. "Tell her what happens if she stops being a good little girl."

Will met her eyes for the briefest instant, then looked down at the floor. "He knows who your mother and grandmother are," he confessed.

Renata felt as if she'd been slapped. The blood drained from her head. "No!" she cried out. Dane grabbed her hair and tugged her head backward, and she cried out again. He shoved the muzzle of the pistol into the hollow under her jaw and chuckled.

"Easy, baby. Don't get him riled. Just hang in there. I've got an idea." Renata prayed that whatever he was planning would work. She didn't want to faint from fear. The rank smell of Frank Dane's cigar-tainted clothes choked her nearly as badly as the unnatural position he'd forced her neck into.

A second later, Will let out a violent curse and hurtled toward Renata and Frank Dane. As Dane pushed her away and aimed his gun at Will, Renata saw Lucky streaking out of the room. She dropped to the floor and tried to decide where to go from there. Will crashed heavily against the wall near her. He stood bent over her, breathing heavily. She could smell his fear and didn't dare look up into his face to see what he intended to do next. Dane still had his gun. Did Will have his? If he chose to use it, which way would he go?

The deafening sounds of the burglar alarm startled a cry from her. Ray must have done something to the circuitry.

The local police would arrive within minutes. Renata stayed crouched on the floor, shaking. This was far from over. What was going to happen now? Would Dane run? Would Will? What would either man do if he felt he had nothing more to lose?

The door swung open and Gabe risked losing eye contact with Crandall to try to warn whoever was coming in. This wasn't the time for heroics. He wanted his officers alerted without endangering anyone else, without Crandall becoming aware. No telling what the doctor holding the gun would do.

A nurse bustled into the room, leaving the door open behind her. "Yes? What can I—?" She halted, gaping at the gun in Crandall's hand. "Doctor, what on earth are you doing?" Gabe winced at the nurse's outburst. He didn't want to set any matches to Crandall's fuse.

"Stand over there and shut up."

With the gun, Crandall motioned the nurse across to the far side of the room. Gabe hoped she'd comply, and felt a quick flash of gratitude when the nurse not only obeyed but put her arm around his mother's trembling shoulders.

Now what? Crandall didn't seem to know, either. His red-rimmed eyes glared at each of them. Twice, he checked a sneeze, and snarled a curse at Lissa, who flinched each time. After several nervous glances at the open door, he moved behind it, so that he couldn't be seen except by someone across the room from the entrance. With his gun aimed at Lissa, Crandall seemed content to wait until visiting hours ended and the hospital became quiet for the night. But the longer they waited, the more convinced Gabe was that Crandall was weighing his options and coming to the frightening conclusion that he didn't have anything to lose.

Renata stared in horror as Frank growling curses over the din of the alarm, pointed his gun at Will. "You bastard! You think you can change your mind on me?"

Unable to act, terrified to watch, she squeezed her eyes shut. Seconds later, the gunshot exploded over her. Renata's heart slammed into her ribs and her ears rang. She felt herself whimper but couldn't hear her own voice. A moment later, with her ears clearing a little, she looked up to see Will slumped against the wall and a dark patch spreading on the front of his uniform shirt.

"Will!" she cried out.

Will looked down at her, surprise, anger and fear mingling in his expression. She watched him press his hand to his chest. He opened his mouth as if to speak, but snapped his mouth shut and jerked his head toward Frank Dane. Renata followed Will's gaze and felt her heart stop. Dane's gun was now leveled at her, the round opening of the barrel staring at her with lethal intent.

With a yowl, Lucky streaked from the other side of the room and launched himself at Dane's face. Jagged red scratches rose in his skin almost instantly. Dane bellowed and swatted Lucky away, then swung the gun toward the kitten, who had landed stunned on the floor.

"Run, Renata!" she heard Ray yell over the clanging of the alarm, over the pounding of her own heart.

She couldn't. Lucky had tried to save her and Frank Dane was going to shoot him. She couldn't let him do that. Ignoring Ray's anguished shout, she threw herself at Dane's legs, hitting his knees from the side. He lurched away from her but stayed on his feet, cursing his outrage. Renata saw Lucky scramble to his feet and tear past them and up the stairs, but she couldn't get up fast enough to get herself away from Dane's gun.

She stared into Dane's small, recessed eyes and froze, frightened beyond thought. He gave her a slow, vile grin. Thunder barked, stunning her ears. Lightning flashed through her. White heat seared her, tearing her breath from her lungs. Pain crested over her, a boiling tidal wave of pain. Helpless, she felt it lift her. From a distance, she heard Ray's voice holler, *"No!"* She saw him racing toward her. Crashing into numbing blackness, Renata reached blindly for him. Her last conscious thought was that now they were together for all time.

* * *

"Gabe! Melissa!" Paul Sykes skidded to a halt at the open doorway before Gabe could signal him to Crandall's presence. Paul was panting, and obviously focused on something urgent. He didn't even look into the room after meeting Gabe's eyes. "Renata Moretti was shot at Melissa's house," he blurted. "She's coming into emergency now."

Lissa made a smothered sound and clenched his hand harder. Renata, shot! Gabe forgot Crandall and his gun. "How is she? What the hell happened?"

Paul was already starting to turn away. "Don't know yet. I'm on my way to scrub. Something about that Frank Dane character, and a State trooper. We've got all three of them coming in by ambulance. That's all I know." He pivoted and faced into the room again.

Out of the corner of his eye, Gabe saw Crandall tensing, and knew that the thread holding him was close to breaking. He forced himself to keep his expression neutral while Paul talked to Lissa and Crandall glared.

"Melissa, do you know her family? Can you call? You can tell them she'll be in surgery. I'll talk to them when I'm done. She was lucid for a while on the way over. The paramedics said she kept asking for someone named Ray, and something about a woman named Celeste."

Paul pivoted and rushed back into the hall. Gabe met Lissa's frightened eyes and never felt so helpless in his life. He looked at Crandall and knew all hell was about to break loose. The man's face was white, and he was shaking, his mouth working but no words coming out. *This is it. He's lost it. He's gonna kill us all.* The thought went through his head even as he tried to deny the possibility.

"No!" Crandall suddenly bellowed, wrenching at the door.

Gabe felt the shock waves that rippled through the room. His father made a low, growling sound of rage but didn't move a muscle. His mother bravely stifled a sob. The nurse hushed her softly. Gabe squeezed Lissa's hand, and gave his parents and the nurse one last look, then turned to face the man who had forgotten his pledge to do no harm.

Wild-eyed, Crandall stared back at him for a long moment, the gun shaking in his grip. Just when Gabe was planning to push Lissa out of the way, Crandall bolted clumsily out of his hiding place. He pushed past Lissa, knocking her across Gabe's chest. By the time she'd righted herself, Crandall was gone.

"Get those cops onto this floor now," he barked at his father. "Have security seal the hospital entrances and exits." His father was out the door almost before he'd finished speaking. The nurse followed at a run.

"Linda, what was the name of Celeste's fiancé?" Lissa asked, her voice breathless, her eyes wide.

"Henry Crandall," Gabe answered instead. His mother and Lissa exchanged odd looks. "He told me, when he thought I was still out of it. Tried to kill me, but Paul interrupted before he had a chance. Gives me the creeps to think that buzzard could have been my father."

"But he wasn't," Lissa said. "Oh, Gabe, Renata is still in danger. She . . . She knows all about Celeste and her lover and Crandall. He murdered them, and she found out he's connected to Frank Dane, too. I think he's going to try to kill her."

His three officers and the hospital security guards couldn't cover the entire building, and Crandall was a loose cannon. If he was after Renata, he could take out Paul and anyone else. The man was like a rabid dog, deadly and totally beyond reason or caution.

"Mom, give me the phone." She was placing it on his chest before all the words were out. He punched in the number of the State police and requested immediate backup. Then he lay back to wait helplessly and pray that it wasn't too late.

Ray clung to Renata, willing her to stay alive. She'd been calling his name, sounding weaker each time, from the instant before Dane's gun went off until now. He answered her again, the way he'd been doing the whole time, and finally, she went quiet. For a second, he thought he'd lost her, but then she smiled and he felt her relax. It could have been whatever they'd given her before the ambulance ride to the hospital, but he liked to think she heard him and felt calmer.

She was being wheeled from the emergency room, into an elevator, to the surgical floor. As the elevator rose, Ray tuned out the voices around them, talking about Renata's condition, and her chances. Instead, he concentrated on murmuring to her how important it was for her to live.

He didn't dare question his luck being with her like this. All he could think of to explain it was that he'd been stuck in the Garvey house, waiting to find Celeste. Now that he'd found her, as Renata, he wasn't bound to the house but to the woman. At least, he hoped so, because he wasn't going anywhere until he knew she was safe.

The elevator stopped and the doors slid open. *"Hang in there, baby,"* he whispered. One of the people in white pushed the gurney into the hallway. *"Stay strong for me, Renata."*

"Ray?" Her voice was so thin. She moved her head from side to side, her eyes searching.

"I'm here, baby. Can't you feel me holding you?"

A cry from down the hall made him look up. Suddenly, there were people screaming and shouting and scattering in the corridor. The sight of the man with the gun, bearing down on them, sent his memory tumbling back through the decades.

He was balancing on the wooden stepladder in the foyer of the Garvey mansion, reaching for a burnt lightbulb in that spidery brass chandelier and trying not to fall on his head. Old Lady Garvey was out with her housekeeper, buying candy for Halloween. His transistor radio sat on a marble table with heavy carved wooden legs. The DJ finished yapping and started the next song, "Earth Angel," by the Penguins. Ray hummed along, thinking about Celeste. That was their song, and she was his angel. They were going to slip away and get married in two more days. He couldn't wait to see her face when he gave her the diamond ring hidden in the furnace room.

Damn! A car was rolling up in the driveway. Old Lady Garvey! She was gonna pitch a fit over the radio. She hated rock 'n' roll. He'd have to apologize. They needed the cash she paid him for odd jobs.

The front door creaked open. Those hinges needed oiling again. He turned carefully to say he was sorry for disturbing the peace. . . .

It wasn't Old Lady Garvey. It was Henry Crandall, the doctor Celeste's father wanted her to marry. *How did he know I was here?* Crandall lifted his arm, pointing something at him. Ray squinted, trying to see more clearly. *What the hell does he want?*

Fire slammed into his chest. It tore through him, stealing his breath. The force of it threw him backward off the ladder. The floor smashed up at him. The world exploded into heat and pain. Stunning, blinding pain.

"Celeste," he whispered.

"Celeste is mine!" Crandall snarled. "Mine! I won't let you ruin everything!"

Ray felt his last breath slipping away. The heat turned to cold. The light turned to darkness. Somewhere, far away, the song "Earth Angel" played softly. *Oh, angel, I'm sorry. . . .* He was weightless, drifting out of his own dying body. All that was left was his love for Celeste.

"Henry!" Ray muttered. *"Dr. Henry Crandall murdered me."* His vision cleared and his killer was standing over Renata with a wild light in his eyes and the gun still in his hand.

"Stand back or I'll shoot," Crandall ordered. "I don't have anything to lose by killing one more." Somewhere nearby a woman was weeping. Others were trying to hush her. Fear vibrated in the corridor.

Ray felt sick. He would do anything to trade places with Renata, anything to save her, but he didn't even have the strength to let her see him. He couldn't tackle Henry, couldn't grab the gun from him. Didn't have a body to shield Renata.

"What do you know?" Crandall growled at Renata. "What do you know about Ray and Celeste?" Her eyes were closed. Ray could feel her pulse weakening. Panic gripped him. She was slipping away. He held her tighter.

Her silence must have frustrated Crandall. He leaned farther over her and howled, "Tell me, damn you!"

Renata's lashes quivered. Her lids fluttered open but her dark eyes looked unfocused and confused. Feeling desperate, Ray held her and looked around for help. There were several cops and security guards creeping toward them, but Crandall didn't seem to notice. Ray hoped the others had enough sense not to do anything sudden, to make things worse.

As Ray watched, Renata focused on the contorted face hovering over hers. "Henry? I know you killed Ray Lowell because I loved him." The steadiness of her thin voice surprised Ray. Her words seemed to hit Crandall like bullets. He stood there, frozen in shock, sweat sliding down his face, while Renata kept talking softly. "I know about the false death certificates, too, Henry. You killed me because I found out. I didn't want to take all those sleeping pills. What did you do to Mrs. Garvey, Henry? She was so nice to Ray."

"Celeste?" The word came out in a hoarse croak.

Crandall's face went sheet-white. He moaned, his mouth working convulsively. The gun now dangled loosely from his limp fingers. Renata whispered something even Ray couldn't quite hear. Crandall hunched over her, whispering her name, his voice harsh and rasping. Suddenly, he sneezed hard, again and again. "Cat!" he snarled as the cops snuck up behind and grabbed for him. They weren't quick enough.

Cursing, practically spitting, Henry pushed the gurney out of his way, then shoved it back toward the cops and waved the gun at Renata. Ray knew it was useless for him to think he could protect her, but he braced himself over her body anyway. He could feel her growing weaker with every breath. *"Hold on, baby. Hold on. Don't you dare die now!"* he ordered. *"I love you, Renata. Stay with me!"*

Dimly, he heard the cops trying to reason with Crandall, heard other voices ordering people to stay back. A man in green scrubs joined the cops and asked Crandall to let Renata go to the operating room with him. Melissa appeared from somewhere and added her gentle voice to the others. None of it mattered if Renata didn't make it.

A gasp from someone made him look up. Henry Crandall bolted the few feet to the doorway to the stairwell, disappearing as the heavy door swung shut. The cops started after him. The hospital people bent over Renata, checking her, reassuring her. Ray felt them pressing in on him and clung as tight as he could without hurting her. The man in the green scrubs told her he was Paul Sykes, a friend of Gabe Bautista's, and that he was going to operate on her now.

"Everything's going to be all right, baby," Ray told her. *"Promise."*

Renata gave the surgeon a weak smile as the gurney started moving again.

The gunshot from the stairwell sounded muffled, but loud enough to startle cries from the people in the hallway. Ray felt a shock go through Renata's body. Everyone froze again. A moment later, one of the cops opened the door from the stairwell and quietly asked for a doctor. Around them, people were buzzing, but Ray didn't have to hear the news. He knew his killer had just tried and convicted himself, then carried out the ultimate sentence.

That was it, then, for Henry Crandall, and for the ghost of Ray Lowell. It was time for him to say good-bye.

One last time, Ray kissed Renata. She said his name softly, as soft as the brush of an angel's wing, and a tear slid from her closed eye. Ray watched her being wheeled down the hallway and out of sight through swinging doors. Then he waited for whatever was going to happen to him.

Chapter
Eighteen

A week later, Ray was still waiting.

Anticipation made him jumpy, so he paced a lot. Then the complaints from nurses and patients about cold drafts made him feel guilty. He'd been haunting the floor of the hospital where Renata was recovering from surgery in one wing, and Gabe was recovering in another. He saw Melissa every day, but she didn't seem to be able to see him anymore. That made him kinda sad, but it was just as well.

After all that talk about *something* happening to him once he solved his own murder, he felt like a jerk still hanging around. It would be different if he knew why he was still there, or if he knew what came next. Every night, he expected something with lightning or white light would happen, like in the movies. And every day, he was back drifting between Renata and Gabe, and stirring up cold air currents.

He really thought he was done. Thanks to Lucky's razor claws and good timing, Renata was going to be okay. The bullet had missed her heart, passing clean through just under her shoulder. He hoped Frank Dane would rot in hell, along with Henry Crandall. McDonald had rallied after that bastard shot Renata, and drew a hidden pistol to get even. Frank had arrived DOA. The trooper was in bad shape, but he'd live. 'Course, he'd probably be spending some of the rest of his life behind bars. Ray figured crawling on broken glass wasn't good enough for the slime who betrayed Renata. But at least it was over.

And there he was, waiting, not knowing what for, watching over Renata, pouring all his strength into helping her heal. He only left her room when the nurses or doctors did things he got queasy just thinking about, like changing her bandage and checking her wound. Then he'd go look in on Gabe and ponder the twist of fate that gave him a son older than he was. So far, he hadn't found the nerve to find out if Renata could see or hear him. If she couldn't, he didn't want to know.

Finally, the hall lights dimmed. Visiting hours were over for another day. Ray slipped inside and settled into his usual spot in the corner beside the bed. Renata lay propped on pillows, her eyes closed, somewhere between awake and asleep. The door swung open and a nurse wheeled Will Mc-Donald into Renata's room. Then she bustled out again, leaving Will alone with Renata. *Now what?*

The guy called Renata's name softly. She blinked and looked at him, her eyes unfocused.

"I've been worried about you," he said. "They told me you were doing all right, but I wanted to see for myself. And to apologize."

No kidding. Ray deliberately frosted Will, then grinned when he shivered.

"Apologize? You saved my life," she whispered.

McDonald hung his head. "That cat saved your life when he jumped on Frank. I'm the one who almost got you killed." Ray couldn't believe the guy's humility. *Hell, why not take the credit? Got her shot, damn it! No almost about that!*

"I used you, Renata. I led him to you to save myself."

The hurt in Renata's eyes made Ray want to do something painful to McDonald. "I know," she said. "But at the last minute, you tried to stop him."

"It wasn't enough. I . . . I made a full confession and re-signed from the force. They're waiting until I get out of here to start the investigation."

"Oh, Will!" Ray could hear the tears in her voice.

The door swung open. It was the nurse who'd brought McDonald in. "Time for lights out, you two," the woman said. Her cheery tone grated on Ray. *About time to turf this rat,* he thought, feeling grim.

"Will, no matter what you intended, you did risk your life to save mine," Renata called softly. "I won't forget that. I'll make sure the investigators know, too."

Ray couldn't decide whether to be furious with her for feeling sorry for the bastard, or to think she was pretty damn special for being so forgiving. Right now, with McDonald's confession hanging in the air, Renata was lying awake. Ray hung back until her eyes closed and her breathing got deep and regular. She was stronger now, but it scared him to think how close she'd come to dying. She still looked pale and fragile, like a china doll, but she wasn't in so much pain any-more. Usually, whenever she slept, he stretched out beside her and wrapped her in his arms, willing her to heal. Maybe that was why he was still here.

He looked around before he climbed into the bed beside her. There were new flowers in Renata's room, from her grandmother and mother. They showed up together twice every day. The grandmother reminded him of Old Lady Gar-vey. The mother was like a cheerleader who'd forgotten she was in her fifties. There was a lot of tension between those two, but they agreed completely on one thing: they loved Renata. He couldn't fault them for that. And he'd found he could add the strength of their love to his own when he poured his energy into her.

It must be working. This morning, the surgeon said Re-nata was healing so fast, he'd discharge her in a few days, if she could find someone to look after her for a while. Melissa said Renata could stay with her, but her gran insisted on tak-ing Renata home with her. Ray had a moment of panic about his plans for Renata's future until a huge load of flowers came with Mayhew's name on the card. As soon as Gran

saw that, she started encouraging her to stay with Melissa.
Ray hoped it wouldn't take long for Mayhew to make his
move. After all, he was handpicked, and no dummy.

Shortly after sunrise, Renata stirred and started to wake
up. Ray slipped out to the hallway and drifted down to
Gabe's room in time to hear Paul telling Gabe he could go
home that morning. That was good news for Gabe, but Ray
was going to miss the motorcycle magazines Melissa
brought from Mayhew's shop. Gabe and Melissa were officially engaged, with the wedding set for New Year's Eve.
Their parents weren't ever going to be best friends, but
they'd managed to make peace with some long-distance
calls. Hell, even Lucky knew what to expect for the rest of
his nine lives. Melissa took him to the vet for neutering and
installing a microchip. As compensation for his loss, he got
a medal from the mayor and his picture in the paper for
being a hero. He was knee-deep in catnip mice and liver
treats.

Ray settled into a corner of Gabe's room and stared out
the window, watching the last few autumn leaves falling out
of the trees. He was the only one who didn't have a handle
on his future.

"I'm not riding in a wheelchair." Gabe glowered at Paul.
Paul grinned back. "I'm fine. I'm walking out of here."

"Hospital rules, pal. Get your butt in the chair."

Paul handed him the last of the potted plants. It had taken
two off-duty cops three trips to distribute all the plants and
flowers he'd gotten around the hospital. Gabe looked at the
plant, felt a sudden wave of unsteadiness, and decided he'd
sit this one out. Paul released the brake and pushed him to
the elevators.

He'd already stopped at Renata's room to tell her they'd
be waiting for her at Lissa's house. Now, he was meeting
Lissa in the lobby. When he got there, he expected her to
greet him with a smile and a kiss. Instead, her face looked
drawn and she seemed so edgy he was afraid she'd fracture
if he touched her. By the time she'd thrown herself into his
arms, she was crying. His first thought was that something

had happened to Renata. She shook her head against his chest, and kept crying.

"Lissa, tell me," he had to say twice before she sniffed and looked up at him.

"Gabe, it's Dave Mayhew. He . . . He had a heart . . . heart attack early . . . this morning. While he was . . . jog . . . jogging."

He couldn't have heard right. "What? Lissa, say that again." She did, still choking over the words. Gabe felt something cold and heavy settle inside him. He looked at Paul, who looked as stunned as he felt. "Find out what's happening, okay? We'll wait."

Paul nodded and headed to the information desk. Gabe slipped his arm around Lissa's shoulders and led her to the chairs near the gift shop. They sat, holding hands over the chair arms between them, and waited. Paul spoke to the receptionist, then picked up the phone and spoke to someone. Gabe watched Paul and tried to comfort Lissa, but he felt sick. Damn, he'd gotten to like Mayhew. And according to Lissa, Renata liked him, too.

After a few minutes, Paul walked toward them. He looked grim. Gabe held Lissa's hand tighter and braced himself.

"I just talked to the cardiologist who admitted him. He had a congenital heart condition that was like a time bomb. It's amazing he lasted this long." Lissa started sobbing all over again. Gabe felt his own eyes sting. "His grandmother got here a little while ago. She said Dave refused to think of himself as an invalid. He insisted on living normally and wouldn't consider a transplant. It doesn't look good. Damn!" Paul clenched his fist.

Lissa lifted her head from his soggy shirtsleeve. "Poor Dave." Her voice was thick with tears. "And poor Renata. I don't know how to tell her. First Ray, now Dave."

Paul looked at Gabe. "Who's Ray?"

Gabe shook his head. "Believe me, you wouldn't believe me."

Ray hovered beside Dave Mayhew's body. He could feel Mayhew fighting to keep his damaged heart going, but he was losing. What about Renata now? Mayhew was supposed to take care of her for Ray. The guy would have been good for her, and he had fine taste in motorcycles. The doctors were saying Mayhew had been living on borrowed time for years. Poor guy, he was just about to catch the brass ring when his ride stopped short.

The heart specialist and a couple of other docs were talking to Mayhew's grandmother. Ray heard the doctors say the words *donor* and *harvest* and *recipient,* which spooked him. They wanted to get to work soon, but Grandma wasn't ready to face that yet. Ray hoped she'd stall them. Maybe Mayhew's natural time was up, but he had an idea that could give them both a second chance.

Renata sat on the edge of the hospital bed and cautiously slid her good arm into the sleeve of a cotton knit cardigan Melissa had brought from her cottage. Her left shoulder protested if she moved too quickly, or tried to use her left arm, but she was tired of lying around the hospital like some shrinking violet. She needed to be busy, to keep her mind occupied, to get over losing Ray again.

The door opened slowly. "Hey, you were supposed to wait for me to help," Melissa scolded gently. She helped Renata slip her left arm back into the sling around her neck. "A nurse is bringing a wheelchair." Renata nodded and reached with her right hand for her purse and gym bag. Melissa grabbed them first. "I'll carry your things."

"I'm not helpless." The words came out sharper than she'd intended.

"Humor me. I was sent to help you. You don't want Paul and Gabe to accuse me of slacking off, do you?" Mel grinned.

The trip home exhausted her, but Renata welcomed the excuse to crawl into the guest bed and sleep. She had hoped that, back at Melissa's old house, Ray would somehow return to her, but she couldn't sense him anywhere. He was truly gone. In the hospital, she had dreamed of Ray almost constantly, dreams so vivid that she could feel him holding her in his arms, healing her, giving her strength.

She didn't dream at all that night. In the morning, she felt stronger physically. The pain in her shoulder was steadily subsiding into an ache that was tolerable. The pain in her heart had become tolerable with the hope that she'd given Ray the peace he deserved. But she felt so empty inside. At least Celeste had carried Ray's baby, even if she'd given him up. She knew a tangible symbol of their love would live on in that child, who was now the man, Gabe. Bizarre as it seemed, Renata acknowledged, she was jealous of her former self. She wasn't foolish enough, however, to think Gabe would appreciate her maternal instincts being directed at him.

Lucky pounced on a sun patch in the guest room, then chased his tail while Renata dressed. When she was ready, she followed the rambunctious kitten and the scent of fresh coffee into Melissa's kitchen. Gabe and Mel, kissing while standing near the sink, broke apart when she cleared her throat. Their guilty expressions made her laugh.

"'Morning, sleepyhead," Melissa said. Gabe winked at Renata over Mel's shoulder. "How are you feeling?"

"Better, thanks." With her eyes, with her heart, she asked her friend, *Is Ray really gone?*

"Good. Sit down. I'll get you some breakfast."

Mel met her eyes, and Renata read the message clearly: *Yes, he's gone.* For a long moment, their gazes held, and Renata felt her friend's empathy, her shared sadness. Then Melissa turned away, allowing Renata to draw her feelings into herself. She could sense Gabe's unspoken curiosity, but she wasn't ready to explain that she was mourning a ghost. When Lucky curled up in her lap, purring loudly and kneading her legs, she was grateful for the diversion.

Over hot coffee and oven-fresh cinnamon buns, Renata listened to Melissa's cheerful voice. Mel had acquired several interesting clients in the past few days, and was excited about the way her practice was becoming so quickly established. Renata was grateful for her friend's tact in offering her something besides her own troubles to ponder.

"Speaking of new clients," Renata said, striving to sound casual, as she poured herself a second cup of coffee, "have you heard from David Mayhew lately? I haven't seen him since he sent that gigantic flower arrangement to the hospital. Gran was very impressed."

She had finally decided to keep her promise to Ray, and give Dave a chance, if he was interested. She wasn't ready to fall in love on the rebound, but she felt she owed it to Ray to try to find love again.

Melissa started to cough. Gabe patted her back. They exchanged a look that struck Renata as suspiciously secretive. Neither of them spoke. Neither of them met her eyes, either. Suddenly, Renata felt a frisson of alarm.

"What is it?" she demanded. "You're hiding something from me. Mel, what is it? Has something happened to David? Tell me!"

Her voice rose shrilly as she read the confirmation in Melissa's expression, and her stomach clenched in dread. She didn't know if she could bear any more bad news, but she did know she had to face whatever had happened. For all she knew, they were only hiding the fact that David had run off with the woman who'd sold him those beautiful flowers. But somehow, she didn't think anything like that would make Mel blanch and Gabe look desperate to be somewhere else.

"Tell me!" she repeated after their silence dragged on, stretching her nerves taut.

Melissa came to sit on the kitchen chair beside her. She took Renata's right hand in both of hers. Her eyes glistened with tears. "Renata, we were afraid to tell you until you were better. David . . . David had a heart attack a few days ago, while he was jogging. It . . ." Mel blinked and a tear slid down her cheek. Renata stared at her friend, unable to comprehend what she'd just said.

"It was . . . bad, Renata. Very . . . bad. He was born with a heart condition. And he's . . ." Melissa sniffed. "He's on . . . life support, but Paul sa . . . said it's just a matter of time." Mel caught back a sob. "Oh, Renata! I'm so sorry!"

Renata simply couldn't believe what Melissa had told her. David was Gabe's age. Thirty-five-year-old men didn't have heart attacks. Did they? She shook her head, feeling as fuzzy-brained as she had when she'd been pumped full of morphine after her surgery. This had to be a dream. It couldn't be real. She couldn't accept that David could . . . No. It was impossible.

"No, Mel. That can't be true. David is fine." She pulled her hand from Mel's. The sudden movement jarred her injured shoulder, but she hardly noticed the twinge of pain. Lucky gave a squeal of protest and jumped off her lap. "He's fine," she insisted. "Ray promised . . ."

"Oh, honey, I'm so sorry," Melissa said again, her voice thick with tears.

Gabe came to stand behind Mel, his hands resting on her shoulders, his bright blue eyes—his mother's eyes—clouded with concern. "Renata—"

She stood up so quickly that her chair fell over backward. Without stopping to set it upright, without stopping to look at her friends, she bolted out of the kitchen. First Ray. Now David. It was more than she could face. She had to get away, had to think, had to stop feeling. Her anguish pursued her. In her blind rush from the house, she bumped her left side into the frame of the doorway. The pain clutched at her with razor-sharp talons, but she didn't care. No, she welcomed the physical pain. It was better than the searing emotional agony.

Renata steadied herself against a pillar on the front porch, then hurried down the steps and along the winding drive toward the street. She told herself that if she went fast enough, she could escape the grief that seemed determined to lodge in her heart. By the time she reached the end of the driveway, she knew she was wrong. Sitting on a boulder at the edge of Melissa's property, Renata gave in to her exhaustion and her tears.

Poor David. Was his heart condition the reason he'd retired so young? Ray had chosen David to take his place. He hadn't made that gesture lightly. He had been telling her he wanted her to find the kind of love they'd shared in another life. To find happiness again. It hadn't been fair to Ray or Celeste to be murdered all those years ago. It wasn't fair for David to be dying now.

Renata cried for them both until she had no more tears left. Then she sat with her head in her hand, the chill in the November air finally penetrating her armor of shock. With a deep, shuddering sigh, she wiped the tears off her cold cheeks. A bold and cheerily insistent *cheep* caught her attention.

The fat sparrow on the ground barely two feet away from her chirped again. He tipped his little head and regarded her with bright, dark eyes, then chirped loudly. To her surprise, Renata felt herself smile. The sparrow fluttered his wings, settled his feathers, and chirped at her once more.

"Okay. I get the message," she answered softly, reluctant to frighten him. "Thanks."

The bird hopped a short distance away, then flew into a nearby tree. Renata lost sight of him, even with the new glasses Melissa had brought for her, but she could hear his distinctive chirping as she rose and trudged back to the house. Yes, she had gotten the message. It was time to get on with her life.

When Renata walked back into the kitchen, Gabe could see she'd been crying. He also could see she'd made some kind of decision. There was a look in her reddened eyes that was resolute. She even managed a smile for him and Lissa.

"Mel, Gabe, thanks for inviting me to stay with you, but I have to leave."

He felt Lissa getting ready to protest and squeezed her shoulder lightly, silently suggesting she give her friend a chance to talk first. Renata was an incredibly strong woman. He had a lot of faith in her. Her expressive eyes told him she understood and appreciated his intervention.

"I can hire a nurse if I can't take care of myself, but I have to be on my own to sort myself out and start over. And I do have to start over. I can't keep living in the past, mooning for Ray or mourning David. Would one of you call a taxi for me? It won't take me more than five minutes to pack up my stuff."

The second Renata was out of sight, Gabe turned to Lissa. She was sniffling and fumbling with her phone book. Gabe stewed over being helpless, while Lissa phoned for Renata's taxi. When Renata came back into the kitchen, she hugged them both with her good arm, then picked up Lucky and cuddled him.

"Promise you'll call if you need anything," Gabe told her. She smiled and nodded, but he had a feeling the only calls they'd get would be social. Renata wasn't the type to ask for help. "How long are you on sick leave?"

"At least a couple of months. Depending on how I feel, I may get back to that literary agent who called about my writing a book about Frank, Henry, Celeste, and Ray. True crime is hot these days. It'll give me a way to put all my ghosts to rest," she said with a brave smile that didn't quite reach her eyes.

"Don't forget to save New Year's weekend for our wedding," Lissa told her. "I want you there with us."

"I wouldn't miss it. You know that." He saw the sheen of tears in Renata's eyes. "And Lucky should be the ring bearer." She gave the kitten a final hug, then whispered a teary "Bye!" and hurried out before he could offer to carry her bag. A moment later, he heard the front door shut. A second after that, Lissa gave a cry and launched herself into his arms.

Gabe held Lissa close and waited for her to stop crying into his shirt. This was one of those times he almost envied women for being able to let out their feelings. All he could do was stand there feeling helpless, for Lissa and especially for Renata, and get angry. Angry at the greed and evil of men like Frank Dane and Henry Crandall and angry at the selfishness of Will McDonald. He was also angry at the twists of fate that could break a woman's heart and snuff out a decent man's life much too soon. But getting angry wasn't going to do anyone any good.

The rumble of a heavy touring motorcycle caught his attention. Someone was riding up the driveway. Arm in arm, Gabe walked Lissa to the living room. They stood by the big window that replaced the one shattered on Halloween, and watched the rider dismount. Renata was sitting at the bottom of the porch steps, waiting for her taxi, and watching the man in black leather. Gabe didn't recognize him until he took off his black-tinted helmet. Even then, he didn't believe it.

Beside him, Lissa murmured, "I think I'll cancel Renata's taxi."

Frozen in shock, Renata felt her sense of balance shifting dangerously as the motorcycle rider hung his helmet on the handlebars and turned to her. His gaze locked with hers. With her breath trapped in her lungs, she stared into his eyes as he strode toward her. When he stopped at the foot of the stairs, towering over her, she had to tilt her head way back to look up at him. Disbelief made her dizzy, but she didn't dare believe.

He nodded toward her tote bag. "Where are you going?"

She had to swallow before she could force out a simple answer. "My place."

"I'll take you. But first, we've got something to do here. C'mon." He held out a black-gloved hand. She reached for it, then pulled her hand back. He frowned. "What's the matter?"

Renata felt at a distinct disadvantage with him looming over her like that. She rose, feeling awkward with her injured arm in its sling, and went to the top stair, bringing her to his eye level. "I heard you had a heart attack." To her dismay, the words came out like an accusation.

Regret clouded his eyes. "Damn! I was hoping you wouldn't find out before I could explain."

"Explain? Explain what?" She took a breath, trying to get the shrill tone out of her voice. "Melissa and Gabe told me you were on life support."

The grin he gave her was endearingly crooked, and shockingly familiar. "Would you believe I got better?"

Chapter Nineteen

Renata clutched the porch pillar tighter, fighting a wave of dizziness. "What do you mean, *you got better?*" she demanded breathlessly.

He gave her a hint of a smile. "Come inside with me."

David peeled off his leather gloves and tucked them into a pocket of his jacket. Renata followed his movements with stunned eyes, noting that he looked the same as he had the last time she'd seen him. Tall, broad-shouldered, narrow-hipped, flat-bellied, long-legged. A description that could fit David, or Ray, or Gabe, or almost any quarterback or pitcher. But there was a feline power to his movements that she hadn't noticed before. A definite cockiness to his stance. It was attractive. And it was all unsettlingly familiar. She hesitated.

"Renata, come with me." He spoke gently, but she read his determination in his eyes, felt it when he closed his hand around her good arm and turned her toward the front door. "I have something to show you."

Renata dug in her heels. "You have something to *tell* me, you mean," she countered, vowing never to forgive him if the heart attack story had been a hoax.

"That, too. But not out here. You look like you're going to fall over. Inside." He wrapped his arm around her waist and nearly lifted her against his side. With her shoulder still aching, Renata didn't even consider struggling. But she dearly wished she could kick him or something, without jeopardizing her own security, or what was left of her dignity. His body pressed into hers with each step he took. He was very solid. Awareness rippled through her, despite her annoyance, as he clutched her to him. A few more steps and he was releasing her in Melissa's front hall. Her new glasses slipped down her nose. She pushed them back into place and opened her mouth to tell him off. He didn't give her a chance.

"Wait here," he ordered.

Renata stood and gaped while David walked into Melissa's living room as if he owned the house. She heard Gabe clear his throat, heard Mel's softer voice, heard David reply too quietly for her to make out. He came back to her with a purposeful expression on his handsome face.

"C'mon downstairs," he said to her, then called into the living room, "Remember, give me thirty seconds."

Curiosity overrode her resentment of David's high-handed behavior. She let him lead her down the bare wooden stairs to the basement where she'd first encountered Ray only two weeks before. David's hand felt warm and strong around hers as she followed him into the furnace room. With his hand on her good shoulder, he turned her to face him. Regarding her with a suspiciously familiar smile in his black-lashed hazel-green eyes, he gently removed her glasses and tucked them into his inside jacket pocket. Then, while she stood blinking up into his eyes, she heard the achingly sweet opening notes of "Earth Angel."

Renata's heart leapt. Her breath caught. She stared at David, searching for answers. Then he wrapped his arms around her, holding her gently, and began to dance.

Ray couldn't control the tremors that raced through him as he held Renata close, trying to be careful of her injured shoulder. She was warm and soft and smelled like flowers and the delicate musk of a woman's skin. He'd only imagined this before. The reality was far more potent than his wildest fantasies. His body was hard and throbbing long before she moved closer and pressed herself to him. Her soft moan, the way she leaned into him, aroused him even more. He wanted to go on holding her, dancing with her, like this forever, but he didn't think he'd be able to last more than one more repeat of this song. Not the way he ached for her.

The music ended. He stood with his arms around her. She was trembling, too. When the song began again, he lost the patience to keep dancing. If he didn't kiss her, really kiss her this time, he was going to explode. Unable to hold his hand steady, he tipped her chin up and lowered his head to meet her lips. A tiny spark signaled their first contact, but the electricity was no illusion. Her lips were soft, yielding, warm under his, and so sweet that he felt intoxicated. Deliberately tormenting himself by going as slowly as he could, he trailed kisses from her mouth to her jawline, to the satin skin of her neck.

"I've been waiting so long to taste you," he murmured. "The reality is better than the fantasy."

Renata drew back and stared up at him. Her dark eyes were like deep pools drawing him in. "Ray?" she asked, her voice quavering.

"Sort of," he amended reluctantly. Her steady gaze demanded an honesty he wasn't sure he could summon. "Mostly?"

"*Sort* of? *Mostly?*" she echoed. "Who *are* you?"

"Sort of David. Officially. But mostly Ray."

She shook her head. "I don't understand," she answered in a low, ragged voice that made him feel awful for teasing her.

"David was dying, Renata. He didn't have much time for this life. I stepped in and healed his heart. He's a . . . a part of me, but mostly, I'm Ray, and I love you." He swallowed hard, praying he hadn't frightened her away with the bare truth. "I know it'll take some getting used to."

Eyes wide and glistening with tears, Renata backed away from him. His heart sank.

* * *

Renata stared up into David's . . . No, Ray's face. "How? Why?"

He shrugged and twin red spots showed in his lean cheeks. "According to the tea-leaf lady in the shop next door to mine, I was supposed to be reborn as David, but because I had all that unfinished business, I got stuck here. So the tea-leaf lady claims that left David born with a bad heart to hold my place."

She felt the hot trickle of tears sliding down her cheeks, but didn't bother to wipe them away. They were tears of joy for Ray and herself, tears of sorrow for David.

Ray suddenly stripped off his leather jacket and threw it onto the cement floor. His white T-shirt clung to his torso, outlining muscles that actually rippled when he moved. It was, she thought dazedly, rather impressive.

"Renata, I told you about the money in the wall," he said. She nodded. "I know you're having trouble believing me, but I can prove I'm telling the truth."

She realized he'd misunderstood her reactions. Before she could gather her wits enough to reassure him that she did, indeed, believe him, he'd crouched at the wall behind the furnace and was using a penknife to dig between corner bricks. She moved to where she could watch him, curious and fascinated by the sight of his strong arms as he worked.

"Hah!" He turned toward her with a dusty metal box. Excitement lit his eyes. "I hid a diamond engagement ring and wedding band along with a few thousand dollars in cash, and got murdered before I could get them. If they're in here, will you believe me?"

Renata nodded. She didn't have the heart to spoil his triumph by telling him she already believed him. Instead, she stepped closer and watched his lean fingers unfastening the catch on the box to reveal a stack of money and something small knotted in a delicate lacy white handkerchief. Ray paused and looked into her eyes, then cupped the small bundle in his hand.

Overwhelmed by emotions, Renata took the metal box from him and placed it on a nearby carton. Then she covered his hands with her uninjured one and bent to kiss his knuckles where the bricks had scraped them. At the touch of her lips to his skin, she heard his sharp intake of breath, heard him say her name in a reverent whisper. She lifted her head for his kiss.

"Renata? I canceled your taxi." They froze mere inches apart at the sound of Melissa's voice from the upstairs. "Gabe and I are going out for a while. C'mon, Gabe." Footsteps thudded overhead, followed by Melissa yelping, "Gabe! Stop that!" and a giggle. Then they heard him say, "Hey, Mom! Dad! Behave yourselves down there! You don't want to set a bad example for us youngsters!"

Ray sighed with exaggerated heaviness. "Kids these days, huh?"

Two sets of footsteps sounded overhead, moving away from the door to the basement. Then the heavier steps returned. "Hey, you two!" Gabe called. "I've been told New Year's Eve is a good time for a wedding." Without another word, the upstairs door shut firmly, and Gabe's footsteps retreated.

Ray quirked an eyebrow at her. Reading his thoughts in his eyes, she smiled. He dipped toward her again and she let her eyes drift closed. His breath was warm on her skin. His lips were soft, sensuous, teasing on hers.

"I can take a hint," he murmured against her lips. "I'm thinking about going upstairs to that guest room and making love to you with our eyes open. How does that sound to you?" He trailed nibbling kisses along her jawline and down to her throat, sending shivers of heat along her nerves.

"That sounds . . ." His tongue dipped into the hollow of her throat, stealing her breath. "That sounds like something I've been dreaming about," she told him, unable to speak above a whisper.

The walk up two flights of stairs seemed to take forever, with frequent pauses for teasing kisses, and yet, when she stood beside the guest bed, Renata could hardly recall how they got there. Suddenly, she was nervous. This wasn't a fantasy or a dream. Ray had seemed so real before, but only when her eyes were closed. Their lovemaking had been an illusion. Now, he was a very real, very solid man, and there was no question that he had a man's hunger for her.

As if sensing her uncertainty, Ray gently drew her down beside him and slid his arm around her. She tucked her face against him, savoring the scents of leather, fresh air, and male skin.

"I want to make love to you, but I won't rush you. If you need time to get used to me, or if your shoulder is too sore, I'm willing to just hold you."

The opening notes of "Earth Angel" began to play again. Straightening, she looked into his eyes and smiled at his earnest, worried expression. "I think we've waited long enough for two lifetimes. Besides, they're playing our song."

He smiled and released her to slide to his knees in front of her. Renata watched as he untied the handkerchief with trembling fingers, revealing a blue velvet box. Inside the box sat an old-fashioned gold ring, set with a single small diamond, and a matching wedding band sculpted to surround the solitary diamond with smaller stones. Ray took her left hand gently in his, and slipped the engagement ring onto her third finger. It was a perfect fit. She smiled even as tears filled her eyes.

He pressed a kiss to her hand, then stood towering over her. Without a word, he untucked his T-shirt and pulled it over his head, then bent and unlaced his boots. Daringly, Renata reached forward and touched the smooth golden skin of his broad, bare back. He paused for a moment, letting her stroke him as she pleased, then hurriedly tugged off his boots and stood again. When his hands went to the snap and zipper of his leather jeans, Renata held her breath.

"Better not just yet," he muttered, leaving the jeans zipped but unsnapped. His grin sent a warm tingle of anticipation through her. "You need to catch up."

His touch gentle, his kisses diverting, Ray eased her out of the sling supporting her left arm, and carefully unbuttoned and peeled off her blouse. She felt a moment of panic that he'd be repulsed by the damage done by the bullet, but he removed her doubts with tender kisses over her neck and shoulders. When he raised his head to look into her eyes again, she was startled to discover he'd managed to unhook her bra without her noticing. He gave her a smug grin as he took it off her.

"So beautiful," he whispered. "Lie back. Let me love you."

It was an offer that felt so right, so *destined,* she couldn't imagine refusing. With one of his arms cradling her, and his mouth on hers, she sank backward onto the bed. His lips parted hers, and his tongue slid into her mouth, hot and wet. She met each slow, arousing thrust with an answering slide of her own tongue, her eyes closed to savor the sensations swirling over her nerves. Ray's fingers circled her breasts, drawing ever closer to her beaded nipples. His teasing fingertips stroked each peak to a tingling bud. And then he tore his lips from hers and captured one breast in the wet heat of his mouth, exciting a startled cry of pleasure from her.

"Open your eyes, Renata," he demanded, lifting his head. "I want you to see me exactly as I am." She opened her eyes and met his gaze. He smiled. "I don't want any questions in your mind as to who's making love to you," he murmured.

Her answering smile turned to a gasp when his hand slid up under her denim skirt, along the inside of her thigh. His palm was warm and rough, his touch firm. He held her gaze and cupped his hand between her legs. Renata fought the urge to close her eyes and gave in to the exquisite sensations he was creating with the slow, knowing pressure of his palm. Just when she was certain that he was going to take her over the edge, he stopped.

Confused, she blinked up at him. A moment later, her confusion vanished when he unfastened her skirt and deftly managed to remove it, along with her socks. Renata watched Ray's face as he looked down at her, and read love and desire in his taut expression. With her right hand, she reached up and stroked the slight roughness of his face and the lightly furred muscles of his chest. He caught her hand in one of his and pressed it against him. She felt the strong rhythm of his heart vibrating through her and blinked away tears at the thought that his heart had nearly failed him.

"What would you say to a double wedding for New Year's Eve?" There was a touching hint of uncertainty in his low voice.

"I'd say yes," she answered without any uncertainty.

"Good answer." He grinned crookedly. "After waiting all this time, I don't think either of us wants a long engagement."

Ray drew back and stood, then unzipped his leather jeans and pushed them off. His black briefs followed. Feeling both daring and nervous, Renata studied him. He was beautiful, and powerfully aroused. He knelt beside her and drew her hand to him. She closed her fingers around the thick, hot length of him and smiled at the low groan her touch elicited. A moment later, her bikini panties were gone and his fingers were delving into the melting heat between her legs. He caressed her to a shattering climax, his low voice urging her higher, reminding her to look into his eyes until the wave of pleasure washed over her and keeping her eyes open became impossible.

He gave her only a few seconds to recover, to drift back to earth, using the time to tear open a cellophane packet and prepare himself. Bemused by his forethought, touched by his concern, she smiled and whispered her thanks. To her surprise, his lean face darkened. "I didn't protect you once upon a time," he told her. Then he grinned. "Gabe's an okay kid, but I want you to myself for a little while, before we start thinking about a family. Okay?"

Smiling, she nodded her agreement, then gasped as Ray gathered her into his arms and lifted her onto his lap. She clung to him with her good arm and let him guide her legs around his waist. The feel of his shaft against her sensitized flesh shocked and aroused her. Greedy for as much of him as she could get, Renata pressed her breasts to his chest. He moaned softly, and the sound sent waves of excitement radiating into the core of her body. She felt both vulnerable and protected, felt as if she were surrendering and conquering at the same time.

Ray's mouth claimed hers in a deep kiss that drove all conscious thought from her mind. He lifted her and gently eased into her. Renata let her eyes close. "Look at me," he ordered hoarsely. "Look at me."

She forced her eyes open and looked into his as he joined their bodies. The swift shock as he thrust deep startled a cry from her. For a moment, she felt overwhelmed by the reality of his body bonded so intimately with hers. But when he said, "Sorry. Sorry. Oh, baby, I didn't want to hurt you. I wasn't sure," in a choked whisper, she kissed away his apologies and hesitation, following her woman's instincts to take herself and her true mate toward fulfillment.

A long time later, when their breathing had almost settled back to normal, he murmured, "You really are only mine."

Renata smiled. "Mmm-hmm. It's *déjà vu* all over again," she said as "Earth Angel" began to play once more.